Cover art by Robert Kraiza

Title page and chapter header art by Rachael Ward

Editing by Erin Nordin, The Word Faery

Proofreading by Antara Dutt, Tessera Editorial

For Jordon, my door, my slip of light, my scrap of unreadable paper, my one red leaf the snow releases in March. My life opened the day I met you and I will love you until the world caves in.

And, of course, for all those who ache.

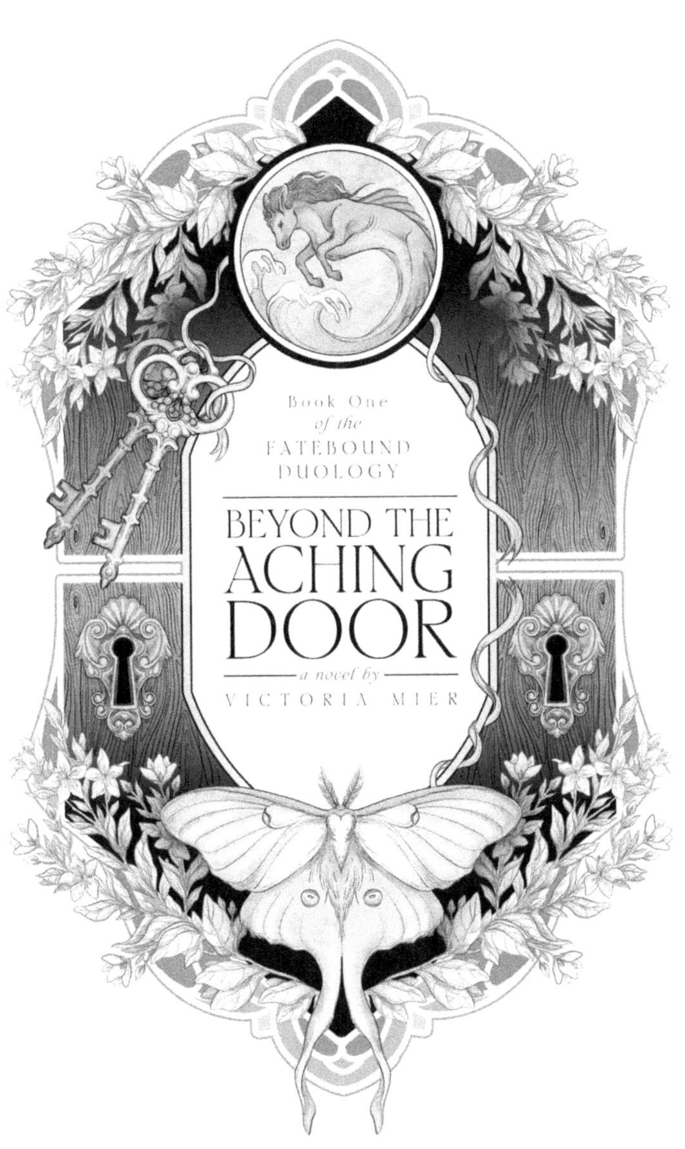

Book One
of the
FATEBOUND
DUOLOGY
BEYOND THE
ACHING
DOOR
a novel by
VICTORIA MIER

Content Warnings

- Grief
- Off-page murder of unhoused people
- Missing/presumed dead father
- Depiction of inpatient hospitalization
- Brief, non-gory violence
- Suicidal ideation
- Descriptions of sexual desire
- One on-page sexual encounter focused on feelings/sensuality

Chapter One

The September day dawned golden and glorious, ushering in a cool breeze, sunlight thick as molasses, and the third drowning in five days.

"Hey, Raegan," the barista—Sam, was it?—greeted as she approached. "The usual? Don't typically see you so early."

Four more text messages from her editor lit up Raegan's phone in rapid succession. She sighed. "No, I'm gonna do a sixteen-ounce drip today," she replied, digging her knuckles into still-sleepy eyes. "To go. The strong shit, please."

The barista rang her up, and Raegan paid, digging into the pockets of her long woolen overcoat for a crumpled dollar bill, which she dropped into the tip jar. She skirted the small crowd of customers awaiting their orders at the pick-up counter, instead moving to lean against one of the café's floor-to-ceiling windows. On the other side of the glass, the sidewalk teemed with morning rush-hour traffic: men in suits and screaming schoolchildren and people running late for their bus. All things she normally avoided by not waking up this fucking early.

Her order appeared on the counter, and Raegan snatched it, taking a large gulp that seared her tongue. She slammed on a travel lid and made her way to the side door. Outside, the remaining puddles and water droplets from last night's rainstorm shimmered in the sunlight, winking at her as if secrets sailed on their shallow depths.

She felt the buzz of more texts arriving and ignored it, though she lengthened her stride, suspicion curling in her belly. Her editor, Henry, trusted her the most out of his team of reporters, valuing her quick, ruthless mind, and unerring ability to connect the dots. And Raegan felt pretty sure Henry's early morning distress call, today's drowning, and the lead crime reporter's emergency gallbladder surgery were all going to tie up in a neat little bow. A bow that might very well knot itself around *her* neck.

When her phone rang half a block from the subway station, Raegan sighed, moving her coffee into her left hand and shifting the weight of her leather shoulder bag. She dug the phone out from her pocket, unsurprised by the name on her screen.

"I'm about to get on the subway," Raegan said after answering the call. "How many times are you going to call me, Henry? You could at least tell me why you want me in the newsroom right this second. I hate waking up early. Almost as much as I hate surprises."

"I'll explain everything when you get here," Henry replied, his voice even despite Raegan's venomous tone. "Sorry. It's a shitshow."

"Isn't it always?" Raegan drawled, making use of the last few seconds ticking down on the crosswalk display. She took a running step to clear the puddle around the curb, the heavy lug soles of her boots thudding on the sidewalk. Up ahead, the mouth of the subway station yawned wide.

"Look," Raegan said, interrupting something Henry was saying about a meeting with the managing editor of the paper. "I'm about to head into the station, so I'm gonna lose you. See you in a few, okay?"

"Yeah, sounds good," Henry replied, distracted. Raegan could make out what sounded like a loud conversation, or an argument, in the background. "See you in a minute."

Raegan hung up, shoved her phone into her pocket and then descended the stairs. The subterranean dimness was a welcome relief—the sun had been stabbing its yellow fingers into her eyes all morning. She wove through the station's bowels, arriving at her platform with only a light sheen of sweat dampening the small of her back.

Gray concrete hunched all around her, abandoned Styrofoam containers and torn plastic bags scuttling across the tracks below. Other subway riders dotted the platform, mostly consumed by their phones, a few with their noses buried in books.

The screech of an incoming train shattered the air. She watched it approach, the dull silver of its mechanical hide glinting in the darkness of the subway tunnel. After boarding, she settled into a seat. The scratched orange fiberglass was slippery beneath her overcoat. She tilted her head back and drew a deep breath. The air smelled only faintly of piss at this hour, a pleasant surprise. As the train pulled away from the station, she tried her best to ignore the pop song blasting from someone's phone. Every day, Raegan got a little closer to strangling people who didn't think headphones were necessary in public spaces.

As her destination grew closer, a migraine thudded in her skull and irritation boiled poisonous in the pit of her stomach. God, it was only Wednesday. She sunk into her seat as the subway slowed to a halt, the sticky floor gluing the soles of her boots to the ground. Raegan scanned the busy platform through the windows in that way she usually did—always searching, just in case.

The outline of a tall figure leaning against the station's wall snagged Raegan's attention. The person read as masculine, clearly and aggressively so, at least a head taller than the other commuters milling about. He was dressed in nondescript but well-fitting black clothing; the way the fabric pulled at his broad shoulders spoke to hard-earned, coiled muscle. He carried no bag, and his casual stance—one hand in his pocket, weight evenly distributed—seemed deadly somehow.

As Raegan looked more closely, transfixed for a reason she could not place, she took in dark tumbles of wavy black hair, an unusually angular face, and a full, sculpted mouth that contrasted with the sharp jaw and knife-like cheekbones. The subway door slid open, and their gazes met for the barest of seconds. Even in the flickering underground light, she could see his eyes were a deep, unusual shade of gray, like the ocean in a storm.

All thoughts of the early morning and her frustration with Henry's weirdness and even the jarring chorus of the pop song melted away entirely. Raegan's heart leapt, familiarity crawling up her throat. A busker's violin music slipped through the subway car's open door like a silk scarf, the notes sweet as honeycomb. An entire sea swelled in her chest. Her breath caught, a broken-winged swallow in her throat, and desire crept up from between her legs. Pain bloomed in her fingers from how hard she was gripping the edge of her seat, nails scrabbling for purchase on the slippery surface.

And then the doors shut and the train rambled off. Raegan collapsed back, her breath coming in hard and fast. Her muscles flexed, ready to do whatever was necessary to get back to him. An alien thought rose in her mind: all she had *ever* done was try to get back to him. She squeezed her eyes shut, trying to breathe through the yearning unspooling in her chest. Dropping her head into her hands, Raegan fought hard to stay in the moment, in her body.

"Breathe," she murmured, suddenly incapable of remembering anything her therapist had told her to do when her mind scrambled to assign meaning to the meaningless. "Just breathe."

CHAPTER TWO

When the train's automated voice announced its arrival at Market East station, Raegan scrambled to her feet before the subway could even come to a halt, eager to leave the liminal space of an underground tunnel on the second to last day of September. This month always felt like a hinge, creaking open wider and wider until she had no choice but to face another October and another anniversary of the worst thing that had ever happened to her.

The subway spat her out into a huge indoor mall clad in tiles the color of dried blood and dotted with wells of dusty fake plants. All of it familiar, simple, real, which allowed Raegan to convince herself that nothing had happened at all. She'd seen an attractive stranger and had a little daydream. She'd been up early, functioning on only a few hours of sleep. Maybe the caffeine hadn't set in yet. As she trudged up the flight of stairs to the newsroom's back door, Raegan banished that odd, lilting yearning further and further away with each step.

At the landing, she scanned her keycard and pulled the door open. She was greeted by drab gray carpet, a sea of cubicles, and ridiculously tall ceilings, courtesy of the building's past as an industrial plant. Raegan released a long breath, her shoulders relaxing. The newsroom always soothed her. It was a monument to fact—a place where only the truth mattered.

People watched Raegan as she made her way to her desk. Even the sports guys stared. Her ease faltered. When she came around a sharp corner, nearly home free in the features section, the food critic stood up in his chair and gaped at her. Raegan lost her patience.

"Okay, what the fuck?" she demanded, dropping her bag onto her desk with a thud.

The food critic pulled a pen out of his pocket for no apparent reason. "Vince is laid up with the gallbladder surgery, so they made you lead on the drownings."

Raegan yanked her coat off, throwing it across the back of her chair. "That probably pissed some people off," she replied, looking over her shoulder with an arched brow. The copy editor across the aisle from her suddenly became very interested in his cell phone.

"Sure did." The food critic sniffed. "I mean, you're very young. With all due respect."

Raegan wanted to bat the words away like a stupid fly, but anger boiled in her stomach, red-hot against her insides. Warmth rose to her face, venom accumulating on her tongue. "I'm thirty, for fuck's sake." She massaged her temples as her migraine thundered louder in her skull. "And you write about food. With all due respect."

The food critic nudged his glasses farther down his nose in surprise, taking her in. "You're thirty? I thought you just graduated college."

Raegan gritted her teeth, reminding herself that there would be an uncomfortable number of witnesses were she to murder her colleague right here, right now.

"I hardly think Raegan's age matters," a cool voice said from behind her shoulder. She felt the surge of anger slow, more smoke than fire, at the arrival of Henry Washington.

"You might recall, Colin, her excellent track record and multiple awards. Or maybe you don't, because as Raegan mentioned, you *do* write about food, which renders your opinion on investigative journalism a bit meaningless, doesn't it?"

Colin made a small noise and sat back down. In a mirror movement, Henry pulled a chair from a nearby cubicle and sat in it.

"So," Raegan said, leaning back against her desk, arms crossed. "You're putting me on the drownings, aren't you?"

Henry's mouth twitched with amusement. "Yes," he replied, looking up at her. "The fact that you already figured it out makes me confident in my choice. Your appalling lack of a work-life balance also helps."

Raegan drummed her fingers across the peeling surface of her desk, emotions warring for dominance in her chest. Without glancing at Henry, she dragged a hand through her hair and squeezed her eyes shut.

"What? Did *he* get to you?" Henry asked in a low, incredulous tone. "Office politics have never seemed to bother you."

His words barely registered. With her eyes closed, the darkness loomed closer, and though Raegan knew she stood in the familiarity of the newsroom, she felt as though she could just as easily pitch herself into the void. Apprehension ate away at her excitement with sharp teeth that threatened to tear open old wounds.

"Unless it's not office politics you're worried about," Henry continued, clearly just as good at connecting the dots himself. "Does this hesitation I'm sensing have something to do with the fact it's almost October?"

At that, Raegan had no choice but to open her eyes. The return of the overhead lights sent her migraine into a howl, and she clenched her jaw, gaze meeting Henry's. She said nothing, daring her editor to keep going. He must have recognized something in her expression because he stared out the large windows instead of looking at her. Raegan glanced down at her hands, examining the raw, red cuticles.

"Look," Henry said, still gazing out the window. "There's whispers from the police department that this is a potential serial killer. I trust you to report this in a way that will keep people safe."

Raegan said nothing, lifting her coffee cup to her mouth even though she knew it was empty. The newsroom was quiet this time of the morning. She normally didn't arrive until closer to noon, typical for her section; a late start made it easier to cover events that didn't begin until eight PM or later. The soft hush made her feel exposed.

Glancing up, she found Henry looking at her. "It's been almost twenty years, Raegan," her editor said, concern and fondness creasing the skin around his brown eyes as he took her in. "Are you really going to do this every October for the rest of your life?"

She narrowed her gaze at him, opening her mouth to speak, but Henry held up a hand. "Actually, don't answer that," he said, leaning forward, elbows on his knees. "Take a day. I can hold the wolves back for a bit. Have your annual mope and then let me know tomorrow. Okay?"

Raegan chewed the inside of her lip. A war brewed within her. She wanted this opportunity. The desire to sink her teeth into whatever was going on in her city burned hot and bright. But she also wanted—*needed*—to follow her mourning practice. It didn't matter how many years it had been; Henry would understand that if he'd ever lost someone in the way she had.

"You made me get out of bed and rush here just to tell me I could have a day to think about it?" Raegan asked, arching a brow.

Her editor laughed, picking at a loose thread on his blazer. For a moment, he avoided answering her, but then his dark, warm eyes met hers. "Appearances, Raegan," Henry replied, gesturing to the offices ringing the outer corner of the newsroom—the ones that belonged to the managing editor, editor-in-chief, and head copyeditor. "I fought for you on this. Had to make it look like you wanted it bad, too."

"It's not that I don't—"

"I know," Henry said, cutting her off, scratching the side of his head. "But I wanted to buy you some time."

Raegan sank into her chair, one arm resting on her carefully organized desk. She crossed her ankle over her knee and stared her editor down. "You're going to tell them I said yes, aren't you?"

"I am," Henry replied solemnly, folding his arms. "People are *drowning* in the middle of a city, Raegan. They're drowning on the goddamn pavement. How in the hell is someone like you going to resist?"

CHAPTER THREE

Henry was right, like he usually was. She couldn't ignore the buzz that started up in her skull when he suggested she have a look at the latest crime scene.

"If you tell me tomorrow you're not in a place to take the lead, fine, I'll handle it," Henry said, getting to his feet. "Besides, getting you to today's crime scene is mostly why I dared to awaken the beast from her slumber."

"It was a smart move." Raegan pulled her freshly charged voice recorder from a drawer, though she doubted anyone would let her get them on record. She shoved a notebook and two pens into her pockets before dry-swallowing some ibuprofen for her migraine. "You're thinking if you let me get a taste, I probably won't be able to let go."

"It's possibly the first serial around these parts in some time." Henry sounded amused despite the dark topic, skirting around her statement.

Raegan stood, searching for her press badge. She almost never used it—didn't usually need to with her work in features —but it might help her not get kicked out of an active crime scene. Or it would *definitely* get her kicked out, depending on which cops were at the location.

"It's a fucked up killing method," she said, trying to focus on the story, seeing if it would distract her from the other tale that she ached to tell this time of year. "They've been trying so hard to pass it off as a series of oddly similar accidents, I almost started to believe it. I mean, drowning? In puddles? And these men, yes, they're vulnerable due to being unhoused, but they're not small."

"The guy this morning was 6'2" apparently, well over two hundred pounds," Henry said, leaning against the half-wall of her cubicle. "Even if the victims were drugged or otherwise incapacitated, they shouldn't be drowning."

"I think the puddles are deeper when the attack occurs," Raegan said, reaching around to the back of her waistband to make sure her knife was there. "And then they dry up. Or something."

Raegan could feel her mind pivoting, less a dark sea and more a dagger, all her frantic energy finding something to settle on. She loved journalism because it could devour her completely and she wouldn't have to poke her head out into her personal life for days, maybe weeks. She'd more or less won awards for being obsessive and antisocial.

"I meant what I said," Henry began, breaking her train of thought. "If you can't take it on . . . I . . . I just know this time of year can be tough."

Raegan set her jaw. "Yeah." Her mind threatened to lose its focus on things that were not her life, the hard-won mask slipping for a moment. "Serial killer drownings will certainly lighten it up."

Henry hesitated, a pained look crossing his face. "Hey, I'm sorry—"

"No," Raegan said, waving her hand. "It's fine. That was supposed to be a joke."

He smiled. "Well, unfortunately, it wasn't very funny."

"Do you have the address of the newest crime scene?" she asked, shoving anything that wasn't work-related out of her head.

"Already emailed it to you." Henry beamed at her like he had just sent her a particularly cute video of a puppy, not the location of a dead body.

Raegan was already refreshing the email app on her phone. Despite her hesitation, the thrill of the hunt began to sing in her body like an old hymn.

"I'll see if they'll tell me anything real," she said, pulling her coat back on and grabbing her bag from the ground.

"You do have a way with people," Henry called after her. "It's kind of creepy but usually effective."

She looked over her shoulder and flashed a grin, a real one for once, before disappearing around the corner.

Raegan had known the second she saw the address that it was going to be weird. People who struggled with homelessness did turn up dead in her city but not usually in wealthy neighborhoods. The places that got their streets plowed first during blizzards for no reason other than median income could not be expected to bear the unsightliness of housing inequality, much less an actual crime scene.

In the slanting morning light, the alley off Delancey Place looked more like a European side street than a crime scene. Wisteria vines draped across whitewashed brick arches, and moss grew thick and lush between the mortar. But there was the crime scene tape all the same, and a man about her age in a medical examiner's jacket bent over a clipboard.

"Excuse me," Raegan said, turning on her smile. "I'm a reporter and was just wondering if you could tell me a little bit about what's going on."

"I'm sorry," the man replied without looking at her. "I'm not supposed to talk to the press."

Before she could reply, he threw a cursory glance over his shoulder. Only then did he turn, tucking away his pen and considering Raegan, eyes sliding down her frame. "It's not that I wouldn't want to help *you*, trust me."

Internally, Raegan shrugged. She could work with that, at least.

"Oh, I totally understand," she said, letting out a sigh and fiddling with her notebook as if she had never opened one before. "I'll go see who else I can speak with. I'm just hoping for some context, not a quote. And my editor said an experienced medical professional like yourself would be the best, since this is apparently . . . strange."

He considered her, and she let him look at whatever he wanted to. "If you're not quoting," he began, taking a step closer. "I can see why you wouldn't want a random officer giving you a rundown."

"No quotes," Raegan confirmed, smiling. Her face hurt.

"It's bizarre," the medical examiner murmured. "The guy drowned. Like, lungs full of water, pulmonary distress, blue skin. But we found him in a puddle. A tiny, shallow puddle, and there's no indication the body was moved."

Raegan studied him carefully, wanting to make sure he wasn't bullshitting her.

"I'm dead serious," he told her, holding up his hands. "I'm out here because we need to collect about a million samples to figure out how this happened."

"Weird," Raegan conceded. "Thanks."

The medical examiner was digging in his pocket for his card, encouraging her to give him a call if she needed "anything at all" in a tone Raegan did not like, when two police officers rounded the corner. One of them was, of course, Detective Bartley.

"Shit," she exhaled through gritted teeth, the smile gone, her voice dropping an octave back to its natural tone.

"Miss Overhill? Is that you?" the detective called. "Raegan Overhill!"

His voice alone made her nauseous, the sound of it like a siren call for old memories to stir and sit on her shoulders, their weight heavy and taloned.

"Hey, Detective," Raegan replied even though her head swam. She walked over to where the detective stood closer to the sidewalk, leaving the medical examiner dangling his card.

"They got you doing crime?"

"They do," Raegan replied. "Vincent has to get his gall-bladder taken out. I don't know how long I'll be on this. It's uh . . . something, isn't it?"

"You know I can't comment just yet," Bartley told her, "but yeah, it's weird. I can set you up with the press liaison for something more concrete."

Raegan considered. Some journalists would be relieved to know a member of the police who didn't think they were a vulture or a piece of shit, but nearly twenty years ago, Detective Winsome Bartley had been in charge of the case surrounding her father's disappearance.

He never found a goddamn trace of Cormac Overhill.

And so it seemed the detective felt he owed some kind of personal debt to Raegan. She was fine with working people and getting what she needed from them. But she didn't cross lines and she didn't want *anyone* to think a cop did her favors because she'd lost her daddy.

It didn't help that Raegan was staunchly of the opinion that if the cops liked her, she wasn't doing her job right.

"Oh, I can reach out for that later, but thank you," she replied, crossing her arms and looking at him a little harder. "I was hoping an officer on the scene might be willing to give me something short. I'm worried this is going to freak people out, you know, impossible drownings with Halloween coming up."

"How'd you know they were impossible?" Bartley asked, drawing himself up and staring down at her, the warmth seeping out of him like a cloud passing over the sun.

"I mean, I don't, technically," Raegan said, uncrossing her arms since he'd already given her the confirmation so easily. "But we're in an alley in Society Hill and there's a drowning. So. Impossible, yeah?"

Bartley relaxed then and let out a chuckle. "Okay, you've got me there. I guess it does seem pretty spooky, huh?"

"It sure does, Detective," she answered.

"Well, let me get you a brief statement," he said, motioning for Raegan to wait. While she did, she texted Henry that she was getting something—not very much, no more than a breaking news item, but something.

Another officer came by to tell her what she'd already suspected: the victim was unhoused. No one in the neighborhood recognized him, not the folks at the corner liquor stores or the outdoor cafés, so no ID yet. This was presumably not his usual haunt. His cause of death hadn't been determined yet.

"But a suspected drowning?" Raegan pushed.

"No," the cop told her. "I mean, there's some medical signs of that, but obviously that couldn't have happened, so we're not referring to it like that."

"No, of course not," Raegan said. "Hey, have you ever seen anything like this?"

The officer weighed her up, his bushy brows furrowed as she held his gaze. "No," he admitted slowly. "No, ma'am, I have not. But I'm sure there's a reasonable explanation."

"Sure," Raegan said with a noncommittal shrug. "Well, thank you for your time."

She double-checked the spelling of the officer's name, begrudgingly gave Bartley a wave, and then headed back to the subway. Her platform was oddly deserted despite the busy morning hour, and she dropped her weight into the cold fiberglass seat with a thud. The memory of the earlier subway ride —the ecstasy that had crept through her, the way her blood had hummed upon seeing the stranger—threatened to resurface, so Raegan kept her eyes trained on her phone. She scrolled through social media and was treated to photos of a high school acquaintance's wedding. Everyone looked happy and normal.

Raegan kept staring at her phone even when the reception cut out in the bowels of the tunnels, willing her own reflection in the small black square to not betray her. Someone across the car from her dropped their bag loudly on the ground. Another passenger at the other end was singing a song she thought she knew. Raegan focused on remembering the title, or maybe the artist, or even just conjuring an image of the album cover.

When her cell service returned and the subway pulled out of the deeper tunnels, a text from her ex-girlfriend appeared. Raegan inhaled and then exhaled so slowly that her vision swam for a minute. Swallowing, she tapped the text alert.

Hey, Layla had written. *Thinking of you. I know this time of year is hard.*

Raegan snorted, tried to run a hand through her hair, and got a ring caught in her curls for her trouble. Once she had painfully extracted her hair from the setting of the ring's stone, Raegan almost succeeded in telling herself to just say "thanks" to Layla and move on. She had almost succeeded in reminding herself that she didn't have to answer at all.

But Colin's reaction to her taking the lead on the drownings and the way the medical examiner suddenly wanted to help when she played a silly girl and the useless guilt that wracked Detective Bartley's face every fucking time he saw Raegan all came flooding back, buzzing in her skull like a thousand wasps that would only quiet once some venom was expressed.

How noble of you, Raegan typed back as the subway pulled

into her station, *to check in on someone who is - how did you put it - so hard to love.*

Raegan banished her phone to the farthest recesses of her coat's deep pockets and exited the subway car. Despite her empty train, the station was packed and she was forced to file slowly toward the escalator. When Raegan finally stepped onto it, she pulled her notebook and a pen from her pocket, intending to scribble down some notes while the escalator moved at its glacial pace.

Instead of making notes, Raegan chewed on the top of her pen, apparently working her jaw too hard because the ink exploded everywhere. She cursed under her breath the entire way to the station's bathroom. As she did her best to scrub the ink off her mouth and neck, then off her hands, she caught a glance of herself in the dim lighting. Dark circles had invited their kin over for supper beneath her eyes. Black ink dripped from her mouth. It was familiar, somehow. Goosebumps rose across her skin as her mind keened. She choked on her next breath, hands flying to grip either side of the dirty sink.

Raegan held herself there for a moment, harsh coughs shaking her shoulders, eeriness coiling in her gut. For a second, she felt sure that if she looked at the mirror, she would not recognize her own face. A feverish chill traced its fingers up her spine.

But then the moment passed, quick as an autumn shadow. Raegan scrubbed the rest of the ink off her skin, and the thoughts of Layla and Bartley and her father from her mind. She would focus on the crime scene, on the story, on the *facts.*

There was probably a reasonable explanation why a six-foot-two man had drowned in a tiny puddle. That's what the officer had said. But the crime scene had felt just like that old story her father used to tell, and Raegan knew better than anyone that sometimes things just happened with no reason-able explanation. And sometimes, with no explanation at all.

Chapter Four

Her Wednesday did not improve—not that Raegan had been expecting such a boon. She buried herself in work, shirking off her promise to join a colleague for lunch at the pub down the street. In her defense, she was nearly finished with a long-form piece she'd been working on for almost four months and wanted to give the copy editors a good chance to review everything. Raegan had learned a long time ago that when you accuse the powerful of bad things, you better have all your ducks in a perfect fucking row.

Day dissolved into night, the approach of October waiting for her just beyond the building's door, grief and memory and shadow hanging in the eaves. When the newsroom quieted and her long-form piece was in Henry's inbox, she slipped out the back entrance and headed for the train station. But instead of the subway, Raegan boarded the commuter rail. Her destination was at the end of the line, deep in the suburbs. Over the years, her ritual had become refined, exact, and it was important to get as far away from her real life as possible. The few people she allowed to be close to her were tired of hearing it, her therapist had to have been exhausted by the tale, and what no one realized was that Raegan was sick of it herself.

But grief is a story, and it is one that demands to be told.

Which is how Raegan found herself in a cozy, if run-down, bar somewhere in New Jersey, signed up for an open mic night. The story was best presented to the unsuspecting as fiction. It seemed safer that way—like maybe it wouldn't worm itself into the listener's marrow if they thought of it as only an exercise of imagination.

She settled down on a stool at the bar and nursed a too-sweet cider, pretending to listen to the performer on stage. Despite the cool weather outside, the bar was unpleasantly warm and everything was sticky. After what felt like two years of spoken word poetry, Raegan had no choice but to peel off her overcoat and lay it across her lap. Condensation beaded on her bottle of cider. The story rattled inside of her like a caged thing, feathered wings beating against her ribs. Raegan reminded herself to sit like a regular person, to look normal and well-adjusted. In a place like this, only a few seconds of holding herself as if she were protecting an old wound could bring men sniffing—for daddy issues, for insecurities, for painful places they could poke and prod to get what they wanted.

But then the host called the pseudonym Raegan had signed up under, and she breathed a sigh of relief, quickly followed by an inhale sharpened with anticipation. She left her coat draped over the stool and pulled her mane of auburn curls off her damp neck as she approached the microphone. No one looked like they cared at all about the open mic, so Raegan didn't bother with the little introduction she some-times had to give. Instead, she straightened her shoulders and looked out at the small bar: the mismatched chairs, the wobbly tables, the low ceiling, and orange-hued lights. Then, she took a deep breath and began.

"When my father was young, he met a man on a train platform. The man wore an old-fashioned three-piece suit. The sun was just beginning to set, the sky leaking spilled molasses.

"The man asked my father for a cigarette. He pronounced it 'cig-ah-*rette*,' stressing the last syllable instead of the first two. My father obliged, but when he offered a light, the man only stared down at the cigarette. He rolled it between the fingers of his left hand once, twice, three times, before tucking it into his pocket.

" 'Not even going to smoke it?' my father asked.

" 'No,' the man answered.

"My father fell silent, moving a step or two away from the man. He stamped his feet against the ground to ward off the winter chill. The platform remained empty. He couldn't see any trains in the distance. His gaze eventually drifted back toward the man.

" 'Aren't you cold?' my father wanted to know. My father was like that.

" 'No,' the man answered, his eyes roving down the tracks. He took out an old pocket watch from the folds of his tweed blazer. He rolled it between the fingers of his left hand once, twice, three times, before tucking it into his pocket.

"As my father watched, the train station began to change. The bricks became new, raw-red in the low light. The benches morphed into old-fashioned wrought iron, crisp and black. The colors of the sunset turned sepia.

"With a start, my father realized there was a train pulling into the platform, though he hadn't heard the engine. The man in tweed approached the door.

" 'Do not follow,' the man warned. My father noticed that despite the winter air, there was no puff of frosted breath when the man spoke.

" 'Who are you?' my father remembers asking, though perhaps he already knew the answer.

"The man stood in the doorway, pulled the cigarette back out of his pocket, and rolled it between his fingers. He lingered for a moment but did not answer, and then he disappeared into the darkness of the rickety train, its sides heaving like an exhausted animal.

"For so many years, my father remembered the man, the train platform, the sepia-colored sunset. All my life, he paused when we said the Apostle's Creed in church, right before the 'I believe' lines. It was just a small pause—

"one,

"two,

"three."

Raegan's mouth felt dry as paper, her heart a war drum. The story was true. Her father was gone, and this story was the only thing she had. And so, she would keep telling it, again and again and again. It was her way of looking for a door, a curtain to walk behind, a secret place she could go, and maybe her father would be there, waiting. If that kind of door existed, she told herself, she was the kind of person it would appear for. And she would walk through it without looking back.

Of course, no door appeared in the wall of the run-down tavern as she paid her tab and gathered up her coat. Nothing in the parking lot either, nor the train station, not even with its flickering lights and empty platform. No matter how many times Raegan begged for a door, no matter how hard she looked, nothing sprung its maw open with a creak that sounded like a lullaby. So, she kept telling the story because it was closer to a door than anything else she had ever known.

What she didn't know—couldn't know—was that the story was an invocation of sorts, a calling of the quarters, a setting of beacons, and when she told it, Fate herself swooped low from the never-places and listened to the story fall from Raegan's mouth like wine.

The next morning, the story still wrapped around her marrow, Raegan headed into the newsroom to tell Henry she'd take the lead. October drew closer now and her mind would still contort like a fish on dry land as it approached, but the desperation always settled after she told the story.

Thursday offered a cool, delicious gloom—the kind of early autumn chill that made the hair on the back of Raegan's neck stand up—the just-beginning-to-turn leaves emphasized by the backdrop of gray skies. She'd somehow beaten Henry to the newsroom, so she headed out to the front of the building to pay a visit to her favorite food truck.

Rich was stationed on his usual bench, stained duffle bag at his feet, feeding the pigeons from a crumpled seed packet. She hated running around behind the police and trying to do their work for them. But it was worth a shot.

"You need a cup of coffee or anything today?" she asked as she approached. Rich looked up at her, his salt-and-pepper hair catching the low, gray light. An already-emptied seed packet threatened to teeter out of the pocket of his faded coat. It had been blue once, maybe.

"Only if you would be so kind," the older man said, smiling up at her.

Raegan hated talking to strangers—a constant source of mockery in the newsroom, which she always admitted she deserved—but for some reason, when Rich had asked her for something to eat after one of her first days at the paper, she'd not only obliged but asked if he wanted company.

They had gotten to talking about the city—Rich knew more about its recent history off the top of his head than most people—and they'd been friendly ever since. She'd tried more than once to connect him with resources, but he always shrugged it off.

"You got it," she told him, heading across the wide expanse of pavement to the nearby food truck, the towering buildings casting weak shadows. A few minutes later, she walked back over with two steaming cups of coffee and handed one to Rich.

"I have a question that might be upsetting," Raegan said. "Is it okay if I ask you?"

Rich looked over the lid of the cup inquisitively, nodding.

"There was a murder or accidental death or something yesterday morning," Raegan said. "An unhoused man. He was found in an alley over by Delancey Place, but Rich, the thing is, all the physical evidence says he drowned. In a tiny puddle. In Society Hill. Have you heard anything about this?"

The moment she brought up the puddle, Rich's hands began to shake so hard he had to put his coffee down.

She felt a rare pang of guilt for possibly upsetting him. "We don't have to talk about it."

"No, no, it's fine," Rich said, smoothing out his pants with long strokes, again and again. "It's just . . . I think this has happened before."

Raegan immediately leaned in closer, her heart hammering. Rich was no official source, but he had never made up stories before, as far as she could tell. She didn't think he'd start now.

"Drownings? In puddles? You've seen this before?"

"I think so," Rich told her. He had picked his coffee back up but was still clearly uneasy. "Look, don't go quoting me—"

"No, Rich, I wouldn't, honest," Raegan said, fighting to keep her tone as even and soothing as possible. "I'm worried about your safety."

"Okay, okay, just don't get all news lady on me, that's all."

Biting back a smile at his wording, Raegan assured him she wouldn't. She settled her elbows on her knees, both hands around her coffee cup. The liquid burned through the thin blue-and-white patterned cup, searing her palms. Raegan breathed into the pain, telling herself to stay in her body no matter where Rich's story went.

"Back in the early '90s, I think, maybe the late '80s, I had some friends who drowned," Rich began, a little shaky, his gaze trained straight ahead. "Some friends like me, you know. There were people saying something was coming out of the puddles, out of the sewers. That all sounded like crazy talk to me. Something that was offering to take people to a better place, a nice place, with a warm bed and where you'd get a full belly."

For a moment, Raegan squeezed her eyes shut, trying to feel the breeze on her face. Her blood thrummed in her veins, mind curling around this lush impossibility.

"Lots of people said no," Rich said, sitting back on the bench, his gaze dipping toward Raegan. "I mean, something just pops out of a puddle and says, 'hey, youse, I'll give you a nice place to lay your head?' No, sir. That sounds suspicious, first of all, and second of all, how is something even popping out of a puddle in the first place?"

Rich's voice wavered, as if the fantastical bent of this tale made him self-conscious. Raegan turned to look at him, nodding for him to go on. She hoped the look in her eyes said that she believed him.

"Then I had some friends who said it kept coming back, every time it rained, every time there was water on the ground," Rich said, the words coming out in a jumbled exhale. "At first they'd see it in real deep puddles in potholes, you know, where it was maybe possible some maniac had climbed in there, but then it would be in just a little water gathered up on a bench, or in the reflection of wet glass."

One leg bouncing, Rich took a long sip of his coffee before continuing. "Sometimes it looked like a weird horse head and sometimes it looked like a beautiful lady," he said, glancing away as he spat the words out as quickly as possible, as if he didn't believe them himself. "In my opinion, the ones who said yes saw the beautiful lady. Think about it—a pretty lady offering a bed and a meal? Can't say I would've said no if I saw it, whatever it was."

At that, Raegan's eyes tracked to Rich. She tilted her head and raised one eyebrow, a question on her lips.

"And I never did see it, before you ask," Rich said, batting the air with one hand as if to swipe away the possibility. "Not once. But I watched people I knew see it over and over again, and they got . . . they got real strange, like it was wearing them down or something. I don't even know half their names—they were just friends, you know, pals that wouldn't take your shit if you walked away, people who knew which bench was yours. And then just—poof. Gone."

Rich hunched over for a moment, wrapping one arm around himself. Raegan let the silence stretch for a moment, not sure what to say.

"You're telling me a good number of people just disappeared?" Raegan eventually asked, her tone low. "No bodies, unlike this time?"

"I mean, I don't think so," Rich replied, looking over at her. "But, you know, the city was bad back then so dead homeless people . . . I don't know if anybody would have cared at all."

Raegan dropped her head into her hands for a second, her thoughts racing almost as quickly as her heart rate. Nausea unfolded in her stomach even though her blood sang with the thrill of it all. She'd have to corroborate this, of course. She'd dig into the archives, and if she had to, she'd reach out to Bartley. He was a senior detective. If he didn't know about these drownings, he was certainly friends with someone who would.

"People hardly care now," she admitted, her eyes softening as she turned to look at him. "Can't help but wonder whether, if the last victim had turned up somewhere less posh, maybe nobody would've noticed."

Rich shrugged and took a sip of his coffee. "Anyway, that's all I know," he said, seeming lighter now that he had released this story from wherever he'd been keeping it. "I can see if anyone else remembers anything, but it was a long time ago and a lot of people just go away one day."

"I'd appreciate that," Raegan replied, getting to her feet. "If you could bring it up when you see friends, that'd be great, but please don't stress yourself about it."

She slung her bag over her shoulder and considered Rich, looking for any part of the story that he might only be telling with his eyes.

"Will do," Rich replied. "You take care."

"You, too, Rich. Be safe." She pulled her coat closer against the incoming late September wind and grabbed the paper bag containing her breakfast from the food truck's counter, though her appetite was threatening to vanish entirely.

"Raegan!"

She turned, surprised, to see Rich standing a few feet from his bench, waving her down. For a moment, she paused, unsure, and then walked the steps back.

"Yes?" Raegan asked, hungry for another layer of this story.

"I just remembered something," he said, looking excited. "There was an Irish fella who used to hang around back then. I remember, he told everyone to stay away from the puddles. Called it a kelp, I think."

Something twisted in Raegan's gut, and her mouth went dry. "Rich," she breathed, trying to settle herself. Her mind keened, drunk on the poison of October and the way the world always bent strangely this time of year. "Do you . . . do you mean a *kelpie*?"

Chapter Five

"That's it!" Rich said, punching a finger in the air. "A kelpie. Does that mean anything to you?"

Of course it did. Her father had raised her on folklore and fairy tales the way other kids were raised on little league or the family business. Raegan's lungs tightened as she stood in a mundane place she knew so well, watching a folktale wander into the real world on damp, backwards hooves.

"Yes," she said slowly, trying to ration the air left in her lungs. "It's a mythological creature from Scottish folklore. They're usually not very nice. But they also don't usually show up in puddles."

"Maybe this is a puddle kelpie," Rich said, shrugging.

"Maybe, Rich," Raegan said, a forced, faint smile crossing her lips. "Hey, thanks for remembering that. It's really interesting. I appreciate it."

"No problem. I'll try to remember other stuff, too."

She needed to be back in the newsroom for two reasons: work, and the familiar tug to wilder, stranger things uncoiling in her chest. Raegan's mind was a vast, dark place, and like all places where shadows multiplied, she could not always trust it.

"

Right now, her heart pounding, palms damp, Raegan found that her mind wanted to tell her many impossible things. She knew full well those things were large enough to devour her.

"Thank you," she said to Rich, her voice coming out shakier than she would've liked. Rich waved at her as she walked away. Raegan tried to breathe, in and out, in and out. Surely, some Irish guy who was struggling or just superstitious made the connection between the mythological water-horse that dragged people to their deaths and people dying of drowning in a city. It made sense, in a storytelling sort of way. That was all, wasn't it? She tried telling herself people turned to folk beliefs or myths when they were scared, but she couldn't make it stick. Not here. Not in a modern city in the Western world. She supposed a kelpie could be an explanation for a recent Irish immigrant, but even then . . . she was unconvinced.

When Raegan returned to the newsroom, that's exactly how she explained it to Henry. He agreed, of course, shrugging off the kelpie bit in its entirety. Raegan knew it was the logical thing to do, and she repeated that to herself about eighty times. And yet, there was that magnetic pull in her bones, the call and response whenever the world around her lilted off its axis.

"I'm more concerned that this has potentially happened before," Henry said, his arms crossed, looking up at Raegan from his seat. "Does this mean you're taking the lead?"

His cubicle and desk were, per usual, littered with sticky notes and marked-up proofreading flats. He called it "organized chaos," but it made Raegan's anxiety spike just looking at it. Three old coffee cups were stacked in the corner, and she was pretty sure something was growing in one of them.

"Shut up," Raegan said through a mouthful of bagel, tearing her eyes away from Henry's desk. "Obviously I'm taking the lead. Anyway. I don't disagree with you. That's the big thing here: has this happened before? But also, let's say these aren't explainable accidents. Let's say, for a second, it's a serial. Has someone been dormant all these years, or is this a copycat of a killer no one knew about? And is there going to be something enlightening in the kelpie myth that this killer is inspired by?"

Saanvi, another reporter, stopped her march to the kitchenette so suddenly that Raegan could've sworn her ballet flats skidded on the carpet. Saanvi walked backwards to Henry's desk, her pretty brown eyes going wide. "What did you just say?" she asked in a hushed tone, leaning toward Raegan.

Henry looked at Raegan, unwilling to answer Saanvi, probably because he considered it Raegan's story and thus her call. But Saanvi and Raegan were friends. Or as close as Raegan got to friendship. They texted. They had gone out for drinks a few times, including a few months ago when Layla broke up with Raegan out of nowhere.

"You heard right," Raegan replied, her tone grim.

"So the bodies *are* connected," Saanvi whispered, her eyebrows flying to her hairline. "I was really hoping they were just a series of unrelated accidents. I mean, what else could it be? It's not like we have any oceans nearby for Timingila to wander in from and have a feast."

Raegan and Henry looked at her blankly.

"Sorry," Saanvi said, waving an elegant hand, her gold bracelets jingling. "Big aquatic beast in Hindu myth. Can swallow a whole whale. What's a kelpie?"

"Oh, kelpies aren't that big," Raegan said, perking up at having someone to discuss folklore with, not surprised Saanvi was more interested in it than Henry. "A river horse, basically. People try to ride it or whatever and it carries them to their deaths."

"Shit," Saanvi said, dragging out the "i" between her teeth. "A kelpie-inspired killer. That's a new one."

"If that's what is even going on," Henry interjected.

"They're good questions. Now you just have to answer them, Raegan."

It was normal for Raegan to pose the questions she had about a story to Henry to make sure she was on the right path. She never expected answers—that was *her* job. But this time, she was really hoping Henry would explain it to her. That he would assure her nothing supernatural was going on, that she was probably overreacting, and that there was no reason for the mention of a mythological creature to leave her feeling so untethered.

"You want to grab lunch with me?" Saanvi asked, sensing the editor-reporter chat had ended. "I have chai going on the stove."

Raegan wanted to bounce more ideas around with Henry, mostly for the sake of feeling less unhinged, but Saanvi's homemade chai was an absolute treat she was not willing to pass up. She told herself more caffeine was maybe not the best idea, but that didn't stop her from wrapping up the other half of her bagel and following Saanvi into the kitchenette.

"Besides serial killers," Saanvi said over her shoulder as she rummaged in the fridge, "how are you?"

"I've been better," Raegan conceded, grabbing two mugs from the cabinet. "I have a . . . personal thing. Anniversary of a death in the family. And Layla texted me that she was 'thinking of me' during 'this hard time.' "

Saanvi whipped her head around so fast she almost dropped the jug of milk. "Eww," she said, the disgust on her face so intense Raegan held back a laugh. "You've got your own shit to work out, but after what she said, she doesn't get to pretend she cares."

Unearned relief swept through Raegan. She had told Saanvi about the argument that led to the breakup, but she had excluded key elements. Because Raegan just needed someone on her side, even if it was only because of a selective retelling.

"Yeah, that's kind of what I thought," she replied, sliding the mugs toward Saanvi, not willing to say more.

"Like, who gets mad because you don't say the 'L'-word after four months? That's just not how dating works in America," Saanvi near-shouted, sloshing milk into the pot of chai and turning up the burner. "And then turns around and says it's too hard to try to love you?! No way." Saanvi turned to face Raegan, one hand on her hip.

"I think you're angrier about this than I am," Raegan said, a smile fighting its way onto her face because Saanvi was angry about the things she *had* depicted honestly.

"No," Saanvi replied, pointing a wooden spoon at Raegan. "You just keep everything pent up. Trust me. I know what that looks like."

Raegan settled onto a chair, pulling the sleeves of her sweater up and then back down, unwilling to discuss her own problems with the irritatingly perceptive reporter. "How are you?" she asked instead, looking up from the faux marble table.

"Since you've been thinking about murder all day, I will permit that little deflection," Saanvi said, raising a perfect eyebrow. The chai was boiling now, and Saanvi removed it from the heat, strained it and then ladled the tea into mugs, handing one to Raegan.

"Thanks," Raegan said, breathing in the aroma of spices and black tea.

"Thanks for appreciating my chai," Saanvi replied, wrapping her hands around the warm mug. "Your kind usually prefers weak-ass bagged tea." She made a retching sound and then took a long, luxurious sip.

Raegan laughed, trying to anchor herself to this: a hot cup of tea with a friend in the ugly but cozy newsroom lunchette. Simple, normal, natural.

"I keep forgetting to bring you some Glengettie," Raegan

said. "It doesn't stand a chance against your chai, but it's pretty good."

Raegan took a swig from her mug, enjoying the familiar flavors made by her friend's hands. The pair sat in comfortable silence, the noise of the newsroom churning behind them. Then someone was calling Saanvi's name from across the room—it was Erin, one of the breaking news writers.

"Sorry," Erin called, jogging over. "Possible active shooter situation just came in on the scanner. We gotta get to University City."

"Shit," Saanvi said, jumping to her feet. "I guess you get two cups of chai, Raegan."

"I'm not complaining," Raegan replied, already reaching to grab Saanvi's mug. "Be safe, both of you. Text me if you need anything."

Saanvi waved at Raegan and then followed Erin, the pair already pulling out their phones and yelling something to their editor. Raegan sat back, staring at the empty chair across from her for longer than she realized. Her mind strayed to Rich's words and the crime scene and the knot in her stomach that sat as heavy as tar.

Raegan had almost wanted to, but she didn't even try to explain to Henry or Saanvi that she could feel something, a tiny seed that should be uncomfortable and scary. But it wasn't. The kelpie felt like hope, like proof that fantastical things could happen, that truth was stranger than fiction.

Gods, she was reaching. Some Irish guy probably got high or drunk and started blabbering about kelpies, and here she was, all these years later, taking it fucking seriously and slapping it onto her wounds like a bandage.

But the seed of the kelpie was deep in her lungs now, throbbing with every breath, filling up the empty places inside her ribcage—the places that had opened when her father disappeared completely and never came back. The parts of herself that Raegan had quieted over the years were awakening, beginning their choir of furtive whispers that there was more to this world, to herself, and to her father's disappearance. If she just looked hard enough, the hushed voices said, she'd find it.

So Raegan decided to look.

Chapter Six

She spent two hours digging through the newspaper archives. Some reporters found the archives creepy, housed in the annex, an eerily quiet building blanketed in outdated hues of brown. The windows reminded Raegan of archers' windows in castles—arrowslits, she thought they might be called, though she couldn't remember where she had learned the term. Very little natural light leaked in, leaving the space reliant on yellow-tinted overhead fluorescents that hummed and blinked irregularly.

She was seated at a sticky-surfaced worktable with two cartons of back issues when she finally unearthed a possible mention of an uptick in "vagrant deaths." The wording alone made her blood boil. But the timeline was right. She pulled the issue and was planning to call Bartley until she saw it was already after 6 PM. Raegan closed the door to the archives and sighed. Her therapist had been encouraging her to have a better work-life balance, but now the two halves of herself had entwined themselves together, the disappearances and Rich's mention of the kelpie weaving separate fibers together. Raegan no longer knew how to unpick them or how to tell them apart.

That feeling, she supposed, was what drove her to leave the newsroom with a particular destination in mind, just as the sun began to slip behind the horizon. She did not get on the subway like she should've, and instead hopped on the commuter train. She sat on the old brown seat in silence, forehead against the cool glass, her breath fogging up the window. Outside, the darkness was blue-black and velvet, studded with traffic lights and streetlamps.

The ride took about fifteen minutes, all of which Raegan spent feeling as though she was exactly where she was meant to be, following some sort of trail, unwinding the fibers. But the moment she exited the train and stepped onto the platform that she once knew so well, all of the sureness went out of her. She walked down the stairs to the street level slowly, like she was in a trance, the heels of her boots clanging on the metal steps.

Raegan turned off the busy commercial corridor and into a quiet northeast neighborhood. The sidewalks were lined with streetlights that mostly worked. Leaves had already begun to dust the street, joining forces with the loose trash to clog the sewer grates. The houses were lit up on the inside, cars tucked away in their short driveways.

And then Raegan found herself standing in front of a pretty brick twin. The sycamore tree's leaves danced up and down the walkway like ghosts welcoming her back. She followed their tumbling path and rang the doorbell before she'd really thought about it. Raegan was almost surprised when someone answered. It was easier to imagine the house as torn down or abandoned, all the memories there locked away somewhere unreachable.

A woman opened the door, her thick cream cardigan closed around her frame, the warmth of the house backlighting her into a nearly black silhouette. She said nothing for a long moment.

"Raegan? What are you doing here?" The surprise in

Bronwyn Overhill's voice stung her daughter, though Raegan supposed she didn't have much of a right to feel that way.

"Hi, Mom," Raegan replied, her voice suddenly an unused hinge no one had bothered to oil. "Can I come in?"

"Of course. Is everything okay?" Raegan's mother asked, opening the door fully and ushering her inside. As much as she didn't want to, Raegan's walls came down just a little bit at the sound of her mother's weathered Welsh accent and the golden light trickling out of the house.

"Yeah," Raegan replied with a shrug. "I'm fine. Honest."

"It's just, you know, close to the anniversary, and you've had trouble before," Bronwyn said, shutting the door behind Raegan but not moving out of the small entry hallway. She scrutinized her daughter.

"I'm fine, Mom," Raegan replied, fingernails biting into her palm. "I just, uh, I'm covering a story and I wanted to see Dad's books. You know, the ones you didn't destroy."

Bronwyn stopped dead in the entryway for a moment, her mouth pressed into a firm line. "You know, your therapist said you shouldn't—"

"My children's therapist from fifteen years ago, Mom?" Raegan demanded. "We're still going off that?"

"Well, that's all the information I have because you don't tell me anything—"

"And this is exactly why," Raegan snapped, trying to ignore the way the house—her childhood home—pulled at her with soft, tiny, pleading hands.

Bronwyn let out a sigh, turning away from Raegan to walk into the kitchen. She couldn't help but notice the room was the same as ever: the compact swoop of counter and islands jutting out into the living room. All the wood was a distressed white with worn brass finishings. Teapots and tea boxes exploded from every corner, some obscured by the pothos vines Bronwyn loved so much. If Bronwyn had known a guest was coming, even just her own daughter, she would have cleaned and wiped the sink dry for reasons Raegan still didn't understand. Instead, a plate and a teacup sat in the metal basin.

The space was warm and cozy with lit candles everywhere. It smelled of cinnamon, like it always did, and Raegan could see the big, warm quilts on the couch in the next room. She wondered if her mother knew how desperately she wanted to just wrap herself up in one, how much she'd like to admit that she was not okay and she hadn't been for a long time and they should just put the kettle on and sit down.

She said nothing instead.

"I just want to know you're okay, Raegan," Bronwyn said, tears already welling in her eyes.

Raegan met her gaze, taking in the soft features and the waves of brown hair and the quivering lower lip.

"I know this time of year is hard, whether you want to admit it or not, and you know what," her mother continued, pulling her sweater tighter around her frame, "it's hard for *me* and you're the only person who understands. It was only ever the three of us, and now it's just the two of us."

Raegan recalled the weekend escapes Bronwyn used to plan when the anniversary got close. They would go apple-picking and shopping at TJ Maxx and out to dinner at a nicer chain restaurant, and they'd watch movies and cry and laugh and then cry again. The grief counselor said Raegan was adjusting well, all things considered.

Her heartbeat rising, Raegan remembered the day she found the books—or, at least, what remained of them. Occult tomes and folklore collections and cheap reprints of ancient texts, all marked up and dogeared by her father. Raegan had come home early from a friend's house to find Bronwyn in the process of burning a pile of Cormac's books in the firepit out back. *Burning* them. Like just throwing them out wasn't enough, like they had to be utterly destroyed, wiped from the face of the earth. Raegan begged her mother to stop and rescued what she could, but Bronwyn just yelled over and over again that it had to be like this because she couldn't lose her daughter, too. To *what*, Raegan did not know, and her mother didn't tell her.

After that, Bronwyn continued to avoid answering any of Raegan's questions. There were no more autumn nights spent making apple pies with their bounty from the orchard. They barely even spoke, and less than a year later, Raegan announced she was going to school in Boston. And that was that.

"I know it's hard for you, too. I know. I just . . . I don't know how to manage your feelings and mine all at once," Raegan said.

Bronwyn was softly crying, pretending to put dishes away. A spoon slipped out of her grasp, loudly clanging down onto the base of the drying rack.

"Mom. I just want to see the books," Raegan sighed. "We agreed you would keep them and I could come look at them. It's not for anything with Dad. It's for a story. The books are out of print and hard to find. They could help with the research I'm doing."

"What could they possibly have to do with an article you're writing? You're a goddamn newspaper reporter," Bronwyn demanded, wheeling on her daughter, a dish towel flying in the process.

Raegan considered her mother for a second, infuriated that Bronwyn was strong enough to allow her emotions to surface, to experience them and maybe move through them. If Raegan acknowledged all the grief clinging to the inside of her ribcage and the anger tucked between her lungs, she felt sure she would drown.

So she took a deep breath and tried to explain. "There's been some weird murders," Raegan began, immediately wishing she had lied instead, "and my editor and I think the killer may be influenced by a certain mythology."

Bronwyn's eyes went wide, her fingers digging into the dish towel in her grasp. "For god's sake, why the hell are you working on something like that?" she demanded. "That can't be good for you."

"Well, Mom, it's because this is my job and I'm not as delicate as you are," Raegan shot back. Immediately, remorse flooded her like a river, but she had never been very good at taking things back. Raegan watched as hurt unfolded on Bronwyn's face, but then her mother set her jaw and pointed down the hall.

"Everything is in his study like it has always been," she snapped. "Please just go look and then leave me alone."

"Yeah, okay," Raegan breathed, trying to walk out of the kitchen as quietly as possible. She tried to put her mother out of her mind as soon as she'd crossed the threshold—a weight she could not carry at the moment. Instead, she headed for her father's study. Raegan hated it as much as she loved it.

The small bonus room near the back of the house would have been a storage room for most people, but Cormac declared it his study, and that was that. The room had not changed: the big leather chair, small desk, ancient banker's lamp, and bookshelves packed to the gills. An old, knockoff William Morris-patterned paper adorned the walls. The faded green carpet was plush from disuse.

When she walked in, Raegan took a deep breath and wondered if it smelled like her father. She didn't really remember what he smelled like. She did remember the stories he'd tell and the hikes in Pennypack Park and this game they'd play where they'd have a tea party but she was a queen and he was her royal advisor. They'd stop wars and give secret support to the brave rebels and sometimes they'd just purchase more unicorns for the castle grounds. As she got older, Raegan always felt like she should stop playing, like she was too old for it, but she never did. They played it the day before he disappeared.

Trying to swallow the emotion gathering in the back of her throat, Raegan began looking through the books. She had a memory of the one she wanted: a big, old book on Celtic mythology. She didn't know for a fact if it was out of print—a lie invented for her mother—but all her Google searches had come up empty, so she assumed it was a rare edition or something along those lines. And it gave her an excuse to be back in the study.

She pulled each book out individually, even ones clearly labeled on their spines, looking for the right title. Ten minutes later, it hadn't appeared. But the big *Grimm's Fairy Tales* he used to read to her had. As had the old photo album that she didn't have the heart to crack open. And there was the pockmarked copy of the children's book about not being afraid of the dark. Raegan pulled it from the shelf, turning the wide hardcover over in her hands, feeling each little tear in the dust jacket.

"Look at this little boy—he's not afraid of the dark, either!" Raegan's father used to say, pointing at the characters on the pages.

He would read the text, but he loved to embellish, too, making up little side stories or pointing out details in the background of the illustrations. More than once, Raegan had wondered how she'd had such wonderful parents and still turned out the way she did. It seemed unfair to them, mostly, but also to her. Hers was a good childhood, spent in the woods with plenty of stories and bonfires in the little firepit out back, Saturday mornings at the flea market and summer days at the shore.

She should've been normal.

"So many of these brave kids aren't scared of the dark," Raegan's father would say. *"Do you think we should try to be more like them?"*

"I do!" Raegan would cheer, no longer afraid of the dark because her fictional friends had gone first.

The old lamp in the corner blinked, drawing Raegan out of the memory. The light fizzled again, and darkness yawned like a door. Raegan froze, her mind going blank with panic. A few heartbeats later, the light returned, but she was left shaken and caught in another memory: accidentally locking herself in the little dirt-floor basement almost twenty years ago.

She had been eleven. It was early spring—the spring before he disappeared—and both her parents were outside doing yard work. Raegan had thought she was no longer afraid of the dark, but when the door swung shut and locked behind her from the outside, the fear came quick and deep. She yelled but to no avail. She tried to remember the things her father had told her, but a primal instinct took root and she could do nothing but beat on the door. It could've been ten years or ten seconds, but at some point, her dad came inside and heard her.

He was quick to console her, scooping her up in his arms and making gentle shushing noises. But Raegan had worked herself into a hopeless terror, even if it was over something as simple as an accidental lock-in. Cormac found himself unable to calm her down. None of his old tricks worked. So he resorted to a new one.

"Do you want to know the old Welsh saying for when you're scared of the dark?" her father asked.

Raegan tried to slow the crying, now transforming into wet hiccups. *"There's a—a saying fo—for it?"*

"Oh yes, Rae-Rae, I can't believe I haven't told you before! It's a spell of sorts. Magic. It's a way of greeting the darkness, of saying hello. It goes like this: 'I greet you, Mrenin, as I walk within your shadow and your stead.'"

Raegan began to calm down, still hiccuping but standing on her own, skeptical as always. *"That sounds silly. How do—does it help?"*

"It helps, you see, because sometimes the darkness is simply a strange realm, and in all strange realms, you need a guide, do you not?" her father had told her. *"Think of this saying as a*

request for a guide to the darkness. Then it can be known and mapped, and once we know something, it can't be scary, can it? All you have to do is remember the phrasing and it will keep you safe. You have to remember it, though. By heart. It's very important to remember it."

Raegan scrunched up her tear-stained face, unsure if she believed it made any sense, but her father always seemed to know what to do and what to say.

"*Okay, so anytime you go into dark places, just say, 'I greet you, Mrenin, as I walk within your shadow and your stead.'*"

He made her repeat it until he was sure she knew it, and even at eleven, Raegan felt this was more serious than her dad was letting on, so she made a note of it in her favorite notebook, which was decorated with at least ten unicorn stickers. She had a decent grasp on Welsh, being the child of two immigrants from Wales, but couldn't place *mrenin*. So later that night, after she was already supposed to be asleep, Raegan pulled out her flashlight that she kept stored away for late-night reading and took out her Welsh dictionary. She flipped through to the *M* section, bringing the flashlight closer to the small text.

mrenin - noun. **1)** meaning a monarch or leader, but usually, a king.

CHAPTER SEVEN

Raegan snapped the children's book shut. The hair on her arms stood on end. Something turned over in the depths of her being, and she could've sworn she physically felt another memory stirring inside of her head, though it did not reveal itself.

There was, she knew, only one thing to do.

Raegan shelved the book and strode out of the study, doubling back through the kitchen. Her mother was no longer there, much to her relief. Walking between the small island and the cabinets, she came to face the basement door. It hadn't changed—wide, white vertical planks and a black, iron flip latch. She took a deep breath, looked over her shoulder to make sure her mother was still in another part of the house, and opened the door. This time, she turned the flashlight on her phone to its brightest setting before closing the door behind her. No use in taking chances.

Working her way down the narrow, twisting stairs, Raegan came to stand on the dirt floor. There were a few storage containers, the rack by the stairs filled with pots and gardening tools. The air that met her nose was slightly damp, vegetal and cool. The space looked very normal, and smaller than she remembered.

Raegan felt silly, the electricity having evaporated from her skin. But she took a deep breath and turned off her phone flashlight anyway. And then she said it, her heart careening faster and faster with each word.

"I greet you, *mrenin*, as I walk within your shadow and your stead."

For a moment, the air thickened, the shadows growing oily and slippery. Something stretched, a door tried to open, and Raegan stopped breathing. The darkness around her turned to silk scarves, caressing her skin like a lover, so liquid and strange that she thought she might be going mad.

But then it dissipated, gone as quickly as it had come. Raegan was standing in her childhood basement, reciting weird Welsh sayings that she'd only just remembered she knew. Dirt scuffed the toes of her boots, and her breathing was heavy. She rubbed her forehead harshly, muttering to herself, and almost turned to leave.

All at once, she remembered the crawl space. Well, barely a crawl space—just an odd little spot near the front of the basement where the room crested the hill in the front yard. It was more like a dirt shelf, a small area between the ground and the slats of the subfloor above.

Just in case. She was down here already, wasn't she?

Turning her phone light back on, Raegan walked toward the crawl space. She couldn't remember the last time she'd come near it. She knew sometimes her dad would stash his favorite mead from Ireland there, using it like a shelf, but there were no mead bottles there now.

She peered over the ledge and there it was: a shadow, a lump, something that did not belong. Raegan dragged an old wooden step stool over, climbing the first few rungs to get a better look. The shadow turned out to be a little unicorn toy, definitely one of hers, from years ago. But how had it gotten up there? And why was it standing perfectly straight, its tail to her, the horn pointing upwards? She supposed she could have put it there, but why? When?

She twisted her phone around, trying to get a better look. And then she saw it: precisely where the unicorn's horn pointed, there was something resting on the beams. Something about the size of a large book, wrapped up in burlap.

Raegan froze. The object looked as though it had been purposely left there, the unicorn pointing an arrow toward its hiding place in the rafters, in a place few would ever think to look. Her mind reeled but her body, acting independently, reached for the package. It came free of the rafters easily, and she held it close, like a line to a drowning man.

"What the fuck," Raegan mumbled. "What the *fuck*."

She lowered herself to sit on the step stool, slowly unwrapping the burlap fabric from the object with shaking hands. It was a book. Adjusting her phone light, Raegan read the title out loud.

Celtic Mythology: Forgotten Tales, Old Stories, New Skins.

It was exactly the book that had popped into her mind: the old book on mythology with its green cover and embossed text. She flipped it open and was shocked to find it just as she'd remembered it with huge ink illustrations in grayscale and a gorgeous script title at the top of each new entry. The Banshee, the Spriggan, the Fey.

And there it was, The Kelpie.

The page showed a creature rearing its head out of a wave. The artist had chosen to depict it so the reader could see both above and beneath the water. On the top of the page, a horse's dark head broke the surface, black eyes situated strangely on its face. Beneath the surface, where its hind legs should've been, was a long, aquatic body, ending in a powerful, razor-sharp tail. Its gaze portrayed a deep, frightening intelligence. Even just looking into the illustration's eyes made Raegan's mouth go dry.

The text beneath identified kelpies as shape-shifting water creatures of Wales, Ireland, and Scotland. They were tricksters, dangerous and wily, often dragging people to their deaths. Sometimes they could be tamed with magical silver bridles, and sometimes they chose to live as mortals.

Raegan had known these aspects of the kelpie's mythology but the book continued with information she had never heard before. Setting it down on the stool and squatting in the dirt before it, Raegan adjusted her phone light, skimming over the words.

"Kelpies," the text read, "could see things that mortals couldn't. They lived in the Rivers, a vast system of water that extended well beyond bodies of water mapped by humans. They could be anywhere and everywhere, and though they mostly kept to their own kind, kelpies were occasionally called upon during wars or skirmishes, particularly by the Unseelie Fey."

The current that had begun to rush through Raegan earlier in the day strained against her dam of reason. She flipped through the pages again, discovering an envelope secured to the endpaper at the front of the book. It was crafted from thick, creamy paper, and written upon the flap was her name. In her father's handwriting.

Anticipation thrummed, her throat closing off, as Raegan dove her fingers into the envelope. It took her at least a full minute to realize it was empty, and only after she'd nearly torn the page in half by accident. Sorrow spiked dark and sour in her stomach; every place she searched for her father always came up empty, deserted, offering only a ghost.

Frustrated tears welled, and Raegan wiped them away harshly with the back of her hand, pawing through the book once, twice, three more times, her hands shaking. She held it aloft and shook it, hoping a wafer-thin letter might dislodge from its pages and suture her wounds closed after all these years.

Instead, her mother's voice came from behind her. "Raegan?" Bronwyn asked. "What are you doing?"

Startled, Raegan spun, forgetting to conceal the book in her panic. "Sorry," she replied, fruitlessly trying to slide the book under the front of her jacket. "Just lost in memory, I guess."

Bronwyn considered her daughter for a long moment, eyes narrowing in concern, but then she relented. "Lots of memories in this house," she sighed, folding her arms. "Did you find the book you were looking for?"

Raegan forced her face to remain neutral. Could her mom not see the giant book in her arms? Sure, it was dim in the basement, but light now flooded in from the open door at the top of the stairs.

"Uh, no," Raegan replied. "It's okay."

"Well, why don't we head upstairs?" Bronwyn asked, clearly unsettled by having found her daughter in the dark of an unlit basement.

"Sure," Raegan shrugged, taking a few steps to meet her mother. Even as they crested the stairs and emerged into the warm glow of the kitchen, Bronwyn did not seem to notice the book. At all.

"Sorry you couldn't find what you wanted," Bronwyn said, slipping her hand into a tea canister, not bothering to hide the sliver of relief in her voice.

"It's fine," Raegan said, fighting to sound even remotely normal, tracking every movement of her mom's eyes. "There's some information online. I just figured Dad had such a big folklore collection, so . . ."

"So you came all the way out here just to check? Without calling? Without making sure?" her mother asked, crossing her arms, forgetting the tea and leaning back against the counter.

"I was already in the neighborhood," Raegan replied. "I

thought it might be nice to just drop by." Her words were automatic, rote, all her attention focused on the way her mother could not see the book she'd unearthed from the basement.

"Well, why don't you stay for some tea? Since you're here?" Bronwyn asked, lighting up. For a moment, Raegan's bones hummed with a desire to do exactly that. The scent of the black tea and her mother's preferred dish soap curled around her, gentle and comforting. But she couldn't stay. Not now. Not with the song of the kelpie in her blood. Not with a book on magical creatures no one else could see. Not with a missing letter from her father she dared not ask her mother about.

Her mother wouldn't understand. Her mother would say she was having an episode, raving about an invisible book and a missing letter from between its pages. Her mother would call people. Her mother couldn't fathom how Raegan needed to see this through before she did anything else.

"I'm sorry, I can't. I lost track of time. Just wanted to come home but forgot about how much work I have," Raegan said, a faux apology.

And then the warmth was gone, her daughter yanked back away from her as quickly as she had shown up, so Bronwyn sighed and went back to the sink. "Of course."

"Maybe sometime soon. You know, closer to the anniversary."

"Maybe, *cariad*. We'll see. You get home safe."

"I will," Raegan said, and then she was out the door and walking down the quiet street before the cinnamon and the tea and the quilts could get their claws into her.

She told herself not to cry, but a hitching sob came out of her ribcage all the same. Her father *had* left something for her. Right? The unicorn toy, the way the book had been hidden in the rafters, wrapped up in rough brown fabric, the letter her father had clearly penned to explain away all her pain.

It had been left for her. Which meant he hadn't wanted to leave. Which meant something had happened, maybe something with the train station and the man in tweed, and it was up to Raegan to figure it out. *Finally.*

CHAPTER EIGHT

Raegan unlocked her front door, still in a tear-choked daze from her discovery. The train ride home had been nothing more than a blur, her arms wrapped around the book so tightly her muscles had begun to shake.

She shoved old mail and last night's takeout to the side, laying the book on the kitchen table. She took a moment to run a hand across the beautiful cover, which seemed to shimmer beneath the warm kitchen light. Here, in a more ordinary space, it rang out so clearly as not belonging. The book's otherworldliness was harsh against the surrounding normality: the small café table, the dingy tile counters, the antique velvet wingback she hoped might be a nice spot for a cat to curl up on one day, when she got her shit together.

Before she knew it, Raegan's fingers were already turning to the page about the kelpie, hungry for more unusual things that did not fit with her apartment where there was only fifteen minutes of hot water and two dead philodendrons.

There it was—too faint to have been noticed in the base-ment, written in pencil by her father's hand. Beside the instructions for summoning a kelpie, which the book detailed but ultimately warned against, was a simple phrase:

"Particularly good for finding lost things. And of course, traveling between worlds".

Raegan sat back in her chair, feeling a little bit like she was having a mental breakdown, but mostly like she'd finally cracked the fucking code after more than ten years of depressive swings and angry outbursts and a broken family and crying on public transportation because she'd seen a man in tweed or the sunset skewed a certain sepia way.

She had always known that there was something different about her father, that he walked paths others didn't see, despite his normal appearance and job as a librarian. After all, he had told that story so frequently, so meaningfully, always beckoning Raegan close as if there was some secret hidden within it that she hadn't figured out yet. When she'd found her mother burning his books that fateful evening years ago, Raegan knew her father's disappearance was not as it seemed. It sounded crazy, of course, to her few high school friends and her therapist. And to her mother, who was still grieving and wanted to accept that her husband had simply walked out because then she could be angry, and anger was sustainable in a way that misery was not.

Raegan wanted so badly to believe that this was *something*. She knew it could be dangerous, but fuck, what did it matter if she entertained this for a few hours and left it alone when it yielded nothing? She did not want to lose the way she felt, like she was so close to something, like the air was thick, molasses-golden, enchanted and sparkling.

Her therapist's voice popped unbidden into her head, reminding her that she wouldn't leave it alone, that Raegan purposefully believed in impossible things to make what had happened easier. It was a coping mechanism, and it wasn't a healthy one, and someone like Raegan was not capable of *just* entertaining a thought like this one. It would become her entire reality, and she would drown in it. It had happened before, when she was in Boston, but she had buried that deep and told herself it wouldn't be like that again—the inpatient stay and the scratchy hospital gown and the fuzzy socks.

Raegan took a deep breath and really thought about whether she wanted to keep reading. She decided she did, but not before she put the kettle on. Somewhere between getting a mug and a teabag, the mug got filled with whiskey instead. When the kettle clicked, Raegan faithfully took it off its circular stand. But then she just stared at the little stainless steel kettle, unsure what to do with it now. She considered pouring the hot water over her hands to see if they would bloat and glisten like tea leaves, if that would make anything more or less real.

Instead, she found herself back at the table, mug of whiskey in her hand, a few gulps already downed, as she began to read the summoning. It called for a body of water, an offering, and a few words in Gaelic that she knew how to pronounce, but not much else. By the time she had read the passage multiple times, including the warning about how kelpies were dangerous, more than half the mug of whiskey was gone and her courage had exponentially increased.

Raegan thundered down the stairs to the front of her building, whiskey in hand, book tucked under her arm and a small folding knife shoved into her pocket. She rounded the corner into the alley, relieved to see the large puddle from the rain last night still intact in a pothole where a number of cobblestones had sunk down into the earth.

"Okay, this is insane," she muttered, and she told herself it was good she thought it was crazy, because that meant she was still sane, right?

For a moment, all held still. Raegan breathed in the car exhaust and that cool, rich scent indicating autumn had arrived. The skyline glimmered above the roof of her building, and a car speaker's bass thumped somewhere farther down the block.

And then Raegan did it. She made a small nick in her thumb, because she wasn't a fucking idiot about to slice open her entire palm, and dripped the required three droplets of her blood into the puddle. Then came the whiskey; she took a swig of her own and dumped the rest into the water, where it swam on the surface for a moment. It was supposed to be mead, but even Raegan didn't have mead at the ready, so whiskey would have to do. The streetlight flickered. She said the words.

Silence blanketed the alleyway, and Raegan could've sworn she felt her heartbeat in every fiber of her being.

Nothing.

Her vision swam with black dots because she didn't dare breathe.

Still nothing.

Raegan kicked at the water with one boot, shouting something incomprehensible. Suddenly, she was sober. Her hands tightened around the book, and for a moment, she considered chucking it into the puddle, but thought better of it—because honestly, what the fuck had she expected, anyway? She turned on her heel to make her way back to the door. Her eyes stung, anger catching at her throat like a clawed hand.

And then, just faintly, from over her shoulder: "You called."

Raegan turned, the hair on the back of her neck standing on end. There, from the puddle, rose a horse's head. It was inky black, the skin tar-like, the edges of its ears softly scalloped. Its forelock was little more than a piece of seaweed, murky green and bloated with water.

Disbelief bloomed in Raegan's mind. Her mouth went dry, and her hands, for some reason, curled into fists. She stared at the being that had emerged from the puddle, wishing with all her heart that it was real and that she hadn't just drank too much whiskey and passed out on the couch. It *looked* real. It looked realer than her, if she was honest, even with only its head and a short portion of its thick, arched neck above the surface. Puddle water ran down its muscles in rivulets, highlighting the odd nature of its flat, greenish-black coat.

"Did you summon me?" it demanded, more harshly this time, in a voice that sounded like crashing waves. "It is very rude to summon me and then walk away."

"I didn't think you were real," Raegan whispered, walking a few steps closer to the thing in the puddle.

The kelpie, having apparently heard her, made a scoffing noise. "We are of the same place," it told her. "I tasted it in your blood. Why would you, of all people, doubt a kelpie's existence?"

Now that this situation was real, or at least assumably real, or maybe realer than it should be, all the warnings in the book came rushing back to Raegan. Fear stirred in the pit of her stomach, a tenseness aching in the small of her back.

"Hey," Raegan said, not moving closer, planting her feet shoulder-width apart. "Don't drown me."

The kelpie met her gaze, eyes dark as river silt. "What *do* you want, then?"

Raegan was quite aware that the kelpie had not said it wasn't going to kill her. She thought of a million things to ask the supernatural creature in front of her, the thing that shouldn't be real and yet here it was, ripe with knowledge of worlds unseen and things she had thought impossible, but only one thing came out:

"Have you seen my dad?"

The kelpie held her gaze, dispassionate, like it couldn't believe she'd summoned a goddamn kelpie to ask such a basic question. "Who is your father?" it finally asked.

"Cor-Cormac Overhill," Raegan stuttered, pulling out her phone and scrolling to a photo of her father: her favorite one, the cropped portrait for the library, where he was smiling and happy.

"Overhill," the kelpie repeated, like it was gaining traction. The kelpie lifted its head out of the puddle, straining to look at the image Raegan displayed. In the back of her mind, she wondered what she would look like to someone passing by on the street, showing an iPhone to a dripping wet horse head in a puddle, or maybe to nothing at all.

"The name is familiar," the kelpie intoned, "but I cannot place it."

"He disappeared years ago," Raegan replied, hazarding another step which brought brackish water and the thick iron smell of blood to her nose. "He read me folklore, and he had all these books with notes. He had this experience at a train station with someone, something. He said you're good at finding lost things and for traveling between worlds." Her heart pounded and her breathing came so quick for someone just standing still.

The kelpie stared. "Child, what is your name?"

There were definitely rules about giving out true names, she knew, but fuck it to hell. "Raegan Maeve Overhill," she said, her blood pounding in her neck.

And after a long pause: "Now *that* means something to me. One moment, please." The kelpie's head sank below the surface, leaving only ripples in its wake. Raegan waited. She would wait for days, for years, because this was the only thing that mattered, the only thing that would ever matter.

She didn't know how long it took, but when the kelpie returned, it held something in its mouth: a tiny, silver key.

"This is for you, probably left some number of years ago," the kelpie said after spitting the key toward Raegan's feet, where it settled like a small fish, dripping with black water. "My kind experiences time differently, you see. All at once and nothing at all. Never in that straight line. We thought you would come sooner. Your kind does not live very long, marching your little line."

"What's it for?" Raegan demanded, breathless, aching to grab the key, but her instincts would not allow her to lean down so close to the creature and grab it.

"I do not know," the kelpie replied. "I only know it is for you."

"That's it?" Raegan asked, wondering if she had begun to push her luck. "You have no idea where I'm supposed to take this or what it opens?"

"No," the kelpie told her, its black eyes expressionless.

More questions crawled up Raegan's throat—it was, after all, her nature and her trade. "Did my father leave it?" she wanted to know, her gaze dropping to the key again.

"I cannot say," the kelpie said, its tone as final as a wave against rock, sounding to Raegan like an otherworldly, slightly Scottish version of John Malkovich, a comparison that might've made her laugh if not for the gravity of it all. "It is possible I have not yet experienced its arrival yet. Perhaps the Rivers spun whoever left it out of their little human line. I do not know. It is not my purview. I only know it is yours. It was lost, and now I have returned it."

Silence hung, tight as a drum, and Raegan forced herself to quell the other questions and thoughts spinning around in her mind. So far, she was not dead, and she should probably quit while she was ahead.

"Thank you," Raegan said, chewing the inside of her lip. "I'm sorry. I've been rude. I'm . . . I'm having a weird night."

The kelpie considered her from its puddle, tilting its large head to the side as if to get a better look. "I can see you are confused, indeed. I bid you a good night. Be more careful if you call the River Folk again," the kelpie said, beginning to slip beneath the slick water.

Raegan leapt forward to snatch the key from the ground

and then took a large step back, not knowing how far out of the puddle the kelpie could climb if it wanted to do so.

"Wait!" she said, unable to pin the question down inside her. "Are you the one drowning people in puddles?"

It was a stupid question to ask, mostly because the answer was obvious—something she already knew, the reality of it like a harsh and sudden fever on her skin. And it was the kind of question that could get her killed. The kelpie sank a bit deeper into the water, obscuring everything but its eyes and ears. Its words came out clearly, despite its submerged mouth.

"I must consume."

"So," Raegan hazarded, her heart against her ribs, "that's a yes?"

The kelpie considered her with dark, oil-slick eyes. "Would you like to see?"

"Nope, no," Raegan backtracked. Her heart hammered as she stumbled another step back across the broken asphalt and cobblestones. "Definitely not. You are dismissed, I guess. If you remember anything about my father, send me a message in a bottle. Or something."

The kelpie continued its unblinking stare, eyes like a toad's. "Kelpies are not particularly good for answers. Only lost things. They are not the same. You have the key now, and the key will tell you where to go. I would not worry too much."

"Not to be rude, but that's pretty easy for you to say," Raegan said, gesturing at the kelpie's magnificent otherworldliness, its ancient eyes and riverstone skin.

"I suppose navigating the world is indeed much easier when you are an illustrious being like myself."

For a moment, Raegan thought the kelpie was making a joke, but its expression was serious, as far as she could judge. What she could not judge was whether it meant her any true harm. It said it didn't, but it was a being of half-truths and puddles as deep as oceans. She did not believe its words for a moment. Her father had taught her better than that.

"I appreciate that you, uhh, kept this key for me," Raegan said, trying hard not to stammer and failing. "You are released."

"I do not require your release," the kelpie replied. "I am under no power of yours. I can go when I please. You may summon me, or others like me, but after that, with no protective spells or sigils in place, we can do as we please."

Raegan blanched and realized that, of course, the supernatural creature she'd half-assedly summoned after half a mug of whiskey could have killed her.

"Of course, I would not drown *you*," the kelpie added in such a matter-of-fact tone that it startled her. "I dare say the King would not be pleased. We have a covenant, after all. Merry meet, Raegan Maeve Overhill, and merry part."

With that, before Raegan could ask anything about a king or a covenant, the kelpie slid back into the water, completely disappearing. After a long time—longer than she'd like to admit—Raegan worked up the courage to peer into the puddle. It was shallow, shallower than she remembered it being when she came outside. There was a beer bottle cap in the bottom. For a moment, she considered stepping in it, just to be sure, but nausea rose in her stomach at the idea of actually doing it, so she retreated.

The walk up the stairs to her apartment was long and strange, each step taking much more effort than it should have. By the time Raegan reached her door, she realized the coming dawn was already casting odd shadows outside, even though she could've sworn it couldn't be past midnight. Losing time, she knew, was no unusual thing when it came to encountering beings of myth. She told herself that all things considered, it was nearly normal.

Raegan locked the door behind her and pulled off her shoes. Her apartment had not changed. There was no mark of her encounter, of the step she had taken beyond the veil. She was utterly alone with the weight of otherworldliness on her shoulders. After seeing an actual mythological creature in the flesh, Raegan would've thought she'd be alive with energy, crackling with possibility. But she found she was exhausted, as if the summoning had drained her or retrieving the key had taken more than she realized.

There was always a price.

Raegan shuffled to her bedroom and began to undress slowly, almost in a trance. She made no attempt at brushing her teeth or anything of the sort because she did not think she could handle water. Not in a sink, not coming from a faucet, nothing, even though her mouth was dry after the gulps of whiskey. Thankfully, she was asleep the moment her head hit the pillow.

But this was not the inky-black nothingness she had always associated with deep exhaustion. Instead, this sleep was thickly webbed with dreams. They marched in, unstoppable and all at once, unfolding like new, sticky wings fresh from the cocoon.

She walked across an autumn meadow, the fur cloak on her shoulders nearly as heavy as the sense of duty and purpose that filled her ribcage. The skies hung low and gray. Her destination, she knew, was the river in the distance—wide and rough-currented, winding along the foothills of the mountains that rose to touch the bleak gray. The air spun thick with woodsmoke. To her left, just beyond her vision, walked a companion—no, much more than a companion. She knew the person walking with her through that meadow would follow her into the depths of hell if she asked. Hesitating, she turned to look at them.

But then the dream cracked down the middle, darkening as if to signal the end of one scene before another began.

Her vision was blurred, blinking in and out of blackness. The remains of a fire, barely more than embers, and the haze of dusk lingered in the distance. Wherever she was, night was coming, and it was coming soon.

Then the world tilted, seemingly of its own accord. No, she realized, it was not the world—just her. She was being carried, slung over a rough shoulder like a carcass. Her mouth was dry and metallic-tasting. Something uncomfortable pressed into her skin, cold and sharp. It took her some time to pull her reeling mind together, but she eventually understood it was the chain-mail of the man who carried her.

There were more men, moving in a pack around her. They all smelled of blood and metal and sweat. They moved up a hill at a quick pace, headed for a stone structure. She could not get a good look at it, but it was familiar, she knew.

The man carrying her readjusted her weight across his shoulder, sending a quick jolt of searing pain through her body. Her vision spiraled into black again.

When she awoke, it was only because someone was scream-ing. For a long, dim second, she wondered if maybe it was her— her final song, her last resistance, but she knew only a few moments later that the sound could not be coming from her.

It was no scream. It was a howl, a horrible sound, long and low and full of rage and despair all at once. It sounded like retribution. It was not human, and it rang through the space as if the stone hallways would always carry a memory of it.

She blinked—or at least, she thought she had only blinked; the darkness was terribly soft and inviting—and the men were gone. The smell of damp earth and woodsmoke and black pepper overtook her. Then there were strong arms around her, and she knew suddenly that she was dying. She did not understand why she hadn't realized it earlier. It was obvious that her body hurt, that it hurt so very badly. Life was seeping out of her like syrup, clinging to everything but her.

Whoever held her, she loved them. She understood that more than anything else. She knew it fiercely. Hot tears trailed down her face, more of relief than sadness. She had been so afraid she *was going to die alone, laid out on a rough wooden table like an offering.*

But the arms were tight and strong and she was not alone. A voice like heather on the hills and dusk over the lake spoke to her, over and over again in her ear. Like a chant. A ritual. A prayer, maybe. It stopped the pain.

"Outlive me. Please outlive me. I love you too much." She strained, trying to see the face of the person whom she knew she loved, to take it in one last time. But then her vision slipped away and there was only a curl of black smoke and the smell of things long dead.

Chapter Nine

Raegan jolted awake, the sheets glued to her sweat-slicked skin. The darkness of the room swam and snaked around her as she fought to make out any familiar shapes: the fake fern in the corner, the overstuffed reading chair by the window. For a long, looping moment, nothing came to her. There was only the same infinite blackness she had seen in the dream when life trickled out of her body.

The dream. She sat straight up, unease digging cold fingers into her stomach. Groping around the nightstand, Raegan found her phone and unlocked the screen. It was 3:33 AM on a Friday in October and the dream was back.

The night terror of being a near-dead body hauled around like a sack had haunted her since childhood. When she was younger, before her father had disappeared, it had come to her nearly every night. Some of her earliest memories were running as fast as she could to her parents' bedroom on unsteady toddler legs, trying to use her limited vocabulary to explain what had happened in her dreaming mind.

As she got older, the dream filled her less with terror and more with a sense of longing that far outpaced her age. Raegan was absolutely sure that all she needed to know was the identity of whomever held her as she breathed her last. Then everything would fall into place. The world would be set back on its axis. She so often peered into the faces of crowds at intersections and examined every commuter on a train platform because she was always looking. Searching. Hoping. Her father had told her she was probably missing someone from a past life. When he'd disappeared, the dreams had stopped abruptly, another finite ending.

And now here the dream was, resurrected and realer than ever. Raegan could not recall tasting blood in a dream before, nor the intensity of the scents that had surrounded her. She swallowed, her mouth dry, a metallic tang still present on her tongue.

Why, she wondered, lifting her damp braid off her neck with one hand, had the dream returned now?

The events of the evening came rushing back to her at all once, like a levy let loose, and she remembered: the book and the kelpie and the summoning and the key. Raegan lunged for the nightstand, open hands hunting for the key, hungry for it, desperate and wild and aching like she had never ached before. A cruel voice in her head chided that it was just a dream—or worse, a full mental breakdown—and that there were no books left by her father, no tiny silver keys made from pure molten hope.

Then the cool pang of metal met her hot hand and she clutched the key to her chest, feeling its contours with her fingers, convincing herself everything had to be real because here it was, pressed against her skin. She waited until the metal warmed to her touch before she flicked her phone light on. The key was still there, resting in the palm of her hand, winking silver in the light.

More awake now, Raegan conceded that she could have hallucinated the kelpie part. Maybe the key had been in a puddle or on a doorstep somewhere. Maybe she'd just snatched it up and concocted the rest, desperate for the world to slant strangely in her favor. She should probably call her therapist.

Raegan lay back down, flat on her back, stiff as a board. She rested the key on her breastbone and forced herself to breathe in and out, soft and slow. Knowledge settled deep in her marrow: this—whatever it was—was her door.

And goddammit, she was going to walk through it.

For the first time in her career, Raegan relished her Sunday-to-Thursday work schedule. She set an alarm and resolved to attempt a few more hours of sleep. She would need to be fresh to follow through with this. The key was only a small token. She would need more to get wherever she was going. The key grasped fiercely between her fingers, Raegan turned onto her side and closed her eyes. Sleep, she told herself. And then: she would walk into another place, another time.

The screen read 8:32 AM when she woke up next—a far more reasonable hour. She rolled over and buried her face in the pillow, wondering if she still had a single foothold in reality, then wondering if she even cared about the answer.

She decided not to dwell on the question of her sanity. For now, she would assume she'd summoned a kelpie and it had given her a key, because there was nothing else to be done. She would not question what she had seen and heard with her own eyes and ears. In the old stories, that's how throats were slit and bad deals were agreed to, Raegan knew. She'd stay diligent. Stay sharp. Treat this like any other story, journalistic or folkloric or otherwise.

Of course, she conceded to herself as she threw her legs over the side of the bed and sat up, she had never wanted any other story to be true quite so badly before.

The face that greeted her in the bathroom mirror looked older. Avoiding her reflection entirely would've been preferred, but it felt necessary to look into her eyes and see if she still saw herself staring back. Her freckled skin was sallow, and her cheeks looked gaunt. Her hazel eyes were dark, and they glittered strangely in the light. All in all, the only thing looking back was an exhausted, sleep-deprived Raegan Maeve Overhill. For now, it seemed, she was still wearing her own skin.

She brushed her teeth using the smallest amount of water she possibly could, re-braided her hair, and then headed into the kitchen. Glorious autumn light greeted her, the suncatchers on her window spinning out rainbows across her apartment. The antique keys on their threadbare velvet ribbons greeted her knowingly. A crow cawed loudly outside. Raegan felt suspended in the moment, held aloft by molten light and fate-threaded keys and black feathers. She knew deep within her bones that something was happening, just the way she had always wanted, and she vowed to not let it slip through her grasp.

The crow cawed again as it took off from its perch, sending a silky black shadow gliding across her window that made the suncatchers wink at her. Elation bucked in Raegan's chest, and she forced herself steady, focusing on the tiny silver key in her palm.

She set the key on her little café table and filled the electric kettle with water, not daring to look into the depths of the small container. It was a worthwhile risk. She needed caffeine —her body felt like it did after an election night or when edits on a longform stretched until 4 AM. But she'd bet her brain had produced more serotonin in the past twenty-four hours than it had in the last ten years.

"I didn't need SSRIs, just a quest," Raegan joked softly to herself as she spooned sugar into her mug. While the water reached a boil, she took her medications anyway and then returned to the table to examine the key more closely in the better light of the kitchen.

On one side, the key read "Property of First United Bank."

On the other, three digits protruded from the silver flesh: "333."

Chills spread like frost along her neck as she remembered the hour she had awoken. Or perhaps she had misremembered, conflating the two numbers to add an extra punch of meaning to all of this. Raegan let out a sigh, forcing herself to focus on the concrete information in front of her.

The key had to be for a safe deposit box, didn't it? She sank into the chair, pulling out her phone and ignoring the kettle on the counter when it clicked. After a few furious Google searches, Raegan confirmed her theory. A few more well-phrased searches led her to the conclusion that the bank was one she was familiar with—and just a few blocks from her mother's house. Her father's good friend had managed it years ago, and perhaps still did.

Raegan rose, heeding the siren call of caffeine, and poured not-quite-hot-enough water into her mug. Standing at the counter, she chewed on her lip until it bled. There had been no safe deposit box when the police helped Bronwyn settle things after her father disappeared. There could be an easy explanation, like her mother lying—which she had done before—or some bureaucratic thing.

Taking her mug with her to the table, Raegan sat back down and turned the key over in her hands. She knew there was only one way to see this through. But myth-making was often the most delicate at the beginning: doors you missed the first time weren't there when you doubled back for them, and fast-growing vines obscured the path you thought you had sighted from the other end of the meadow. If she was going to pull the curtain back and attempt to see beyond it with her mortal eyes, she would have to act hard and fast.

Raegan sipped her tea, ignoring the way the heat stung the raw spot on her lower lip. She told herself to contact her therapist. She told herself to let a friend know where she was going, maybe even share a significantly pared-down account of the last few hours. She told herself that her medications could sometimes cause hallucinations, though she'd never had them in the five or more years she'd been on the same regimen. She told herself to count to ten before she made any decisions.

On the count of four, Raegan was on her feet, sprinting to her bedroom to pull on an old, worn jeans that clung to her curves and a loose t-shirt. She darted to the door, yanking on boots and jamming her arms into her favorite leather jacket. As she swiped her keys from the catchall bowl, the framed portrait of her father on a nearby bookshelf caught her eye. Their gazes met.

"There better be a reason for all this shit," Raegan said out loud, surprising herself with how calm her voice sounded. "Or I swear to god, when I find you, I'm going to be so pissed off."

And then she was out the door, thudding down the steps. If she made the next train, she could be in the northeast in less than twenty minutes, the bank only a few minutes' walk beyond the station. She silently thanked the newspaper for the monthly train passes it bestowed upon all its journalists—the good ones, too, with no zone restrictions.

The early morning sun turned everything to molten bronze, even rusted-out chain-link fences looking more like the chainmail of a hero. The city was just beginning to wake, sparrow-song still discernible over the hum and bleat of traffic and humanity. The air was cool against her face, tipped with the coming seasons of frost and chill.

She told herself not to sprint to the station but then conceded that a jog would be reasonable. After a nail-biting, foot-tapping, obsessive-phone-checking train ride and a concerted effort to not look absolutely unhinged as she bounded out onto the sidewalk, Raegan was standing in front of the First United Bank in Fox Chase.

The bank occupied a squat brick building that was typical of the neighborhood. The busy boulevard whizzed behind her, horns blaring and pedestrians scurrying like beetles. A cream cornice crowned the building's roof, marred with bird feces and debris. Raegan lingered on the sidewalk, eyeing the tinted glass doors, feeling like what waited beyond could save her or destroy her.

She gripped the key tighter, forcing herself to take a deep breath.

"Hey," a gruff male voice called from behind her. "Hey there, baby! Looking mighty fine in those jeans this morning!"

Raegan narrowed her eyes and glanced over her shoulder, clocking a middle-aged man making his way across the cracked sidewalk toward her. Anger surging, she slipped her hand toward her waistband, where she always kept her knife.

"Hey," Raegan replied, timing the visible unfolding of her knife with her words. "Fuck off. *Now.*"

The man blanched and then snarled something half-heartedly at her, waving his hand in the air as if she were a fly he wanted to bat away. His complaints were lost to the roar of traffic just behind him. Raegan gritted her teeth and turned back to the bank, trying to find her footing again, fighting to remain in the current of the book and the kelpie and the key.

Setting her jaw, she tucked the knife back onto her waistband and took the last few steps across the sidewalk and into the bank. The air-conditioning, too cold for the morning hour, hit her in a rush of chill. The space was carpeted in a worn-out navy. A phone rang in the distance, and a photocopier droned down a hallway to her left. Though someone was using the ATM in the lobby, no one else was in line for the tellers.

Raegan wavered a few paces from the counter, wishing she had answered a million questions before walking in. What had been the name of her father's friend? How did you ask to see a safe deposit box? What was she going to do when they denied her, or when there was no safe deposit box at all, or when the only thing inside the box was empty space that she could not fill, no matter how hard she tried?

Myths, Raegan reminded herself, were rife with messy beginnings. She set her jaw, gripped the key so hard in her pocket that its teeth bit into her palm, and walked up to the teller.

"Hey, good morning," Raegan said, leaning casually against the counter. The teller was older, male-presenting, and she made a snap decision to play a damsel in distress. "Um, I've gotten myself into a bit of a situation. I hope you might be able to help me out?"

She was about to pull the key from her pocket when someone walked out from the back offices—a tall, balding man with a kind face. Their gazes met, and recognition turned over in Raegan's mind.

"Well, my goodness!" the man called, making his way over. Raegan noticed that he dressed like her father—worn-in slacks, a buttoned cardigan, reading glasses tucked into a breast pocket. She also noticed he was not American—Scottish, she thought.

"Could that really be Raegan Overhill?" the man asked as he drew closer. Was it possible to get so lucky that her father's friend not only still worked at the bank but walked out right when she arrived?

"Oh, hi. It's me!" Raegan said, taking her hand out of her pocket. "I'm sorry—you were friends with my dad, weren't you? I'm embarrassed. I'm totally blanking on your name." She smiled then, the kind of smile she saved up for situations like this: dazzling, disarming.

"I thought it was you," the man said, clearly delighted, coming to stand on her side of the counter. "And please, don't fret about my name—it's David. Your father and I met at the book club he ran at the library. I miss him very much. And aren't you just the spitting image with that hair!"

"I miss him, too," Raegan told David, surprising herself with how much she liked his deep, warm voice and the way he hunched his shoulders a bit to make his height less intimidating. "I stopped by to get myself out of a pickle. Maybe I could see what you think and catch up a little?" She resisted the urge to bite the inside of her cheek while she awaited his response, every muscle in her body tense.

"Of course," David replied easily, waving her deeper into the building with one hand. "Why don't you come into my office and sit down? We can have a cuppa, if you'd like."

"I would like that very much," Raegan said, following him down the carpeted hallway.

He stopped at the third door on the left and gestured her inside. She stepped into the bland office, sweeping her gaze over the low bookshelf, filing cabinets, and two chairs in front of a big desk. There were no windows and the overhead light was too bright. She did not sit, instead hovering in the blank space between the two chairs.

"So, tell me about this problem you're having," David asked, sitting down at his desk. He pulled his glasses from the pocket of his cardigan and put them on, like he was ready to solve the issue at that very moment. Raegan silently pleaded to whatever goddess would listen that this would go the way she needed it to.

"Look," Raegan started, rubbing her temple for a moment, "I found a key in my dad's study. I think it's for a safe deposit box here. I know he's been gone a long time and it's probably silly I'm even checking in on this. I just miss him."

David sat back in his chair, some of the joviality seeping out of his face as he visibly paled. He looked like he was trying to find the right words, and Raegan waited, letting the silence blanket the room.

"Your father . . ." David began, immediately trailing off. He readjusted his glasses. "Your father was a bit odd. It was endearing. Everyone liked him, you know that—I'm sure you remember. About a year before . . . before it happened, he asked me to set him up with a safe deposit box. I did. I didn't particularly think anything of it—both of your parents, like me, are immigrants, and we have papers and documents that need to be kept safe."

Raegan lowered herself into the left chair. She could hear her heart thudding in her ears. For some reason, her eyes tracked to the carpet between her boots. It was stained. An old coffee spill, she thought, before she fought off the dissociation, pulling herself back to the present.

"But then he made a stranger request," David continued. "He asked me to keep the safe deposit box here, no matter what happened, and that if one day you turned up with a key, to make sure you got access."

"That's not usually how this sort of thing works, is it?" Raegan asked, looking up at David. Suspicion pricked her, but she didn't know if she was simply being unfair. Her father always had a way of gently shrugging off the regular rules, no matter where he was.

"No," David admitted, steepling his fingers. "No, it's not, but it seemed harmless enough and he had never asked me for anything in our many years of friendship. He had done so much for me—he was there for me when my wife left, and he essentially introduced me to my whole social circle. It was the only thing he had ever asked of me. I told the police when he went missing, but they never followed up. I probably should have told your mother—your poor Mum—but Cormac had been so . . . serious about it, and serious about it being for you. Frankly, I haven't thought of it in years. But now . . ."

"Now here I am," Raegan said, her tone low and soft. They considered each other across the expanse of David's desk, where folders were piled up and a mug emblazoned with "FEARLESS READER" sat abandoned off to the side.

"I'm sorry," David said suddenly, rubbing the back of his head as he looked away from her. "I never thought your dad was in danger. I just thought he was being his usual odd self."

Raegan folded her hands on her knee, waiting for David to

look at her again. When he did, she saw guilt in his gaze, as if he thought her father requesting the safe deposit box was some sort of harbinger he should've identified. She saw sorrow, a deep sadness that his friend was gone, disappeared, and he hadn't been able to do a damn thing about it.

Straightening her spine, Raegan took a deep breath. "David," she said, her tone sharpening.

He sat up, leaning forward onto his desk as if her next words would be some of the most important he'd ever hear.

"I need to see the box."

Chapter Ten

Time suspended itself within the four walls of the First United Bank, all the ordinary workings of such a mundane place cast aside for something greater.

David moved first, drumming his fingers on the desk. "Right. Of course you do. Come with me." With that, he stood and took a few long strides across the room, checking at the doorway to see if Raegan was behind him. She hadn't gotten out of her chair, her fingernails digging into the upholstered arms.

"It's right this way," David said, gently gesturing down the hallway. Something in his gaze had softened, and embarrassment swirled in Raegan's gut. Did she look like a deer in the headlights? Did she look like a lost child, hoping her daddy had left something behind for her?

Raegan forced herself to her feet, the soles of her boots quiet on the carpet as she followed David down a long hallway. When it came to a T, David veered to the left into a shadowy corridor. They marched in silence until a large gray door loomed at the end of the hallway.

"This is the safe deposit room," he said, pulling out a key

ring and flipping through a number of keys. "We'll go inside, I'll show you to the box, and then you'll be able to view it privately. You can let me know if you'd like to leave the contents here or if you'd like to withdraw them."

"Okay," Raegan said, surprised at how hoarse her voice was.

Darkness greeted them before David took a step inside and motion lights kicked on, illuminating a modest room with a table in the center. The walls were covered with safe deposit boxes, all neatly numbered. It reminded Raegan of a mausoleum.

She followed David inside, stopping at the table. She was pretty sure that's what people did in movies and wondered how accurate those depictions were, though now was not a particularly useful time to be curious about it.

"What's the number?" David asked, pushing his glasses back up his nose.

"333," Raegan said, not daring to reach for the key in her pocket just yet. David nodded and set off for a section of the boxes, clicking his tongue as he scanned the numbers. She could see from across the room that all the boxes in the row started with three.

"Ah," David said, pulling a small silver box from its place on the wall. "Here you are." He placed the box on the table. It looked normal as far as Raegan could tell. The earth did not seem to shift on its axis. No ancient knowledge bubbled to the forefront of Raegan's mind.

"Right," she exhaled.

"I'll be just outside," David said, tucking the key ring back into his pocket. "Come on out whenever you're ready."

Raegan nodded, turning back to gaze at the box. When David closed the door behind him, it felt like the entire universe disappeared. It was only her and whatever was inside the box. Or whatever wasn't.

"Just open it," Raegan told herself between gritted teeth. She clutched the key in her pocket. Her heart raced and her stomach flipped. She swallowed hard, squeezing her eyes shut for a second.

Then she stepped forward and inserted the key into the tiny lock. It turned over with a quiet click. A drawer slid out. Before she could stop and think, before she could even allow a single feeling to raise its head in her body, Raegan pulled it open.

Inside were thick sheets of paper, folded in on themselves letter-style. She reached in and plucked them from the metal case. Inhaling shakily, she unfolded them and laid them flat on the table, one by one.

There were seven papers in all. They were large and the material was substantial, bringing parchment and vellum and ancient libraries to mind. On Raegan's first glance, the writing upon them appeared to be scribbles. Endless loops and mad lettering, all amounting to nothing.

She narrowed her eyes and looked closer, leaning over the table. Madness unfolded in front of her, presenting instead furious notes and graphics and circles and half-sentences, unusual drawings in miniature and things crossed out and reworked. There was complicated math that far surpassed Raegan's abilities and instructions for what looked like hand positions or symbols. One page was full of notes about the appropriate accommodations for different moon phases and the positions of certain planets. The last two pages were just illustrations: a large set of ornately wrought, towering gates and a circle with complicated symbols around it.

Her mouth dry, Raegan smoothed the papers against the table again, straining her eyes to look at the minute details in the margins of the pages, often trailing off onto the next sheet. She could not make head or tail of it—some of it didn't even seem to be in English. Even places where she could understand some of the individual words proved too esoteric overall for her to riddle out.

The circle with the symbols, though . . . She had no idea what it meant and certainly had little knowledge of the symbols themselves, but it was a pentacle. Raegan was sure of it. A casting or summoning circle, a magical fetish of some kind, though she had no idea of its purpose.

She dragged a hand through her hair, clenching her jaw. All the logical parts in her were saying that her father had simply suffered some kind of mental health crisis that led to his disappearance. But with each breath, each heartbeat, Raegan became surer and surer that this was real, whatever it was.

"Magic," she admitted to herself, barely more than an exhale in the quiet space. She suddenly became aware of how much time had passed since David had exited the room. Moving quietly, Raegan folded the papers back up and gingerly placed them inside her pocket, tucking the key beside them. She rubbed her eyes hard, trying to mimic the appearance of having just been crying. Then she pulled herself together and walked out. At the threshold, silence yawned wide and hungry, the space at her back feeling infinite and full of dangers.

Then David appeared in the ordinary hallway with its ordinary carpet and ordinary overhead lighting. "Oh, Raegan, are you alright?" he asked once he'd taken a look at her face.

She swallowed. "It's just some original copies of my dual citizenship papers," Raegan said, pushing her voice out low and hoarse. She swiped at her cheek as if wiping away a tear. "I don't know why I thought there would be something more fantastical in there."

David looked at her, startled, and opened his mouth to say something. Then he seemed to remember he was speaking to the daughter of the man who'd disappeared without a trace and closed it again. "I think we both worked ourselves into a bit of a tizzy," he said, ushering her down the hallway. "We both miss your father very much. It would be nice for there to be some magic to it all, wouldn't there? You can have a seat in my office and take a breath."

"Thank you," Raegan said as they rounded the corner, a woman in a tan pantsuit breezing past them. "I think I just need to go home and cry for like an hour." The papers sang a quiet chorus of rustling sighs from deep within her pocket.

"Is there anyone you can call?" David asked, stopping in front of his office, discomfort settling across his face. "Anyone I can call for you?"

"No, no," Raegan said, straightening and taking a deep breath. She raised her gaze to David's and gave him a grim little smile. "I'm fine, I promise. Well, okay, I'm not. But I will be. I'll be fine to get myself home."

David wavered, looking unsure. "Alright," he finally said. "Please be safe. Don't hesitate if you need anything. I'm sorry it's all turned out this way."

Raegan shrugged, taking another step down the hallway and away from David. "That's life, isn't it?" she said.

David sighed, leaning against the doorframe. "That's life," he echoed. "Be safe, Raegan."

"I always am," Raegan replied, walking backwards toward the bank lobby. "Thank you again." Then she turned and strode across the lobby, out through the doors, and into the crisp morning. She stood for a moment on the pavement, squinting at the bright sunlight. Triumph surged through her body like a tidal wave, and she slipped a hand into her pocket, a thrill running down her spine when her fingers met the thick folds of parchment.

Raegan took a deep, ragged breath, her mind racing. "Okay," she said to herself. "Okay." And then she walked down the block at a reasonable pace, looking for all the world a somewhat morose woman who'd just had another hope dashed. She turned at the corner, casting her gaze back at the bank. It sat squat on its lot, unmoving. No one came out of its dark-eyed doors. No one made frantic phone calls on the pavement outside. No one seemed to give a single shit about what had just transpired.

She took a deep breath, zipped her pocket closed, and broke into a run.

Chapter Eleven

Raegan took her apartment's steep stairs at a full-out sprint, bursting through the door for the second time in less than twenty-four hours. She removed the papers from her pocket with careful, shaking hands, placing them on the café table next to the book.

"Okay," she murmured. "You can figure this out." She peeled her leather jacket off her damp skin, pulled her hair into a bun, and grabbed her laptop from her work bag. Her stomach growled for food, but she ignored it, logging into her computer instead and bringing up the old faithful: Google.

It wasn't long before she found herself with about a million tabs up at once, attempting to decipher individual symbols, taking copious notes the entire time. She quickly realized the contents of the papers made no sense together, which didn't surprise her, but she was doing her best to parse out each symbol's meaning in the hopes of discovering a broader intent or message.

Raegan knew a lot of this was way over her head—most of her search results were concerned with high ceremonial magic, the kind associated with secret societies and dusty old white men. After a few hours of research, she came to the realization that the contents of her father's safe deposit box would be a challenge for a lifelong occultist to understand. She was good at figuring new things out—it went with the journalist territory—but every time Raegan thought she had a grasp on a symbol or a tiny part of a note, she'd find another piece of information that contradicted it. She tried casting her net a bit wider, but all she found were spells for making a straying boyfriend come back and a large group effort to hex the government that she briefly admired.

Raegan shoved her chair back, face hot with frustration. She chewed on a hangnail. She thought about making a cup of tea. She considered visiting the occult bookshop tucked into the city's northwest hills to ask the bookseller with a thousand-yard stare and a tattoo of a door on their shoulder about her father's papers, but decided she didn't want to risk another person knowing about what she'd discovered. She ignored more rumbles from her stomach. She stared at the sheets of thick, creamy paper, willing them to divulge their secrets.

And then it dawned on her: she had recently gained the ability to summon an actual magical creature. Embarrassment flushed her chest for not thinking of it sooner. Summoning the kelpie again would be dangerous, no doubt, but she felt out of options. Raegan knew herself well enough to know she wouldn't sleep, wouldn't eat, wouldn't do anything else except focus all of her energy on the contents of her father's safe deposit box. So really, she reasoned, summoning the kelpie was the less dangerous option.

Raegan quickly searched for some basic protective sigils to use and scribbled them into a notebook. She doubted their efficacy against the creature with oil-slick eyes and riverstone skin. But she supposed it was better than nothing.

Tucking the notebook into her back pocket, Raegan pulled a bottle of whiskey off the shelf, wishing she had taken some time to figure out where the hell to get mead. She checked her waistband for her knife and skimmed the ritual for summoning the kelpie again, though it felt etched in her brain or maybe like it had always been there and the book had only helped her remember.

Then Raegan opened the door, abandoning her jacket on the couch, and walked down the stairs to summon an ancient being from a puddle. More time had passed during her research than she'd realized. The glorious day was fading into early evening, dusk hunched on the horizon like a bat's wing clinging to a branch. Her neighborhood was busy with the thrum of Friday happenings, so Raegan followed the alley to the back of her building, where it tucked itself into another structure. A chain-link fence stretched to her left, encircling a dumpster and a large tree stump. A dog barked in the distance. She felt the hum of the subway from the metal grates lining the street as she searched for a suitable puddle on the blistered blacktop.

The only puddle was quite shallow, and an old paper plate sat at its bottom, but it would have to do. She hoped the kelpie would not be offended by her choice of water source as she scraped protective sigils into the asphalt using a piece of chalk she'd improbably found in her kitchen junk drawer. Then she poured the whisky, squeezed the small incision on her thumb to produce blood droplets, and spoke the summoning.

A preternatural hush fell around Raegan as she said the final phrase, like the rest of the world had been silenced. This time, sober and sharp-eyed, she noticed something change in the atmosphere; it was not unlike the process of putting in contacts. A slippery, shiny film overlaying something else, only noticeable for a moment before disappearing completely.

The dumpster and the tree stump and the chain-link fence faded away. Her heartbeat was loud in her ears, and she could've sworn that for a long, stretched moment there was nothing at all in the world but the drumming of her own blood.

Then the puddle water went black. The paper plate slunk

from view, and there, right before her, was the kelpie: oil-slick skin, eyes wide and expansive, bulging from its head like a toad's, the seaweed forelock, the deep primal feeling unfolding in Raegan's gut that told her she was in the presence of an ancient thing.

"Hello," she said, involuntarily taking a step back. "I drew some sigils this time. To be more careful. Like you said."

The kelpie rose out of the water, rivulets of black running down its thickly muscled shoulders, its eyes trained on the ground around the puddle. Raegan held her breath as it studied her handiwork.

"I already said I would not harm you," the kelpie intoned, raising its eyes to hers. "But you do understand I could simply wipe those away? With the water? In the puddle? That you summoned me from?"

Raegan sucked in air, her stomach dropping out like she was on a rollercoaster. Fear pricked her skin, a thousand hot needles. "Oh. Yeah. Not my best work. Um, but you're still not going to drown me, right?"

"No, I shall not," the kelpie replied, slinking back into the puddle until only its head was exposed. "You are lucky I've already arrived at that decision. Otherwise, it would be simple to drag you into the depths."

Raegan wiped her damp palms on her jeans, resisting the way her entire body told her to run and to keep running. "Lucky, indeed, thanks to your benevolence," she said, bowing her head to the ancient creature. "I . . . I had a question I was hoping you'd be able to answer, if you would consider extending your kindness again."

"Do you plan on disturbing me every time you seek knowledge? I am no Questing Beast," the kelpie replied, shaking water out of its mane.

"Um, I'm not planning to," Raegan said, edging farther away from the puddle. "Honestly. I've just hit a very unexpected roadblock and I did not think anyone else would be able to tackle this problem. There are few, if any, that hold your wisdom."

The kelpie held her gaze with its black eyes, working its heavy jaw. She couldn't read its expressions, but she hazarded a guess that it was considering. "This is the last favor, Raegan from Over The Hill," the kelpie said. "I hope it is worth it."

She hoped it was worth it, too. "My father, the one who went missing, he left me these papers in a safe deposit box. The key you gave me—that's where it led me." She caught herself, wondering if the kelpie knew what a safe deposit box was, so she added, "The key you gave me opened a box with these papers in it."

"Yes," the kelpie replied, its tone flat. "I understand how safe deposit boxes operate."

"Sure, okay," Raegan said, nodding, thinking it was not unreasonable to assume a mythological creature was unfamiliar with banking. "I suppose I should understand there is no limit to your knowledge."

The kelpie shifted in the puddle, the arch of its heavy neck cresting. "You may stop with the flattery. It has become exhausting and hollow," it said, sounding bored. "Show me the papers of which you speak."

Raegan hesitated. So far, this interaction was going in her favor, but keeping a healthy distance between herself and the kelpie's strange, fathomless eyes seemed wise. To show her father's papers to it, she would have to step right up to the edge of the puddle.

Gritting her teeth, she told herself there was no point in any of this if she wasn't willing to be brave. She gathered the papers in her hands and took small steps toward the puddle, her eyes trained on the kelpie.

"Here," Raegan said, slowly shuffling through the pages, holding them up like a picture book for a child. "Tell me if there's any you want to have a closer look at."

The kelpie let out an exasperated sigh and then raised itself a bit farther out of the puddle. When it leaned in to look, it suddenly paid sharp attention, as if it had been expecting a crude cartoon and had instead gotten a Monet. "*This* is from your father?" the kelpie demanded, its eyes flicking to hers. Her palms damp, Raegan reminded herself not to stare into the endless blackness of its pupils.

"I believe so," she replied, her voice shaking. "At the very least, it was in a safe deposit box that he owned."

"Raegan from Over the Hill," the kelpie said, its voice authoritative and booming, the kind of voice she could imagine commanding armies, "what you hold in your hands is an incredibly complex spell, the likes of which your kind rarely attempts."

Silence cloaked the alley, as downy and hushed as the first snowfall of winter. Raegan fought the faintness growing at her knees and the black dots that threatened to crowd her vision. If her heart beat any faster, she thought, she might faint.

"A spell," she repeated, her mouth dry. "A spell . . . to do *what*?"

The kelpie pulled away, settling back into the puddle, the arch of its neck disappearing beneath the water. "That I cannot say," the kelpie answered. "You see, your kind *practices* magic. To do so, you need spells for channeling and harnessing power, as you are too simple for anything else. The greater creatures of this place, such as myself—we *are* magic. We do not use the spells or incantations of lower beings. I have seen enough of human spellery to recognize that this was a complex, intense effort, but no more. It is beneath me, you see. Wolves need not grasp the workings of an anthill."

Raegan's throat felt like it was closing off, and her head threatened to explode. She wondered if her world was collapsing or finally coming together.

"Right," she said, placing the spell carefully into her pocket and then beginning to pace in front of the puddle. "So how do I find out what the spell was intended for? Like, is there a local witch or something I can speak to? I'll pay."

"That spell far surpasses a local hedgewitch," the kelpie replied, its black eyes narrowing in concentration. "Allowing another human to view it will be dangerous on a number of levels."

Raegan waited as the kelpie's jaw worked back and forth.

"You must take this to the King," the kelpie decided, once again raising its pitch-black gaze to hers. "He is less friendly and charming than I, but no one else can be trusted. Tell him Rainer sent you. My name shall grant you safe passage."

Raegan narrowed her eyes at the kelpie. "I appreciate your help," she said slowly, choosing her words carefully. "But why are you allowing me to use your name? What's the price for such a thing? You already bestowed your last favor on me."

The kelpie shot her an appraising look and said nothing for a long moment. Its mane dripped river water onto the puddle's surface, the soft plops the only noise in the space. The smell of brackish water and decaying bones in deep, dark places flooded the alley.

"There is no price."

"I very much doubt that," Raegan laughed, putting one hand on her hip. "I mean, come on. Do you expect me to believe that?"

The kelpie closed its eyes and sighed, sending ripples out through the puddle. She pulled her hand off her hip, hoping she hadn't annoyed the creature so much that it'd decided to take back its promises not to harm her. Historically, she had that sort of effect on people.

But then the kelpie opened its mouth, closed it again, and Raegan realized it was simply searching for the right words.

"All that has passed," the kelpie began, sounding each word out, "between you and I feels familiar, and more so, important. Both times we have met, I have heard the hum of a Fatesong and felt my Threads plucked by an invisible hand.

Which can only mean that you and this spellcraft are Fate-kissed. Gods-touched."

The world threatened to fade entirely to black, the ground trembling beneath her feet. Of all the things that Raegan yearned to be, the most sacred of them was this: Fate-kissed. Important. Worthy of a quest. Allowed a peek behind the curtain. Permitted to steal a glance through the worn spot in the tapestry.

"Gods-touched," she breathed numbly, her entire body humming.

"Yes," the kelpie said. "There is no doubt Fate has Her hand in whatever is unfolding, so you must go to the King. He and Fate often travel the same narrow Threads. He knows much in the way of your human magic."

"So this king, he's . . . human, too?" Raegan asked, clutching the spell papers tightly.

"Do not be absurd," the kelpie snapped, snorting through its long, equine nose. "Of course he is not."

"Right. Of course not. Does he have a full name?" she asked, trying to retain the tone and body language of a supplicant. "Or an address?"

"I am not sure what name he goes by these days," the kelpie replied. "But go to the place I tell you to and he will be there."

The kelpie told her an address without asking if she was ready, and she almost dropped her notebook from whipping it out of her pocket so quickly to take the information down. Raegan's hands shook wildly, her handwriting taking up a whole page with its overblown loops and unsteady lines. Before she could say or do anything else, the kelpie was slipping beneath the water, just his eyes remaining, two midnight jewels.

"Wait," she pleaded, feeling like a child who understood nothing. "What do I even say to him?"

"You are Gods-touched, Raegan from Over the Hill. You

already know the words. Just say them." In the space of a blink, the kelpie was gone and the puddle was just a puddle. Raegan clutched the notebook with the address to her chest. She couldn't decide if she felt more like the loneliest or the luckiest person on the planet. Settling on both—they were not mutually exclusive, she thought—she began the climb up the stairs to her apartment.

Raegan locked the door behind her and laid her father's papers out on her coffee table, where she thought they would be safest. Stepping into the kitchen, she rummaged through a cabinet and plucked a protein bar from a box. She collapsed on her couch, pulling the green knit blanket around her like armor. Her mouth dry, she forced herself to eat at least half of the protein bar before she did anything else.

Mid-chew, Raegan realized that the kelpie had told her his name. Rainer. She shot to her feet, tripping when the blanket snagged at one leg, darting toward her laptop. Snatching it off the bistro table, she returned to the couch. She knew from her father that creatures like kelpies almost never revealed their names—names were sacred. Names were a form of control, and things like the kelpie never gave up control.

Curious, she searched "Rainer" on Google. There was nothing about kelpies—which she had expected—but a few of those sites for naming babies informed her that the name had Germanic origins. It was formed of two words: "advice" and "army." She scrolled a little farther and saw another entry; this one claimed the name meant "warrior from the gods."

Raegan thought of the kelpie and its river-green skin and its self-importance, and wondered why her very first call had summoned not just any kelpie, but an important one. A warrior, a source of wisdom, one that could feel Fate's tendrils down its back.

A being that could look at Raegan and say, definitively, clearly, without a shred of doubt in its lucid black eyes, that she was Gods-touched.

CHAPTER TWELVE

Raegan slammed the laptop shut, catching crumbs from the protein bar between the screen and the keyboard. She cursed under her breath and cracked the laptop open just far enough to sweep them into her hand. Getting to her feet, she threw the crumbs in the garbage can under the sink. Then she paced back and forth in her small kitchen. She stopped at the window above the sink. In the sweep of nightfall, it was more like an obsidian mirror, reflecting her face and the lights from her living room.

"Am I losing my mind?" Raegan asked herself in a low whisper. Before her reflection could contort or give her an answer she didn't like, she poured herself a glass of water and meandered back to the couch. On her way, she saw the notebook with the address sitting open and sat down to look it up.

As she had suspected from the street name, the address was in Old City, tucked away in the far corner near the river. Raegan toggled to Street View. The building was typical of the neighborhood: a lovely antique row house, made from brick and adorned with well-maintained details like shutters and a decorative cornice. The carved front door was painted a deep shade of black. A glass insert in the middle of it read "ARAWN ANTIQUES" in gold-gilt lettering.

Raegan bit the inside of her cheek, pulling up another tab to search for the antique shop. She paged to the Google Maps listing. The hours were by appointment only. It looked like the shop had been there for at least a year or more, but there were no reviews and no website.

"Who doesn't have a goddamn website these days?" she muttered, grabbing her phone to see if there was any trace of the business on social media.

She got nothing, so decided to call the listed number. Unsurprisingly, it went to voicemail, though she held her breath the entire time it rang. The voicemail was an electronic recording. It informed Raegan that the shop was open by appointment only, encouraged her to leave a detailed message about what she was looking for, and that the owner would contact her if any current inventory matched her request.

Raegan briefly considered making something up, but then the voicemail beeped and she panicked and just hung up instead. She toggled back to the Google Maps listing and looked at the name again.

"Arawn," she muttered, narrowing her eyes. It rang a bell. She plugged it into Google. The top hit was a Wikipedia page, which informed her why the name sounded so familiar. In the *Mabinogion*, a collection of Welsh mythological stories, the king of the Otherworld was called Arawn.

The King.

"You cheeky little shits," Raegan said between gritted teeth, addressing every supernatural creature in existence.

It was too late to go to the address now, partially because of the late hour—it seemed she'd once again lost time by summoning Rainer—but also because Raegan wasn't keen to confront the possible king of the Otherworld at night. That activity, she reasoned, was better saved for a bright morning.

She closed the laptop—more gently this time—and

tucked her legs up on the couch, pulling the blanket around her. She stared at the wall and chewed her lip, trying to get her head around what was happening, or maybe what *wasn't* happening outside of her head. With a sigh, Raegan concluded that constantly debating whether or not she had completely lost her mind was probably not helpful. Occasional check-ins on her sanity seemed normal, but sitting on the couch and torturing herself over it was useless.

With that decision made, she untangled herself from the blanket and got to her feet. She stretched, a few spots in her back cracking, her neck complaining about all the tension it had been holding. A hot shower would probably help. Water still made her feel weird given the whole kelpie thing, but Rainer probably couldn't crawl out of a showerhead, she reasoned.

Raegan immediately wished that thought had not popped into her head as she turned the water on, checking the back of the door for a fresh towel. Then she closed and locked the bathroom door and undressed, the clothes and the body of a woman who knows magic exists feeling entirely new to her. Like she had been reborn.

The bathroom steaming up broke her reverie; it was the cue that her fifteen minutes of hot water had started. She stepped into the shower, trying to ignore the water pooling around the drain, tying her hair up because wash day wasn't until tomorrow.

A little while later, Raegan exited the shower, wrapping herself in a soft towel. She savored the simple power of hot water and the smell of her favorite soap: spicy peppercorn and bergamot with just a hint of oakmoss. Taking a deep breath, she conceded she felt marginally better and somewhat saner.

By the time Raegan had brushed her teeth and gotten ready for bed, the soothing effects of the shower had worn away. Even with the lights off and the weighted blanket positioned perfectly, she found herself just staring at the ceiling, her muscles humming with anxiety.

She told herself to sleep. Tomorrow she would go to the person Rainer called "the king," who would immediately interpret her father's spellwork. Then she would somehow use the spell to find her father and everything would be okay again. Her mother would stop looking at her like somehow, vaguely, this had been Raegan's fault all along. She could stop scanning the face of every stranger on the street. She wouldn't get the breath knocked out of her in those rare moments that she heard another Welsh accent. She and her mom and her dad would all go to their favorite pub in Old City, the one that her parents swore looked just like one in Wales, and they'd drink all night and repair all the old wounds and make up for lost time.

And then of course, magic—*magic*—would still be real, and it'd be thanks to her father that anyone knew at all. She and her father would explore the limits of it and tell the whole mundane world about it. How many systems of oppression could be toppled, she wondered, with magic?

What was meant to be a comforting series of thoughts to lead her into slumber quickly spiraled out of control, and Raegan found herself riddled with even more anxiety, trying to contend with the idea that something as beautiful as magic could exist in the horrible world she knew.

Seeing no other useful remedy to the situation, she flopped on her side and pulled open her bedside drawer, retrieving her vibrator. Sex, particularly casual encounters, had always been a relatively safe place for Raegan—all the intimacy with none of the attachment, none of the personal backstory. But she was not particularly interested in dealing with another human being tonight, so she'd have to make do on her own. Besides, her bed *was* getting more comfortable by the moment, and an orgasm would probably only make her sleepier.

It did, though that stranger from the subway—all obsidian waves and oceanic eyes and ivory muscle—rose into her mind unbidden before she could push the thought away. A little embarrassed, she curled onto her side. Raegan closed her eyes, and exhaustion began to weave its way into her mind, quieting the thoughts and pulling her gently into a softer, darker world. As she drifted into sleep, she could've sworn that for a moment, she felt the weight of a muscular arm on her waist and the smell of woodsmoke in her nose, though it was gone the moment she focused on it, sleep tugging at her again.

But Raegan was not permitted to enjoy a peaceful rest. Instead, Fate leaned down and sang of older places, of different times, of wilder dreams.

Raegan was herself in the dream, she was fairly sure. The braid over her shoulder was thick and long and auburn, and her body felt the way it always did. She wore a dress with a belt, and she was happy, she realized—within the confines of this dream-world, at least. She stooped over, pulling a plant from the ground, shaking the dirt from it, and tucking it into a pouch at her waist. The sun warmed her back and the cool breeze blew gently and everything felt right with the world. Distantly, Raegan recognized that this was a new dream, or at least as far as she could remember. She fought to stay with it. Of course, that was the exact moment it burst like an irate bubble.

The next image unfolded slowly—she was walking down a sidewalk on a pretty spring day. It was London, she thought, or someplace similar. A line of schoolchildren came marching around the corner, and old-fashioned cars drove by. The women in the park she passed by were perfectly made-up, chasing after children in three-inch heels. Startled, Raegan looked down at her own clothing and saw a smart, buttoned blouse tucked into wide-legged pants.

It had to be the 1930s, maybe 1940s, she thought. Her body marched down the sidewalk of its own volition, and she turned the corner to enter a café. She stepped inside, her eyes adjusting to the dim interior. As they did, a man turned away from the counter and walked toward her. For some reason, something that she couldn't place, her heart stopped and she felt sure that she knew him, that she had been looking for him for so very long. He kept walking toward her, and when he caught her gaze, she knew without a doubt that she had seen those ocean eyes before. Elation rose in her chest, as sharp and sweet as a glass rose.

"Excuse me, I'm so sorry to interrupt," Raegan said, her voice coming out accented and unfamiliar, thick with emotion. "Do I know you? I have to know you. I think I've been looking for you."

The man was so close now, and she took him in with a greedy gaze, savoring his well-cut suit, his broad shoulders, the dark hair swept away from his forehead, the brows that knit together as he searched her face. Raegan glanced down, embarrassed at her fervor, and noticed his hands were shaking.

"No," he said hoarsely, as if choking out that single word was all he could manage. Then he straightened, his face relaxing. "No, miss, I am sorry. I do not think we are acquainted." His voice was deep and lush and dark; she could have sworn she heard a bit of Welsh peeking through the harsher London accent. "In fact, I am sure we are not," he added.

Raegan could be wrong, could have seen incorrectly in the low light, but his sharp jaw clenched when he spoke, like he was trying to swallow traitorous words crawling up his throat. For a moment, she swore his eyes shone with something she could not identify.

Before she could say anything else, he was out the door and walking briskly away. She watched him go, watched the way he moved with an unusual, lithe sort of grace, his long strides devouring the ground beneath his feet.

When he was out of sight, Raegan found herself choking down a harsh sob. For no reason at all, she felt that she had lost everything. Those brief moments in the presence of that startling man felt like watching a passing comet—the sudden awareness that so much heat and light and warmth and wonder existed just out of her reach. But then the comet sailed by and she was left to reckon with the cold, dead darkness of her own universe.

Grief unhinged its jaws and threatened to devour her whole.

Raegan awoke with a start, her fingers gripping her sheets so hard it hurt. With a shaky breath, she released the fabric, raising one hand to her face. Her cheeks were damp with tears. She sat in the darkness trying to regulate her breath, trying to grasp the dream—a café, a man, someone she knew, someone she had always known, someone she needed to find. All feelings she was already well familiar with.

Rolling to her side, Raegan massaged her temples and wondered why her dreams couldn't be about normal shit. Or better yet, she thought, she'd like to be one of those people who didn't remember their dreams at all.

Knowing that normality had never really been in the cards for her, Raegan reached over to check the time on her phone. The light from the screen washed the room in shades of deep blue and gray. Her phone screen read 6:33 AM. It was a reasonable time to get up, she told herself, a time in the morning many regular, functioning adults awoke on a regular basis. She knew sleep would not return to her.

Raegan stood and stretched, her body protesting movement at such an early hour. She shuffled her way to the kitchen, filling the electric kettle and clicking it on. Her gaze went to the papers from her father's lockbox, gathered safely on the coffee table. She only knew a precious amount more than she did yesterday, but that was going to change. She was going to get dressed, she was going to go to the address from Rainer, and then—

Her phone rang shrilly, and she knew based on the hour that it had to be important.

"Raegan? It's Henry," came her editor's voice through the speaker.

"Henry. It is Saturday."

"I know, I know, I'm sorry—there's been another drowning," Henry replied, his voice still tinged with sleep. "You should go to the scene."

Fury simmered in Raegan's stomach, sending spikes of heat through the rest of her body. She clenched her jaw, extraordinarily pissed for a number of reasons: for forgetting the kelpie had not denied killing people, for taking the lead on a possible serial killer right before discovering that magic was fucking real, and lastly, for having to talk to another person before 8 AM.

"I can't today," Raegan found herself saying, which was not something she had ever said before.

Henry's sharp inhale of surprise made her uneasy. Silence greeted her from the other end. Her heart hammered, and she felt herself begrudgingly caving before Henry even said another word.

"Where is it?" Raegan asked, defeated. "I'm sorry. It's just . . . the anniversary's coming up . . . I saw my mom yesterday . . . It's pretty early—I'm just kind of out of it. I'll go."

"Look, Raegan, you're one of our best reporters. I don't think you've ever missed a deadline. If you're having a shit day, you're having a shit day, and I can get someone else to cover it. It's just, you know, if someone else gets something breaking—"

"Yeah, I know, I might not be lead anymore," Raegan said, but she already didn't feel like the lead, because she hadn't done an ounce of research after finding the book in her parents' basement, and that was going to show very, very quickly. "Look, I'll do it. Today is just rough, and obviously I wasn't expecting to work. What's the address?"

"You *are* off on Saturdays," Henry said, and she could hear him doing that thing where he pulled his glasses off and rubbed his eyes, deep in thought. "I'll cover it. If anyone asks, you were puking. Stomach bug. If I get anything wild, you'll still stay on lead."

Raegan wanted to tell him it did not matter to her at all if she stayed on this story, but that would be a dramatic departure from the person she had been just a day and half ago when she'd seen Henry last, and she knew she had to keep that close, stuffed away in her ribcage.

"Thank you, Henry, seriously. I really appreciate it. I'm sorry."

"You don't need to be sorry. Just send me updates tomorrow."

"I will," Raegan promised. "Seriously, thank you."

Henry told her to take care, and then she was alone in her kitchen, the tea kettle puffing steam and her mind running in a million directions. Though she was grateful to Henry, she was still *angry*—angry that anything would dare distract her from the path she was walking. Most of all, Raegan was angry that Rainer—her Virgil, essentially—had to be a goddamn murderer.

Muttering under her breath, she turned sharply and filled her sink up with water. She had no idea if it would work, but she grabbed the whiskey bottle and her knife because she was going to summon the kelpie again, right here in her fucking kitchen, and she was going to tell him to stop running around and murdering people.

Her fury should have cooled by the time she finished the incantation. She should've realized her mistake when the tips of Rainer's scalloped ears rose from the sink water. And she certainly should've turned back when the kelpie's black eyes met hers.

"I thought," the kelpie said, its tone flat and deadly, "we agreed we would not be speaking like this again."

"I would appreciate it if you stopped murdering people! I have other things to do!" Raegan shouted, slamming her fist on the countertop.

The kelpie looked taken aback, blinking at her silently for a heartbeat. "It is the way of things," the kelpie replied, pulling itself up, the entirety of its head rising out of the water. "I spread out the death. I do not plague one location for too long. I take only those who wish to go. But as I told you, I must consume."

Raegan realized, not for the first time, that the creature was *very* large—but in her kitchen, it seemed even more obvious. The kelpie's massive head obscured nearly all the morning sun from the window behind the sink, casting it in an ominous backlight.

"And *I'm* telling you to stop murdering innocent people and making it so goddamn obvious!" she shouted. "Why don't you kill a bad person? There's so many fucking bad people in this city. But you're killing vulnerable folks, people who haven't hurt anyone, and then you're leaving the bodies behind like a fucking amateur?"

Rainer tilted its head down, like a warhorse about to charge, and then it held Raegan's gaze. She narrowed her eyes at the kelpie, crossing her arms. They stayed like that for a few moments, neither moving, Raegan barely breathing, the only sound the echo of the water cascading off Rainer.

Right when she was losing her resolve, the kelpie sighed and looked away. "You are not wholly incorrect," the kelpie said, its tone low and quiet. "I will consider your input. Do not summon me again."

The kelpie began to sink back down into the water, but not before Raegan drew herself up, all her anger and sadness boiling over, and leaned into the kelpie's long face.

"Rainer," Raegan said, "I command you to stop killing."

"It does not work like that," the kelpie sneered, but Raegan thought she saw the whites of its eyes, so she tried again.

"Rainer, by the power of your name freely given, I bind you and I command you to preferably stop killing people, or at the very least only kill objectively shitty people, hide the goddamn bodies, and *stop making more work for me.*"

The kelpie shrank back then, moving from side to side in the sink, frothing water everywhere with its distress. "Where," Rainer began, the words ground between its many teeth, "did you learn such words?"

Realizing the kelpie's reaction probably meant it had worked, Raegan stood a little taller. "I'm Gods-touched, Rainer," she spat.

She watched as the kelpie took a long, shuddering inhale, sending waves of ripples out into the sink. Tiny waves lapped at the counter.

"Very well, Raegan Maeve Overhill," Rainer said, as if to demonstrate it had her name, too. "I will stop feasting in your city. For now. As long as you walk your silly little line. Which will not be long, and I am only bound for as long as you breathe."

"Sounds great," Raegan sneered. "Now go."

The kelpie blinked its black toad-eyes at her. "It would do you well, Raegan from Over the Hill," Rainer said, "to be wiser in this dangerous world. It is dark and terrible. You know little of it and even less of yourself."

And then the creature was gone from her sink as if it had never been there at all.

Chapter Thirteen

The water drained away of its own volition, clear and a little soapy, not the opaque black-green it had been just moments ago. Raegan stared at the bottom of the deep sink for a long time, begging the drain not to elongate its jaws and release a monster into her apartment.

When the hairs on the back of her neck stopped standing on end and she noticed the sounds of morning traffic returning, Raegan set about getting her first cup of tea prepared, trying to push all thoughts of the furious—and terrifying—kelpie aside now that her adrenaline had receded. But when her tea was fully steeped, she found herself frozen, the milk carton hovering above the cup. She stared into the black liquid, wondering exactly how much water the kelpie needed to reappear. As she kept a steady eye on the mug, something about the way the steam reached up in elegant plumes, sly and curled at the tip, was achingly familiar.

Rolling her shoulders, Raegan poured the milk into the tea, giving it a quick stir and downing it while staring out the window above her sink. There were still a few gulps left when she slammed her mug down on the counter and went to get dressed. She had no idea what to wear for a rendezvous with someone—something?—called "the king," but she eventually settled on fitted black pants, lace-up leather combat boots that came up to just below her knee, and a long, dark overcoat. After a lingering look in the bathroom mirror, Raegan elected to leave her hair down; the wild, dark auburn curls tumbled over her shoulders like armor.

Gathering her keys and phone, she cast a glance at her father's papers laid out on the coffee table. Raegan collected them carefully, gathered them in a manila folder, and then slid them into her work bag, which she then stowed beneath the coffee table. There was no chance in hell she was taking the spellwork straight to this king. She would decide when—and if—the time was right for such a thing. This king would have to prove themselves worthy of such trust.

With a long inhale, her heart pounding much faster than she would ever admit, Raegan opened her door and exited her apartment, thudding down the three flights of stairs to the ground level. The day greeted her overcast and damp, the street stickered with wet leaves. She took a deep breath of the air, smelling woodsmoke somewhere. And then she stepped out onto the sidewalk, the breeze catching at her hair. She felt as if the world turned ever-so-slightly on its axis, like a strong headwind had filled her sails for the first time in years. She was sure, so sure, that the soft gray breeze was singing her name. What had the kelpie called it? Threads. She felt like her Threads were being pulled, a strange song played across her skin. Raegan stood for a moment, admiring the sensation, the vastness of it, the way she felt as if she were an entire ocean.

And then she put her hands in her pockets and headed for the subway station.

"Raegan." The voice came from behind her, not on the wind but a tongue, and it was one she did not recognize. She did not know if it was the strangeness of her morning or simply a wish, but Raegan thought that the voice had a heavy North Welsh accent. Just like her father's.

Her stride faltered, but she kept going. Ignoring it, she thought, would be a good test.

"Raegan!" More insistent this time, barked from a hoarse throat. Otherworldly or not was another question, but there was no mistake that something had spoken. Raegan froze. Squaring her shoulders, her jaw clenched tightly, she turned on her heel and looked down the sidewalk.

A few paces from the door to her building stood a woman. She had dark, curly hair streaked with steel and green-gray eyes. Her complexion was pale, lightly dusted with freckles, and she wore a loose button-down and jacket over dark pants. She stood off to the side, a lit cigarette in her hand, as if only moments before, she had been leaning against Raegan's building, just waiting for her to come down the stairs.

The woman was undeniably familiar in a way that made the back of Raegan's throat close off. "Do I know you?" Raegan called, crossing her arms over her chest.

The woman took one slow step closer, her boots making no noise on the sidewalk. Raegan mirrored the step in reverse, keeping a solid distance between them.

"Yes and no," the woman replied. Her voice was low and raspy. "It's a long story."

"Most stories are," Raegan said, locking gazes with the stranger.

"Could we maybe go inside and talk?" the woman asked, gesturing to Raegan's apartment building.

Raegan let out a scoff. "Fuck no. I don't invite strangers into my home." That was categorically untrue. She had a long history of inviting strangers into her home—more specifically, her bed—but she figured the lie would go over just fine, considering she had never seen this woman before in her life. She hadn't, *had* she? The more Raegan looked at her face, the more her thoughts clouded.

The woman stared back, taking a long drag on her

cigarette. And then finally: "That's wise," she said with a sharp nod. "Maybe somewhere more public?"

The woman walked closer, and Raegan allowed it this time, studying her features: the large green-gray eyes, the square chin, the delicate hands, the tight curls. Suddenly, she realized: except for the hair, this woman looked like her father. But that wasn't possible. Her father had no siblings. No family, really—dead parents and an estranged uncle.

"Why do you . . ." Raegan asked, her voice trailing off when the woman came within a few steps of her.

At this distance, the resemblance was uncanny, though dark circles clung beneath the woman's eyes. She looked ragged. Raegan always remembered her father as being full of life, but nostalgia was a hell of a drug.

"Why do I look like Cormac?" the woman asked, one sharp brow arching. "Because he was my brother. I'm your aunt. And before you say anything—I imagine your father never brought me up. He may have even said he was an only child."

Raegan's mind swam, her eyes becoming unfocused for a moment before locking in, unreasonably, on a yellow oak leaf, its fingers stained brown by the cold snap. Then she brought her gaze up to the woman, who had returned to her cigarette.

"What are you doing in the States?" Raegan demanded, ignoring the rest of the situation for now. If she had an aunt that her father had never told her about, there was likely a good reason, possibly a dangerous one, so she'd start easy.

The woman stared her down, eyes gone gray as the wind kicked up, tugging at both of their clothing. A muscle in her jaw jumped before she exhaled. "Because you did magic," she replied simply, as if it were the most obvious answer in the world. "I'm here because you did magic. I felt it. And I got here as fast as I could. Because if I felt it, then . . ." The woman's voice trailed off, the wind gobbling it up. Raegan tilted her head at the stranger's words.

"Then . . . what?" Raegan asked, confused.

The woman's eyes widened, surprise—and fear, Raegan wagered—was clear across her face. It was the first time in their conversation that the stranger had not guarded her expression. "Hell," the woman spat out. "You don't know?"

"I don't know . . . *what*, exactly?" Raegan asked.

The woman grimaced. Raegan noticed the other hand that held the cigarette by her side was shaking.

"Gods, I don't know how to make you believe me," the woman said, taking another step toward Raegan, her eyebrows pulled together. "But if you don't even know what impact doing magic could have, you and I must talk *now*."

Raegan studied the woman. Her distress and fear seemed genuine. Only one of her pant legs was tucked into her boots. Raegan was fairly sure a bit of mascara was smudged beneath her eyes. Fear was hard to fake. When people attempted it, they usually forgot that most folks don't like showing fear and kept it in their expression for too long. In reality, almost everyone did their best to wipe it off their face immediately— which was exactly what the woman had done.

"There's . . . there's a café a few blocks from here," Raegan said, the words climbing out of her throat before she could stop herself. "It has some quiet nooks. We could talk. If you tell me your name?"

Unexpectedly, the woman looked at her and grinned— dazzling, utterly disarming, and Raegan recognized her own smile on a stranger's face. "Maelona," the woman replied. "My name's Maelona Overhill."

"Okay, Maelona," Raegan said, shifting her body weight in the direction of the café. "Let's go talk."

Raegan turned and headed down the street without checking if Maelona was following her. After a few steps, she sensed the woman slightly behind her and she could smell the cigarette smoke. She appreciated the space, and that Maelona didn't try to talk as they walked because Raegan needed that time to get her head on straight. Her heart was pounding nearly out of her chest, and her fingers itched to call her mother. She thought better of it after a few moments; even if Bronwyn had information about Maelona, Raegan would likely have to wade through a large emotional reaction before getting to it.

And if her father had lied about having living family members . . . ? That thought sunk like a stone to the bottom of Raegan's stomach. If that were true, Raegan absolutely did not want to hurt her mother with the idea that her husband had been lying to her. There was already enough grief.

Above, the skies roiled and darkened, mist eventually working its way down from the heavens and onto Raegan's shoulders. Despite herself, she sighed. Wearing her hair down was essentially a guarantee of precipitation.

The café was just up ahead when Maelona spoke suddenly, jarring her. "It reminds me of home, sort of."

When Raegan turned to look at her, brow furrowed, Maelona gestured to the street around them. "I've never been to Philadelphia before. I thought it would be like other big cities in the States. It's not, not really. I like it."

"Dad always said that," Raegan replied. "I was born and raised here, but I still think Philly feels very different from other major cities."

"Phil-ee," Maelona echoed. "Is that a nickname? For such a short word?"

Raegan laughed, despite herself, pulling the café's door open. "Five syllables is long in English," she replied. "It's a term of endearment, I suppose."

"Right," Maelona said, forcing a smile that looked more like a grimace. "Can I smoke in here?"

"Nah," Raegan said with a shake of her head. "Feel free to finish up, though. I can go get us a table?"

"Yeah, that would be great," Maelona said before taking another long drag. Up close, she was taller than Raegan but thinner. Raegan would wager that beneath her loose-fitting clothing, Maelona was almost skeletal, at least based on the bones that jutted out of her wrist just below her sleeve cuff. She watched the woman for a moment longer before someone came through the door and thanked her for holding it open. Raegan mumbled a response and walked inside.

Ray's Café and Tea House was one of her haunts when she couldn't stand to be alone in her apartment but only had the tolerance for strangers. Its awning was stained, and the red neon letters in the window always flickered. The interior hadn't been updated in years—no big glass windows or cold white walls with minimal black lettering. Unlike most cafés in the area, it was warm and cozy and friendly.

Raegan chose a table tucked into a corner, taking the seat that allowed her to see the majority of the café and the door. Just in case. Outside, Maelona crushed the butt of her cigarette under her boot's heel in a practiced maneuver. Then she put her hands in her pockets and walked inside. Her gait was slightly hitched, like she was covering for an old injury. Raegan noticed that the woman walked with her head down, shoulders hunched, as if she were perpetually trying to avoid being seen.

When Maelona reached the table, she didn't quite sit down; it was more like all her joints finally gave up and she just fell into the seat. She said nothing to Raegan, taking in the surroundings.

"I like this place," Maelona said eventually, her fingers tapping an anxious melody on the tabletop.

"Good," Raegan replied. "Because you're paying." With that, she pulled up the laminated menu like a shield, perusing the offerings that she already knew very well. When a waiter arrived to take their tea order, Maelona asked for the strongest siphon coffee and Raegan got her usual Earl Gray.

"Would you like to put in any food orders?" the waiter asked, tucking their pad back into their apron.

"Maybe in a few minutes," Raegan replied. "I think my aunt still needs to decide." The waiter nodded and headed for the counter, leaving Raegan alone with the woman who claimed to be family.

Silence fell over the table. Maelona was chewing the inside of her cheek, looking out the window. In this light, Raegan could see the lines that etched her skin. If this woman was actually her aunt, Maelona shouldn't be much older than her late fifties. There were parts of her that made her seem younger —the frantic energy, the wild mane of hair, her choice in clothing. But the deep exhaustion in her features spoke of someone at the end of their life, not a little past the halfway point.

"We should get the pork and leek dumplings. They're good," Raegan announced, for once being the one to break the silence. She relinquished her menu-shield, placing it on the table.

"It's seven in the morning," Maelona replied, arching a brow.

"I said they're good," Raegan repeated, more sharply this time.

"Fine," Maelona agreed, immediately deflating like Raegan had a feeling she would. The woman's fingers danced on the tabletop again, and she stole glances at Raegan periodically until their drinks arrived.

When they did, Maelona peeled back the lid on Raegan's teapot as if something might be hiding within its white ceramic belly, but she looked appeased and put the lid back with a soft clink. Then she grabbed her coffee cup with shaking hands and took a long drink. Maelona placed it back on the table, misjudging the saucer and sending a black tidal wave over the lip of the mug, eliciting a quiet curse. Raegan wordlessly handed her a wad of napkins.

"So," Raegan said eventually, folding her hands on the

table, looking expectantly at Maelona. "Apparently we have very important things to discuss."

Under the harsh indoor lighting, Raegan saw Maelona's face pinch, the movement outlining the worry and stress that seemed to be permanently sculpted into her skin. For a moment, the only sound in the café was the quiet chatter up front and a low, lilting melody that slunk in the front door from a passing car. It was orchestral and full of hurt and want, as delicate as a curl of smoke, reaching into the space like a column of fog.

Then a long sigh left Maelona's body, seeming to rattle her bones. She dug the heel of her palm into one eye; Raegan noticed that her long, spindly fingers shook.

"What's important," Maelona finally said, raising her gaze to meet Raegan's, "is that magic is real and it's dangerous. You know that, though. Because you've done it."

Raegan clenched her jaw, waiting, but then she saw Maelona was not making an accusation, only a statement. Her heart leapt against her breastbone. How could Maelona possibly know she'd summoned the kelpie? And from across an entire ocean, nonetheless?

"By doing magic," Maelona continued, searching Raegan's face, "you've thrown away the protection we sacrificed *everything* to give you."

Unease swept through Raegan's body, a brackish tide teeming with sharp-toothed mouths. Questions speared her thoughts—what kind of protection was Maelona referring to and who exactly was the "we" that had sacrificed so much. She squeezed her eyes shut for a moment, willing her mind to quiet. When she opened them, Maelona had leaned her upper body across the table, so close—too close—to Raegan, something half-mad gleaming in her gray-green eyes.

"You have made yourself known," Maelona said, her voice edged with a rough rasp. "And the Protectorate have seen something that looks like one of theirs—unoathed, untrained, and thought long-lost."

The older woman paused again, her brows coming together in a heavy V, looking like the weight of the world rested squarely on her shoulders.

"So they're going to come for you."

Chapter Fourteen

"Who?" Raegan asked, holding Maelona's gaze. "Who is coming for me?"

At that, Maelona reeled back as though she'd been struck, something like outraged horror shadowing her expression. Raegan could feel her heartbeat in her throat.

"You don't even *know*?" Maelona hissed, eyes wide, face pinched. Her shaking hands curled into fists on the tabletop.

"What do I not know, Maelona?" Raegan replied, trying to keep her voice calm and level. "Help me out. That's what you're here for, right?"

Maelona leaned back in her chair, looking stricken with despair. Her jaw worked, gaze darting to the sidewalk. The moment stretched taut as a bowstring. Raegan waited, turning over the information she had from the book and the kelpie. She had a sharp, sinking feeling that it would not be even close to enough.

"This is worse than I thought," Maelona finally said, her tone quiet and hoarse.

"If things are so bad, *help* me," Raegan implored, throwing everything she had into the words. But Maelona only fell silent again, her mouth settling into a firm line, eyes trained on the sidewalk beyond the window. Raegan watched, confused, until she realized with a queasy, feverish jolt that Maelona was searching the block outside. Almost as if she were looking for someone.

"You know nothing, and we're nearly out of time," Maelona mumbled, sounding dazed, her eyes appearing to follow the slow track of a large raindrop traveling down the windowpane.

"Hey. Who the fuck is going to come for me, Maelona?" Raegan demanded again, switching tactics, going back on the offensive.

Maelona did not even register that Raegan had spoken. Instead, she turned in her seat and examined every single patron of the café, lingering on a mundane-looking man in a navy suit who sat at the counter. Raegan fought away rising panic. While she felt certain Maelona had answers, she was *not* sure if Maelona was sane, or her real aunt, or actually here to help.

When Maelona turned back, her gaze fell heavy as a millstone on Raegan. "Do you even know about the Protectorate?" she demanded, her eyes wild. "Do you know about the Fey? The Gates? The Timekeeper? Do you know the fucking *King* is here, in the States?"

The king again. First from the kelpie, and now from Maelona. She almost caught a memory, something deep in the recesses of her mind, but it slipped out of her grasp, leaving her feeling adrift.

"Where is my father?" Raegan asked, voice strained, finding herself unable to summon any other words. She wished she were less predictable, but anytime she felt unmoored, her compass pointed due north—right to that aching hole in her chest.

"He's dead, Raegan," Maelona snapped, but there was no venom in it. She looked drained. "If you're holding on to some idiotic hope, let it go. He risked everything to have a normal life with you and your mother, but the Gates called too sweetly in the end."

Raegan's breath caught and she studied Maelona carefully. She certainly seemed to believe what she'd said—that Cormac was gone. Raegan wound her hands into fists, ignoring the nausea rising like a tide in her stomach. No. She'd know; she would've felt the warm, bright light of him leave this plane. She would *know*. But all Raegan knew for sure was that her father's story wasn't finished, no matter what Maelona said.

Besides, throwing out that her missing father was actually dead was a good tactic. The resulting emotions could make Raegan weak, pliable. She grit her teeth. She would be neither of those things. She would cling to hope, not sorrow. Hopelessness had never done much for her, anyway.

"Is that what you were trying to do when you broke the protective warding?" Maelona asked, weariness shadowing her face. "Scrying for your father, just in case he wasn't really gone?"

Raegan inhaled, still steeling herself against the idea of her father being dead. The thought, she knew, was parasitic—it would latch its teeth into her and lay claim to her mind if she allowed it access. So she shut it out, pressing her lips together and letting her gaze drift away, hoping Maelona would see whatever she wanted in the non-verbal response and keep talking.

"Unlike you, Raegan, I am inducted and oathed," Maelona laughed, sharp as porcelain shards. "I'm trained to deal with the Fey. I'll only accept a clear 'yes' or 'no.' "

"Yes," Raegan gambled, wiping damp palms on her thighs beneath the table. It wasn't technically untrue. "I was looking for him."

Maelona choked out a scoff, glancing away to search the crowds on the sidewalk again. "He and I sacrificed so much for you," she said, words thick with exhaustion. "And you've fucked it all up looking for someone who's been dead more than a decade."

Silence hung between the two of them, the sounds of the café all but faded away entirely from Raegan's ears. She wanted to scream that her father wasn't dead—couldn't be. But she clamped her jaw shut instead.

"And I suppose you're looking at a dead woman as we speak," Maelona added with a humorless laugh, throwing one hand up in the air as if she didn't have a care in the world, as if death had always been lingering on the threshold. "If—or more likely when—the Protectorate learns I've been helping you all these years, and your father before that, there will be hell to pay."

Raegan took a few seconds—one long inhale, one long exhale. Then she sharpened her words to see where Maelona might bleed.

"I find it difficult to believe you put your life on the line for *me*, someone you hardly know," she said, her tone harsh and unbelieving, one eyebrow raised haughtily. She braced herself for a reaction, and Maelona did not disappoint—with a wordless snarl, she slammed a fist on the table, rattling the porcelain.

"I couldn't save my own fucking brother," she hissed, her eyes flashing, all of her tension and anxiety unfolding into rage instead. "Let me at least save *you*." Maelona stared Raegan down for a long, skittering heartbeat or two before she deflated, shoulders sagging beneath her coat. "The Protectorate wants you," she continued, sounding weary again, though her hand on the tabletop was still curled into a fist. "But I'm not going to let them have you. I owe Cormac that, at least."

Raegan clenched her teeth, trying and failing to slow her heartbeat. She needed to be clever and quick. She had to keep Maelona talking; she needed every bit of information the woman had to offer.

"Why would they even want me?" Raegan countered. "Like you said, I know so little." But hearing that name again —the Protectorate—rattled her. Something almost like a memory slithered in the dark recesses of her mind. The sensation was formless and wordless, but she could feel it against her skin, a gossamer touch of another world.

Before she could catch the fleeting thing inside her head, or even open her mouth to ask another question, the chimes on the door to the café rang, announcing another patron. Maelona's head snapped up to look, her shoulders hitching with tension. Raegan peered beyond Maelona, catching sight of a mountainous man in a pinstripe suit of a murky, indeterminate color. She felt quite sure she'd never seen the man before in her life, and yet her chest constricted sharply, dread dragging cool fingers up her neck.

Maelona moved so fast Raegan could hardly track it. She shot out of her chair and bent low over the table, her body obscuring Raegan's view of the man at the door. Then her hand wrapped around Raegan's forearm and pulled with surprising strength. Without a chance to brace herself, Raegan was yanked halfway out of her seat.

"Come with me," Maelona hissed. "*Now.*"

Raegan's initial response was resistance—she planted herself beside the table, feet set shoulder-width apart. Instead of pulling harder, Maelona stepped in close.

"What could you possibly know of the Protectorate's reach and power, Raegan?" she asked in a low, dangerous voice. "Of the things they will do to reclaim what they believe to be theirs—*you*?"

At that, Raegan relented, mostly out of shock. She raised her eyes to meet Maelona's. "Not enough," she admitted quietly.

From the front of the café, she heard a voice—rough around the edges, clipped with faux politeness, thick with an English accent. Revulsion bloomed in the back of her throat.

Suddenly and fiercely, Raegan needed to be away from here—away from that mountain of a man in the pinstripe suit. Her life, she was sure, depended on it.

So she let Maelona drag her by the wrist to the back of the café. The long, narrow space ended in a small hallway, the fronds of twin palm trees draping across the entry like a curtain. Raegan opened her mouth to tell Maelona she'd only ever been back here for the restroom and had no idea if there even *was* an exit. But the older woman spoke instead.

"When your father disappeared," Maelona said, her voice low, fingertips like a vice around Raegan's forearm. "The Protectorate didn't consider for a moment that he'd been killed in action, even though that's usually how we meet our end. No—Cormac had sown so much doubt and discord with all his starry-eyed ideals about magic that we were told to hunt him as a deserter."

Maelona yanked Raegan along, picking up the pace as they passed the door to the bathroom. The rest of the hallway was a dim, unknown space. Raegan had nearly managed to find some semblance of calm when Maelona's grip on her arm tightened. Then the taller woman swung Raegan against the wall, a strong hand wrapping around each of her biceps.

"They made me *hunt* my own brother like a fucking dog," Maelona hissed, her face inches from Raegan's, eyes wild in the gloom. "And if I found him, I was to kill him—and you and your mother."

Raegan's mouth went dry, adrenaline seeping hot into her veins. So Maelona was trying to scare her—that much was clear. She quieted her thoughts and searched Maelona's face. All she found was ragged dedication and the kind of rabid gleam she imagined was not unlike a wounded animal's eyes when backed into a corner.

As if she were confident she had made her point, Maelona relaxed her grip on Raegan, continuing down the hallway. Up ahead, the wall curved, culminating in a large metal door. An exit into the alley, Raegan hoped.

"But you're not here to kill me," she said, forced to break into a jog to match Maelona's long, purposeful strides.

"Neither is the Protectorate," Maelona replied without looking at her. "Not anymore. You're too useful. War is coming. And all good little soldiers must report for duty."

Maelona shoved Raegan toward the door, releasing the grip on her arm. The force of her fingers might've left bruises, but Raegan felt no pain—only the blood pounding in her veins.

"You need to run, Raegan. Get as far away from this as you can. You're unoathed, which means you're still free," Maelona said, almost imploringly. "Give me your phone."

Again, Raegan hesitated, her heart thudding so hard her chest hurt. Going off gut instinct and not much else, she handed her phone to Maelona, unable to hide how hard her hands were shaking. Maelona took it and began to type with unsteady fingers.

"I will contact you," Maelona said, stealing another furtive glance over her shoulder before handing Raegan's phone back to her. "Do not trust anyone and do not do more magic. Not now, not ever. That's the price of your freedom, and if I were you, I'd pay it."

Raegan hesitated, a cold hand slipping over her heart. To give up magic—the thing she had always been searching for and had *finally* found—was too steep a price.

"But wait—"

Maelona shook her head, reaching behind Raegan to push the door open. "It's not real magic, anyway," she said. "It's poison loaned to us by the Timekeeper to do his bidding in places he can't reach." With that, Maelona grabbed Raegan by the shoulders and shoved her out into the damp mist, slamming the door shut behind her.

Raegan stumbled backwards over a set of concrete steps,

bumping her hip hard into a large dumpster. The pain barely registered. She caught her balance just as frustration swept through her. Charging back up the steps, she banged the heel of her palm against the metal door. When Maelona didn't answer, she yanked the handle, but to no avail—it was locked.

Raegan bit down on her tongue, resisting a childish urge to throw her head back and scream. Instead, she ducked deeper into the rain-sodden alley behind the café. Pulling her coat shut, she navigated the maze of overfilled dumpsters and broken glass to the mouth of the alley. She edged along the building's wall, her heart a war drum in her chest.

"They're coming from the front, love."

Raegan's stomach dropped out, a wave of panicked nausea rushing through her. She spun, nearly tripping on a torn trash bag, to face whoever had just spoken. There, swathed in the gloom of the alley, stood a woman. She was taller than Raegan, built in an elegant way that reminded her of someone, something, somewhere.

The woman smiled, the lines around her mouth creasing. Raegan found it impossible to tell how old she was—the stained gray hoodie, grime-caked sneakers and patched jeans gave little away.

"Yes," the woman said with a sharp laugh, gesturing to herself, her voice reminding Raegan of old-time starlets with transatlantic accents. "I'm not what I used to be. Surely not what you remember. But they're coming from the front. You're safe out here for a few more moments."

Raegan's mouth was impossibly dry, her heart thudding so hard in her chest it had begun to hurt. Her palms were slick. Apparently, this moment was the breaking point at which her brain refused to take in more new information. She stood dumbly, unable to take her eyes off the woman. Beneath the dirty hood, the woman's face was full of sharp planes and odd angles, bronze skin and unusual golden eyes.

"You best be going, *brenhines pennaf*," the woman said,

her voice firmer this time. "Before they see. Shoo. Out you go."

A sorrow too heavy for any one person to hold fell over Raegan's shoulders like a winter pelt. "Where am I supposed to go?" she asked, surprised by the sound of her own voice—thin, hoarse, utterly lost.

The woman stepped closer, hollow-eyed wistfulness dancing across the ancient planes of her face. "Oh, love," she replied. "Where else? To the King, of course."

Chapter Fifteen

Raegan hovered at the mouth of the alley, her gaze locked on the hooded woman, wondering if she should run. Her muscles quivered—she felt every inch a deer standing at the edge of a meadow, wondering if the hunter's arrow was nocked.

Yes, Raegan decided. She should run. With one last look at the woman, she turned onto the sidewalk away from the café, her boots thudding hard on the pavement. But she was not going to run away.

No. Raegan was going to run *toward* whatever this was—toward magic, toward her father's secrets, toward the king. The remnants of rush hour parted like the Red Sea for her. She sliced through the neighborhood, reaching the threshold of the city's oldest section. She slowed at a busy intersection, her breath rattling in her chest, throat raw.

When the light changed, she took off again, not minding the way she had to gulp air in painful gasps or how her calves began to protest. Transformation was never easy. The blocks passed in a blur—pavement giving way to cobblestone, glass and steel architecture melting into neat, squat, brick and stone houses lined up like teeth, their wooden shutters creaking in the wind.

When Raegan reached the cross street she was looking for, she paused on the corner, her skin a wildfire. Her eyes tracked down the block in search of the address given to her by the kelpie. The thought sent a shard of ice into her chest. The sureness she had worn like armor only moments ago, faltered.

Raegan set her jaw and squeezed her eyes shut, letting out a long breath. She would be insane to barrel into this, wouldn't she? She should go back to her apartment, lock up tight, and wait for Maelona to contact her. She should not waste everything her father had put into motion, no more than she should squander whatever Maelona had suffered to keep her safe.

Absent-mindedly, Raegan reached into her coat pocket. Her fingertips hit the tiny silver key of the lockbox. She pulled it out, turning the object around in her palm. Its metallic surface caught the weak sun, sparkling like a coin at the bottom of a fountain. She wrapped her hand around it tightly, allowing the teeth of the key to dig into her skin.

Despite everything, it was not in her nature to let this go.

Raegan stepped off the street corner and onto the block where Arawn Antiques should reside. Her strides were long and slow now, her eyes hunting, wanting to spot the building before she dared walk closer. Perhaps the structure itself could tell her something, some story in its window-eyes, a tale scarred into its brick.

And then Raegan found it, standing at the far end of the block: a handsome row house thick with decorative wood accents, all painted a deep, shiny black. The front door was set to the left, adorned with a large silver knocker. Two windows were to its right, both with the shades drawn. Satisfied, she took a deep breath, shoved her hands in her pockets, and headed toward it.

And then she felt it: Fate playing her like a violin, her Threads taut, singing a melody that almost brought her to her knees. The air was thick with woodsmoke, which made no sense this deep in the city, and the gray, gloomy sun was steady on her back. Everything seemed to slow down, sticky as molasses, steady and purposeful and gilded like amber. Only a few more paces, and then Raegan would be standing directly across the street from this place that called to her with the gravitational pull of a black hole.

Movement at the end of the block, just past Arawn Antiques, caught her attention. Raegan jogged around a café's outdoor tables that blocked her view. And then—from around the corner, on the other side of the street, out of the mist—there he was: the stranger she had seen on the subway platform.

Tall and muscular with his dark tumbles of wavy black hair, unusually angular face, full, sculpted mouth, and knife-like cheekbones. He was dressed differently than when Raegan had seen him from the train; instead of casual black clothing, he wore a white button-down shirt cuffed at his elbows, dark pants, and Chelsea boots. He moved down the block with a strange, lithe grace that swallowed Raegan's attention.

"Please," she begged to no particular deity, her mouth dry, her eyes tracking his movement down the street, her heart pounding louder, and her hands shaking more and more with each step he took closer to the door of Arawn Antiques.

A symphony as sweet as honey wine slipped through the air, swelling like the sweep of a rolling hill as Raegan watched the man scale the steps to the front door, his long legs devouring the distance as though he were merely stepping over the curb. When he reached for the door knob, Raegan did not question the instinct that told her to move.

She gathered each fragile hope she had ever dared to allow into existence in her unsteady hands like glass eggs, and then, without hesitation, she sprinted across the narrow cobblestone street with wild abandon as he disappeared behind the door.

Scrambling up the steps, Raegan felt a thrill run through her when she realized the shining black door with its ornate silver finishings had not yet fully closed. Before she could think about it, before she could do anything but allow the oldest and deepest ache in her chest to pull her forward, Raegan pushed through the door and collapsed into whatever waited beyond it.

The door shut behind her. Darkness crowded in. It was as if her ears had been stuffed with cotton and she had been blindfolded. The space she had boldly entered was nothing but darkness. She drew herself up, waiting for her eyes to adjust, but the moment never came. The only thing she noticed was the faint smell of woodsmoke and black pepper.

Terror slid a cold hand onto her neck, but Raegan forced it away. "Hello?" she called. Her voice rang out much louder than she thought possible or logical. "Rainer sent me."

Nothing for a heartbeat, but then something stirred, maybe, in a far corner. The darkness beneath her feet seemed to slide, to move of its own accord, inky black and curled at the tips, like elegant plumes of steam drifting from a cup of tea.

The shadows closed around her, suffocating. The misty autumn morning felt a thousand years away. In her head, Raegan heard Maelona's warnings. She felt like a kid again, trapped in the damp dark of that childhood basement, except this time her father would not come to her rescue.

Oh. Of course.

Raegan straightened her spine and planted her feet firmly on the floor. She swallowed hard, just once, and then she opened her mouth to speak. "I greet thee, *mrenin*, as I walk within your shadow and your stead."

A beat, a moment of hesitation, and then Raegan's mind turned over like a serpent, sending words to her tongue that she could've sworn she did not know.

"This darkness is your dominion, and to you I surrender,"

she recited. "Do me no harm."

The shadows subsided, slipping away like tendrils, and as they did, Raegan was forced to accept how unnaturally dark it had been only moments ago. She understood that it was never a matter of her eyes adjusting. This darkness was no mundane thing. It was a different kind of shadow entirely, slippery like silk and soft as velvet.

"No harm shall be done."

The voice came from the center of the shadows. The sound of it was like rain on wet stone, or heather on the hills, or dusk over the lake. The voice was low and deep and regal, and god, for some reason, she thought it sounded like home. The shadows slunk away farther, as if pushed aside like a curtain. Raegan found herself facing the stranger from the subway platform, and she was transfixed.

He was even taller up close, all spring-loaded muscle beneath porcelain skin. His black hair fell in elegant waves. And his eyes. Eyes that Raegan somehow knew, had known from even before the subway platform—ocean eyes, gray and fathomless. Something emanated from him, pulsing out from his being, and it made her head swim. *Power*, she realized. It was power. Pure, raw, unadulterated power.

She stood stock still as he approached her slowly, leaving space between them. It wasn't space he would have any trouble closing in a heartbeat, Raegan knew, but she appreciated the courtesy. Closer now, the scent of woodsmoke and rain and black pepper was strong and unbearably gorgeous.

"Rainer sent me," Raegan breathed. She was repeating herself. Her heart was in her throat.

He appeared to be looking at her too intently for the words to register anyway, those impossible eyes searching her face, as if he didn't trust that it actually belonged to her. His dark eyebrows drew together, something like disbelief came across his features. Then he clenched his jaw, a muscle jumping.

For a moment, Raegan thought his full lips might part and he would utter something like, *"Welcome home, I have been waiting for you. I have always been waiting for you. Like the heather returns to the hills every year, so I have hoped you would return to me."*

He did not. Instead, he steadied his expression, all cold grace, and gathered himself. "It is always a pleasure to meet an acquaintance of Rainer's," he said, his tone cool and professional.

The way he reached his hand out to hers was not. It was tentative, delicate, unsure, like it was a dry winter day and he was afraid of shocking her. Meeting his gaze, Raegan pressed her palm into his and found that he had been right to worry about a spark. Electricity flooded her body, and outside a birdsong crescendoed, like everything the bards used to sing about had fallen into place, like this was the very moment the gods had been waiting for all along.

"Have we met before?" Raegan asked, the words tumbling from her mouth before she could scoop them up and put them back where they belonged.

"I do not believe so," he told her, his expression inscrutable. An accent she could not place hung heavy on his words, though she did not think she'd be remiss to equate it to Welsh.

"Who are you?" Raegan asked, the smell of black pepper and woodsmoke and rain, that torrential kind of rain during autumn, making her head swim. She wondered distantly if her question was one that could even be answered in full.

"I am known as the King," he told her, and even though it came as no surprise, her heart still raced wildly in her chest.

Up close, the planes of his face were not human. Too symmetrical, yet too feral. The aquiline nose was too perfect, the features too angular and too sharp. He was beautiful in the way all deadly things are.

"What may I call you?" the King asked. His careful words

neatly sidestepped the long history of trickery between their people. *If* he was what she thought—though she had little doubt she was standing in the presence of the Fey.

"Raegan. Raegan Maeve Overhill," she replied once she found the strength to look up at him and meet his gaze again.

The King arched a dark brow at her, the corner of his mouth curving up into something unkind. "You should not give a full name to things like me."

The words on their own were only a warning, but the twist of his mouth and the cold gleam in his eyes was a taunt. Raegan leveled her gaze at the King, though her heart was pounding against her ribs.

"You would have learned it from the kelpie if not from me," she replied, lifting her chin. "If you are going to take from me what is not yours, at least have the decency to take it directly."

Something akin to amusement rolled across the King's angular face like a heat wave. His gaze slid down from the crown of her head to her shoes, then back up to her eyes. "Why are you here, Ms. Overhill?" The words were lazy, looping, something about them reminding her of the Cheshire cat.

"Do you conduct all business in a poorly lit lobby? Or do you have somewhere more comfortable to sit?" Raegan demanded, letting steel slip into her tone.

Hospitality, she knew, was important to the old things, and playing that card gave her a tiny shred of control over the situation. Surely it would lead her deeper into the King's space, but she did not feel it wise to continue this conversation in a shadow-filled room. For a long, stretched moment, the King simply watched her appraisingly. Raegan's heart thudded louder and louder until she was sure he could hear it, too, but she held her ground.

"Please, do follow me," the King said in a dry tone, gesturing with a lithe, powerful hand.

Raegan clenched her jaw and took a tentative step toward

the King as he turned on his heel. He moved through the darkness, and she maintained as great a distance from him as she dared. The King had not agreed to her request verbally, only asked her to follow him, and she had not missed the technicality.

Surprise flooded Raegan when she emerged from the shadows into a small side room. Lit by mundane electricity, the space was much cozier than she had anticipated—like something she'd create for herself, given a much larger budget.

An ornately carved Victorian couch upholstered in meadow green velvet stretched along one wall. To Raegan's right, ferns and vines hung around the large, high windows she had seen from the street. A gorgeous, neatly arranged desk sat in the far corner. In the middle of the space, a circular table with two chairs waited. Books were piled on one side of the table's well-worn surface. She snuck a glance at the spines, but the gold lettering there did not appear to be either of the two languages she could read.

With a jolt, Raegan cut her survey of the space short, realizing she had lost track of the King. She whipped her head to the left, dismayed to find he had been standing just off to the side, arms folded across his broad chest, watching her the entire time. The stance caused the shirt's fabric to pull at the King's shoulders, outlining his lithe, muscular build. Despite everything about the situation, heat pooled in Raegan's belly.

"Didn't expect something so cozy," she sneered, trying to recover.

"Most people do not get this far," the King countered, unfolding his arms. He waved toward the table with one hand —an impossibly elegant, long-fingered hand. Raegan could not imagine those hands shaking or jostling a coffee cup. "Please have a seat."

It was not a request. Unsurprisingly, the King spoke with the quiet, cool authority of someone used to being obeyed. Raegan had been planning to sit anyway, so she meandered over to the table, trying to make it clear with her slow pace that his command had little to do with her choice. She sank into the chair with its back to the window, giving her the most open view of the doorway and the rest of the room. The chair was hard and uncomfortable, which she imagined was intentional.

Only once Raegan was seated did the King close the distance with one long stride. He lowered himself into the chair across from her and crossed his ankle over his knee. Here in brighter light, the King's inhuman beauty only grew more apparent. She knew it was embarrassing and she wanted to stop, but all Raegan could do was gape at him. He shouldn't be real. He was only meant to be some attractive stranger she met on subway stations and in dreams. He was not supposed to be made of such gorgeous alabaster flesh and strong, powerful bone.

Raegan caught his gaze inadvertently, and immediately found herself nearly lost in his eyes: an impossible shade of gray, the color of an ocean in a storm. She swallowed down the familiarity that crawled its way up her throat, a déjà vu so violent she had to shake her head to clear it.

For the barest of moments—probably when he thought she would not notice—the King's expression softened and Raegan saw something other than cool detachment. There was a haunted sort of longing in his gaze, as if he desperately wanted something he knew he could not have.

Raegan suddenly wished to weep, like she might at the conclusion of a very long and arduous journey, but any emotion the King had perhaps shown was entirely gone. He folded his hands on the table silently, waiting for her to speak, and she watched him carefully, wondering if her gut feeling could be trusted.

It seemed too improbable: that she had always been looking for him and now, finally, here he was.

CHAPTER SIXTEEN

Raegan drew a shaky inhale and turned as if to examine the Victorian couch, trying to pull her mind back to herself. Whatever strange feelings surfaced from deep within her marrow were irrelevant. She was meeting with a faerie king, who was likely older than castles and mountains and countries. Leaving in one piece, let alone with what she needed, would take every ounce of her wit. She shifted her gaze back to the King, who took it as an opening.

"Whatever you seek my assistance with," he said, tilting his head to the side and watching her closely, "must be very important for you to choose such a perilous path."

Raegan held her tongue. A car horn sounded outside, which she couldn't quite reconcile with the otherworldly being in front of her. "Yes," she said eventually, steepling her fingers as she rested her wrists on the table. "But considering the gravity of the situation, Rainer insisted upon involving you. I chose to honor the kelpie's counsel, despite an audience with the King being far from my first choice."

She would do what she always did. Be in control. Know more. Have more aces up her sleeve. Or at least she'd try.

"Nor should it be," the King returned, one elegant eyebrow arching up for a moment. "Particularly not for your kind. We owe each other no allegiance."

It was a very polished way of saying that Raegan's race and the King's people had been warring for a thousand years, but she was admittedly more focused on how the arch of the King's brow sent warmth to her core. For an instant, she would've sworn beyond all reason that she'd seen him arch that brow a million times before.

"There is an artifact I'm hoping you might be willing to examine," Raegan explained, her tongue heavy, trying to navigate the situation at hand despite her confused tangle of emotions. She knew she should focus on how terrifying the planes of the King's face were. On finding her father, who she refused to accept was dead until she could confirm it herself. A basic tenet of journalism—believe nothing, trust no one. "But it is a delicate situation," she continued, "and I'm hoping to establish some basis of trust before permitting access to the artifact."

He looked at her with dark, heavy-lidded amusement, his expression gone wolfish. He glanced away for a second and then back at her, head tilted again, the gray eyes now nearly entirely black. "I cannot begin to imagine," the King said, his voice sharp as a sword, "what would cause a human to trust *me*."

One of his impossibly powerful-looking hands reached across the table to emphasize his words. The veil of politeness was gone. The creature in the room with her was all wolf, all snake, all predator.

And then he drew back, the aggression gone from his broad shoulders, his weight shifting back into his seat. Raegan studied him, her heart racing, the chair's back pressing painfully into her skin.

"Overhill," he said, his tone measured again. "I imagine

this will frustrate you, but this is not something I wish to entangle myself with."

"What?" Raegan demanded before she thought better of it, as if she had already forgotten his politeness was only a mask. "I've barely told you anything at all. How can you decide so quickly?"

"I cannot help you," the King repeated, shifting so his body was now angled toward the door. "Please give my regards to Rainer."

Raegan's face grew hot, her mind reeling at this dead end. Where could she even go next if the literal Fey king failed her? She had thought coming here might spell an early death or that she'd have to promise him her firstborn. But she'd never thought that her audience with the King would be so brief. It'd never even crossed her mind. Granted, Raegan had not stopped to think about much more than going beyond the shining black door that had called to her so sweetly.

"No," she spat, leaning forward onto the table. "No. I refuse to accept that."

The King stared at her. Raegan stared at the King. For several long seconds, she felt the entire world condense to this building, this room, and the startlingly beautiful gray eyes of the ancient being across from her.

"You must accept it," the King said, his words long and low, drawn out, dark and deadly. *Or else*, he did not say, though Raegan supposed something as dangerous as the King never needed to tack on the extra words. The threat was implied. Always. Her mind raced to grab onto anything, anything at all, even if she was just stalling. Her fingernails bit half-moons into her palms, and she was entirely too warm in her overcoat. It did not help that the longer she shared this space with the King, the more she felt something unfolding in her chest that she did not understand.

"I know you," Raegan spat like an accusation, like it was a

reason to so openly disobey a being clearly used to commanding others.

"No," he responded, his face blank. "You do not, and I must ask you to leave."

Raegan did not understand what drove her to it, what madness possessed her to make the choice, but she reached across the table and seized the King's hand with her own. "Why are you lying to me?" She intended the words to come out angry, demanding.

Instead, that strange thing in her chest unfolded sticky, cocoon-fresh wings, and her words were half-strangled with grief, an ocean of tears breaking the levy behind her eyes.

She watched as the King's long fingers curled reflexively around hers, as if their palms were two sides of a locket. The rigid line of his shoulders relaxed. With their skin laid flush against each other's, Raegan was struck by how the map of his tendons and veins was more familiar than anything else she had ever known. A peculiar feeling hung in the air: Threads were plucked and pulled, and Fate sang a very old song, soft as a lullaby and treacherous as the jaws of a wolf.

As it did whenever Fate sang this particular tune, time slid its scales out of order, a snake latching fangs onto its own tail, a river flowing backward and sideways and not at all.

Raegan no longer sat in a small room in Old City. Instead, she found herself on a heathered hill at sunset, August in all its glory around her, two strong hands tangled in her auburn curls, her body pressed against one much harder and larger than her own.

Then the hill was gone, and instead she walked alongside someone through an autumnal meadow, woodsmoke heavy on the air, a rushing river before them. The feeling of finality was thick in her marrow, as weighted as the wool cloak upon her shoulders. She knew without a shred of doubt that whoever walked beside her, silent and resolute, would unwaveringly be with her until the very end.

The meadow collapsed into a bonfire, surrounded on all sides by deep and ancient woods. She could feel the warmth of liquor in her veins and the exhaustion thick in her body. The side of her cheek rested on someone's powerful shoulder. The firelight danced, revealing no one else seated around it. She lifted her head, took a breath, and kissed the person next to her before either one of them could think better of it.

The bonfire simmered and snuffed out, the darkness of a dim, stone-walled room swallowing it whole. A single candle burned in one corner, a wide pool of wax beneath it, the flame almost spent. Silvered pre-dawn light slunk in through the window. Her mouth was against someone else's, desperate and keen, her lips swollen from the intensity of the exchange. And then her own voice, whispering, "I am yours until they come."

The stone-walled room pitched, and a voice penetrated the very edge of her consciousness. "Overhill."

The voice was low and deep and masculine, richly accented with a lilting roll that sounded like home. The stone room pulled away, fading out into nothing.

And then she was panicking. She had no idea where she was, who she was, what the gray light leaking in from the window meant, what the cacophony of sounds just beyond the walls could possibly be—a thousand footfalls and the blow of a hundred horns.

"Overhill," the voice came again, calm and steady. "Could you picture your home for me, in your head? What color is the door?"

She fought against the river of her own mind, peppered with meadows jeweled in dew and banquet halls hung with silken dressings, the lightest breath of a kiss against the nape of her neck, her heavy waves lifted to one side by a lithe hand.

"Overhill," the voice repeated, still just as calm. "Where do you keep your tea?"

"In the cabinet," she mumbled, fighting to stay with the voice, to not be swept away by the feeling of a gray warhorse charging beneath her, the sensation of her hand on the pommel of a sword.

"Which cabinet?" that beautiful voice wanted to know. "Picture it for me. Please."

And then she saw her small kitchen with its deep sink and scuffed white cabinets and the tiny window overlooking the street and the brown leather couch waiting just beyond it and the little bistro set she had dug out of a restaurant's dumpster.

A heartbeat, and then powerful arms closed around her and everything else was gone.

The world faded back in slowly. Warmth first. Next the brush of a hand on her cheek. Finally, words murmured low and gentle against her ear, spoken in a darkly melodic tone: *Let it wane. We cannot keep singing the same song.*

And then Raegan fully awakened, sitting straight up, feeling as though she had come spiraling out of complete and utter darkness. The door of the void closed behind her as she frantically took in her surroundings. She was wrapped in her green knit blanket upon her familiar couch. Her head was woozy. Had she fallen asleep while researching? While writing? Should she be at work? Day and time slipped away from her entirely, a cool river running between her fingers.

She turned her head and looked to her left. A glass of water sat on her coffee table. Curious, Raegan reached her hand out and touched the glass. It was still cold. She couldn't have been asleep that long. With a groan, she swung her legs over the side of the couch and sat up.

Relief sang through her veins when she caught sight of her father's spell papers, still neatly stowed in her work bag. Her phone was on the coffee table, sitting on the book she'd pulled from the rafters. The date on the screen read Saturday, as she'd expected.

Raegan gulped down half the glass of water, wiping her mouth with the back of her hand. She didn't usually nap for this reason—she never felt refreshed when she woke up, just foggy and completely out of it. She reached for another drink of water and nearly choked on it when the happenings of the day came flooding back all at once, as if some door had been opened within her.

Raegan remembered Maelona and her warnings. She remembered her fruitless visit to the King. She remembered that she had left the mundane world behind just like she had always wanted to. And beyond that, deeper, lurking beneath the surface, she remembered heathered hills and charging warhorses and blazing bonfires.

What Raegan did *not* remember was how she'd gotten from the King's space to her apartment. She did not remember walking up the stairs and coming through her door. She didn't remember throwing her keys in the bowl or taking off her coat or wrapping the blanket around herself. Granted, it was cocooned around her in just the way she liked, so it was impossible that someone else could have done it. But why couldn't she *remember?*

"What the fuck did he do to me?" Raegan muttered, fear settling into her bones.

She had gone into the territory of an actual fucking Fey king and demanded something of him. And he had refused. Raegan bit the inside of her lip, her palms gone clammy. Even a refusal was not free. There would have been a price for the audience alone.

She lunged for her father's Celtic mythology book, clutching it to her chest for a moment before flipping through the pages to find the long entry about the Tylwyth Teg. The illustrations that had captivated her as a child depicted beautiful creatures in clothing spun from thunderstorms and necklaces strung with broken promises. Their faces were shadowed, but from what Raegan could pick out, they *did* resemble the

King: knife-sharp cheekbones and elegant necks and shapely mouths.

The beginning of the entry told her the things she already knew: Wales, Ireland, Scotland, and England all had names for and tales of the Fair Folk. Later mythologies in other lands had gentled them into tiny, flitting things in gardens or jovial red-haired men with pots of gold, but there were still those who knew the old ways and hushed the tourists who spoke of the Fey in crowded pubs. They avoided certain hills at twilight. They did not obstruct the way of fairy roads.

Raegan began skimming, pausing briefly over the words "Seelie" and "Unseelie," but the text more or less reflected her existing knowledge. She flipped the page, her clammy fingers sticking to the paper for a moment.

Tilting the book toward the window to get better light, Raegan hunted for her father's spidery handwriting somewhere in the margins. She nearly jumped when she saw his bracketing in pencil around a section of the book's text.

The Age of the Gentry fell and the Age of Man began at the Battle of Camlann. Despite their many eyes, the Unseelie Court could not predict humanity's willingness to unleash the Timekeeper, for in many ways, such a choice was a simple exchange of one eldritch terror for another. The Timekeeper, of course, is order and law and rule, while the Fair Folk are chaos and magic and mayhem. The tenuous alliance between the Timekeeper and the early league of men, now known as the Protectorate, was based nearly entirely on a shared hatred of the Fair Folk. The Tuatha De Danann[1] had imprisoned the Timekeeper beneath the Isles, and men likewise sought to be rid of what they perceived as the Fair Folk's rule.

In return for his release, the Timekeeper granted the men power to wield magic, as well as weapons for their armies. Now often called holy or sainted iron[2], this set of weaponry was imbued with the Timekeeper's power, and as such, had an unprecedented ability to dispatch the Gentry. When the Unseelie Court[3] was defeated, the Timekeeper erected the Gates.

The Gates have transformed over the years under the Timekeeper's influence. First, they merely divided the world in two, providing a dedicated space for humanity to flourish. But the Fair Folk, particularly the Unseelie Court and its most well-known King[4], were displeased both with the Gates' impact on magic and the way men viewed Earth as their possession. Conflicts between the Unseelie Court and mankind resulted in more and more restrictive versions of the Gates, until arriving at the state of affairs today: no passage between the Gates and no magic flow to the human realm.

There is a little-known Third Place that is said to exist between the Realms, a space purely under the Timekeeper's dominion. The purpose and shape of this In-Between is unknown, though this author posits it is simply a no-man's-land that functions as an easy killing ground for anyone foolish enough to attempt dismantling the Gates.

---

1 - The Fair Folk have gone by many names for millennia, but this author uses the Tylwyth Teg and the Tuatha De Danann interchangeably to reference the first generation of the Gentry, the children of Danu.

2 - It is often thought that Excalibur, the fabled sword, was one of these weapons, but all evidence reveals that

Arthur had the blade before the Timekeeper's release, though it, too, was forged with the intention of spilling the blood of magical beings. But that is another story entirely.

3 - Nearly all oral tradition and historical texts indicate that the Seelie Court did not fight. If they had, this author supposes the tide of the war would have almost certainly been turned and the Age of Man would never have been.

4 - This author, of course, speaks of the Exiled Unseelie King. He took the throne from Ragrshydan the Cruel not long after the Gates were erected. Oral accounts and Feyish historical texts indicate that, in a stunning departure from tradition, he was asked by the Unseelie subjects to take the throne and had little personal interest in the acquisition of power. Though the throne was still obtained by the traditional method of slaying its current occupant, this occurrence was the unusual beginning to a very unusual—and powerful—rule. It is rumored he has no true name—part of what makes him so incredibly dangerous—but he has been called Gwyn ap Nudd, Obe'ryn, Annwfyn, and other names throughout time. In modernity, he is most often referred to simply as the King. His bloodlines and history are completely unknown, which is strange considering his immense power and capability. Noble houses of the Unseelie should be clamoring to claim him, but he belongs to no one. The prevailing myth is that the King is one of the Tuatha De Danann—a child of the gods. Of course, this myth is heavily disputed, as all of the Tuatha De Danann are thought to have left this plane with the goddess Danu long before the Battle of Camlann.

Raegan let her head fall to meet the back of her couch, unfocused gaze directed somewhere toward the ceiling. So she had not just met *a* Fey king, but *the* Fey king. The Unseelie

King, to boot—though she had little doubt that the reality was much more complicated, the Unseelie Court tended to be the most antagonistic and sadistic toward humans in folklore. What was he doing in *Philadelphia*, for fuck's sake?

And the Protectorate—the organization she should have been born into—was as ancient as Camelot and presumably just as powerful as Maelona had said. She'd also spoken of the Gates and the Timekeeper, but with essentially no context; at least Raegan had *something* now.

But fuck. This entire situation was a chess match that everyone else had been playing for a thousand years before Raegan had even realized she was a pawn on the board at all. She bit the inside of her cheek. There were parts that she could swallow—the parts that felt more like folklore, like sucking the marrow out of bone and recognizing the taste of the inner story. The Fey-mankind conflict, a god getting involved, and some epic battle were all like ambrosia on her tongue.

The King and the Protectorate and the Gates were different because she had interacted with two of them, and her father had—at the very least—tried to touch the third, which Maelona clearly considered a death sentence. The book that Raegan's father had purposefully left for her—that had led her to the kelpie and to Maelona and to the King—seemed to agree.

Which left Raegan wondering, for the millionth time, why her father had done what he had done.

She cast the knit blanket off her shoulders, stood and stretched, a vertebra in her back cracking. She chewed on her lower lip until she tasted blood.

Her phone lit up on the table. With a strange urgency, she reached out and snatched it. There was one new text message from an unknown number.

It's Maelona. Call me as soon as you see this.

CHAPTER SEVENTEEN

The phone rang and rang, the sound looping in on itself until Raegan started to think that maybe an eternity had passed since she'd tapped the call button next to Maelona's name.

"Pick up, pick up," Raegan hissed, pacing back and forth in front of her couch. "You just fucking texted me."

Then the line finally clicked. "Raegan," Maelona greeted, her voice thick with a hedged kind of hope. "Are you safe?"

"I'm fine," Raegan breathed, dragging a hand through her hair. Words tangled themselves in the back of her throat.

"I can get you out of this," Maelona said, sure and determined. "I've prepared a safe place for us to meet. Soon—it needs to be soon."

"Okay," Raegan said, her pacing slowed for a moment. "Thank you. But I need you to tell me more about my father. Can you do that?"

Silence yawned wide at the other end of the line. She thought her heart might explode through her chest as she waited, biting her tongue.

"It's not a good idea." Maelona's voice was as heavy and

suffocating as damp leaves. "It's safer for you to know less. I'd rather focus on preparing you to leave."

"I summoned a fucking kelpie," Raegan shot back, her pacing turning into stomping. "I think it's a bit late for that, don't you? Besides, I need to know, Maelona. I have a goddamn right to know."

"No," Maelona replied, grounding the words between her teeth. "The wolves are already at our fucking door. It will only make everything harder."

"Then *let it* be harder," Raegan snarled, pouring all her fervent need for closure into those five words.

She heard Maelona let out a long, low sigh on the other end, but then the woman didn't speak again. Raegan caught what she thought was a fumbling noise, followed by nothing. She almost began to panic before she heard the clink of a lighter through the speaker.

"Only your father," Maelona finally said, her accent thicker as she spoke with a cigarette between her lips. "We will *only* talk about your father. And I don't even know how much closure I can give you. I sure as hell don't have any."

"Fine," Raegan replied, clutching the sides of her phone violently with anticipation. "Only my father. I promise."

"Right," Maelona said, her tone curt. "Meet me at the Green Line Café. Baltimore and 43rd. I've set a number of wards, and it's safer in public. At least, it should be. I don't know anymore. This is a risk, Raegan. I need you to know that."

Raegan could not stop to think about the risks. She held the phone to her ear with her shoulder as she darted toward the entryway to pull her boots back on. She noticed for a fleeting moment that they were tucked neatly against the wall, toes pressed into the baseboard, laces stowed in the shaft—so unlike the way she normally kicked them off in any random direction. But then Maelona was saying her name, asking if the coffee shop would work as a meeting place, so she just shoved her feet into her shoes without further investigation.

"You're going to have to give me like forty minutes," Raegan said, almost dropping the phone as she began to lace up her boots. "You're all the way over in Spruce Hill."

"Yeah, that's fine," Maelona replied. "But I'm going to ask you again to let this go. Let *him* go."

"No," Raegan said. "See you." She hung up before Maelona could say anything else.

She pulled the phone away from her ear, releasing her cramping shoulder. For a moment, she stared at the black screen, wondering if perhaps the tiny, rectangular darkness held some sort of an answer or a sign for her.

It did not, so Raegan finished lacing up her boots and reached for her favorite leather jacket, adorned with silver hardware, buttery soft padded-leather paneling the shoulders and sleeves. She shoved her keys and wallet inside its pockets. Then she cast a glance over at her work bag and her father's spell. Despite herself, Raegan ached to tell someone. Part of her was still paranoid that the lockbox and the papers were just cruel delusions. She wanted someone else to touch the thick parchment where it curled at the edges and tell her, *"Yes, this is real, this is so very real."*

She swallowed, her jaw clenched. Maelona would not—could not—do that for her. Maelona would be more likely to set the spell aflame with her cigarette lighter, telling Raegan in that hoarse voice of hers that it was for the best.

Pulling on her jacket, she decided that her father's spell and the King should be tucked away and kept from her aunt. She would go to Maelona *only* for answers about her father and the Protectorate. Pulling the door closed behind her, Raegan stampeded down the stairs and broke out into the autumnal mist. Afternoon brought darkness closer to the city's horizon, smudging soot around all the edges. Raegan scanned the block, eyes sharp for anyone suspicious. Seeing nothing, she shoved her hands in her pockets and began the journey.

After a subway ride that seemed to last forever, she emerged back into the aboveground world and found that the clouds and fog had burned off, allowing autumn sunshine to turn everything bronzen. She half-wished to be angry at the bright, slanting light, but this side of the city was gloriously draped in the season, rows of sycamore trees festooned with reds and yellows. As Raegan walked south, the commercial buildings melted into Victorian townhomes wreathed in creaking wooden porches dusted with leaves, kids' bikes, and boxes of books free to a good home.

She rounded the corner onto Baltimore Avenue, the painted green façade of the café like a beacon in the distance. Her pulse thrummed against her skin. She would be careful and clever, and she would get answers about her father. Then, and only then, would she decide what to do next.

Raegan slipped through the door, taking stock of the airy café, which was characteristically busy. She hadn't seen Maelona at the outdoor tables—not that she had imagined she would. Quickly scanning the room, she noted that one of the coveted seats by the large bay window was open, and considered grabbing it and forcing Maelona to join her. But then Raegan's skin crawled at the thought of being visible to any passersby. She felt like a bug under a rock lifted, high and sudden, into the air by an overly curious child.

Weaving through the tables, she finally found Maelona tucked away in the back corner and made her way toward the older woman, who was doing a decent job of acting as though she had not spotted Raegan the second she'd walked through the doors.

"Hi," Raegan greeted, peeling off her leather jacket, which had become much too warm in the autumn sun.

Maelona looked up from the mass-market paperback she had been pretending to read. An untouched almond croissant sat on a plate before her, but Raegan saw Maelona's coffee cup was already drained.

"A *kelpie*, Raegan? Seriously?" Maelona said in the way of a greeting, running her eyes down Raegan's form, almost like she was checking for wounds or extra appendages. When she did not reply, Maelona narrowed her eyes and added, "Took you long enough."

"This café, while lovely, is very far from my apartment," Raegan said, sitting down across from her. She put her elbows on the table and propped her chin on her hands. "And I don't drive."

Maelona waved the words away with one hand, the other sliding the croissant toward Raegan. "All yours if you want it," Maelona said, looking away for a moment. "Can't get my stomach to settle."

Raegan tore off the end of the croissant and popped it into her mouth, as if to prove she was of a stronger constitution, capable of eating even under extreme duress, though she couldn't remember her last real, full meal. She noted that internally, the way her therapist always told her to. Raegan loved food, and this decrease in appetite could be a warning sign.

"You might want to lay off the coffee if your stomach is giving you trouble," Raegan said pointedly, her gaze shooting to Maelona's mug. Her aunt scowled, but her hands fidgeted with the edge of the saucer.

"Are we safe here? Who showed up earlier at Ray's?"

Maelona looked away, tonguing the inside of her cheek. "We *should* be," she answered, eyes sliding back to Raegan. "But nothing's completely safe. I told you that." A long sigh and then, "A higher-ranking member of the Protectorate showed up earlier. Like I said, they're very interested in finding out who exactly you are. I've concealed you, for now. But—"

Someone dropped a plate nearby, and Maelona cut off whatever else she was going to say, her entire body swinging in the direction of the noise, every muscle tense and ready. Raegan watched—it was like seeing a dog's hackles go up. When Maelona found the source of the noise, she relaxed, turning back to Raegan, who wondered what it would be like to live her life so reactive to every sound, every quick movement, every stir of the shadows. She supposed she might know soon enough.

The thought turned her stomach, and she pushed the croissant a few inches back toward Maelona.

"Right," Raegan said, taking advantage of the pause. "You said my dad risked so much for a normal life, but then . . . the Gates. Why would he go to them?"

A muscle in Maelona's jaw jumped, and she twisted her coffee cup around. "Not going to start with any softballs, I see," the older woman grumbled.

"That's not my style," Raegan replied sweetly. She tucked her hands beneath the table, resting them on her thighs so Maelona could not see the way they shook like leaves tumbling into gutters.

Maelona sighed, the tension in her shoulders rising. "I've asked myself the same question a million times," she finally told Raegan. "I have no good answers."

"He had to have a reason," Raegan pushed, narrowing her eyes. "He was pretty fucking smart."

"About *some* things," Maelona snapped. "Okay, about most things. But not magic. Real magic; not the parlor tricks we now have courtesy of the Timekeeper. The real shit, from way back when. The things the Gentry knew. He was obsessed, and that made him foolish."

A few tables away a toddler suddenly burst into shrieks, cutting off whatever Maelona was going to say. Raegan's head ached. She wished fervently for the notebook and good pen she'd left at home, unsure of how Maelona would react to note-taking. Her aunt wouldn't be the first to freeze or clam up at the sight of a reporter's notebook on the table. But

Raegan needed her process, her way of making sense of things, the clarity she only found at the end of scribbled notes and meandering arrows and three crossed-out conclusions.

The toddler's cries quieted as a man in a brown wool sweater lifted them from their seat, cradling the child in his arms, all sorts of soothing words falling from his mouth as he made for the door. Unexpectedly, emotion swelled in Raegan's throat. She thought of autumns past and long-burned-out bonfires and the smell of her father's cologne permeating a red scarf—

"Raegan." Maelona's sharp tone cut into her thoughts. She turned back to her aunt, heat rising to her face at having drifted away over such a silly thing. Her aunt was watching her closely, and Raegan saw there was no use pretending. Maelona seemed to know exactly what she had just witnessed.

"Raegan," Maelona said again, this time much gentler, something in her expression crumbling. "I've bought us a little time. I'll answer your questions. But . . ."

The woman sighed, squeezing her eyes shut for a moment. When she opened them, there was more sadness and fear in Maelona's gaze than Raegan knew what to do with.

"But Raegan, I need to get you out. I need to keep you safe," Maelona said, steel creeping back into her tone. "Your father's gone. I might as well be, after all these years of hunting one moment and running like prey the next. Let's break the cycle together, yeah? Let's not give the Protectorate another Overhill to devour."

With those last few words, Maelona was the most terrifying Raegan had seen her—the late afternoon light slanting off the silver threads of hair around the crown of her head, the jawline set, spindly fingers quietly resting, the wiry muscle in her forearms coiled and ready.

Surprising the both of them, Raegan reached one hand across the table to grip Maelona's palm tightly. Her aunt's flesh was hot and dry beneath her fingers.

"Thank you for giving a fuck," Raegan said simply, meaning it. The pair exchanged sheepish smiles, faces flushed with the intensity of the moment, before Raegan pulled away.

Maelona cleared her throat and then plucked her paperback from where it had been discarded beside her coffee cup, paging through it to retrieve a slim sheet of folded paper. Raegan thought there might have been some handwritten words on it—phrases, mostly, it seemed—but then Maelona smoothed it down flat on the table, obscuring it from her view.

"I pulled a few ideas of where you might go and the paths you might safely take," Maelona said, her eyes jumping as she scanned the sheet before her. Then she looked up at Raegan, the hollows under her eyes a bit brighter, the deep crease between her brows not quite as sharp.

It only lasted a moment, because then Maelona's gaze skipped just to the left, out into the café over Raegan's shoulder. The air around their table changed completely, Raegan sensed, her stomach plummeting.

"Listen to me very carefully," Maelona said, her tone like ice as she tucked the paper back into the pages of her book, gaze locked with whatever threat loomed behind Raegan. "If you only listen to one thing I ever say to you, please, let it be this."

Raegan sat stock-still in her seat, her pulse howling in every crevice of her body, muscles tensed and ready.

"Raegan," Maelona continued, voice as flat and cold as a frozen lake. "*Run.*"

Chapter Eighteen

Nothing else had changed inside the café. Raegan could still hear the hum of the espresso machine and the clink of mugs on saucers. The college students studying in the corner had barely moved an inch, and the tiny dog sheltering beneath the table next to her hadn't awoken from its nap. The ambient chatter and soft lull of the indie rock music playing over the speakers all remained the same, the smell of fresh coffee and sweet syrup filling the air.

And so Raegan hesitated. By the time she had actually managed to fling herself from her seat and in the general direction of an exit, Maelona shouted something, holding up one hand to send what Raegan could only describe as a shockwave through the air. Maelona's other hand reached over to grab Raegan by the scruff of her sweater, swinging her around so that Maelona stood between her and whatever had appeared at the door.

"Get down!" Maelona yelled, turning toward Raegan to flip their table on its side, creating a small spot of cover.

Adrenaline thick in her veins, Raegan scrambled behind the table, pushing her back against it, trying to make herself as small as possible. Her mind was racing to keep up; no gunshots or explosions or even the calmly-delivered news of a bomb threat had preceded the chaos. Whatever was going on, Raegan was not wired for it.

Something shook the café hard—not an earthquake, something else—and she hazarded a look to her left, wondering if there was fuck-all she could do for everyone else in the building. If they were in danger, it was certainly her fault.

To Raegan's shock, the once-bustling café was absolutely empty, entirely devoid of the people and the lipstick-stained coffee cups and sugared pastries it had held only moments ago. Before she could process such a development, something tore through the air, whistling past her. Raegan tried to track its movement, but there was nothing to see, only something to be felt, and it raised the hair on the back of her neck and made her teeth vibrate.

Magic, Raegan realized, near-delirious. Magic that her bloodline could work on this half of a world that had been broken into two.

"Overhill!" The voice thundered from behind Raegan, unnaturally loud and coarse. Something bloomed sour in her stomach at the sound of it. She almost answered, spat back a curse or insult reflexively, but Maelona spoke first, and Raegan realized she was not the Overhill being addressed.

"I told you I had this handled!" Maelona snarled. Her aunt's words sent distrust spiraling through Raegan's chest, but she told herself to hold steady. "Why are you storming in here like this?"

"Handled?!" came the scoffing response. "I think you had little intention of bringing your brother's whelp into the fold."

Raegan clenched her jaw and forced herself to detach as much as she could from the shouted words. For now, the explosions of magic had stopped. She should take the opening.

Rocking back onto her heels, still concealed behind the

table but ready to spring from a crouch, Raegan scanned the back of the room for any exits. Her heart raced faster as she saw none, but then her gaze landed on the wraparound café counter. Surely there had to be an exit in the kitchen just beyond it. She hoped it wasn't a dead-end alley, but Raegan didn't see any other egress point besides throwing a chair through a window, which she imagined was harder than it looked in the movies.

She wiped her damp palms on her pants, locking her gaze with the counter. Her body felt like a car trying to turn over— as if her muscles knew exactly what to do in this scenario, as if she had handled it a million times before, but she just couldn't get the process started.

Taking a deep inhale, Raegan prepared herself to run for the counter, but not before she caught movement out of the corner of her eye. Maelona was losing ground, it seemed; her aunt now stood abreast with the overturned table instead of three strides in front. Whoever had come for them was fanning out like a pack of wolves around the café: a nondescript man in an even more nondescript suit of an indeterminate color was slinking along the far wall. Raegan could see another—taller, thinner, but strangely homogenous—picking his way through the café to her immediate right.

Regret landed heavy in the pit of Raegan's stomach. There would be no vaulting over the café counter to freedom. Maelona had told her to run, and she had hesitated. Now here they were, everything wasted.

"Could we please handle this in a civilized fashion?" the heavy, guttural voice from before asked, suddenly so much closer.

Raegan heard Maelona's sardonic snarl of a laugh in response. "You stormed a building filled with civilians," she snapped, "and used battle magic against your own kind. We're well past that point."

"Some might argue we passed that point when your traitor

of a brother defected and you *watched him go*," came the response, like a machete through the dull, unnaturally still air.

Raegan felt stupid and childish continuing to cower behind a small, overturned café table, so she slowly rose to her feet, turning to face whoever was confronting her aunt. The man who had showed up at Ray's only a few hours ago now stood just inches from Maelona's face, though he towered over her, dressed in that dusty pinstripe suit. His light eyes, straight, noble nose, and heavy, mountain-like build rang a thousand bells of familiarity in Raegan's brain, but none sang in a timbre she could comprehend.

"There she is," the man snarled, turning his gaze toward Raegan. "The prodigal child returns."

"Bedwyr," Maelona said, putting one arm out in front of Raegan. "Leave her out of this. She is not fit for the role we play."

The man—Bedwyr, Raegan knew, had maybe already known—hardened his expression, eyes boring into hers, like he was searching her for something she did not even know she possessed. Panic rose with Raegan's pulse—the disappeared people, and the men spreading out like wolves, and the chaos, all forgotten. She knew this man. And she absolutely despised him. She did not think she had ever been so certain of anything in her life.

Bedwyr's gaze snapped back to Maelona for a moment. "I'll be the judge of her fitness to serve," he said, and then the man reached out and grabbed Raegan by the forearm.

The moment his fingers brushed the sleeve of her sweater, she felt something deep within her snap. Her father had given up everything to create a life for her away from the Protectorate. Maelona had taken a number of risks that Raegan doubted she could even begin to comprehend. And here the Protectorate was, rearing their ugly, pinstriped heads and taking what they wanted anyway— the most exhausted trope played out again and again in human history.

Raegan was not a thing or a whelp or a jewel to be snatched. Above all, she knew with a strange and absolute certainty that this man Bedwyr had dared to lay his hands on her before, and she would burn herself to ash before he did it again.

Something within her gave way, like a valve or a dam or perhaps a levy, and before she knew it, Raegan was screaming—screaming like there was nothing to do but scream, her head thrown back, her hands contorted into claws, heeding the blackened waters' call. Her own voice fell alien in her ears, less a human cry and more the thunder of a swollen river over-taking everything in its path.

The sounds of pipes bursting, metal turning in on itself, water rushing free and unbidden, filled the room, and there was, somehow, what looked like a tsunami of river water—brackish, strangely woven with silver threads—sweeping in from the kitchen.

Everything moved in slow motion, frame by frame. Bedwyr saw the wave and looked back at Raegan in surprised confusion and—unless she was flattering herself—fear. He yanked his hand away from her, instead snatching Maelona by the wrist. The two disappeared in a blink, as if the café had folded in on itself and devoured them whole.

Raegan noticed a few other besuited Protectorate blink out of existence like Maelona and Bedwyr had. The ones closer to the kitchen—the ones who were not fast enough—were instead swallowed by the rush and swell of black water.

It was not the darkly quiet peace Raegan had always equated with drowning. Instead, the water slipped a thousand hands around their limbs, dragging them down, forcing tendrils into eyes and mouths and lungs. She found herself frozen to the spot, facing the towering wall of water, knowing she could never outrun it.

For a moment, the wave crested and took the shape of a woman with many arms, each fist grasping a Protectorate body. The watery hands brought four men to its gaping mouth, devouring them one by one, crushing bodies into the damp darkness that hungrily awaited.

Then the wave-woman collapsed into a silvery stream that swept the café, rushing toward Raegan. She remembered reading that even ankle-high water moving fast enough could knock a person off their feet, so she braced herself for impact. But when the water reached her, it seemed to split around her boots, flooding everything but her. She watched it dance around her, wondering what such a thing could possibly mean.

Eventually, some of the floodwater slipped through the door or down through cracks in the floor, leaving only a few inches that shone silver in the low light.

Raegan wasn't sure how long she stood there, taking it all in: the broken chairs and shattered pastry case, the soaking wet antique rug balled up against the door. The only sound in the space was her quick breathing and a few irregular pitter-patter drips of water.

She clenched her fists, begging for the sharp bite of her nails in her palms, hoping it would be enough to tell her what was real and what was not. She pressed in until the pain was quite real, but the destroyed café and dripping water did not change. Panic climbed her throat. Her aunt, her only lifeline, was gone. She had utterly fucked any escape plan—the Protectorate knew she existed, knew Maelona had tried to hide her, and Bedwyr seemed intent on harvesting her like an overgrown orchard.

"Breathe," Raegan told herself, but her body hardly obeyed. She was breathing, yes, but the gasps were short and hard, certainly not conducive to soothing.

Shouldn't there be sirens? Horrified pedestrians peering in? Anything? The street outside was empty, the wind blowing gusts of gray, dried leaves against the café's doors.

"Steady," Raegan murmured, closing her eyes for a

moment, half-daring to hope that when she opened them, she'd find herself waking up in bed from a bad dream.

No such luck—the same scene greeted her and the wrongness of it all mounted quickly, fanning the flames of panic. And then, somewhere in the haze of her thickly thudding heart and racing mind, Raegan felt eyes upon her.

Chapter Nineteen

She spun on her heel, almost slipping on the damp hardwood. Emerging from the gloom of a far corner, draped in shadow, was the King. She noticed his impeccably tailored black suit for a heartbeat before she caught the expression on his face: eyes wide as he searched the wreckage, long-legged strides quick and urgent. For a brief moment, the King seemed to be cloaked in panic instead of deadly authority.

And then his gaze met hers and the eyes turned hard, a muscle in his jaw leaping. The King said nothing, looking at her with an expression Raegan thought might actually be loathing.

"Where the fuck did you even come from?" she sputtered, her heart rate spiking, her hands clammy.

Though he offered no reply, the tall Fey creature moved forward with terrifying grace, picking his way through shattered plates and broken chairs. Raegan watched him, breathless, until he came to a halt a few feet away from her. She told herself there was absolutely no point in noticing how beautiful his hands were—vascular, powerful, and long-fingered.

"Do you know what happened here?" the King asked,

looking down at her, his tone armored in the cold authority she'd been expecting.

"Uhh, me, apparently," Raegan stammered, leaning against a still-upright table, only for it to give under her weight.

She caught herself with a jolt, the movement splashing water on her pants. The King watched her silently. When she said nothing more, one of his dark brows arched up expectantly.

"The Protectorate," Raegan began, to which the King nodded grimly, as if she were just confirming what he already knew. "They came for me. A man tried to grab me. I . . . I got mad, I guess. Something just sort of snapped. I think it was me? I was so angry, I screamed, and then all this water rushed in from nowhere."

The King tilted his head to the side, looking at her with more interest. "You did this?" he asked, gesturing with one sweeping hand at the destroyed, water-logged café.

Raegan nodded, swallowing hard. "I think so?" she replied, assuming it unwise to lie to such a being. "They still took my aunt, though, and she was the only source of information I had. A lot more helpful than you, by the way."

Nothing on the King's face registered her small jab, though something outside the café caught his attention and he narrowed his eyes. "We should go," he said, not taking his gaze off whatever he saw. Raegan tried to follow his sight line, but she didn't see anything at all in that general direction which would be a cause for alarm.

"Oh, it's *we* now, is it?" Raegan demanded, not quite capable of stopping herself.

The King's eyes tracked to her, and one side of his mouth curved up for a split second. "Do you want to leave this place alive or not?" he asked, voice low and cool.

"I suppose when you put it that way . . ." Raegan conceded, trying to fish her soaked leather jacket from the ground. When she looked back up, the King was closer—much closer. The scent of black pepper and damp stone and autumn rain washed over her, dispelling the brackishness that had been sitting in her nose.

To her surprise, he extended his hand to her. She eyed it like a snake in her boot.

"Why are you helping me?" she demanded, holding her ground, her fist tightly wound around the damp collar of her jacket.

The King considered her question. Raegan had a strong sense that he was not thoughtfully reviewing her request, but instead deciding whether to answer at all, and how much truth to reveal if he did. She wondered if it was true that the Fair Folk couldn't lie. She wondered if the King got around that by just not saying very much.

"At this exact moment, it is advantageous to me," he finally replied, distant and professional, as if they were discussing a real estate deal.

"Temporary allyship works for me," Raegan conceded with a shrug, reaching out to take his hand. The moment their skin touched, she stiffened and nearly blacked out; it was as if a tidal wave of every human emotion slammed into her all at once.

The King made a low sound of frustration and released her hand, hooking his arm through hers instead. The fabric of his suit jacket and her sweater dulled the tidal wave considerably, and Raegan straightened.

"Come," the King commanded, turning toward what was most certainly not an exit, but for once in her life, Raegan hardly felt she was in a place to question anything.

Besides, to her chagrin, she was more focused on how deep and velvet-cloaked the King's voice became when he issued a command. Raegan began to imagine him uttering the same word under very different circumstances, but then he yanked her roughly over a pile of obliterated furniture.

"Jesus fucking Christ," Raegan snapped, grabbing his arm with both hands to avoid losing her balance entirely. "I am half your goddamn size."

Instead of an apology, the King merely gazed down at her from between infuriatingly long, dark lashes. "Less than half," he observed in a detached tone, and then he scrutinized a section of wall. "You will not like this."

Raegan opened her mouth to protest, but then the entire world collapsed inward, darkness closing all around her. She felt like a rubber band pulled all the way to its breaking point, stretched and stretched and stretched until all she knew was the inevitability of her entire being snapping in two.

And then she stumbled out into a very normal alley. The sun was bright and thick in her eyes. Raegan wasn't immediately sure where she was, but she could hear the hiss of a bus coming to a stop and the chatter of people going about their everyday, mundane, utterly human lives.

More importantly, she felt incredibly ill, worse than she'd felt in a while—like she'd developed a bad hangover in thirty seconds. She doubled over and choked back a dry heave. The King no longer had his arm hooked through hers. Instead, having grabbed the back of her sweater in one large hand as if she were a naughty kitten, he dragged her toward a line of trash cans tucked against the opposite brick wall. He flipped open one lid with his free hand just in time for Raegan to throw up the contents of her stomach. She wasn't sure how her body had so much to regurgitate; she'd had, what, a few cups of tea and a bite of Maelona's croissant?

Raegan wiped her mouth with the back of her hand, beginning to straighten before another intense wave of nausea hit her. She doubled over again, her stomach finding more to expel. Somewhere through the nausea and the bone-deep exhaustion, she realized the King was holding her hair back, the tips of his fingers brushing the nape of her neck. The sensation sent a jolt of longing through her that she didn't understand.

When she finally felt as though there was nothing left in her stomach, Raegan stood up straight. The King's fingers lingered in her hair for a second too long, tracing the spirals of her curls. She should have responded with a barbed comment, but was preoccupied with stopping herself from leaning into his touch. Yearning rose unbidden and thick in her ribcage, dark and sweet as molasses.

The King released her, taking a step back. She fought to find her balance, her sanity, her dignity, standing for a moment or two, woozy and exhausted, the light too bright and the world too loud and the King too achingly familiar.

She blinked. The King extended a hand, offering her a handkerchief, because of course he just carried those around. Raegan took it, taking care not to brush against his skin as she did. She glanced down at the square of fabric before wiping it across her lips. It was a dark gray, subtly shimmery like a pearl.

"Appreciated," Raegan said, stuffing the handkerchief in her pocket. She pivoted to lean against the brick wall, shielding her eyes with one hand to look over at the King.

In the late afternoon light, his unusual features were even more prominent—the aquiline nose, the full mouth, the sharp jaw, the ivory skin, the black hair falling in waves to the base of his neck, where it curled up against his skin. His beauty was dangerous, sharply edged, and like Bedwyr, the King felt familiar in a completely impossible way. Unlike Bedwyr, who had looked at her with an emotion Raegan couldn't decipher, the King was gazing down at her with a very obvious expression. It was the way one might look at the bug in their apartment they thought they had already successfully squashed.

But he was quiet, no icy words dripping from his sculpted lips, so Raegan pounced. "Why are you following me?" she asked, her voice like a knife.

It could have been the slanting sun in the alley, the way

shadow and light sliced his face in half, but Raegan swore the King rolled his eyes. "Do not flatter yourself," he replied, leaning back against the alley's opposite wall, infuriatingly casual. "A large contingency of my sworn enemy appeared. Battle magic was exchanged. Old elemental magic reared its head. An unstable pocket realm flared into existence. Naturally, I came to investigate."

"Yeah?" Raegan asked, her stomach still queasy. "And what did your investigation yield?"

He watched her, not unlike a wolf wondering if its prey could still be played with or if it was better to bring teeth to throat and end it. "That you have caused an impressive amount of problems in a short period of time," the King replied, gray eyes cold as winter.

"Thanks," Raegan replied, batting her eyelashes at him and twirling the end of one curl for emphasis. "Causing problems is my specialty."

One side of the King's mouth curved up again, and amusement simmered in his expression. He pushed off the opposite wall with no warning, closing the distance between them. One long stride carried him so close to Raegan that she was forced to tilt her chin up, the crown of her head meeting the rough brick wall behind her.

"You are not afraid of me," the King observed, his tone low, eyes searching hers.

"No," Raegan replied—not a lie but not a truth, either. Her heart beat wildly, and every primal instinct in her body told her to run. "I'm not."

"Draw the attention of the Protectorate or meddle in the affairs of the Unseelie Court again," the King began, his mouth only inches from hers, his voice soft and deadly, "and it will be the last time you do anything at all."

Raegan's body was panicking, sending adrenaline careening through her veins. Her muscles itched to fight or run or maybe both. And yet the King's physical closeness felt as natural as the return of spring, and it strengthened her resolve.

She tilted her head, gaze dropping to the King's parted lips. "Tragically, meddling is my profession," Raegan returned, matching his tone. "If you'd like me to stop, I'm afraid you'll need to offer me a deal."

CHAPTER TWENTY

The air around her seemed to drop twenty degrees in temperature as silence stretched taut across the space. Raegan did her best to hold her ground, but her back was pressed roughly against brick and the King of the Unseelie Court was looming over her, his eyes nearly black in the shadow of the alley.

And then, just like that, the spell broke. The King stepped back a few inches, and autumnal warmth returned to the air. Raegan permitted herself one shaky exhale. She knew this dance was far from over.

"You," the King began, voice low, though no expression moved across his features, "are a *fool*."

For the first time, true fear swam in Raegan's chest, its long fingers reaching up her throat.

"Was my offer of your life in exchange for ceasing to interfere not a deal?" he demanded. "And perhaps the kindest one I have offered in centuries. Yet you wish to renegotiate."

The King stepped toward her again, lithe as a panther and twice as dangerous. Looking at him now, Raegan was without a single doubt that he was ancient and deadly and beyond anything she had ever encountered before. She did her best to hold his gaze, every muscle fiber in her body shaking.

When the King swooped down into her space, she resisted the urge to shrink back. He was so close that she felt his breath dance past her cheek.

"Name your desire," he murmured, his head tilted to the side, eyes sliding to hers. The amusement had returned, but it was soured now, all the heat wrung out of it, nothing left but cruelty beneath its veneer.

Raegan sucked in as deep a breath as she could muster. It was now or never, it seemed. She forced herself to wait a moment, to review her wording. Precision had never mattered more, but thank the gods she was good with words.

"Assist me truthfully in locating and rescuing my father," Raegan began, forcing herself to meet the King's gaze, "with no trickery or malice, and with no adverse impact on my physical and mental well-being. Once my father is found and safely returned here, to Philadelphia, in this timeline and this year, I will cease any interference with your court and the Protectorate."

Moving quicker than her eye could track, the King planted his palms on either side of Raegan's head, boxing her in against the brick wall. Her stomach bottomed out, and fear landed a thousand hot pinpricks across her skin.

"I could just kill you," he stated, as casually as one might take notice of the weather or a new café opening down the block. His gaze bored into hers, and she bit down on her tongue.

"And yet, you have not," Raegan said, imitating his cocky tilt of the head, searching his expression for something she could identify. "Which tells me that you won't."

It was a hell of a gamble. Fear melted into terror, slippery and insidious as it wound its way through her body.

For a long moment that stretched into a small eternity, the King simply held her gaze, his eyes black as the night sky, expression unwavering. For all Raegan knew, she might already be dead, the last thing she ever saw imprinted on her mind as the final bursts of life and electricity gave way to nothingness.

But then a muscle in the King's jaw leapt and he pushed off the wall, dropping his arms to his sides. Raegan watched his chest rise and fall. She made a decision, hoped to god she was right, and then opened her mouth to speak.

"If you don't want to help me, I could certainly draw the attention of the Protectorate again," she said, crossing her arms. "I'm sure they would be very interested to know the Unseelie King himself is in this city."

The King shot a powerful hand toward Raegan, and for a moment, she was absolutely certain he was going to kill her. Instead, he gently caught her jaw between long, curled fingers, tilting it up as he leaned in closer to her, so close that a passerby might think a kiss was imminent.

"*That*," he said, amusement simmering across his features like a heat mirage, "is much better leverage."

Raegan's body keened at his touch, begging for more, a stark betrayal. She gritted her teeth and exhaled sharply through her nose. "So we have a deal?"

"Yes, Raegan Maeve Overhill. You have a covenant with the Unseelie Court, and I will act in its stead."

The King slipped away from her and made his way down the alley, long legs devouring the distance. Raegan felt frozen to the spot, her body trembling, using every ounce of her mental capacity just to keep up with everything that had occurred in such a short period of time. She wondered if she could help Maelona. She wondered how she could possibly keep herself safe long enough to have a chance at seeing her father again.

For the first time, leaning against the rough brick wall, her breathing harsh and shallow, a nervous sweat ghosting her skin like a film, Raegan dared to wonder about the thread between her dreams and her father and the Protectorate and the King.

The answers were large and formless, obscured by an ominous fog, and she squeezed her eyes shut. She told herself to count to ten and reached eight before she was interrupted.

"Come along," the King called from the mouth of the alley, his voice velveted in authority. "I hardly have all day."

His words deepened the thudding of Raegan's heart, and she forced her eyes open. She feverishly wished for a few moments, just a few, to think over her options, to make a list in a quiet space, but she knew that chance was gone.

She had made a deal with the Unseelie King, and there was nothing to do but see it through. So Raegan gathered herself up and pushed off the wall, walking down the alley as though it were the entry to a labyrinth. Luckily, she had a sight line on the Minotaur, though he hid his beastly half well.

The King waited for her on the sidewalk, standing off to the side, cloaked in the shade of a tree. Raegan almost expected him to be invisible to any other humans, but in the three seconds she paused at the mouth of the alley, it was quite clear that the rest of the world had no issue perceiving the King. Two college girls stole not-so-secret looks at the lithe being in the three-piece suit, whispering to each other approvingly, and a gorgeous passerby with a shaved head and an impeccable overcoat dared to make eye contact and smile flirtatiously.

To Raegan's surprise, the King returned the flirtation with a sly smile of his own—at least before he realized Raegan was watching. Then cool impassivity slid across his features again. "You've finally managed to walk a few meters," he observed archly, his tone so dry it cracked in the air like a whip.

Raegan settled for a scowl she hoped was formidable, though she doubted it. Autumn had swept clouds back across the sky like cream in coffee, and with the sun's retreat, the seasonal chill had returned. The damp leather jacket she still stubbornly carried in one hand would be of no use.

Her lament over her outerwear was cut short as the King's shadow fell over her. Wordlessly, he offered her his arm, even though there were no broken bits of furniture or pools of water. A fanciful thought reared its head in Raegan's mind, but she cut it short, trying to ignore his heady scent of rain and woodsmoke.

She took the King's arm—friends close and enemies closer, after all—and tried to prepare herself for whatever awaited. For now, there was just the sidewalk beneath her feet, though it felt so much more like a rushing river or an impossibly thin thread of Fate. Déjà vu cloaked her; it was as if their steps had been rehearsed and choreographed a thousand times before.

"Where are you taking me?" Raegan inquired, instead of asking if he felt that strange, lilting sensation, too.

"Back to Old City," the King replied. "To my office. I have an object there that should be able to locate your father."

Hope stirred defiantly in Raegan's chest, and she fought to temper it. There were miles to go, she knew, as finding her father was one thing. If he was alive—because there *was* a possibility that Maelona was correct, though she roughly pushed that thought aside—then retrieving him would be another quest entirely. For now, she allowed herself to walk along this narrow Thread beside the Unseelie King.

Moving together, they slipped past a large group of students in high school uniforms, coming to a pause at the curb. Raegan busied herself with the cars that rumbled through the intersection: black, gray, black, blue, blue, yellow.

"We will have to use another portico," the King said, pulling her attention back. She turned to find him looking down at her, dark eyebrows drawn together in what Raegan would almost call concern, if she were a fool. She liked to think she was not.

"It is an established one," he continued, "so you should not be as ill, but you will likely still feel unwell."

The light changed and the traffic halted, and they moved through the crosswalk, passing a food truck on the other corner. Ordinarily, the smell would make Raegan's mouth water, but in her current state, her stomach only churned uncomfortably in response.

"I hope you have a trash can in your office," she replied, lengthening her stride to keep up with the King as they rounded a corner, moving away from the busier corridor of the neighborhood. "A portico is a portal, right? Like what we did earlier?"

"More or less," the King said with a shrug of his broad shoulders.

Raegan waited for him to elaborate or explain how a fucking portal even worked, but of course, he remained silent, guiding them through a calm, leaf-strewn section of the neighborhood until they arrived at an overgrown community garden. A fence stretched across the lot, brown leaves gathered in heaps around its posts. A gap in the fence's line served as an entry point. Trash from the street had tumbled into the front of the garden, plastic bags stuck on branches and flying like flags, takeout containers caught in the tall grass. The rest of the garden fell into darkness, blanketed in the shadows of the row houses on either side of the double-wide lot.

As they approached the threshold, the King hesitated, casting a glance over at Raegan. "Stay close," he instructed, his expression unreadable. "There is more than one door in this place. Some are hungry."

Before Raegan could respond, the King plunged into the gloom of the overgrown garden, their arms still linked together. As she passed through the gap in the fence, the smell of rotting leaves and damp earth overtook her. She could almost believe she had left the entire city behind—the exhaust and grease and steam erased, replaced with the smashed flesh of gourds and soil gone too long untended.

Desiccated leaves crunched underfoot as the King led her through a surprisingly maze-like space. Broken trellises loomed on either side of their path, and garden gates hung askew, chicken wire rusted and peeling.

"Doesn't your kind love beauty?" Raegan wondered aloud, looking around at the rot and decay, surprised the Fair Folk would use this garden as a space for their magic.

To her surprise, the King stopped dead in his tracks, turning to look down at her, inquisitive. He held her gaze for a moment longer than Raegan could handle, and she looked away.

"Is this not beauty?" the King asked, his tone genuine, at least as far as she could tell. "Old roots were cut to the bone here, and yet they reemerge, defiant. Is there anything more beautiful than defiance, than survival? It is the most ancient song and perhaps the sweetest."

The King did not give her a chance to respond; he simply returned to whatever path he had chosen and began to walk. Intrigued by the seemingly open way in which he answered, Raegan tried to watch him more closely in her peripheral vision as they traversed the garden. And she was rewarded for her careful attention: she caught the moment when his free hand reached out to a vine of morning glories, fingers brushing the trumpeted buds.

Silence fell again. Raegan could only hear the soft whisper of the wind in the dead leaves and her own footsteps; the King appeared to move soundlessly through the space. The garden defied logic—they should've hit another building, or a cross street, or anything, by now and yet there was only the unfolding of tall brown grass.

The King slowed to a halt, sliding his arm out of Raegan's. She suddenly noticed a large wooden archway before them—the kind that usually had thick ivy or flowering vines wrapped around it, reserved for places like botanical gardens and fancy spring weddings. This one had no green at all—just a weathered, almost-gray tinge. The wind whistled through it gently, and its legs swayed as though unsteady. She had no idea how she hadn't noticed it as they approached.

The King's voice interrupted her thoughts. "Wait here for a moment," he said, tone low. Then he stepped forward, his hair and suit a harsh black in the drab earth tones surrounding them. He slowed when he reached the archway.

Raegan's vision condensed to the King's shoulders and the fine black cloth that covered them, framed on either side by the sagging wood arch. She thought he said something, though it was hard to tell over the rustle of so many dead things in the wind, and then there was a low pop. It was as though a film had been removed from her eyes and suddenly the garden was riotous with life and color and green. Two elegant trees stood on either side of the arch, their boughs laden with white petals.

The King glanced back at her, as if perhaps she would've taken the moment to bolt, but Raegan only gazed on, spellbound as the trees' petals fell around him like snow. She almost laughed; a creature with such feral beauty, so clearly a predator, dusted with petals as downy as the wings of a dove.

And then the laughter dried up in her throat as she watched him: the petals, the arch, the black cloth, the snow, the door, the black cloak. She had seen this before, a thousand times before, endlessly rooted in this same spot, no snow or petal touching her skin, no door opening at her touch, forever abandoned in the desiccated garden like a rotted-out husk.

"Oberon," she murmured, the name tumbling out of her mouth like a stolen jewel. The ancient thing in the three-piece suit tilted his head, his features stark, and then something in the line of his powerful shoulders softened.

"Steady," he told her, his voice calm and gentle in a way she hadn't thought he would be capable of. "Steady."

She nodded, wiping clammy hands on her thighs. She shook her head to dispel whatever odd feeling had come over her, returning to this place of parched grass and half-dead shrubs. Raegan watched as the King reached forward with an elegant hand, long fingers outstretched, and tapped at the center of the archway. The air rippled like the surface of a pond, moving with an oil-spill shimmer.

She squinted and yearned to take a step forward, to examine and to understand, because watching whatever the King was doing rang so familiar in her bones. But before she could, he pivoted and stalked the three steps back toward her.

He reached over, one hand poised in the air above her upper arm. "May I?" the King asked, looking at her with those ocean eyes in a way that made her very aware of her pulse.

"Sure," Raegan replied, desperately trying to sound nonchalant. She braced herself for whatever feelings would arise at the King's touch, but he had looked away, displeasure coming across his features.

She froze, her heart a rabbit in her chest, wondering what horrors had entered the garden, armed with that vicious, teeth-rattling magic, ready to snatch her up as if she were the only thing worth harvesting in a blighted orchard.

"Your jacket," the King said, sending Raegan's mind reeling. "It is wet."

"What?" she asked thickly, her eyes darting about the space until she realized her damp coat was the source of his irritation. "Oh, this old thing? It's not a big deal. I'm not even sure why I'm still carrying it."

To demonstrate how little her favorite jacket apparently mattered, Raegan mimed throwing it away, accidentally slapping herself hard in the thigh with heavy, wet leather.

"You should have told me," the King replied, leaning across Raegan to brush his fingers on the jacket's sleeve. As he did so, she felt the material dry in her grasp. She pulled it against her chest to inspect it, running her hands over the material. It was supple and clean and good as new.

"Oh, thank—I mean, that was . . . very kind of you and I

am happy my jacket is repaired," Raegan stuttered, nearly thanking an ancient Fey king like a goddamn amateur.

His gaze slid to hers, and something like mischief played at the corners of his mouth. The autumn breeze rattled through the dried-up leaves of a nearby climbing vine, reaching over to tug at his dark waves of hair. To Raegan, the entire effect was dangerous—it made him much less feral-looking, removing a reminder of what he was.

"You may thank me, if you so desire," the King told her. "We have a covenant."

"Just to be safe, I'd rather not," Raegan beamed, pulling her jacket back on, feeling a bit like she was putting on armor.

She knew it was silly, but having the touchstone on her was a relief—the garment had been with her since college and had seen her through more than one sketchy situation. She had come to think of it as her lucky jacket, and she knew the power of such things.

"One cannot be too careful," the King agreed, one eyebrow arched. Then the breeze halted and the mischief drained away, like it took him too much energy to keep it going. Cool indifference settled back across his features as he gently laid a large hand on Raegan's upper arm, meeting her gaze and inclining his head, asking for permission.

"That's fine," Raegan said with a nod, her heart in her throat as she looked beyond the King to the portico's shimmering arch.

The King gave her no warning, no countdown, and certainly did not ask for further permission—instead, he seized Raegan and pulled her along with him into the mouth of the portico, straight into whatever darkness awaited on the other side of its oil-spill skin.

CHAPTER TWENTY-ONE

Raegan emerged from the shimmering darkness sputtering and nauseous, her legs unsteady beneath her. Though she couldn't be sure with her head so woozy, she was fairly certain she had stepped out into another alley, this one narrower and gloomier. An overturned trash can had spilled its litter onto the ground, and browned weeds crawled through cracks in the concrete. She bit down on the inside of her cheek, staring at her shoes, willing her stomach to settle.

"Are you ill?" came an accented, dark and lovely voice. Raegan forced herself to look up and meet the King's gray eyes. He stood only a foot from her, leaning down to examine her current state of affairs.

"It's not as bad as the first time," she said weakly, swallowing back nausea.

"Can you walk?" he asked, brushing nonexistent lint from his impeccable suit with one hand.

"Of course I can," Raegan sputtered, as if the mere suggestion were ridiculous. She took one step and immediately swayed hard to the left, her shoulder clipping the wall. She heard the King grumble something under his breath.

"May I take your arm to guide you?" he asked, irritation creeping into his voice as if Raegan should absolutely have magical travel down pat by the second try.

Reacting to his snide tone, she spat, "No. I said I'm *fine*. God, humans aren't as fragile as you think."

As Raegan straightened, trying to find her balance, she heard the King let out a long, low sigh, as though he were absolutely beleaguered by her presence. Which she supposed he was. He didn't *have* to make the deal, though. He could have just killed her, which he seemed very comfortable doing. In fact, he looked like he was born to commit violence, all that coiled muscle and towering height and capable hands and—

"You presume to know what I think?" the King asked, his tone verging on mocking. "Amusing. I have walked this earth for a thousand years. Your kind cannot even *fathom* such a span of time. Come along."

Irritation grated inside her as Raegan shoved off the wall and kicked an empty can toward the King. It didn't hit him, of course—it just ricocheted off the opposite wall, clattering all the way. The King's gaze tracked the can and then slid to her, eyes narrowed.

"Is it enshrined somewhere in Fey code that you have to be an absolute dick all the time?" Raegan demanded, taking a few stumbling steps toward him.

Again, the shadows fell in just the right way so she couldn't be sure, but she thought the King rolled his eyes in response. It didn't seem like something ancient Unseelie kings would do, but she supposed she wasn't the foremost expert. At least not yet.

Raegan reached the King and moved to sweep past him, though she had no idea where they were headed. Just as she drew even with him, the King caught her by the elbow and leaned low, his lips brushing her ear.

"Take care that I do not tire of your amusements," he warned, fingers gripping her elbow like a vice. The delivery of his words, coupled with his physical proximity, sent a delicate chill spiraling down her spine, but it was not *only* fear she felt —that would be entirely too simple. Then the King straightened, his free hand reaching to take Raegan's other elbow. He pulled her to face him, chest to chest, in the gloom of the alley.

As he examined her, impossibly beautiful and impossibly cold eyes searching her face, Raegan held her breath, trying to summon the courage to break his grasp and run. She was not going down without a fight, no way, nohow. Her knife was on her waistband, but she wasn't sure if she could reach for it and run at the same time, and besides, she didn't think a folding knife would be much use against the King of the Unseelie Court.

But then he spoke a short string of words she didn't understand. Raegan immediately felt warm, as if someone had thrown a heated blanket around her, and the fogginess in her head and sickness in her stomach disappeared. The warmth seeped out of her as the King released her, stepping back. She felt good as new.

"What did you do?" Raegan asked, her tone thick with suspicion, eyes narrowed in distrust.

"Abated your portico-related illness," the King replied. "You are welcome."

"Why the fuck didn't you do that the first time when I was vomiting in a random trash can?" she spat, anger bubbling over inside her.

The King shrugged his broad shoulders. "I did not wish it." He pulled Raegan along by her elbow, exiting the alley and taking a sharp left onto the sidewalk.

"You guys are *just* like all the folklore says you are," she snapped, trying to pull her elbow out of his grasp but finding he was much larger and much stronger than her, which she supposed she already knew, but she found it annoying and wished it were not so.

At her statement, the King laughed. It took her by surprise

—the sound of it was like an autumn bell in an afternoon meadow, as bright and tart as biting into a Honeycrisp apple. "Those stories, which most of your kind are not even clever enough to bother reading," the King began, softening his grip on her but not releasing, "were your fair warnings. And yet here you are."

"Yeah, well, being clever never got me very far," Raegan grumbled in response, dodging a middle-aged man who could not be bothered to look up from his phone as he walked. The King did not answer her, so she took a moment to observe her surroundings.

Antique buildings sat squarely on opposite sides of cobblestone streets. Cars trickled by, rattling on the uneven surface. Across the street, a minivan was trying—and failing—to parallel park. She spotted a familiar café up ahead. Relief flooded through Raegan as she recognized the neighborhood; they were indeed returning to the King's office in Old City. When he'd pulled her through the portico, she hadn't been sure where they were actually going to end up. She was pleasantly surprised the King had told the truth. Though, she supposed he couldn't lie. Or was that pure myth?

"That place makes great lavender lemonade," Raegan announced, desperate for something she knew for sure, pointing across the street. The King followed the trajectory of her hand with his gaze. "And excellent pastries."

"Can your kind go any time at all without thinking of food?" he inquired, only a little unkindly.

"I haven't eaten very much today," Raegan replied, meaning it to come out as a simple statement, but instead it sounded a bit like she was a Victorian orphan begging for just a bit more soup.

The King slowed his step, a muscle in his jaw leaping. "Do you require a meal?" he asked, voice dripping in so much condescension she longed to punch him.

"Not at this time but probably later," she replied, sickly-sweet, quickening her pace to keep up with him as he crossed the street, not seeming to heed the oncoming traffic very much.

"Your people require much nourishment," the King observed. "Is it exhausting? It appears exhausting."

"What, having to eat three meals a day?" Raegan asked, half her question getting cut off by the blare of a car horn. "Honestly yeah, maintaining a human body is a stupid amount of work."

The King laughed again, deep and bell-like, and warmth pooled in Raegan's core. She scolded herself internally, but it was too late: she liked making him laugh, and she was probably going to try to do it again, despite her better judgment.

The King swung around another turn, coming onto a busy, popular street. It was thick with tourists, the historical attractions thronged with lines, the Starbucks on the corner packed to the brim.

"This way is better," Raegan said, slipping her arm through his and tugging. "You avoid all the mayhem of this block."

The King looked at her, eyebrows drawing together as if he thought perhaps this time the human would trick the Fair Folk, but he acquiesced, and in a few moments, they emerged from a tiny, winding side street, only a few footsteps from his office.

"I was not aware of this shortcut," the King said, shooing off someone who was trying very hard to hand Raegan a flier advertising a furniture store.

"You're welcome," she replied as they approached his office. It seemed more ordinary now—just a pretty building in a row of pretty buildings. The black door no longer seemed to yawn wide like an invitation. It was just a door. Strange things, she supposed, would become ordinary to her the farther she waded into the depths of this world behind the world.

The King pushed the door open. Raegan noticed he used

no keys, but she had a feeling the entrance would be locked for anyone else who tried to enter. She focused, bracing herself for that infinite darkness that had greeted her the first time. But as she crossed the threshold, Raegan found only a small vestibule, attractively clad in vintage black-and-white honeycomb tile and a muted dark floral wallpaper.

"Where did all those terrifying, endless shadows go?" she inquired as the King closed the door behind them.

He moved past her, sliding out of his suit jacket, looking at her inquisitively, like he did not understand.

"You know," Raegan continued, making a swirling motion with her hands. "It was pretty dark and spooky the first time I walked in here."

"Yes," the King replied, hanging his suit jacket on a coat rack. "The first time, you were uninvited."

Raegan waited for more information, but it was clear the King considered his response a full explanation because he turned on his heel and walked down the short hallway. Though she certainly wanted to understand the breadth of his power, that wasn't the question she was interested in pressing him on at this exact moment, so she followed him mutely into his office.

It was the same as it had been earlier, though Raegan thought perhaps the stack of books on the table had changed, and there was an envelope with a dark green wax seal placed upon the topmost book. The King flipped a switch on the wall as he walked in, lighting an antique lamp that would've been at home in some dark-academia-wet-dream library.

Raegan wavered at the threshold as the King plucked the letter from the table, turning his back on her and stalking to his desk at the other end of the room. Feeling safer without his eyes on her, she took a deep, shaking inhale, remembering that she was here to find out if her father was alive or dead or something else entirely. Permitting herself a moment of weakness, Raegan closed her eyes on the exhale. She breathed in again, noticing the scent of the space: warm and spicy, orange flower and vanilla and clove.

Feeling a hair more settled, she opened her eyes to find the King pulling a wicked-looking dagger from his desk. Her heart immediately leapt into her throat, hands clammy, fear shooting stakes into her chest. But then he sliced into the green-wax-sealed envelope, and she realized the dagger was only an unnecessarily terrifying letter opener. Or the King simply used a dagger as a letter opener, which seemed both possible and also on-brand.

As she also realized he was going to make her wait while he read the letter, Raegan coaxed her heart rate into a more normal pace. The task was made more difficult by the way she had to fight to look at anything but the King's broad shoulders and his ass, now very much exposed with the removal of his suit jacket.

With his back still to her, eyes on the contents of the letter, the King said, "Stop looking upon me like that."

Raegan's face burned with a blaze of heat, and her mind went white with panic. "Like *what*?" she scoffed unconvincingly.

The King turned to face her, folding the letter with slow movements and placing it back on the desk. "Like you are . . . imagining," he said, sounding out each word as his eyes met hers. No amusement simmered on his expression as it had on other occasions, but Raegan noticed that the skin around his eyes had crinkled just a bit, and she wondered what that might mean.

"Presumptuous," she replied, voice thick with condescension, having recovered herself. She crossed her arms and arched a brow at him, the very picture of scorn.

One stride carried the King to the front of his desk, where he also folded his arms, leaning back against the antique piece of furniture. He crossed one long leg over the other and cocked his head at her. "Are you ill again?" he asked in a tone so perfectly innocent Raegan had trouble believing it was leaving his lips. "Your face is quite red."

"Would you like to continue wasting your precious time flirting with me, or do you want to fulfill your half of the deal and get this over with?" she inquired archly, taking a step toward him.

For a moment, the weight of the King's full attention fell onto Raegan's shoulders like a heavy silk cloak. He considered her, his lips slightly parted, apparently feeling no shame in running his gaze down her frame and then back up to meet her eyes. Her heart beat wildly, and anticipation knitted itself thickly in her chest. The longer he looked at her in that way, the farther her pulse slipped down her body—from her breast to her ribs and then her stomach and then lower, lower, lower.

"Of course," the King replied, pushing off the desk and moving toward a filing cabinet against the wall. All the heat fizzled out of the room, leaving Raegan with a physical chill. She pulled her leather jacket tighter around her body and tried to get her thoughts marching straight again. She was here for her *father*, for fuck's sake. She had a chance to dispel the oldest thing that haunted her late at night. And more than that: a quest unfolded itself before her, rich as ruby and sweet as sin.

Raegan forced herself to look around the King's office; collecting facts and context always made her brain kick into gear. There was so much she hadn't seen the first time— whether that was due to her heightened state of fear and anxiety, or some kind of Fey fuckery, she wasn't sure. A door— slim, iron-latched—stood behind his desk. On the wall diagonal from her hung two swords, a shield, and an enormous battle ax. Raegan didn't know shit about antique weaponry, but she had a feeling all four were very, very old. In the corner, a large fern draped itself elegantly over the edges of its planter, lusher than it had any right to be.

"Antiques dealer, huh?" she asked, incapable of not poking

and prodding. "Weird occupation for an ancient king of unimaginable power."

She felt his eyes on her for a heartbeat, but by the time she looked over, his gaze was trained on whatever he was looking through in the cabinet.

"I would have thought it obvious this is what your people call a front," the King replied, gesturing with one elegant hand to the space. "It is harder to slip through unseen these days. A more plausible costume helps."

He had a way of speaking as though he would rather be swallowing broken glass than having a conversation with her, which Raegan secretly admired. In retaliation, she said nothing, pulling her phone from her pocket as if he could not be more boring. Two hours ago, Henry had texted her to ask if she was doing okay. And then, more in character, his text from forty minutes ago wanted an update on any background research she had unearthed.

Raegan ignored it, switching apps to check her email, finding ordinary newsroom chatter, including some edits back from Henry on a long-form piece. She stared at the email with what she supposed could best be called disbelief. Just a few hours ago, there was almost nothing Raegan cared about more than her work. Now she wasn't even interested enough to open up Henry's email. She slipped her phone back into her pocket and stared at the scuffed toes of her boots, telling herself that three deep breaths would be helpful right about now.

The sound of a door creaking open rang out in the space, and Raegan jumped, looking up in panic. But it was just the King, pushing open that mysterious door behind his desk.

He wavered on the threshold, gaze locked on her. "Ordinally, I would simply request that you wait here," the King began, his eyes narrowing. "But I imagine you would be incapable of stopping yourself from rifling through my correspondence and belongings."

"That is incredibly rude," Raegan replied, offended, crossing her arms, "and entirely correct."

"I thought as much," he said, leaning against the doorframe. "And so I will ask that you follow me."

Raegan reminded herself that just beyond the window at her back lay the world she knew, where her colleagues were filing stories and yelling at politicians on the phone. Where the 48 bus was almost certainly late. Where Rich sat on his bench and Aleksey, the Polish guy who ran her favorite food truck, knew her breakfast order: bacon, egg, and cheese on a toasted everything bagel.

All she had to do was choose. "You want me to follow you where?" Raegan asked, her heartbeat increasing.

"Into my archive," the King replied, gesturing to the shadow-spun, cavernous space behind him.

"Right," she said, thoughts of the mundane slipping away as she moved toward the door and the King, albeit slowly. "Is this some kind of a trick?"

He looked at her long and hard; she could read nothing in his expression.

"I imagine I would not tell you if it were," he finally answered.

"Reassuring," Raegan replied, coming to a halt on the other side of the desk, still a good pace or two from the King and the door.

"Must I again remind you that I do not have all day?" he inquired, one brow arching.

She shot him a look full of long-suffering irritation, once again wishing to pummel his impossibly beautiful, terrifyingly feral face. "After you," Raegan said, gesturing for the King to lead the way.

The tall, dark-haired creature in the black suit nodded, turned, and then disappeared through the doorway.

Chapter Twenty-Two

Raegan wavered. The space beyond the door seemed impossibly dark, blanketed in shadows too thick for daytime. She recalled how the darkness had coiled at the King's call and wondered if the gloom eagerly awaited her footfall, poised to strangle and suffocate. Her agreement with the King had hardly been ironclad, and she knew it. But it should hold.

Still, it felt like placing all of her hopes on a silken thread balanced high above an abyss. She paced in front of the doorway, wishing to god that she had at least tucked a little iron in her pockets before she'd left her apartment earlier that morning. But now here she was, trapped in an enclosed space with a deadly creature, utterly defenseless.

"Overhill." Her surname echoed through the darkness as if spoken at the opposite end of a long, tiled corridor. The voice was unmistakably the King's—she would know that voice anywhere, like heather on the hill and dusk over the lake. For a moment, something about his voice saying her name stirred a memory in the very back of her mind, like the fragment of a dream, but it withered nearly as soon as it had bloomed.

Forcing herself to stay in the moment, in her body, Raegan

took a deep breath and walked over the threshold. To her relief, it was not nearly as terrifying or deadly as she had imagined—more like walking through a bit of mist. Only a few steps carried her to the other side, where the King awaited her.

It was the space and not the Fey king that claimed Raegan's attention. Though she hadn't exactly had enough time to formulate what she might've expected out of something the King called his archive, she supposed this wasn't far off. The ceiling was high and vaulted, dark-stained wooden beams arching across the space. Flickering sconces studded the walls in even increments, casting shifting shadows over the stone-clad floor.

A few paces from her, two leather chairs with high, curved backs sat poised on either side of a reading table, the area marked out by a well-worn antique rug. Just beyond the seating area, a long, gleaming worktable stretched across the room. And beyond that stood endless rows of cabinets and storage; Raegan suspected everything was meticulously tagged and arranged. The space smelled of something soft and lemony floating above a base of the pleasing, musty scent of old books, powdery and almost sweet in her nose.

"This is magnificent," she breathed, turning on her heel in a full circle to take it all in. "Are there books here, too?"

"We are here for one item alone," the King replied, much to her disappointment. "If you would follow me. Stay close."

He began to walk down the center aisle, and Raegan trailed close behind, her footfalls oddly muffled on the stone floor. She tried to peer down rows as they passed, wildly intrigued by what might be housed in this place. Her treasure hunt was cut short when the King slowed and then took a sharp left, having apparently found the row he was looking for.

They walked maybe ten feet into the aisle, single file, until he halted in front of a large curio cabinet. Raegan stood just off to the side, the weight of what she was here to do settling on her shoulders again. She wished with all her might that she were simply here to look at magical things and read strange books, not to answer a question that would wound her no matter the answer.

The King's voice broke the silence: low, hushed words in a language she could not identify. A ball of light appeared above them, illuminating the area they occupied. Between the brightness and the proximity, Raegan could not stop her attention from straying to the King. Something like him should be less real under close examination. As he turned his focus toward the cabinet's lock, she took the opportunity to scrutinize him.

He was impossibly real, the porcelain skin more marked than she had noticed at first. An old scar, barely more than an indentation on the skin, bisected the outer corner of his right eye. And another just above the collar of his shirt, a faint, white line encircling his neck. Raegan shifted uncomfortably at the thought of what could've produced such a scar. She told herself to stop looking at him, but the King seemed absorbed in carefully removing something wrapped in silk cloth from the cabinet, so she figured another moment or two wouldn't hurt. As he moved to stand straight again, the object safely cradled in his hands, she caught just the barest hint of silver around his temples, a stark contrast to the rest of his raven black hair. But still—no one would ever look at the King and think he was more than forty, though thirty-five seemed a safer bet. And yet he had walked this earth longer than Raegan could even wrap her mind around.

The King turned to his right, toward the mouth of the aisle and Raegan. The overhead light disappeared, leaving only the soft, flickering warmth of the sconces. Something about the darkness of the space and the way he faced her, some precious object in his hands, his full mouth set in a determined line, was painstakingly familiar.

"We've been here before," Raegan said before she could stop herself, jarred by the prospect of such a thought.

The King met her gaze as he glowered down at her. His brows drew together, face tight with clear distaste. "No," he replied, shaking his head. "We have only just become acquainted."

"You're wrong," she protested, panic rising in her throat. "Why would you say such a thing?"

His eyes, that impossible shade of gray, held hers. His strong jaw, backlit by the warm glow of the sconces, seemed as familiar as if she had spent a thousand years tracing her fingertips along its curve. The cold, dark intensity of his expression held a casual, unhurried sort of hatred. And yet heat stirred unreasonably in her core.

"Overhill," the King intoned, steel creeping into his voice. "If you would return to the reading area, please. We have the object we require."

Whatever had possessed Raegan slipped away like a shed skin, leaving her heart pounding and her mouth dry. She pressed a palm to her forehead, surprised to notice her hand was shaking. "Right," she said, fighting a wave of dizziness. "I'm sorry. I don't—"

"No need," the King interjected. "But let us exit the stacks."

"Oh," Raegan replied with a start, realizing that she was blocking his path. Mumbling something she couldn't even process herself, despite it leaving her own mouth, she turned and marched to the end of the row and then down the main aisle without stopping to see if the King was behind her.

Raegan slowed to a halt by the reading area, and he breezed past her, placing the object on the table. Though the silk cloth still covered it, she estimated that whatever it was couldn't be much wider than a dinner plate. It stood about two hardcover books in height. Based on the way the cloth fell around the object, it seemed rounded.

"I think it would be best for you to sit," the King said, gesturing toward one of the comfortable-looking, whiskey-colored leather chairs. Raegan nodded, mute, and sank into the closest one. The King, to her surprise, lowered his tall frame into the one beside her. He kept his gaze on the object, moving to unbutton his sleeve cuffs. He began to roll up his sleeves to the elbow, revealing powerful forearms roped in coiled muscle.

Raegan set her jaw and sent a plea for temperance to the Christian god her parents had adopted when they came to this country. Not quite willing to pull her eyes away, she noticed the King's forearms were littered with scars. Many of them had faded to white, almost entirely unnoticeable except for their sheen in the flickering light, but a few stood out more clearly.

"Are you prepared to begin?" he asked, causing her to jump. She yanked her gaze away from his forearms and to his eyes, but he had already been looking at her and she knew without a doubt he had noticed.

Raegan rubbed clammy palms on her thighs. "Begin what, exactly?"

"We are going to scry for your father," the King explained. "Most scrying, even by a talented seer, is not capable of seeing into different realms or through enchantments."

He leaned forward and pulled away the silk cloth, revealing a shallow dish made of a material so black that it seemed to devour the dim light of the space.

"This is Nyx's scrying glass," he continued, folding the cloth neatly and tucking it into his pocket. "It will permit a longer view."

"Nyx?" Raegan asked, disbelief—despite everything—sneaking into her voice. "As in the goddess of the night? We're talking about *that* Nyx?"

"Yes," the King said, his tone measured, as if having a primordial goddess's personal object was an everyday occurrence. Raegan longed to ask a thousand questions about the object's provenance and the King's relationship with Nyx, but all the words died in her throat. None of it mattered. Her father was close now, her quest reaching a pivotal point.

"What do we need to do?" she asked, tone solemn, eyes darting between the bowl and the King.

He raised a few fingers, and the reading table grew in height, bringing it level with her waist. He shifted his chair slightly to face the table more directly, and she mirrored him.

"This object was spun from the fiber of the night sky," the King told her. "It is powerful, and as such, it has teeth. It will take something from you. Dreams. Sleep. Nightmares. I know not—it exacts a different toll from everyone. Do you consent?"

Raegan inhaled, her breath shaky. She had expected a price. There was always a price, but she preferred to know the cost up front. What if it took her recurring dreams? None of them were pleasant, and she didn't know why she felt she must keep them—would she not sleep easier without them? And yet she hoped feverishly that the scrying glass spun from the night sky would not take them from her.

"This is the best option?" Raegan asked, raising her eyes from the bowl to meet the King's gaze.

"Yes," he replied. "To my knowledge. I am not infallible."

Raegan nodded, gripping the arms of the chair tightly, her nails digging into the soft leather. "Okay. I consent to the glass's toll," she said. A thought crossed her mind. "Will it cost you something as well?"

"Of course," the King replied, leaning forward. "It does not play favorites. A toll is a toll."

She thought it made sense that something created by a primordial goddess would demand a price from a random mortal as readily as from the Unseelie King. She respected that.

"Please place your hands, palms up, on either side of Nyx's

glass," he instructed. "I will guide you through the process. You may find it helpful to close your eyes."

Raegan moved her hands as the King instructed as soon as the words left his mouth, but closing her eyes seemed out of the question. She was alone in a cavernous place with an ancient, powerful being.

As if he knew her thoughts, the King caught her gaze. "I will not harm you," he said. "Besides, if I wanted to, I would. Your eyes being open or closed would hold little sway."

Raegan grumbled something under her breath about the King's bedside manner that he certainly heard but chose to ignore. Then he dimmed the sconces with another slight movement of his hand. Her mouth went dry, and she tried to focus on centering herself. She closed her eyes. One breath in, the vanilla-y smell of old books thick in her nose. Exhale. Another breath, this time the woodsmoke and black pepper and rain that clung to the King suddenly in her senses. Exhale. One more inhale, and somehow, the smell of her father's wool sweaters.

When she opened her eyes, two candles—beeswax tapers, slender and non-uniform—floated on either side of the scrying glass. The warm, dancing light across the King's face hit some part of Raegan's mind hard, again that intense déjà vu feeling.

"May we begin?" he asked, his voice low, tinted with reverence like a stained-glass window.

"Yes," she said, nodding, her blood thrumming in her veins.

The King wasted no time—the second the "yes" left Raegan's lips, he began to speak in a language that made her marrow thrum. A few seconds in, she could tell it was an incantation. It could be nothing else, not with the rhythm of it, like a drum beating over and over again, circling back around to devour its own tail. The language did not feel completely alien; it was almost like she had studied it once, long ago.

The King stopped speaking, and then he reached out and tapped the center of the glass, like the motion he had done earlier to open the portico. Suddenly, he looked taxed—the strong line of his shoulders slumped, his perfect posture gone, hands moving to grip the sides of the table. She wondered what power it took to say that incantation, to pluck magic from this half of the world that had none.

"Picture your father," the King said, his breathing a bit too heavy for someone sitting still. "His face, his clothes, the sound of his voice, the way he walked, the color of his eyes, the smell of his soap. Every memory you have. Allow the glass to see."

Raegan nodded, letting out a long exhale and, despite her better judgment, closing her eyes. She recalled everything she could: the stories he would tell, his favorite green cardigan, his round tortoiseshell glasses, his hair—even redder than hers—and the sound of his voice, accent lessened by his years in the States. She remembered how he'd taught her to sew a button back on, and when they'd found a hagstone in the nearby park's creek, and how they'd look at his wedding photos together. She remembered that he'd taught her to spill salt or seeds in front of the door and to always carry iron. She remembered the scent of his cologne: oakmoss and cedar and hay.

Raegan was not sure if it was simply the situation or if the scrying glass was influencing her in some way, but she felt a few hot tears slide down her face. A cry was building at the back of her throat—all the old anguish, the not-knowing, the fear of *never* knowing, the grief with no coffin to bury, the mourning with no wake—but she pushed it back, holding herself steady.

She opened her eyes, the world blurred and watery. She nodded at the King, and he reached forward, lightly placing his fingertips on the outside of her wrists and turning her hands over to cup either side of the scrying glass. As seemed to always be the case, his touch elicited a wave of emotion in her deepest recesses, but she swallowed it down, sharply focused on the task at hand.

"Do you permit me to see with you?" the King asked, reverence still clinging to his tone. "I do not wish to intrude, but the glass knows me well and I can guide its gaze."

Raegan balked. She knew he was asking, and there was no pressure in his voice or his body language, but she had expected to be the only one to see whatever the glass held. But she had also never scried before, and it seemed foolish to turn down the assistance of something like the King.

"Alright," she agreed, her voice shaky, trembling around the edges.

"I will need to lay my hands over yours," he told her. "If you permit it."

Raegan realized she would have to keep whatever the King stirred in her at bay, but she thought she could handle it. She supposed any being of the King's power likely summoned such a reaction when touching a mere mortal.

She set her jaw. "Yes. I permit it."

The King inclined his head and reached out with his powerful hands. For a moment, just when his palms were almost touching the back of her hands, she could've sworn he hesitated or steeled himself or something—which she furiously tried to file away for later questioning. But then the King's hands—cool, heavy, calloused—were on hers, and her mind tilted and keened.

Her father. His favorite cardigan and the way he'd perch his glasses on his nose and the sound of his voice, warm and lilting. Her father and wherever he had gone, leaving this empty place in Raegan's chest that could not be filled with anything, no matter how hard she tried.

"Look into the glass," the King instructed, his voice seeming to surround her from all angles. "Look and see."

Raegan shifted forward, her hands still gripping the sides of the glass, and leaned over the reflective black surface. She was surprised when the King did the same, the crowns of their heads almost touching. For a heartbeat, both of their reflections appeared in the dark glass, until the King spoke another word that made Raegan's bones hum. The surface shifted, a hundred shadows twisting like limbs.

And then, there in the devouring black of Nyx's scrying bowl, was her father.

The view was framed on either side by gray metal, and it took Raegan a few beats to realize she was looking at her father through a window. He seemed to be seated next to it. Salt tinged his deep red hair. His face, more lined than she recalled, seemed relaxed, at ease, as if he were simply gazing out a window at a lovely view.

Anger and hurt boiled in Raegan's stomach, but then her thoughts latched on to something peculiar—her father was wearing the exact same clothing he had on when he'd disappeared. It could be a coincidence, but it was odd to see the same tweed blazer over the cream sweater, the dark green pocket square tucked against the brown fabric. Raegan tried to push closer, to look for more answers.

The moment she strained, leaning closer to the glass, a split second of unreasonable foreboding bloomed in Raegan's mind. Then, a sensation like being slammed into a brick wall, and next, nothing at all.

CHAPTER TWENTY-THREE

Raegan bolted upright. Her head rewarded her for it with a sharp ache and pinpricks swarming her vision. She ripped the blanket off and pushed herself painfully to her feet. Black spots crawled across her eyes, a thousand flies, and she swayed, her balance slipping away.

Two large hands caught her by the waist. "I recommend you lie back down," said a cool, dark voice from just behind her.

"Fuck your recommendation," Raegan spat at the King. "What happened?"

"Sit down," he replied, venom creeping into his tone, "and I will enlighten you."

Raegan ground her teeth, annoyed to have met someone apparently resistant to her communication style, which seemed to work on almost everyone else, even if they didn't enjoy it. She tried to think for a moment, her mind still woozy and heat rising to her face at the feeling of the King's hands on her waist. His touch had no right to be so intoxicating. Every fiber in her being yearned to lean back against his chest. God, she hated the Fey.

"Fine," she snapped, groping for the chair's arm and lowering herself onto the seat. An ottoman had been pushed up against the front of the chair, creating enough space for someone her height to recline. As her vision cleared, Raegan noticed a still-steaming cup of tea on the table where the scrying glass had been. Her gaze flicked to the crumpled woolen blanket on the floor.

"Did you tuck me in and make me tea?" she demanded incredulously, glancing up at the King, who had moved to stand in front of her. "What the fuck?"

In response, he shot her such a withering look that she actually shrank back a bit. "You collapsed on a stone floor," the King began, steepling his fingers, one brow raised. "Your shoulder hit the ground first, your head in quick succession. You did not wake for several minutes and then began to shiver uncontrollably. Considering our agreement, no, I did not leave you unconscious on the floor. Have I done something in violation of our covenant?"

With each word, the King's tone grew icier and icier until his expression turned so hard and full of hatred that Raegan averted her gaze, choosing instead to look down at her hands. Silence stretched between them.

"What happened?" she asked, raising her head to look at the King again.

"Drink," he said, pointing to the teacup.

"You said if I sat down, you would tell me," Raegan replied, slamming a fist on the chair's arm. "So fucking tell me."

Moving as quickly as a serpent's strike, the King reached across her, snatched the teacup from the table, and shoved it into her face, all without spilling a drop. "Drink," he repeated, as if dealing with a bratty child. "The tea contains herbs—expensive and difficult to obtain, mind you—that will assist your recovery."

Feeling as though she'd been hit by four large trucks

consecutively and also having dealt poorly with the enormous emotional turmoil of what the scrying glass had shown her, Raegan grabbed the teacup from him and hurled it at the opposite wall. It shattered spectacularly, the hot liquid seeping into the stone.

She did not even have a moment to shakily consider the consequences of her actions before the King's hands were gripping either arm of the chair, his body lowered over hers.

"My people do not take kindly to such a repudiation of hospitality," he hissed, their faces only inches apart.

Raegan forced herself to look up and meet his gaze, finding ice-cold rage in his gray eyes. Before she could quell it, a twin flame sparked in her chest—her trauma was being freshly sliced out of her, and he was angry about *hospitality*?

"I will ask nicely one more time," Raegan snarled, leaning forward, her nose nearly brushing his. "*Give me what I want. Tell me what happened.*"

The King tilted his head slightly to the side, and she no longer saw anger in his expression; instead, something dangerously close to desire slithered onto his features. One side of his impossibly beautiful mouth curved, sending a shower of sparks through her chest.

Suddenly and uncontrollably, she craved to be devoured by this creature of silken shadow and impossible power. Her heart beat like a hymn, louder and louder, some half-forgotten, broken-winged hope pulling air into its lungs for the first time in a millennium. She knew against all reason that his kiss was a key, the feel of his skin a portal, and that his body against hers would be her final absolution and her greatest sin.

And then the spell broke. The King yanked himself away from her, staggering a few steps back before his usual grace returned. Raegan dug her fingertips into the leather arms of the chair, her breath coming in unreasonably ragged gasps. When she finally dared to, she tilted her gaze up to look at him. Shock skittered through her when she noticed a wave of his hair had come out of place, falling across his forehead. The moment she saw it, the King raised an elegant hand to tame the black lock.

"Tell me what happened with the scrying," Raegan said, her voice an octave higher than it should be, "and then tell me what the fuck *that* was about."

For once, the King did not protest or try to slip out of responding to her request. Instead, he addressed her in a flat voice, not making eye contact. "Our scrying was successful," he said, slipping his hands into the pockets of his pants. "But something was capable of pushing away our gaze so violently that the action had a physical impact on us both. Even Nyx's glass will certainly gain us no further insight, and now there is something quite powerful that knows we are looking. How that intersects with your father, a mortal, is beyond me."

"Alive, though," Raegan croaked, looking down at her hands. "He's alive? That couldn't have been the past or something?"

The King considered. "Nyx's glass is difficult to fool. I am hesitant to claim anything is impossible, but I would be surprised if we did not see your father alive just now."

Elation rose in her, battling with the wooziness and weakness. Raegan moved forward to sit on the edge of the armchair. "What do we do next, then?"

The King's gaze shot to hers, and the identity he wore so convincingly had locked back into place: sly, cold, slick as a waxed bar top. "We cannot scry again," he replied, crossing his arms.

Raegan did not even attempt to resist the urge to roll her eyes. "Why are you dragging this out?" she demanded, leaning forward, her elbows on her knees. "I know the game you're playing. Okay, let me ask this a different way to satisfy your Fey fuckery: if you can't find my father, who can, and when can we see them?"

The King let out a low sound of displeasure, his eyes

closing as a muscle in his jaw tensed. "I would not ask anyone but an Oracle to inspect this further," he replied.

"Great," she said, getting to her feet. Her balance pitched to the left and her eardrums howled, but she held steady. "Let's go. On our way, you can tell me about . . . the other . . . thing . . . that happened." As good as she was with language, even Raegan wasn't sure how to word it, and she was certainly not willing to admit the depth of what had transpired. Intellectually, she imagined it was another by-product of being around the Fair Folk, but the intensity of what she'd felt in her body made her want to throw sense and caution to the wind.

"You desire me," the King said, suddenly beside her, his voice like a silk scarf sliding around her neck. "Given what I am, my instinct is to use that desire to my advantage. But our covenant is quite clear."

"Men are not usually my thing, so that sounds like bull-shit," Raegan said, her face red, mortified that her emotions and thoughts were apparently splattered across a canvas for all to see instead of properly bottled up and stored out of sight.

She turned to look at him, summoning as much disdain as she could. But the King met her gaze evenly, with no judgment or mocking in his eyes.

"And I am not a man," he replied.

Raegan could plainly see his words were true. She could see that the angles of his face were too sharp, the cheekbones like knives beneath the porcelain skin. Here in this impossible space that held knowledge beyond her comprehension, the King towered over her, gowned in shadow, a beast that had walked straight out of the oldest, darkest folklore. To think such a thing would feel anything but amusement at her desire seemed ridiculous now.

"No," Raegan agreed, her voice firm because she desperately needed this reminder herself. "No, you are not."

The King's face seemed to soften at her tone, though she was not foolish enough to think it was anything but an imitation of kindness. "You need not feel shame," he told her, gaze drifting to the door that led to his office. "You are neither the first nor the last mortal to feel what you do."

Raegan wanted to shoot back a comment about his arrogance, but the King's tone was clinical, no cockiness or pride laced through his voice; he was simply making a statement he knew to be true. So instead, she zipped her leather jacket closed and shoved her hands in her pockets, mirroring the King's stance.

"How do we get to the Oracle?" Raegan asked, anxiety crowding her throat. "I'd like to at least know my father's location by the end of the day. I don't exactly enjoy your company, so let's not drag this out."

Unlike nearly everyone in her life, the King refused to take the bait. Instead, he inclined his head, elegant as always, and held out his arm for her to take.

"I can walk on my own," she spat, stomping two steps toward the door before he caught her by the elbow.

"It is neither a courtesy nor chivalry," he told her, his expression dead and cold. "I must shield us from the Protectorate's attention, particularly with the blood you carry in your veins. It is less taxing to conceal you from their view if we maintain physical contact."

Raegan gritted her teeth, furious with herself as disappointment sang through her body. She should have known. Of course something like the King relied on mortals finding themselves carried away by his power, his beauty, his magic. And to think she'd considered herself above that.

She took his arm roughly, and the King led them back through his office. He slipped on his suit jacket, and then they were out the front door. They walked several blocks in silence, her teeth grinding the whole way as she refused to even spare a glance in his direction. Too many things swam and spun in Raegan's stomach for her to attempt to name them, so she focused on putting one foot in front of the other.

She needed a hot shower and at least ten minutes to cry her eyes out over the sight of her father, living and breathing all these years later, but instead, the King pulled her into an alley. A towering chain-link fence at the opposite end featured a door-shaped cut, the top section of metal twisting into a now-familiar shape.

"I feel like shit," Raegan announced, "so it would be great if you didn't let me suffer again when we go through." Even to her own ears, her voice sounded weary, weighted, torn at the edges like an old sweatshirt put through the washing machine too many times.

The King turned to her, faux-concern etching his features for a moment before he simply nodded. "You will feel no discomfort," he promised before leading her through the trash-strewn alley, a nearby dumpster contaminating the air with the stench of rot. Up above them on a fire escape, a woman was yelling at someone on the phone, her voice shattering the still air.

The King paused in front of the portico, speaking a series of words that curled around Raegan's senses, blocking out the yelling woman and the smell of rotted food and the traffic in the distance. Then, like before, he raised his hand and tapped the air, turning the space before them into a shimmering, oil-slick surface, thin as the skin on overheated milk.

He turned to look at her, one brow arching. Raegan nodded her permission, and then the King swept them into the portico, the world tumbling and twisting all around them. When they emerged from the formless in-between, she waited for the nausea to strike her, but it never came—and neither did any source of light. Whatever space they had entered yawned wide and shapeless, devouring her in its pitch blackness.

Despite herself, Raegan clutched the King's arm tighter, panic rising in her chest.

"We are safe." His voice came from just above her ear, as if he had leaned down to speak to her. "Please stay close. We will be out in the open air momentarily."

Raegan had never thought she was claustrophobic. She'd endured packed elevators and airplanes and tunnels with no issue. But here—wherever they were—the darkness was absolute and pressing, as suffocating as a thick blanket on a summer's day. Fear slunk through her. Had the King found some loophole in their deal? Was this consuming darkness to be the last sensation she felt?

"Steady," the King murmured, his voice gliding through the dark. "We are nearly there."

Raegan forced a deep breath into her lungs. The air was damp, slightly vegetal, almost as if the scent of petrichor had been bottled and left to age. The King guided her around what felt like a sharp corner, and then she noticed weak light in the distance. She thought she could make out a steep set of stairs. Questions lingered on her tongue, but she kept quiet, focusing on navigating the terrain.

The King reached the top of the stairwell first, waving his hand over the lock of a heavy metal grate. It clicked, and then he pushed the grate open, leading Raegan through before closing it behind them. She watched as the grate shimmered and then disappeared entirely, melting into ordinary parched grass, complete with the tattered remains of a plastic bag.

"Let us move with haste," the King said, beginning to walk at a pace meant for legs of his length, not hers. "There are always eyes."

He led them across a busy highway and then beneath the overpass, its cement belly humming with the sound of traffic. The neighborhood quickly shifted into something more residential, row houses lined up shoulder to shoulder, interrupted only by corner stores and bakeries and dental offices. She stayed silent, watching every alley for a portico or the river-black eyes of a kelpie peering from a sewer gate, for any sign that this place held magic she had been too blind to notice before.

When the King turned into a large shopping center—Raegan had definitely been to the Home Depot here more than once—confusion swam in her mind. They made their way across the parking lot to the end of the strip mall, where a nondescript, one-story brick building squatted on the pavement. A door stood in the middle, sealed up tightly behind safety bars. Two square windows bookended the door without ceremony or elegance. Dusty blinds obscured any view inside, except for the admittedly lush plants that dominated the windowsills. A few glass ornaments hung from the larger stalks, but Raegan didn't see anything she recognized in their sly, slinking shapes.

The King slowed, and then after one sideways glance at her, he reached for the door's handle. Somewhere behind her in the parking lot, perhaps from the window of a car or a passing boom box, Raegan heard a beautiful song soar through the air, the notes moving in a fiercely triumphant crescendo so powerful that tears pricked the back of her eyes.

And then the King opened the door.

Chapter Twenty-Four

The feeling in Raegan's body was not dissimilar to passing through a portico, but slower—more of a gentle pull through a long space than the violent squeeze of the portal. This time, she stuck the landing, appearing on the other side with her arm still entwined with the King's, not even a little off-balance.

The surroundings that greeted her could not possibly have existed in the same shopping center as a Home Depot and the DMV. The dark blue ceiling, painted with gold leaf depictions of stars and planets, was at least thirty feet high. Creamy marble floors stretched across the space, covered in a few places with plush rugs in cool jewel tones. Flowering plants filled every corner and crevice, fairy lights twinkling between their stems. The space seemed to be lit entirely by the chandeliers that hung from the ceiling, appearing to be nothing more than shallow, engraved gold bowls emanating a soft glow. The air carried the scent of thunderstorms and cold vanilla and Italian lilac—chilly and fresh and floral.

Raegan pulled her attention away from the grandeur of the setting when she felt the King slip his arm out of hers. She turned toward him to see he was already walking a few paces to a long, gleaming marble counter that ran along the left side of the room. A stunning mosaic portrait of a woman devoured the upper portion of the wall behind the counter. Her skin was rendered in what looked like abalone shells, her long dark hair falling in twists, her hands holding a shallow dish and a sprig of a leafy plant.

"My liege, it is a pleasure," a voice called out, jarring Raegan from her admiration of the mural.

From a hallway she hadn't noticed, a short, nondescript man with deep olive skin and horn-rimmed glasses, dressed elegantly in a tailcoat, appeared. His attention was focused entirely on the King, and at least to Raegan, he seemed genuinely happy to see the ancient being.

"I did not realize you were coming," the man said, walking to stand beside the curve of the counter closest to them, a slow smile on his face. "Have I made an error? I ask only because the Oracle is currently absent."

"What?" Raegan asked, her tone sharper than she meant it to come out.

The man's gaze swung to her. They made eye contact, and the man tilted his head, brow furrowing. His expression stirred something in the back of Raegan's mind—something about the tailcoat and the olive skin and unremarkable features made her think they'd met before.

"Do you know when the Oracle will return, Keeper?" the King asked, leaning on the counter with one elbow. He was always so sure of himself in every room he entered, his power and authority a given, and it firmed Raegan's resolve to outsmart him. Somehow. At some point. Maybe.

"I know not, my lord," said the tailcoat man—the Keeper, Raegan supposed, growing increasingly frustrated with the lack of actual names—bowing his head to the King. "I understand she is dealing with an important situation involving the Seelie Court's accusations against one of her Sister Oracles."

"Ah," the King scoffed, shaking his head. "I imagine they will keep even Octavia occupied for some time."

"Unfortunately, you are likely correct," the Keeper replied, pulling a heavy leather journal from beneath the counter. "I have no interest in rushing you out—in fact, I have more of that whiskey you enjoyed so much last time. But if your visit is purely for business, I am happy to note that you stopped by and ensure you are one of the first the Oracle sees upon her return."

Frustration simmered in Raegan's stomach. Was all of this a game—the scrying glass and the Oracle and whatever was going to come next? Just a way of wasting the stupid mortal's time until the King figured out some way to dispatch her or until she gave up?

"I'm looking for my dad," Raegan asked, stepping up to the counter. "Can't imagine it would be hard for you people to find a random mortal."

In her peripheral vision, Raegan saw the King press his mouth into a firm line. "There are complications," he said after a beat or two. "I attempted to locate the man using Nyx's glass, and something quite powerful shattered our divination. I feel only the Oracle can safely explore this situation further."

As soon as the King started talking, the Keeper leaned forward onto the counter, listening to every word raptly, his eyes occasionally darting to Raegan. In the moments she met his dark brown gaze, she felt sure she was dealing with a creature more complex and ancient than it appeared; something in his eyes betrayed a deep, calculating intelligence. She reminded herself of whose side the Keeper was likely on, and the fact that it was certainly not hers.

"I do not wish to press a sensitive issue," the Keeper said, drawing back, crossing his arms over his tailcoat, looking between the King and Raegan, "but our Apprentice here is nearly an Anointed Oracle. Though you should share your concerns and allow her to make the final decision, I do think it is worth consulting her, if you would like."

To Raegan's surprise, the King looked toward her. The soft overhead light cast shadows onto his face, underscoring how out of place he looked in these surroundings of jeweled opulence. He belonged on the page of an ancient book, rendered in shaking charcoal. Or on a battlefield, the earth rent beneath his feet.

"Any Apprentice to an Oracle is a talented, experienced seer," the King told her, "and an Apprentice close to her anointment is nearly an Oracle's equal, though there are certain talents she cannot access. Those abilities are not ones that should impact your search, but I cannot say for sure."

"Seems like it's certainly worth a shot, right?" Raegan asked, surprised that he'd bothered to explain anything to her. Then distrust climbed up the back of her neck and she looked at the Keeper. "Is what he just said true?" she wanted to know, narrowing her eyes at the Keeper. He and the King were clearly friends, at least judging from the whiskey offer, but if the finely clothed being was Fey, she imagined he could not outright lie.

"It is a true and accurate summation," the Keeper said with a nod. "I assure you."

"Then fine," Raegan said, shrugging out of her leather jacket to signal she was settling in and following this through. "I'd like to see the Oracle's Apprentice."

The Keeper nodded, exchanging the heavy, bound parchment for a few looser sheets and an ink quill. He placed them on the marble surface, offering the quill to Raegan. "Please sign in," he told her, gesturing to the parchment. "Just your name."

As she glanced down, a line appeared. There were names above it, she could see, but they blurred when she tried to look at them directly.

"*Just* my name," Raegan scoffed, looking back up at the Keeper. "Are you kidding me? You're the goddamn Fair Folk."

To her left, she heard the King let out a soft sound that could've just been an exhale but sounded suspiciously like a laugh.

"Your caution is wise and warranted," the King said, leaning over her to pluck the pen from her hand. When his fingers brushed hers, Raegan's entire body trembled, images blooming at the back of her mind, just as blurred as the names on the paper. "But I assure you, it is simply standard practice." He slid the parchment a few inches down the marble counter, then he leaned over the thick paper and wrote on its creamy surface. Realizing this was a chance at his true name, Raegan darted a step over, eyes hungry.

Upon the parchment, in elegant, looping writing, the King had written: "Oberon, High King of the Unseelie Fey."

Oberon. She had already known that, she thought. She had maybe always known that. She'd said it herself earlier, hadn't she? Seeing his name and title written out made Raegan's vision blur, sleeping things stirring deep within her, snippets and flashes dappling her mind. She gripped the edge of the counter, the stone cool beneath her fingertips, and yanked herself back to the present through sheer force.

"Is Oberon your true name?" she demanded, attempting to take the offensive stance, but the way his name fell from her mouth felt as sacred as sacrament.

When she turned to glance at him, the King was already watching her. There was an intensity in his gaze, thick as wildfire smoke, that sent a lightning strike of desire down her chest. She might have held his gaze for an eternity had the Keeper's voice, bold and sure, not come from behind the counter.

" 'Tis the truest name he's ever had," the Keeper said, "though that is hardly a polite question for our people."

Raegan turned to give the Keeper a dirty look, but when she met his gaze, she saw humor twinkling in his brown eyes.

"It is enough to bind me to the rules of this place," the King replied, sliding the parchment back toward Raegan. His expression had returned to neutral, the smoke cleared.

"Oh, so I *am* agreeing to something," she snapped, throwing a hand up in the air with annoyance.

"By entering the sacred space of the Oracle, you agree to the laws of the Keeper," the King said. "It is certainly no more than what your kind signs away regularly for medical treatment and such."

Raegan wondered what the High King of the Unseelie Court knew about medical consent and intake forms, and also *why*, but she turned her attention toward the Keeper instead. "What are the laws that I'm agreeing to?" she asked him.

Without saying a word, the Keeper reached a hand forward and flipped the parchment. As Raegan looked at it, words appeared on the back. She sharpened her mind, ready to disentangle complicated, meandering language meant to confuse. Surprise jolted her when she saw the rules essentially boiled down to: payment was due at the time services were rendered; Oracles and Apprentices and all other seers were to be treated with the utmost respect at all times; service could be refused for any and all reasons or revoked at any time; and finally, entry and service were subject to the discretion of the Keeper.

"This feels deceptively simple," Raegan admitted, reaching for the quill. She did not want to fall for a basic con. She also did not want to miss an incredible opportunity to search for her father, available to her because she had somehow managed to force a Fey king into a deal. That didn't exactly seem like a situation that came around frequently, so Raegan sighed and, before she could torture herself with further thoughts, put pen to paper and wrote down her name.

"Excellent," the Keeper said, his shoulders squared. "I will summon Seer Cordelia. I believe you are already acquainted with her, my liege. In the meantime, please, have a seat."

The Keeper gestured to a luxurious seating area across from the counter with a stately, wide sweep of his hand, and then he turned to disappear back down the hallway, which was too dimly lit for Raegan to see very far into its depths. She did, however, notice that from between the split of his tweed coat sprang a long, curling tail covered with downy brown fur.

Despite herself, she stared wide-eyed for a moment before following the King to the seating area. He had settled onto the far end of an emerald velvet couch. A wingback clothed in impossibly pearlescent, creamy leather sat on the other side, and nearest to Raegan was a graceful rattan chair with a tall, curved back. On closer inspection, she saw the material seemed to be living tree branches, slender as her finger, woven delicately into the desired shape.

In the end, Raegan chose the other end of the velvet sofa. The marble-topped coffee table before her was adorned with a vase of fresh flowers so spectacular that she thought a number of the species may not even exist in her world. A bowl that looked more like a giant silver shell held oranges, pomegranates, and pink apples; a note in spidery font indicated they were quite real and to please, help yourself. Glossy hardcover books were stacked high, their spines inscribed with gold gilt lettering. Her fingers itched to slide one out from the pile.

"Cordelia Iravani is a talented diviner." The King's words came from beside her, at the other end of the couch. She looked up from the pile of books to find his gaze locked on hers, something heavy in his expression. "But she may not be able to reach what you are seeking," he continued, crossing his arms and studying her.

Raegan assumed this was some sort of test of her resolve, so she met his gaze and held it, one hand reaching to pluck a pink-skinned apple from the bowl. She gave it a little toss and then took a large bite from its flesh, a satisfying crunch echoing in the air. "Then you are gonna be stuck with me until you find someone who can," Raegan told him, her voice as sweet as the fruit's flesh. She smiled at him as she chewed, then almost choked as a thought dawned on her. "*Fuck*, did I just eat faerie food?" she demanded of the King, her eyes surely as wide as the silver fruit bowl.

To her surprise and horror, the King threw his head back and laughed, the sound of it like a deep silver bell echoing through the space. Dread stirred in Raegan's stomach. She had come so far just to fall for a trick so simple.

"I apologize," the King told her, his laughter ceasing, "for laughing at you. I found your expression very amusing."

"I'm delighted to have entertained you with my terror," Raegan snapped, the apple sitting uselessly in her hand, juice running down her fingers. "But answer the fucking question."

The King's gaze slid to hers, lazy and sly as a curl of smoke. "No, Overhill," he replied, "it is not faerie food. We are not in Faerie. You are not trapped here forevermore."

He lifted his chin to look out around the space, and Raegan followed his gaze to the gleaming marble floors, the inky blue celestial ceiling, the rich jewel tone fabrics and the ever-present sound of softly falling water.

"Though I suppose it would not be such a curse, would it?" he asked, his tone brightened with a blush of levity.

"There's worse places, but I've been described as 'fiercely independent' since I was four years old, so I don't take well to confinement," Raegan replied. To show how quickly she had recovered from her admittedly very real moment of fear, she took another bite of the apple. She chewed and then— crossing one ankle over the other and leaning back against the plush velvet of the sofa—asked, "Can I call you Oberon? I'm certainly not going to run around referring to you as 'my liege' or 'your highness' or any of that shit."

For a moment, the King—the most collected, terrifying, and even-keeled person she had ever met—resembled a deer in the headlights. But like every other time Raegan had thought she'd caught something beyond his cool, deadly demeanor, it was gone in half a heartbeat.

"That is acceptable," the King said with a slight incline of his head.

Footsteps echoed on the marble, and Raegan looked past the King to see the Keeper and a tall woman clothed in sweeping robes of blue velvet approaching them.

Getting to her feet, a half-eaten apple clutched in one hand, Raegan tried to steel herself, anxiety churning in the pit of her stomach. The King stood as well, brushing out slight wrinkles in the sleeve of his suit jacket with the back of one hand.

With all her might, Raegan fought to calm the panic rising in her throat, begging every deity she knew for two things: to find her father safe and unharmed, and to squash the small, strange part of her that ached unreasonably for the King.

CHAPTER TWENTY-FIVE

Raegan had shoved as much of the panic back down into her stomach as she possibly could by the time the Keeper and the seer reached the seating area. Tucking her leather jacket under her arm, she strode toward the pair, meeting them a few feet past the couch, out in the sea of creamy marble. Shadows fell to her left, and she knew without looking that the King had come to stand beside her.

"May I humbly introduce Seer Cordelia Iravani, Apprentice of the Third Oracle," the Keeper said, sweeping into an elegant little bow.

The seer beside him was tall—not just an optical illusion from standing near the short-statured Keeper—and impossibly graceful. Her black hair fell in perfect waves that Raegan strongly suspected were perfumed with scents like jasmine and neroli and bergamot. Every visible inch of her deep bronze skin was perfect. Her dark amber eyes were expertly lined in kohl, cheekbones highlighted with a shade like molten gold. The lush blue velvet of her robes—chic and alluring on her, when they would surely look costume-ish on someone else— highlighted her white teeth and inviting smile.

Raegan bemoaned the continued attractiveness of the Fey,

watching in confusion as Cordelia stepped forward, her arms open to embrace the King. Shock nearly drove Raegan a full step back, and snideness danced at her mouth as she awaited the King rebuking the seer.

But the King returned Cordelia's embrace, holding her tightly against his chest for a moment. Raegan's character assessment of the King apparently consisted of multiple blind spots, which she begrudgingly noted as she watched the interaction with rapt attention, hoping to fill the blanks.

"Cordelia," the King said warmly, continuing to lightly hold the seer by her shoulders as the Fey woman stepped back. "What a pleasure to see you."

"The feeling is mutual, my liege," Cordelia replied, smiling up at the High King of the Unseelie Court like he was an old college friend. "I don't think we've seen each other since you first arrived in this city, have we? Are you well?"

"I have been better," the King replied, releasing the seer. "But I suppose it comes with the territory."

"Heavy is the head that wears the crown," Cordelia replied, a hint of sarcasm creeping into her tone. Raegan delightedly realized the seer was mocking the King.

"No court, no crown," he replied, one ink-black eyebrow arching. "I am king in name only, and we both know that."

Cordelia swatted at the King's bicep, a devilish grin spreading across her face. "Well, you maintain my fealty," she said, ducking into a mock curtsey. "For what it's worth."

"More than an entire legion," the King answered, confusing Raegan to her core when he winked.

Were they flirting? Were they close friends? Was this some sort of weird Fey social dance? Had Raegan read him completely wrong—an unheard-of occurrence? She stood mute, rooted to the marble floor, wondering how this darkly charming, gregarious person had managed to snatch the King's body without anyone noticing.

And wondering why she felt *jealousy*, of all things.

"Hardly. But I appreciate the confidence," Cordelia replied, her gaze trailing to Raegan for the first time. "And who do we have here?"

"This is Raegan Overhill," the King said. "We are hoping you might be able to locate her father, though there are some complications."

"Yes," Cordelia said, nodding, clasping her hands together. "The Keeper briefed me. Why don't we head to a more private area, and you can fill me in on how you got mixed up with a mortal looking for her father."

With that, the seer turned on her heel and strode toward a tall, arched doorway at the back of the cavernous room. Raegan made a face at Cordelia's back but began to follow her anyway—begrudgingly, of course. She turned in surprise when she felt the King gently brush her shoulder as he kept pace beside her.

"There is little need for such condescension, Cordelia," the King said, his tone somehow both charming and deadly at once. "You know I have lived much of my life beside humans."

Cordelia turned to look at him, walking backwards in her high heels, which Raegan admittedly found impressive. "Maybe that's why you're so fucked up," the seer suggested wryly, sliding her hands into the folds of her velvet kaftan. Her amber gaze slid to Raegan. "No offense."

Raegan decided to play nice, telling herself that it had everything to do with finding her father and nothing to do with how gorgeous Cordelia was. "None taken," she replied. "Humans *are* very fucked up. Granted, you lot don't seem much better, but I'll take responsibility where it's due."

"You're funny," Cordelia said, though she wrinkled her nose as if she had smelled something bad. She turned back around on her heel, crossing beneath the large archway. "Follow me to the right, please."

Raegan trailed the seer, noticing that beyond the archway, plush rugs ran down the middle of the marble floors, devouring the sound of their footfalls. A long, dim hallway stretched out before them, lit by flickering torches. The ceiling was the same as within the parlor, but the blue was inkier, as if the sun were lower in the sky. The gold leaf constellations had taken on a pearly hue.

Both sides of the hallway were lined with smaller archways, their openings obscured by sumptuous velvet curtains. Raegan stifled the burning desire to pull some of them back, to see how this place worked and what was going on beneath the surface. Instead, she continued walking, concerned about the way she felt reassured by the King's dark, silent presence at her side. She tossed the core of her apple into a tall silver container that she belatedly realized may, in fact, not be a trash can at all.

Cordelia reached an archway that looked no different from the rest and paused, pulling the curtain aside and stepping within; it seemed clear that they were to follow. Raegan wavered at the threshold.

"She's a peach," Raegan said in a low tone to the King once Cordelia had melted into the darkness. "Hopefully she can at least find my father."

"My apologies," the King replied, surprising her. "She is not overly fond of your kind. She will get her barbs in—she is young—and then she will be professional and complete the tasks we require of her."

"Speaking of that," Raegan said, aware that they were likely lingering in the hallway for too long. "What will this cost? Another thing like the scrying glass?"

The King shook his head. "It is a monetary cost," he replied. "I will handle it."

Raegan looked at him in disbelief, her voice rising. "And then what will I owe *you*? Do you think I'm an idiot?"

The King let out an exasperated sigh, looking at her with exhaustion. "Do you happen to have twelve Feyrish silver coins on you?" he asked, one brow arched.

Raegan made a frustrated noise, tossing one hand in the air. "You know the answer to that."

"Then allow me to take care of it," he replied, reaching forward to pull the velvet fabric back. "I consider it part of our deal."

She crossed her arms, fixing him with her best "don't bullshit me" stare, but likely on account of being more than a thousand years old, he just stared back at her, utterly unfazed.

"Fine," Raegan snapped, ducking past the section of curtain the King held open for her. Gloom greeted her on the other side, punctuated by several small candle flames. She paused, waiting for her eyes to adjust, and when they did, Raegan could hardly absorb all of the magic within the space.

The ceiling was made of the familiar velvet fabric, but it was tented and pointed like the top of a circus tent. The fabric hung down in rippling waves, flashing different colors in the warm candlelight. At the far end, Cordelia sat at a round table that could have been made entirely from moonstone—it was near-translucent, rich with a pearly shimmer, a deep blue dancing in its depths. The air within the space was cool and refreshing. Beautifully illustrated charts covered the walls—moon phases and astrological constellations and maps and things that Raegan had never seen before in her life, including a diagram of a nautilus shell marked with instructions to be followed at each turn of its labyrinthine insides.

Most importantly, the room *hummed*. The space seemed to throb with the ebb and flow of something she strongly suspected was magic. Being on this side of the curtain felt like what Raegan imagined pure oxygen might feel like in her lungs.

"How is this possible?" she asked, turning to the King as she tried to reconcile what she saw before her with the information she had gleaned. "Don't the Gates completely bar magic from our side of the world? And wouldn't the Protectorate be able to smell all this like blood in the water?"

The King did not look at her, but she saw the corner of his mouth curve up into something dangerous. "It is advantageous," he said slowly, "for some to believe those things. The truth, as it usually does, lies somewhere in between."

Raegan opened her mouth to ask more, but then Cordelia's voice interrupted them. "Come," she called. "Sit. Tell me how I can be of assistance."

The seer looked impossibly powerful and beautiful seated on the other side of the moonstone table, her palms placed flat on its surface, her form backlit. When she tossed some of her dark, heavy hair over her shoulder, exposing the skin of her neck and her collarbone, Raegan was admittedly distracted.

"I need to find my father," she managed to say, coming to stand at the edge of the table, ignoring the two soft-looking chairs. "Oberon helped me scry for him in Nyx's scrying glass, but something very powerful pushed us out. We were hoping you could help."

Cordelia looked from Raegan to the King, who had come to stand at Raegan's side, in disbelief. "The Unseelie King let you use Nyx's glass?" the seer demanded, her eyes widening. "And permits you to address him so informally?"

The King lowered himself into one of the chairs with a heavy, near-theatrical sigh. "Yes, Cordelia," he replied, his tone becoming arch. "I have never been one for formalities. Additionally, you may be familiar with deals. Overhill had something I wanted, so I bartered for it."

"You must have wanted it quite badly," Cordelia said, her gaze falling on Raegan, as if to decipher what the King desired from such a small, unremarkable mortal. In her peripheral vision, Raegan saw him hold up a hand.

"I did not come here to discuss my dealmaking with you, seer," he said, expression gone cold. "I came to see if you could assist with finding the location of a mortal."

For a long moment, Cordelia looked between Raegan and the King as if there was some invisible thread between them that could explain the situation at hand. Suspicion still on her face, the seer shrugged and reached for a silver box on the bookshelf behind her. She laid it carefully on the table, removing the lid gently. Raegan watched, her heart hammering in her throat. Cordelia moved with a reverence that made her hair stand on end. She was close. She had to be. She wondered if her father knew she was coming.

Cordelia slipped a sheet of paper—no, not paper, too translucent—from the box and placed it in front of Raegan. She lowered her gaze to examine it, but it gave away no secrets, looking for all the world to be just a sheet of vellum, but with more flash and shimmer.

Then Cordelia placed a quill and ink in front of Raegan. The feather was silver, almost metallic in appearance, and the little pot of ink was a similar shade of pearlescent gray. She raised her gaze, looking at the seer for instruction.

"I will do a simple scrying first to get a feel for the complexity of this situation," Cordelia said, calm and collected. "Based on your concerns and earlier trouble, I want to take this slow. Raegan, if you would please, write down your father's full name and date of birth. As you do so, try to visualize him—actual memories help as opposed to trying to conjure a stagnant image. Anything you can recall clearly works. It need not be significant."

Raegan sank into the chair, feeling like she was underwater, her movements dulled and slowed by the weight of an entire ocean. But she forced herself to nod and do as Cordelia instructed. She reached for the quill and picked it up, finding it to be much lighter than she'd expected. With her other hand, Raegan slid the pot of ink closer and dipped the quill's nub into it, automatically scraping the excess ink off on the side of the jar, though she could not recall having ever used a quill before.

Raegan hesitated only for a moment, and then she began to write her father's name and birthdate, her mind running thick—for the second time that day—with memories. She moved deliberately, breaking each letter down into the lines and half-circles that formed his name, driving the quill deep into the strange vellum paper, as if doing so could make the material absorb more of her father. By the time she finished, tears pushed hotly at the back of her throat. Raegan put the quill down and slid the paper toward Cordelia, bringing the back of her left hand to her eyes and squeezing them shut. She gritted her teeth and told herself not to cry, not here, not now.

Letting out a shaky exhale, she opened her eyes. Her vision still a bit blurry, she watched as Cordelia folded the paper with her father's name upon it. The seer's elegant hands moved with lithe grace, creasing the paper again and again, as if she planned to make origami from it. When Cordelia had created a small, star-like shape from the vellum, the seer opened her mouth, placed the paper on her tongue and promptly swallowed it whole.

Raegan's gaze darted to the King, but his expression held no reaction—not even that slight furrowing of the brows, which she had gotten fairly good at recognizing—so she assumed this was standard practice. Then Cordelia closed her eyes and spoke. The words were in no language Raegan knew, yet they made her bones tremble all the same. Something— magic, power, gods, demons, perhaps all four—fell over the space, whisper-soft, like the feathered wings of some ancient creature.

Next, Cordelia opened her eyes and pushed the silver box to the side. Placing both of her hands flat on the table's surface, thumb-to-thumb, the seer swept her fingers across the glimmering stone. Lines lit up across the table—a map, Raegan thought, though not like any map she had ever seen before.

She bit down hard on the inside of her cheek, blood blooming in her mouth. Her fingers gripped the sides of her chair's seat, nails slicing into the fabric. Her stomach lurched, queasy with anticipation.

Cordelia lifted one hand high above the table's surface and the glittering lines transposed upon it. She loosened her fingers slightly, and a rounded, triangle-shaped stone tumbled from her grasp, stopping sharply just a few inches above the table. The seer spoke another word that made Raegan's teeth vibrate and then leaned forward to breathe on the stone, the way one might to create condensation on a cold window.

When Cordelia sat back in her chair, the stone began to sway back and forth. Raegan watched it, realizing this pendulum had no chain and no feasible, logical way to be moving the way it was.

The pendulum picked up speed, its side-to-side sashay transforming into slow, looping ellipses across the table and its maze of golden lines. Raegan glanced at Cordelia to see if anything could be deciphered about the progress so far, but the seer's eyes were closed. Her face was almost entirely relaxed, except for the erratic way her eyes moved beneath her lids, like moths swarming a sole light source on a dark night.

The moment stretched long and thin, Raegan's heart hammering with anticipation. Just as she was about to look at the King and search for any sign of concern, Cordelia's eyes snapped open. Her irises had turned pale silver, flat as two coins laid over her lids. The seer did not appear to be breathing, though the power Raegan had felt upon entering thrummed louder and louder.

Cordelia leaned forward, palms flat on the table's surface, clear of the glittering lines. Then she straightened, furrowed her brow, and spoke one single, sharp word that felt like a thunderclap.

The pendulum tumbled from the air, clattering uselessly onto the moonstone surface, rolling to the left before lolling into a circle. The seer gasped, pulling her hands away from the table, the silver gone from her eyes as she watched the pendulum slow to a halt just beyond the reach of the golden lines.

For a long moment, no one moved or spoke. Raegan was fairly sure she had stopped breathing, her entire world consisting of the unmoving pendulum and the seer's blatant mixture of surprise and horror.

"That," the King said, breaking the silence, his words like a low-lying storm cloud, "is impossible."

Chapter Twenty-Six

"Yes," Cordelia said, her gaze locked on the pendulum stone. "Even if his location were cloaked or he were in a pocket realm or between planes, the scrying would still show *something*. This . . . Whatever happened, my sight was completely rejected."

Beside her, the King sighed heavily, dragging one hand through his hair in the most human-like gesture Raegan had seen him make.

Cordelia raised her eyes for the first time, looking at the King. "I will attempt a few less obtrusive means," she said, her eyebrows drawn together. "But I hope you understand that you are dealing with something . . ."

"Primordial," the King finished for her with a sharp nod of his head. "Yes."

"What the fuck does that mean?" Raegan demanded, twisting in her chair to address the King.

He considered her, a weariness creasing his expression. "It means, as we suspected earlier, that something powerful and likely very, very old is interested in obscuring the location of your father. Or perhaps more realistically, your father is within the realm of a very powerful, very old thing that does not wish to be found," he told her.

"Hold on," Raegan said, just barely stopping herself from leaping out of her chair. "Does that mean he's definitely alive? Like, for sure?" She swung to face Cordelia, her teeth dug into her tongue, watching the seer closely.

The seer tilted her head slightly to the side, eyes narrowed, in a vaguely animalistic way that mirrored what Raegan had seen the King do more than once. "You mean you are not sure if the focus of these efforts is even alive?" Cordelia asked, her tone short, eyes darting between the King and Raegan.

"Well, no," Raegan said, the words stretched. "I thought you knew that. I mean, we saw him, but it was only for a moment."

"Seeing an image of someone in a scrying glass does not always mean they are alive," Cordelia said, her words barbed and intended solely for the King.

"I may have forgotten that part," the King said, almost apologetically but not quite.

"For Olwyn's sake," Cordelia spat, rolling her eyes. "We should have started there."

Raegan almost opened her mouth to say the words that clung to the back of her throat, but she pressed her lips together instead. She knew deeply, truly, and absolutely that her father was alive. She had always known and had never doubted, no matter how many years went by, no matter the funeral with the empty casket, or the way her mother's endless, gnawing anger finally left her one autumn and she put Cormac's photo on the ancestor shelf, his features lit up by the flicker of the candles. Even Maelona's insistence hadn't swayed her because Raegan had never questioned whether her father lived or not. She'd only ever asked herself why he had gone and to where and if he might ever come back.

"We're going to start from the top," Cordelia announced, pushing a stray lock of molasses-thick hair behind her ear.

"This is going to take a while, and I need you to do exactly as I say."

Despite herself, Raegan glanced toward the King for a heartbeat, long enough for him to meet her eyes and give a small nod. Unreasonably calmed by his response, she turned her gaze back toward Cordelia. "Okay," Raegan said, folding her hands on her lap. "Just tell me what to do."

Taking charge did not appear to be an issue for Cordelia. Over the course of the next few hours, the seer valiantly attempted to determine whether Cormac was alive. She did some weird thing with two eggs—one black as night with iridescent speckles, the other the color of an oil spill—that the King seemed very delighted to be witnessing. She cast lots. She heated wax in an ornate tin cup and poured it into a bowl of cold water, studying the shapes the hot wax formed. She cleaved a silky black chicken in half upon a stone altar and studied its entrails for forty minutes.

Finally, Cordelia insisted upon scrying for Cormac in her own glass, despite both Raegan and the King's protests. The attempt ended in a broken eight-hundred-year-old heirloom divining glass, two black eyes for Cordelia, and a wicked migraine for Raegan.

"Cordelia," the King said, beginning to sound strained for the first time all afternoon. "I think it is best we wait for the Oracle. No more of this."

The seer made a vague, noncommittal sound from the chaise lounge where she was sprawled out, a cold compress laid across her eyes.

"He's probably alive," Cordelia mumbled a few moments later, hoarse and exhausted. "That's all I can give you. The Oracle will know more."

The seer pulled herself into a seated position with a low groan, discarding the compress. The back of her hair was mussed from being pressed against the arm of the chaise. A bit of kohl had migrated to her temple, and though her black eyes had decreased in overall darkness and puffiness, the seer still looked as though she had been through the wringer. "Allow me to walk you out," she said, swinging her legs over the edge of the chaise. "I'm alright, I promise."

"Cordelia," the King said, his low, rich voice firm. "You look the very opposite of alright."

"Fuck you, my High King," Cordelia replied, though there was no venom in it. "I look incredible as always."

The King laughed, clear as a silver bell, the sound of it uncoiling a spool of longing deep in Raegan's core. She ignored it, getting to her feet, unsteady with exhaustion. The King mirrored her, extending a hand to help Cordelia off the couch. Instead of daintily taking it and getting to her feet all on her own as Raegan expected, the seer grappled the King's wrist with both hands and hauled herself off the chaise. Raegan watched the King's tendons flex in his forearm—he had removed his jacket and rolled his sleeves up at some point—and averted her hungry gaze.

"Well, thank you for the entertaining afternoon," Cordelia said, her smile thin. "I suppose it's good to be humbled now and again."

"Thank you for your heroic efforts," the King replied, rolling his sleeves back down and buttoning them at the wrist. He took a few steps toward Raegan, leaning forward to pull his suit jacket off the back of the chair beside her.

"I'd say to call on me whenever you wish, but please don't do this to me anytime soon," Cordelia said, her voice wrung dry, shoulders defeated. Underscoring her words, she gestured for the King and Raegan to follow the Keeper, who had appeared at the mouth of the room.

Raegan fell into step beside the King, picking at the skin around her cuticles, her mind already racing. Securing an audience with the Oracle was imperative. Raegan could only hope the prophetess would not be gone for much longer.

"The Keeper will take care of everything up front,"

Cordelia said, her voice cutting into Raegan's thoughts. "Oberon, if you were anyone else, you'd be getting surcharged to death."

The King paused in the doorway, turning toward Cordelia. Raegan stopped beside him, her shoulder brushing his upper arm. "I am always happy to pay what is owed," he told the seer with a regal incline of his head. "Your efforts will be rewarded with more than coin."

Cordelia took a step closer and grinned; it was dazzling, all molten bronze sunshine and autumn glory. "Favors from the Unseelie Court are the best kind of payment," the seer replied. "Take care, both of you."

Then Cordelia raised her hands to touch the King and Raegan on their shoulders at the same time, a gentle goodbye between three people who had peered a bit too deeply into the void together. But the moment her fingers brushed both the King and Raegan at once, Cordelia's head snapped back as if dealt a violent blow. A low, pained wail escaped her lips, and she dropped like a stone, her legs cut out from beneath her.

Raegan reacted more to the sound than anything else. She spun and jumped to the side, her heart pounding with sudden adrenaline. Thanks to his much quicker reflexes, the King caught Cordelia by the forearm and then the waist, steadying the seer just before her knees could meet the cold marble floor. Everything else happened in slow motion, all noises dulled and softly echoing, as if someone had stuffed Raegan's ears full of cotton.

The Keeper, who had gone out into the hallway ahead of them, came rushing back in, crouching at Cordelia's side. He turned to Raegan and asked her a question, but something—more than adrenaline, more than fear, more than confusion—was building inside of her, and she just stared at him mutely. She knew on a logical level that he was speaking words, but she could not understand any of them.

The King had taken a knee beside Cordelia, holding her

waist and supporting the back of her head with his other hand as she shook violently, her eyes having turned that same silver shade from before, when she'd scried for Raegan's father. Pressure continued to build inside Raegan, a sweeping, soaring feeling, like an orchestra escalating to an overture's climax. It was as if every part of her body were built of strings, cross-hatched and woven together, and a god was trailing their fingers against them, playing an old, sweet song. Her bones reverberated with the swoop and shape of it, her migraine evaporating.

From behind her, somewhere in the hallway, she caught just a snippet of a melody—grand and aching, its valleys low and dark, its peaks as joyous as a hero's return. It sent shivers across her skin, this song—honeyed with Fate and heavy with Sorrow. She felt Time slip out of tune, scales sliding past her skin, a snake devouring its own tail.

It was the seer's voice that broke through the melody, her tremors having apparently abated, her eyes still that eternal, silver-slicked shade.

"Exactly who—or *what*—have you brought into The Temple of the Pythia, High King?"

CHAPTER TWENTY-SEVEN

The Seer's words hung as heavy as smoke in the air, though Raegan could barely process anything with the notes of that melody still so thick in her ears. She could nearly taste it: sweet like mead, metallic like blood, damp like rain. It sounded, she realized, like Fate.

"Our business is our own," the King replied, dark and regal and terrifyingly cold. He pulled his hands from the seer without much concern for whether she could support herself, straightening to his full height. "I have shared the information necessary for the requested—"

The King's words cut off suddenly as the spun-gold song slunk in from the hallway, louder now, undeniable. Raegan watched as the rest of the statement died in the King's throat, his attention focused entirely on the gilded notes slipping through the velvet curtains.

The Keeper, still crouched beside Cordelia, was awestruck —as if he were seeing something he thought long dead, entombed a thousand miles away, never again to rise and walk among the living. "It cannot be," he murmured as he helped Cordelia to her feet.

Upon standing, the seer clasped her hands together,

reverent as a sinner rising from the confessional. "It is," Cordelia whispered, her eyes glimmering with tears. "It's a Fatesong."

Chills cascaded across Raegan's body. A tide roared inside her head, moving with the same swell and swoop as the sacred melody that circled her. She saw jeweled meadows and blackened battlefields and rushing rivers and cities aflame. She tasted mead and ash and blood on her tongue, her throat aching. Fingers digging into the cuffs of her leather jacket, Raegan fought hard to stay in the moment, reminding herself of the marble floor beneath her, breathing in the creamy, aquatic scent of the space—anything to not be swept away in the rush and roar of the song. It sang to her so sweetly, and she knew she would allow it to consume her entirely.

She let out a shaking breath, the melody still wrapped thickly around her. She saw the Keeper take off his glasses and fold them in his hands, the way a gentleman might remove his hat before entering a church. Cordelia had thrown her head back, nostrils flaring, as if to let the golden thrum of the song fill her entire being.

The King, though—looking upon him nearly broke Raegan's heart in half. Somehow, the melody made the shadows hang more heavily on him, the gloom a cloak upon his shoulders. When his gaze met hers, the song swelled, and Raegan found herself looking into an ocean's worth of grief— the King's sorrow and torment so jagged and raw that she thought she could cut herself upon its sharp edges.

And then, as quickly as it had arrived, the melody slunk away like the sun slipping over the horizon at sunset. A soft silence filled the space, punctuated only by the sound of breathing—sharp, quick inhales, impossible to tell from which of the four bodies they originated.

"Oh, and what a song it is," Cordelia breathed. "I heard *Prophecy*. Grand, ancient, eternal . . . inevitable."

Anything Raegan wanted to say withered on her tongue—

and there was *so* much she wished to say; it was as if everything was unfolding just how she'd planned it, but of course she had not planned anything at all, had she? So silence cloaked the space again, and how silent it all felt without that song in her ears, without its thrum filling up the empty spaces in her chest.

"I have heard it before," the King said, each word spoken like an iron stake being driven into the ground. The shadows of the space gathered dark around him, his eyes like black water. "It lies."

"My liege," Cordelia pleaded, her hands reaching out for the King before she snatched them back, as if she thought better of it. "No one has heard a Fatesong in nearly a millennium. We thought them extinct, or more likely, mere myth."

The King's expression grew darker, and he seemed tall, taller than ever, the shadows knitting themselves around him, as if he had perhaps never been flesh and bone at all. "That Fatesong," he began, his gaze trailing to Raegan for a heartbeat, "is rooted in violence and death. When its Threads are followed, when its melody is sung, it brings nothing but destruction."

His words hit Raegan like a pile of large stones. She felt the truth of it in her marrow, the seas of her mind throwing snippets of shattered bodies and slit throats and burning villages onto her shores like broken, battered driftwood.

And yet Cordelia barely hesitated when she reached out to grab Raegan's hands with her own, the seer's entire body radiating with pure, unadulterated hope. "It is *you*," she whispered to Raegan, her eyes flitting between amber and silver, mead and mist. "It sings for *you*."

Raegan let out a shaking breath. The understory had become the overstory, the way had opened, and the door yawned hungry and aching. Before any words could come to her mind—it didn't seem like an event to be trapped by language, anyway—Cordelia folded her fingers into Raegan's and pulled.

"To the Vaults," the seer said, addressing Raegan alone, though her gaze flitted to the Keeper. "There is a Prophecy to be read."

And with that, Cordelia pulled Raegan out through the velvet curtain and back into the hallway. Raegan did not resist. She knew a Fatewind when she felt one, and she would sail this tiny vessel, laden heavy with hope, for as long as it would carry her weight.

Raegan pulled closer to Cordelia, matching her pace, only for the seer to surge ahead, breaking into a run down the wide, softly lit marble hallway. For a moment, Raegan hesitated, throwing a look over her shoulder—where was the King? Instead, she found only the Keeper, standing a few paces from the archway they'd departed from.

"Cordelia!" The Keeper's voice careened through the corridor, his tone sharp.

The seer slowed her pace and turned but did not stop, her hand gripping Raegan's tighter and tighter. "Keeper," Cordelia replied, her rich voice magnificent, like the heroine of an ancient fable. "I heard it. In that Fatesong. I heard the Gates fall."

Even from this distance, Raegan could see the Keeper stop breathing, could see the way his heart leapt into his throat.

"Seer," the Keeper called, his voice lower than Raegan had heard it before, thick as honey. "Truly? You heard them fall?"

In response, Cordelia simply threw her head back and laughed, the sound of it so wild and free and endless that Raegan found herself joining in, electricity buzzing in her marrow like a thousand bees.

"Yes," the seer replied, gripping Raegan's hand, her skin hot and feverish. "The Vaults. Take me to the Vaults, Keeper."

The small man—who was not a man, who had never been a

man, who could not be contained within a plain face and a tailcoat —drew closer to them, only a few of his walking steps somehow bringing him to stand right before them. "It is highly irregular," the Keeper said, though his voice betrayed something else entirely. "You are not anointed as the Oracle. And yet you have offered Fatespeak and now you dare to request access to the Vaults."

Cordelia let go of Raegan's hand and closed the distance that separated her from the Keeper, placing her hands upon the shorter being's shoulders, gazing into his eyes. "The Gates," she breathed before bringing her forehead to his and letting out a laugh that sounded like every wish ever made.

Raegan found herself transfixed by the interaction. She thought it might be like watching two prisoners of war find out someone was finally, *finally*, after all this time, coming for them.

The Keeper gently shook his head, pulling away from Cordelia, who was whispering quiet pleas, one of her hands gripping his. "A Prophecy is not a promise," he said, soft as a dove feather on the breeze. "It is the furthest thing from a promise."

"It is not a promise," Cordelia agreed. "But it is a door. And how long we have been battering ourselves against a wall. How long we have yearned for a door."

Cordelia's words let loose a sob at the back of Raegan's throat. She tried to push it down, pressing one hand to her mouth, but the cry untethered itself anyway, and tears fell softly down her face. The Keeper watched her, as if her reaction were evidence or proof that could sway him, though she knew not which way.

"The Oracle," the Keeper began, hesitant, "would not, I believe, wish us to wait on such a revelation due to her absence. We will investigate the Prophecy this Fatesong has spoken to you, Cordelia, but nothing more until she returns."

Upon speaking the last few words, the Keeper pulled a large iron ring from somewhere on his person. From it hung too many keys to count, some of them positively ancient-looking, the others as mundane as Raegan's own apartment key. With a delighted whoop, Cordelia turned, grabbed Raegan's hand again, and then took off down the hallway, nearly pulling her shoulder out of its socket. But Raegan did not mind the pain; more so, she almost did not feel it, as if even her body knew nothing had ever mattered more than this moment, a moment scaffolded upon every insane choice and wild leap that had brought her here.

As she ran with the dark-haired seer down the velvet-lined hallway, Raegan understood that there was absolutely nothing rational about whatever was happening all around her. She couldn't even be quite sure that this was not some sort of fever dream. But was it possible to feel so alive in a dream? To taste mead and blood and hope so clearly? She did not think her body would sing like this for but a dream.

The light of the flickering sconces grew dimmer the farther she ran headlong by Cordelia's side. Her heart pounding, her lungs aching, Raegan slowed without regard for the seer's desire to sprint ahead. This was her path to walk, yes—but she had never done it alone before, had she? She threw another glance over her shoulder, searching the dim hallway for the King. They had come so far together—would he not see this through? And more importantly, could she see it through without that silent, unwavering presence at her side? She felt as though she were going into battle having just lost a limb.

Cordelia finally slowed to a brisk walk, and Raegan turned to find a door just a few strides ahead. It was not a regular sort of door. It was crafted from wood, yes, but laden with impossibly detailed ironwork. Metal stars studded the wood grain. The top of the door was arched, coming to an elegant point. A large, ornate iron keyhole was set into the door's right side.

Before she could stop herself, Raegan reached her hand out and laid her palm against the door. It felt alive—warm to the touch, softer than wood should be. She felt a heartbeat pulse beneath her fingers.

"Oooh," Cordelia cooed. "The door likes you. Of course it likes you."

Raegan turned to the seer, her mouth half-opened to ask exactly what that meant, but the Keeper was approaching, and Cordelia's attention locked on to his ring of keys. The Keeper's eyes strayed to Raegan, and then he held her gaze. Raegan hadn't taken her hand off the door.

The Keeper's movements slowed, almost like everything was underwater, as his fingertips brushed a large iron skeleton key. Age had blackened its patina. Even from where she stood, Raegan could see it contained none of the fine craftsmanship of the door, no matching arches or stars or scrolls. The key was simply a key.

Beside her, Cordelia seemed to be holding her breath as the Keeper's footfalls brought him to the door's mouth. Time moved strangely, too slow and too fast at once, like a river unsure of which way it was meant to flow. The moment the Keeper inserted the key into the door's lock, a golden melody trilled from above their heads. All three of them looked up at once, but of course all they saw was the celestial ceiling, the heavens painted upon it now a brighter silver, the rich blue background nearly black.

The Fatesong looped long and low, soft as silk, and then the Keeper pushed the door open. Pure, unadulterated darkness waited beyond the threshold—not like the King's, which felt alive with magic. It was dead nothingness, like the empty galaxies before stars blinked their eyes open.

The Keeper waited, holding the door open, his grip firm, almost as if it were an untamed thing that might decide at any time to remember its wildness and devour them all whole.

"Follow me," Cordelia said, her fingers still intertwined with Raegan's. She looked at the seer, her heart pounding, hesitation lacing itself through her euphoria for the first time.

"It's safe," Cordelia added, her amber eyes imploring. "I promise. There will be light once the Vaults allow us in."

But the seer had misjudged Raegan's hesitation. She was not afraid; in fact, she had never felt calmer. But her very essence called out for him, just as it always had and likely always would. Now that she had finally found her dark and terrible king once more, she had no desire to let him go.

Besides, were the shadows not his dominion?

"Where is Oberon?" Raegan asked, her heartbeat spidery and skittering in her chest. Cordelia's expression folded in, the space between her eyebrows wrinkling—it was clear to Raegan that the seer had just now noticed the King was not with them.

The Keeper, however, did not register the King's absence as new, though he did heave a sigh at Raegan's line of questioning. "Our King," the Keeper began, leaning his shoulder against the door, looking as though he was searching for the right words, "will not hear this Fatesong out. That being the case, it is not right for him to accompany us into the Vaults. He cannot help us locate a Prophecy that he rejects."

Doubt simmered in Raegan's stomach, anxiety climbing the walls of her chest. It was not so much that she did not trust the Keeper and Cordelia. As distrusting as Raegan was by nature, she knew something much larger than herself was going on here, and trust was simply not a relevant factor. It was more that she could not imagine going into a dark place without her King.

Tears pricked her eyes, and she forced down a dry swallow to stem the emotion rising in her throat. "But he will be waiting for us?" she asked, looking between Cordelia and the Keeper, trying to keep her tone even. "When we return from the Vaults?"

The Keeper looked genuinely surprised at Raegan's question, his eyebrows shooting up. "Oh, of course," he said.

"Despite his bluster, I hardly believe him capable of leaving you behind."

From beside her, Cordelia let out a little laugh, like she and the Keeper were in on something that Raegan was not. She opened her mouth to ask what the Keeper could possibly mean, but Cordelia tightened her grip on Raegan's hand, took a running step across the threshold, and dragged Raegan into the waiting darkness with her.

Beyond the door there was nothing—a complete and utter absence of anything at all. Primordial darkness, Raegan hazarded, the black matter that made up space, just waiting to be formed by cosmic upheaval or the sweep of Fate or perhaps the hands of bored gods. It closed in on her, hungry and stifling, everything an inherent dichotomy: her living, breathing flesh, and the darkness's great, glorious nothingness.

Then there was a low, shuddering sound—almost mechanical, but too ethereal, like machinery imagined by elves—and suddenly Cordelia's face came into Raegan's view, lit by a lantern the seer held aloft.

"Here," Cordelia said, handing Raegan the lantern, which she accepted wordlessly. "The Vaults are massive, you see, so when you first enter, it takes a moment for it to know which section to spit you out into."

Raegan steadied herself, fighting for some sense of cool composure. She wrapped her fingers tightly around the ring at the top of the lantern, grateful for the way its flickering flame drove away the oppressive dark. "Which section are we in?" she asked, knowing damn well the answer wouldn't mean anything to her. But asking questions calmed her, and more knowledge was rarely a bad thing.

"I cannot believe it," the Keeper said from farther ahead, standing on the edge of the platform that floated in the darkness.

Raegan moved forward to get a better look, and her stomach dropped. The three of them appeared to be standing on a large slice of rock jutting out over a massive archival library. A spiral staircase, crafted from intricately carved wood, wound a dizzyingly long way down to the bottom.

Cordelia rushed to the edge to stand next to the Keeper, the hem of her robes a whisper against the rock. When she reached the edge, she gasped softly. "Unrequited," she murmured.

Steeling herself, Raegan raised her lantern and walked slowly to the edge, taking her time to ensure there were no other drop-off points.

"I suppose it makes sense," the Keeper was saying as Raegan came to stand beside the two Fey beings. "What else could it be but Unrequited? Any Prophecy that mentions the King has surely been pored over a thousand times."

"The Fatesong spoke of them both," Cordelia said, the lantern light casting stark shadows across her face, accentuating her strong features. She looked positively otherworldly. "It sang for her. But I am sure it spoke of them both."

Raegan attempted to digest that piece of information—it was rude, but admittedly useful, that the Fey seemed very content to talk about mortals like they weren't in the room—when Cordelia turned toward the Keeper, her lantern swinging wildly.

"The Fatesong sounded old. *Very* old," the seer said, her words heavy with implied meaning.

"He was not King yet," Raegan said without realizing she was speaking aloud, simply sliding the most logical puzzle piece into place. Cordelia's eyes flitted to her, the seer's expression approving, and the Keeper turned to her, nodding in agreement.

"That makes our task easier," the Keeper said. "Let us examine the sections containing Prophecies made in the span of time between the King's creation and his rise to the Unseelie Throne."

Cordelia nodded, letting out a shaky exhale before gathering up her robes and making for the staircase. Raegan watched her go, wanting to see the path the seer took before she risked further steps upon this rocky ledge that hung in the shadows.

To her surprise, the Keeper caught her gaze and offered his arm to her. She froze, considering, but then walked forward to accept. When Raegan slipped her arm into his, she felt a buzz of power, like a low electrical hum, but it was nothing, of course, like touching the King.

"This must all be overwhelming, I imagine," the Keeper said, his tone diplomatic, as he began to usher them forward toward the staircase. Raegan had lost track of Cordelia, who must have begun to descend the staircase already.

"For a mere mortal," she said, hoping her sarcasm translated. "It most certainly is."

As they approached the edge, Raegan gripped the Keeper's sleeve a bit harder, trying to focus on taking one step at a time. She had never been afraid of heights before, but this was something else entirely. The staircase seemed unending from her vantage point, and darkness clung to every corner. She had the impression the ceiling was very, very high—hundreds of feet or more—but the lack of defined walls made her head spin.

The Keeper began to descend the staircase slowly, halting after a few steps to ensure she was alright. "You are not precisely mortal," he said, deep in thought, "but the Vaults have an impact on everyone when viewed for the first time."

"Not precisely mortal?" Raegan demanded, edging forward a few more steps, wishing she could put down the lantern to grip the railing but not wanting to relinquish the light.

The Keeper made a disappointed noise like she was a child with her hand in the cookie jar, coming to an abrupt halt. "I should not have spoken so freely," he finally said, looking up at her from a few steps down. In the half-light, he looked simultaneously ancient and impossibly young. He could have been eighteen or fifty; he seemed to exist entirely outside of time.

"It's fine," Raegan said, stepping closer, taking advantage of the few extra inches that the higher step she was perched on gave her. "I have that effect on people. I'd love for you to keep speaking freely. Very interested in your previous statement."

The Keeper smiled at her then, a secret little smile, as if this was some sort of running joke between them. "Let us not keep Cordelia waiting," he said. "This is her first Prophecy. She must be quite excited."

Raegan held his gaze for a long moment, again struck by the positively inhuman slant of his features, wondering if his façade would crack. But the Keeper merely bowed his head politely, almost meekly, and then continued his descent down the stairs.

"What makes it Unrequited?" Raegan asked, thinking she could sidestep the discussion of her 'not precisely mortal' status for now and loop back around when the Keeper had gotten comfortable talking about safer topics.

"Unrequited," the Keeper said, his usual elegance back, his voice rising in volume as if he were performing for a crowd, "refers to a Prophecy that has not yet come to pass and has not been seen by other Oracles. Many prophecies with no merit are made by charlatans every day; Unrequited Prophecies are not like that. They are in every way real—Threads shake and Fate sings for them. But then they don't happen, or perhaps, we do not realize they are happening, or they do not happen when we think they will. Even with Prophecies very far in the future, there are normally touchstones that allow us to match them up with some possible future Thread. Unrequited Prophecies have no touchstones, no matches."

Raegan made the mistake of looking down while the Keeper was speaking, hoping they were close to the bottom, but their progress was slower than Cordelia's, and they were still a horrifying distance from the last stair. Her stomach flipped, and she gritted her teeth together so hard her jaw cracked. "Right," she said, fighting to focus on the Keeper. "If there is indeed an Unrequited Prophecy that names the King and me, and it's Unrequited because no one's realized it was talking about *us*, how old would it need to be?"

The Keeper considered, his lantern swinging as he picked up the pace slightly, as if talk of Prophecies without being near them made his hands itch. "At least a thousand years, I'd imagine," he said finally, ducking into another tight twist of the staircase.

Raegan's eyebrows shot up involuntarily as she attempted to wrap her head around the Keeper's answer. "That feels like a long time," she eventually said, sounding out each word. "Is it actually? Like, for a Prophecy? For your kind?"

The Keeper chuckled, glancing back at her for a moment. "A millennium is a long time, even for us," he replied. "A sharp-eyed, long-sighted Oracle could certainly see that far along the Threads, but it would be a very good reason for it to end up in the Unrequited section."

A thousand years. Someone, from all that time ago, had seen Raegan and thought that whatever she might do was worth recording, worth keeping tucked away in the Vaults for all this time. Someone had thought Raegan might brush up against Fate. Someone other than the kelpie she'd summoned from a puddle believed she was Gods-touched. The thought was dizzying, even more so than the fucking staircase they were somehow *still* on.

Raegan said nothing as they turned into another of the staircase's twists, preparing to face the sheer drop into nothing again, but relief flooded her when she saw solid ground awaited her. Ahead, a dark stone floor—solid, not inlaid with tile—spread out for what seemed like miles. Hundreds, if not thousands, of large carved shelves were lined up like dominoes, spiraling in on themselves in some sort of labyrinth. It was not unlike an immense library—the ends of the shelves seemed to denote some kind of filing system, though it was not in any language Raegan could read.

She followed the Keeper into the soft hush of the place, releasing his arm. He set his lantern down at the base of the staircase. Raegan did as well, and saw that Cordelia must have done the same with hers. Then she set off beside the Keeper down the outer curve of shelving. To her right, the shelves rose like trees, massive and towering, and to her left, the sheer cliff face climbed out of her vision. Down on the floor level, the Vaults were lit with a soft, diffused glow that she could not decipher the source of, much like the lobby. The cliff face seemed to shimmer and wink in the light, like it was made of obsidian or another smooth, shining rock.

A series of antique-looking rugs formed a walkway along the shelving, quieting their footsteps. The Keeper passed by a number of rows without a second glance, and Raegan realized he must be working his way back a thousand years, to the time when the King was not yet the King. She tried to remind herself to see how many shelves came *before* the earliest possible date of this Prophecy. Curiosity had always been one of Raegan's gifts—and flaws—and she ached to know how long the Fey had presumably walked this planet.

"I think I've found a good section to start with." Cordelia's voice from up ahead broke the soft silence. The seer stood three spirals in from Raegan and the Keeper, half her body obscured by the shelves.

Without answering, the Keeper picked up his pace, strides lengthening as he cut through the labyrinthine shelves. Raegan followed, her heart suddenly remembering to thud anxiously in her throat. Reaching Cordelia felt like it took all of eternity. Every step seemed to set her back two, like she was battling waves to swim past the break. A heaviness settled across her chest, the burden of all the things she had dared to hope for unfurling weighted wings.

When Raegan finally turned into the curve of shelving, she took one look at the contents of the dark, carved bookcases and glanced at Cordelia in shock. Instead of books or perhaps scrolls or maybe even unfamiliar artifacts, the shelves were heavy with glass containers. Some were nothing more than slim, etched perfume vials. Others were massive, glimmering domes. Most fell somewhere in the middle: apothecary jars and fluted cloches.

Raegan stepped closer to the nearest shelf, her mouth opening in awe as she examined the contents of the containers. Within each curve of glass was some kind of winged creature, seemingly born from paper. In a large dome above Raegan's head stood a raven made from thick parchment. Inside a tiny glass box crouched a dragonfly, its wings painstakingly cut from what she thought might be vellum. She moved a few steps down the tunnel of shelves, her steps slow, utterly spellbound.

Her gaze fell on a bat made from heavily ink-stained paper suspended in a bell jar. Everything about it was so real, down to the thinness of the skin on its wings. Raegan approached, raising one shaking hand to the glass. She half-expected it to crack its eyes open and swivel its ears, though it did not—the paper bat remained mute and still behind the elegantly curved glass.

Raegan continued walking down the aisle, lost entirely to the sparrows and damselflies and griffins and other winged creatures she could not name, all housed behind shimmering glass. She stopped at a dove perched in a stained-glass box before she realized the Keeper and Cordelia wavered a few steps behind her, watching her every move.

She turned to examine them as she had the paper creatures. "How do I find it?" Raegan asked, already knowing,
somehow, that she was the only one who could.

"Keep walking," Cordelia said, her voice hushed and reverent. "You will know when you do."

Raegan nodded and then, like a woman in a trance,
continued to make her way down the slowly-curving aisle. The
carved shelves soared high on each side—so high that she
wondered how she could possibly know if the right Prophecy
were yards above her head, far out of her sight. But she was
deep in the world behind the world, and she knew such
mundane concerns had little place here. So, she walked a
perfect, swooping line in the center of the shelves, her gaze
slipping from side to side, trying to believe as much as the
Keeper and Cordelia did, that she would know the right
winged thing when she saw it.

Time passed. Raegan was fairly sure of it, though it also
could have been but seconds since she'd walked through that
arched wooden door. All the things she understood about the
world seemed to fall away here in the Vaults; everything real,
everything true, balanced on paper wings. The rest did not
matter. So she kept walking, her gaze falling on birds and
insects and dragons.

She was almost about to turn to the two Fey beings at her
back and say that perhaps she was not, after all, who they
thought she was. But then, a luna moth housed in a small
apothecary jar caught her eye. The sharp curves of its wings
were rendered in age-spotted paper so thin she could see right
through it. Despite its delicacy, the moth was larger than her
hand. Two ink stains on the bottom of its wings formed eyes,
or maybe moons. She recalled suddenly that once reaching
adulthood, luna moths only lived about seven days. They
weren't necessarily rare, only sparingly sighted. Alive, magnificent beyond compare, and then gone.

Something like grief unmoored in her chest, and she raised

her hand to the glass. She allowed a few shaking fingers to make contact with the cool surface. As she did, Raegan thought she saw the moth's wings flutter. She yanked her hand back, shocked, staring at the paper moth to see if it might reveal its secrets to her.

"Again." The Keeper's voice came from behind her; he only spoke one word, but it conveyed everything: some kind of honeyed, weighted sorrow, like there was only one option and they were all doomed to keep choosing it, over and over. As if there was nothing else he could do but tell her to raise her hand once more to the glass jar and the paper moth that slept within.

Without turning to look at him, urged only by the single spoken word, Raegan nodded and touched the glass again. She was not surprised when the moth's wings gave a small shake. This time, she kept her fingers there, hot against the cool, smooth surface of the glass. In a few more moments, the moth beat its wings as though coasting on some invisible current. The eye-moons blinked in and out of existence, somehow holding Raegan's gaze all the while.

Eventually, the moth took flight, rising above the base of the jar, its large, curved wings holding its small, down-covered body aloft. It hung there, suspended in the air, glorious wings dipping up and down, up and down.

From behind her, Raegan heard Cordelia let out a gasp, or perhaps more like a breath the seer had been holding for a hundred years. As the moth continued to beat its wings, the Fatesong looped again above them, golden-bright and rich as good soil.

"What now?" Raegan asked, not removing her eyes from the paper creature.

"Take it into your hands," the Keeper said. "Hold it close. To your heart. And then we begin our ascent."

Raegan let out a shaky breath and rested her palms against either side of the jar. The moth responded, its wings beating faster, so she carefully removed the glass dome from the shelf, pulling it close to her chest as the Keeper had instructed. Then she turned—a small, mortal woman in a leather jacket holding a Prophecy spun by an Oracle more than a thousand years ago between her hands.

In a silent procession—Keeper, Seer, Fated—the three began to once more walk the labyrinth, taking the path to return to the surface where the Unseelie King awaited them.

CHAPTER TWENTY-NINE

Raegan's heartbeat kept time with her footsteps, damp palms leaving misty imprints on the jar she clutched to her chest. Blue fell in sweeps of velvet all around her, the seer and the Keeper at her back. The hallway felt longer than it had with her forearm in Cordelia's grasp. She resisted the urge to run once more—the paper moth was so fragile and broken glass so sharp—even though something primal in the pit of her belly demanded a sprint.

The two Fey creatures behind her posed no immediate threat, Raegan knew, and even if they did, fleeing on her human legs would hardly make any difference. She tried to shove the urge away, but it only pulsed stronger, overwhelming every fiber of her being with one thought: *run*.

And then understanding swept through Raegan like a tide, and she shot into a sprint, tucking the jar into the crook of one elbow, palm flat against the glass. She was not running from anything. She was running *toward* something.

Toward someone.

Up ahead, a shadow cut through all the blue, tall and angular and waiting, as always. Tears pricked her eyes, and she ran faster, the sound of her heavy boots devoured by the cavernous hallway. By the time the King's face—brow knit, jaw clenched—came into view, Raegan was nearly upon him. She slowed but did not stop, snatching at his suit sleeve to pull him into Cordelia's workspace behind her. Something about a moth and an apothecary jar and a Prophecy meant they needed to be alone, even if only for a few moments.

Raegan eyed the seer's moonstone desk in the far corner, and instead, gingerly placed the jar on a low coffee table made from an unfinished slab of wood. She tried to force her thoughts into an orderly line, but her legs were weary, leather jacket plastered to her skin from her sprint. Breathing hard, she perched on the end of a chaise lounge—blue velvet, predictably—and turned to look at the King.

Everything slowed as his ocean gaze examined her and then the Prophecy on the table. Raegan waited to see elation or wonder in his expression, but instead, bone-deep weariness was all she found.

"We have done this so many times," the King said, gaze meeting hers, long strides carrying him closer. "No more."

He spoke the words in a low, hoarse tone, intended only for her. She suddenly had the strangest feeling that her skeleton had once belonged to a thousand other people—that her body was barely more than a grave for someone she used to be.

"But this is everything," Raegan said, eyes darting to the doorway, not wanting to waste this small moment. "This is everything I've ever wanted. Magic. Fate. Purpose."

She waited for more of his casual cruelty, for another dose of dark-eyed hatred. But it did not come. Instead, the King closed the distance, standing between her and the Prophecy. The tips of his elegant fingers grazed the underside of her chin. "It is your choice. Know that I will follow you to the ends of the Earth," the King murmured, head tilted as his eyes searched hers. "But we have done this a thousand times, and I never like the ending."

The heat from running and the closeness of the unearthly being sent a flush racing across her face. The King released her, straightening but not looking away.

"Cordelia said she heard the Gates fall," Raegan said, clawing at her jacket as more sweat pooled at the base of her spine. "Isn't that exactly what you want?"

The King ignored the query, moving behind her in a sweep of black cloth and predatory grace, extending his hands to help her out of her jacket. Black pepper and damp stone and woodsmoke rolled over Raegan's senses, conjuring more unnecessary heat in her body. She yanked herself away from the King, rising from the chaise lounge and sending one elbow flying back toward him.

He dodged the attempt so neatly it infuriated her.

"Fuck off," Raegan snapped. "I know how to take off a goddamn jacket."

She waited for rage or offense or distaste, but the King only raised one eyebrow, amusement rippling in his dark eyes.

"Of course I want the Gates to fall," he said after a heartbeat, looking out into the hallway. "But Prophecies come with steep prices. Once you release a winged thing, you cannot cage it again."

Raegan took a deep breath, thinking about the enormous marble-clad lobby of this place and how much it felt like a chessboard. How much she felt like a pawn around these ancient Fey creatures. She opened her mouth to say something but then closed it, peeling the rest of her jacket from her damp skin.

"You came here for your father," the King said, jarring her, his tone regal and authoritative again, edged in thorns. "Finding him is your desire. Everything else—the Gates, a Prophecy, the predicament of my people—has nothing to do with you. Not anymore."

She squeezed her eyes shut, fighting to conjure an image of her father, battling for the King's words to be true. But she knew—and suspected he did, too—that everything was tangled together, a snake devouring its own tail.

When Raegan opened her eyes, Cordelia entered the doorway, velvet robes swishing with her movements. The seer paused for a moment, gaze falling upon the Prophecy. She looked at the paper moth like it held every hope and every promise and every wish ever made. "Our salvation is at hand," Cordelia said, breathless, as she began to circle the coffee table.

In her peripheral vision, Raegan saw the King blanche.

"You cannot mean you intend to release it?" he demanded, watching Cordelia with an expression sharp as a dagger. "You are no Oracle."

"I'm the closest thing you've got," Cordelia snapped, meeting the King's eyes for a split second. "We cannot wait for her return. We cannot waste another moment. The *Gates*, my King. Even from behind the glass, this Prophecy sings so sweetly of freedom."

Any softness Raegan thought she might have seen in the King disappeared entirely at Cordelia's words. Razored shadows slid across his features and his eyes narrowed. But he said nothing—he didn't need to, not with the way he wore authority like a cloak.

"Cordelia," came the Keeper's voice from the mouth of the room. He said the seer's name evenly but with a hint of warning, as if the dark, feral glint in the King's gaze did not suffice.

"Do you want to keep rotting away in a dying land?" Cordelia demanded, her voice distant and watery, like she was speaking from a thousand miles away.

Nothing but the domed Prophecy and the King seemed real to Raegan. Paper body and dark waves and whisper-wings and black cloth. Something that might have been her blood thundered in her ears.

"You are not Anointed, Cordelia," someone—the Keeper, she thought—was saying. "You had no right to offer Fatespeak earlier, and now you seek to do it again? Releasing the Prophecy *must* wait until the Oracle returns. You know this. We've tested enough boundaries by simply retrieving it."

The moth's wings beat up and down, the sails of a ship billowing in the wind. It was the most beautiful thing Raegan had ever seen, delicate and powerful at once. Its song threatened to break her heart and mend every wound she'd ever suffered. The sound was faint, but as she focused on the moth, the golden slip of it filled her ears and her head and her heart again, effervescent with magic, buoyant with promise, heavy with Fate.

Just there, beyond a thin curve of glass, was everything she'd ever wanted.

So she reached out and lifted the lid from the jar.

All that followed happened in slow motion, almost like she was not really in the room at all. The King's powerful hands reached for her wrists a fraction of a second too late, followed by a low sound of sorrow slipping from his parted mouth. The Keeper shouted in protest, grappling for the apothecary glass, but it was of no use.

The Seer, though, looked lit from within—triumph gathering around her like an impending storm. Her eyes, usually a rich brown, turned gold entirely: no pupils, no iris, just gleaming, glinting gold that tracked the moth fluttering above her head in a spiral. Then it banked, landing on the seer's chest. The moth's body rested against her sternum, its wings flattened on either side. The air hung sacred and thick, as if all of Time and Fate had always been waiting on this moment.

Then the Seer began to speak—her voice amplified, booming, louder than it had any right to be, ringing out through the space.

"WHEN THE WORLD IS SPLIT IN TWO, THE MAEVE OF THIRTEEN FROM O'ER THE HILL—NOT FROM BENEATH—WILL MEND WHAT IS SHATTERED. SHE WILL COMPLETE THE WORK OF THE

ONE WHO CAME BEFORE. SHE WILL WALK THE IN-BETWEEN BESIDE THE EXILED KING. SHE WILL TURN BACK THE TIMEKEEPER."

The Seer paused, her robes flowing around her on some invisible wind, looking not unlike a long-lost goddess only now returned to her rightful divinity.

"AND SO THE GATES SHALL FALL."

CHAPTER THIRTY

The words floated on the air like a pair of paper wings, translucent and beating with life. A golden swell of purpose gathered in Raegan's chest. Perhaps all the sorrow that marked her like an ink stain was not meaningless. Perhaps all roads had always led here, into a marble room with three ancient beings who spoke of Fate and Gates and magic.

"You have no idea what you have done, child," the Keeper said, shattering the silence. His voice sounded hollow, scooped out and empty.

The Keeper strode farther into the space from the doorway, and Raegan braced herself for further rebuke. But beyond a ragged sigh, the Keeper remained silent. He snatched the Prophecy's jar from the table and held his hand out to Raegan. Mutely, she placed the glass lid into his hands, gaze straying back to Cordelia. The velvet-draped seer's eyes were still flat, golden discs, but no wind fluttered her robes any longer. Raegan dared not look at the King.

But he stepped into her sight line anyway, moving toward Cordelia, his steps stilted and stiff, lacking their usual grace. He reached out two cupped hands—his fingers were shaking, Raegan noticed—toward the seer. With a soft beat of its wings, the luna moth left its perch on Cordelia's chest, and moved toward the King's palms with an eagerness Raegan felt in her own body. Together, the Keeper and the King returned the moth to the glass jar with startling ease. There was no question in Raegan's mind that the pair had done this before.

The King set the jar down onto the coffee table, resuming his stance beside her. Raegan craned her neck around his large frame, feverish for another look at the moth. When her eyes landed upon it, she saw with a start that it was just a paper thing. No life shimmered along its wings. It looked sad and flat and lonely inside the glass.

"The Oracle will understand," Cordelia said, breaking Raegan's thoughts. When she looked up, she noticed the seer's eyes had returned to their normal brown hue. "We had no choice, and really, we are just in time. I thought I was about to see the last of magic on this side of the Gates wither away entirely."

Confusion spiked Raegan. She narrowed her eyes, arms crossing on her chest before she realized she had moved at all. "Is *that* what's happening?" she asked, though she felt she already knew the answer, an understanding beginning to unfold in her mind. Such an idea, though, seemed impossible with all that she had seen—the kelpie and the King and the portico and all those divination rituals and the absolute terror and wonder of the Vaults.

The Keeper collapsed into one of the chairs by the moonstone desk, rubbing his temples with one hand. "In short, yes," he said, not meeting Raegan's gaze. "When the Timekeeper sealed the Gates, we were cut off from the Otherlands and left with only the residual magic already here. Magic is bleeding from this world—or perhaps it is better to say it is being choked out like a weed."

A delirious laugh clawed its way up Raegan's throat. These impossibly powerful beings needed *her*.

"Why wouldn't the Protectorate allow you to return to

the Otherlands?" Raegan inquired. She turned briefly toward the King. "Not you, obviously. But the rest of your people. The ones who just got stuck on the wrong side of the Gates. Wouldn't they rather that you be far away from humans?"

"How would the Protectorate ensure my own people hated me if they were simply allowed to cross the Gates?" the King asked her, one eyebrow arched, his tone turned rueful. "If I ever manage to return, reclaiming my throne will be nearly impossible. I am the reason the world was cleaved in two. I am the reason the remains of my court wander this half of the planet in exile, constantly pursued by the Protectorate with no hope of making a home. I am why lineages were ripped in half. Only some of us can survive so far from the Source."

"The Source?" Raegan inquired, her legs suddenly zapped of strength. She sank back onto the velvet chaise. "What, like a fountain or a Hill of Tara-esque place? Somewhere that all magic originates from?"

Cordelia's sharp gaze shot to Raegan, amusement playing on the seer's features. "You are taking to all of this with little issue," she said, her mouth curving into a dagger of a smile.

"I read a lot of books," Raegan replied, deadpan, leaning back on the chaise and crossing an ankle over her knee.

"It's an oversimplification," the Keeper said eventually, his brow furrowed. "But yes. Essentially."

She nodded and picked at a cuticle, wishing fervently for a printer, a corkboard, and a massive amount of thumbtacks. Everything happening around her, despite being mystical and absolutely beyond her wildest imagination, should still follow some kind of logic. She wanted to write it all out and pin it up on a wall until she found the connections.

Realizing there was a loose end, she looked up at the King and cocked her head. "How *did* you get exiled, anyway?" she demanded, her eyes narrowed. "The Protectorate would've had to capture you, right? How the fuck did they manage that?"

For a long time, the King simply searched her gaze. And again, he looked at her like he could see right into her, like he already knew all of her deepest secrets and oldest yearnings. Historically, Raegan was not a fan of being perceived. But she fervently hoped to be *seen*. She rarely was. And yet here was an impossible creature, ripped right from the pages of folklore, who looked at her like he knew her as well as the back of his hand.

She said nothing but held his gaze, wondering if she might be able to peer into him as easily he did into her.

"You truly do not remember?" the King asked, lowering himself onto the other end of the chaise in a way that made his suit jacket stretch tight across his broad, muscled shoulders. Something low in Raegan's belly thrummed.

"What could I possibly have to remember?" she demanded, the words stumbling and unconvincing, even to her own ears.

"The Protectorate managed to capture me," the King said, drawing out each word like an arrow from a quiver, "because of you."

Confusion swam thickly in Raegan's mind. She was distantly aware of Cordelia's attention suddenly snapping to her, the seer's gaze intense and hot.

"*Me?*" Raegan asked, her mouth dry. The question managed to leave her mouth despite how, the longer she looked at the King, the more she did not believe her own doubt. Too many conflicting images rose up from the silken depths within her.

A battlefield on a high hill, black smoke rising into the air. Someone who looked remarkably like the King but younger, his hair longer, looking over his shoulder at her, smiling in a way that exposed dimples. A river coursing madly before her, its waters darkened with rage and despair. A low-lit room, a fire-

place sputtering in the corner, skirts hitched around her waist, the gnarled wood of the table rough against the backs of her exposed thighs, the mouth of a raven-haired knight kneeling between her open legs softer than sin. Battlements built from uneven blocks of gray stone drenched in rain, her own voice cursing as she snatched a bow from a dead archer's body, and prayed to every god she knew that she could recall how to string an arrow.

By the time Raegan's mind was her own again and the undeniably vibrant memories—if that's what they were—cleared from her vision, she found herself back in the seer's workspace, the King kneeling before her in a way that was entirely too similar to what she had just seen. She scrambled away from him, her fingers clawing for purchase on the velvet chaise. She fought an urge to pull her feet up and hug them to her chest.

"Steady," the King murmured. "You were gone for some time."

Raegan bit on her tongue until she tasted blood, and did everything in her power to banish the image of the low-lit room with the sputtering fire. She tried to focus on the coursing river and the death and the black smoke. Somehow it was easier.

Dragging the heels of her palms across her eyes, she looked to one side to see the Keeper standing in front of the coffee table, lips pressed together as he watched her. A tray of tea sat on the table, steam curling up cozily from it. Cordelia had taken up residence by the doorway, her gaze trained on Raegan, eyes wide and arms crossed.

Panic eased a hand over her throat. Her skin crawled with a thousand hot pinpricks, and her stomach lurched, sweat gathering at the back of her neck and the base of her spine.

"Tea?" the Keeper asked unhelpfully, extending a cup to Raegan. She eyed him with what was probably best described as unbridled contempt, which she supposed was not precisely fair, seeing as he'd taken the time to make her tea while she tumbled uselessly through her own mind.

But the simple words to politely decline did not seem to exist in her brain. The King, still kneeling before her, raised a hand to gently push the Keeper's offered teacup away.

"Can you tell me your name?" the King asked, his voice costumed in a deep, warm tone. Perhaps it was meant to be soothing. It did not soothe her. Instead, it unspooled threads of heat in her core, a gentle throb erupting.

"Raegan," she replied, shoving a handful of curls off her damp forehead. "You want the year and the current US president too?"

Something entirely too playful pulled at the edges of the King's mouth before he stood, retrieving her leather jacket from the back of the chaise. She noticed another hitch in his movements; a rough spot in the endless grace.

"Though I appreciate your continued offer of hospitality," the King said to the Keeper with a regal bow of his head, "I think it is apparent that Overhill and I have much to discuss. We will take our leave."

Cordelia leapt forward at his words, frowning. "You don't get to shut us out," she said. "There is much to be deciphered about the Prophecy and so much we can do before the Oracle has even had a chance to return. This mortal is the key we've been searching for. I'm begging you—let me see what doors she can unlock."

Irritation spiked hot in Raegan's chest, and she watched, gratified, as the King's jaw clenched, his gaze falling heavy on Cordelia.

"Overhill is not a *key*," the King replied, his voice a thunderstorm rolling across the horizon. "She is a person. I will not have you speak of her as if she is some tool to be tinkered with."

Cordelia took a step toward the King and Raegan, planting herself in front of the doorway. Though she said nothing, her brows drew together and the pinch around her mouth promised unpleasantries.

"Regardless," the King continued, "before anything else, I believe Overhill needs rest."

Relief coursed through Raegan. She felt like she hadn't slept in days. She wanted fresh clothes. She wanted to be alone and *think*. She looked away from Cordelia for a heartbeat and found the King's eyes, heavy as an entire ocean, already upon her.

"And answers," he added, his tone gentler. "I believe some answers are owed. I would have rather avoided this entirely, but that moment has passed."

Then the King extended a hand down to her. Despite every story she had ever read about his kind, she took it. He helped Raegan to her feet, his larger hand engulfing her palm and part of her wrist. His touch sent her swimming in dark, electrifying currents. She fought to stay steady.

"We will be in contact," the King said, handing Raegan her jacket, which she accepted a beat too late. "The finer workings of this Prophecy need attention but in due time."

"They need attention *now*," Cordelia countered, looking toward the Keeper for support as her voice rose. "Are you going to place the needs of a mortal vessel over your own people? If she's really the reason you were exiled, why do you not seek revenge? How far does our once-mighty King plan to fall?"

Faster than Raegan's eyes could track, the King closed the distance to Cordelia, backing the seer into a corner. His broad frame engulfed hers entirely. In her peripheral vision, Raegan saw the Keeper's gaze widen as he rose from his chair in slow, deliberate movements. Quite suddenly, she recalled a childhood afternoon at the zoo when a toddler tipped over the fence of the panther enclosure. The zookeeper had moved just like the strange, neat man in his tidy suit did now: as if his calmness was all that stood between tender flesh and dismemberment.

"Do you want," the King asked of the seer in a tone that scattered chills down Raegan's spine, "to see *exactly* how far I can sink?"

As he spoke, all the shadows in the room unfurled from their hiding places. The diffused, warm light that seemed to emanate from the very core of the Oracle's Temple dissipated, as if snuffed out by the single breath of some forgotten beast's unhinged jaws.

"Cordelia," the Keeper warned, though his veneer of calm was shaken, arms held up in a stiff attempt at soothing. "He is our High King."

"Precisely," the seer seethed. "Which is why he should be willing to dissect this human piece by piece if that's what it takes to return our people to their home."

The King threw his head back and laughed. The sound of it was all wrong in Raegan's ears—none of that autumnal bell she'd heard earlier, only wolfish darkness heavy with warning.

"Child of barely two hundred summers," the King began, his voice thrumming as if every Unseelie regent had risen from their resting places to lend authority to his words, "you see so far but understand so little. Recall that I am Gwyn ap Nudd, the Render of Worlds, the King in Shadow. Do not make the mistake of threatening what is mine."

Something feral and sharp-toothed uncoiled in Raegan's core, a wildfire igniting deep in her core. A secret part of her yearned to see the King rip Cordelia and the Keeper limb from limb. Not for the sake of empty violence but because she was his and he was hers and any blood spilled would be in her name.

She tried not to be disappointed when Cordelia instead stepped to the side of the doorway, features pale with poorly masked fear. Raegan heard the Keeper let out a long, shaky breath as he shifted his weight back, arms dropping to his sides.

Pleased, the King turned to Raegan and offered his arm like they were about to stroll along a grassy promenade. She took it, desire sweeping through her body. He guided them under the archway and into the hall without a backwards glance at Cordelia or the Keeper.

In silence, they strode down the velvet-draped corridor, arriving once again in the marble lobby. Raegan focused on the sound of her boots on the stone floors, fighting the urge to check over her shoulder for a wild-eyed seer in pursuit. The thought did not frighten her, as perhaps it should have; she felt only prickly annoyance. Instead, what bid her heart to race and her head to spin was the King disentangling his arm from hers to place an open palm against the small of her back.

Raegan was no fool. She had an idea of what the misplaced memories and the strange feelings and the Keeper's words and Cordelia's reaction might mean. After all, she *did* read a lot of books.

Brows knit together, Raegan turned toward the King to find he was already looking down at her. Though she saw no cruelty in his expression, none of the tenderness she thought she had caught earlier remained, either. In a sudden rush, doubt replaced the desire.

"Let us depart before Cordelia has any more foolish ideas," the King said, gesturing toward the doorway.

She nodded, wanting to return to the part of the city she knew better, where she had an advantage, where she might be safe. Her mind turned over like an engine in the cold, suddenly calculating and sharp again.

Outside the Oracle's Temple, everything was human and mundane, just as Raegan had left it. Perhaps only she had changed. The yellow light of the setting sun was near-blinding. She shaded her eyes with her hand, trying to get her bearings now that they were back on mortal sidewalk, the familiar sounds of a neighborhood shopping center falling in around her.

The King lingered beneath the tattered awning above the storefront that somehow held endless wonders. A regular person in a green hoodie walked by, a plastic shopping bag dangling from their forearm as they replied to a text. With a start, Raegan dug into her pocket to retrieve her own phone.

Her screen lit up with a missed call and two texts from Henry, a voice memo from Saanvi, and sixteen new emails. Henry wanted to know if she had gotten anything on the story and had grown impatient in the hours since he'd first contacted her. The real world—*if* her world was still the real one—crashed down hard.

And with it came the suspicion of things that seemed too good, too storybook-slick, to be true.

CHAPTER THIRTY-ONE

"Are you fucking with my head?" Raegan demanded, wheeling on the King. Behind him, the Oracle's Temple had disappeared, replaced with the nondescript storefront. "These memories, these feelings, this sense that something bigger is going on—you could make me feel all of it, couldn't you?"

The King watched her with a guarded expression but said nothing.

"Answer me," Raegan hissed, taking an aggressive step toward him. "Could you?"

"It is within my power, yes," he replied, something she could not place flashing across his expression. "But it would take a considerable amount of energy, and I do not view it as a worthy expenditure."

She stomped a few steps down the sidewalk and then halted, remembering the King's words about physical proximity allowing him to better conceal them from the Protectorate. She clenched her jaw and wondered if that was even true or if it was just another way to pull her barriers down.

Dragging a hand through her hair, Raegan leaned back against the storefront's grimy windows. She squeezed her eyes shut. Her instincts were adrift; *nothing* felt real anymore. Everything had taken on a fairytale hue, edges rimmed with thorns and mist. She had no due north.

After a heavy exhale, she forced her eyes back open to find the King standing in front of her, watching her carefully, brows drawn together. She raised her gaze to meet his and hated that, in the ocean of his eyes, she found the only thing that felt real.

"It's smart," she admitted, rueful. "If you threaten your fellow Fey and storm out of there with me by your side, of course I'll think you care about me. You'll build on that trust, and then when the time comes, you'll cash in on it. And I'll probably be dead, but the Gates will be open and you'll have your throne back, won't you?" Raegan held her ground, back pressed against the window, arms crossed over her chest.

The King tilted his head as she spoke, mouth parting. Then he held her gaze for a long, skittering moment before stepping in close, his body mere inches from hers. "It would be so much easier," the King said, his head bowed like a sinner, voice low and reverent, "if that were true."

"Fuck you," Raegan snapped without half the venom she'd hoped to muster.

He smiled then, the curve of his full mouth sensual and the ocean in his eyes turned to slinking smoke. Her body pushed off the window of its own accord, pitching her into his realm of expensive black cloth and coiled muscle and damp stone. Tentatively, filled with as much desire as terror, Raegan laid the flat of her hand against the King's chest, right where his heart should be. He permitted it, watching her with that guarded expression again, though something like hope flickered in his gaze for a split second.

Heartbeats—probably even Fey ones—were practically indistinguishable without biomedical equipment, Raegan knew. And yet the slow, strong waves that pulsed through the cloth and into her palm felt like a song she'd forgotten she knew the words to, devoured by time and circumstance.

But then a shrill note sounded, shattering the moment. Her mind churned and she stepped back, the window meeting her spine. Moments passed thickly before she realized the sound was just her phone ringing in her pocket. Only three people's numbers were set to audibly ring with an incoming call: Henry, her mom, and . . .

Hands shaking, Raegan yanked her phone out, seized with a sureness that the person on the other end of the line was her father, resurrected by her actions, by her fierceness, by her quest. She answered the call without so much as glancing at the screen.

"Hello?" Raegan said with so much desperation that alarm rolled over the King's face.

"Raegan?" came the response. "You alive? I know it's your day off, but it's unusual to not hear from you for this long. And you are reporting on a possible serial killer, so . . ."

The hope she'd harbored in those precious moments spoiled and turned sour in her stomach. Bile rose in Raegan's throat—hardly a fair reaction to the voice of the best editor she'd ever worked for.

"Yeah, Henry, I'm fine," she replied, sagging back against the shop window. "Sorry. I managed to track down what could be a pretty incredible source, if they'll talk to me. I was hoping you were them, returning my call." She squeezed her eyes shut and prayed Henry accepted the lie.

"Well, I'll let you go, then," her editor said, sounding satisfied. "Looking forward to hearing about whatever you've found."

"I'll tell you all about it when I know more," Raegan assured him, trying to sound like the obsessed, workaholic journalist she'd always been. Anxiety gripped her insides and squeezed. She was supposed to be in the newsroom tomorrow, doing her job as if absolutely everything hadn't changed.

Henry hung up, leaving her with two halves that did not fit together—the career she had fought so hard for, and the quest she'd rather die than ignore. Her father had been the same, hadn't he? She did not seem entirely to blame for this glittering madness; it clearly ran in the family.

"Oh, fuck," Raegan realized suddenly, her tone loud and sharp as she looked up at the King. "Will the Protectorate go after my mom?"

He considered her question, head tilting slightly to one side. "Remind me how you remained undetected previously as we walk," the King said, offering Raegan his arm. She took it and hated that she immediately felt safer.

The King directed them north of the Oracle's Temple, a different path than they had approached it from. Raegan appreciated the precaution. As they walked, the neighborhood now punctuated with yellow school buses and children in uniforms exiting corner stores, she explained to him what little she knew of her father's protective warding—via Maelona, of course, who was hopefully still alive—that kept the family hidden.

"I think your mother is safe," he said, solemn. "Your father sounds proficient. I imagine your summoning of Rainer was the only reason the Protectorate detected you. Nothing ever occurred previously, correct?"

"As far as I know," Raegan said, kicking a piece of trash out of her way. The neighborhood smelled heavily of diesel exhaust from all the school buses. A cacophony of songs blaring from car windows, and the sound of storm doors creaking open and shut, filled the air.

"It is unlikely your mother also carries Protectorate blood," the King continued thoughtfully. "There are only a few original families left, and they do not intermarry; most already share some lineage. Your ability to do magic on this side of the Gates is thanks to the Protectorate's oath to the Timekeeper. It makes you much more easily discoverable. I would hazard that your father's working cloaked you entirely, but summoning Rainer shattered the illusion he had placed on you, making your magic as good as a beacon for the Protectorate."

Raegan's eyes went so blurry with the implication of that statement that she had to fight to keep the pavement in view ahead of her. "That means . . ." She trailed off, her tongue thick in her mouth.

It meant she would never know the rush of calling to the waters like she had in the coffee shop again. It meant whatever fantasies she had of being taught magic by a Fey king—unlikely, Raegan realized, but she was also far closer than the vast majority of people—seeped out of her. A tangle knotted itself in her stomach.

"Yes," the King replied, clipped, professional. "As long as the Protectorate reigns, you cannot do magic without inviting them to find you. But your mother should be safe. The Protectorate may be interested in her as leverage, if they can even find her beneath your father's spellwork, which I doubt."

Quite suddenly, Raegan wanted to sit down on the nearest stoop and cry. With all the ongoing turmoil, she hadn't even realized that she'd been holding the possibility of doing magic—real, actual, terrifying magic—tightly against her chest like a consolation prize. A promise to herself that no matter how fucked up everything got—no matter how dead, or maybe just uncaring, her father turned out to be—she had a chance at magic. A rosy-hued, delicately constructed chance, like something out of a storybook or a middle-schooler's daydream.

But now that hope fled, and she felt all the emptier for it. She reminded herself that at least her mother was safe. When she could think a bit more clearly again, hopefully after food and sleep and a shower, Raegan vowed to investigate that topic further.

She tried to bring her attention back to her body—the heaviness in her limbs, the broken glass winking in the street, the weed-choked alleyway the King had turned down. Up ahead, a brick wall sealed off the path. She hesitated, but then she caught sight of the now-familiar archway painted onto the wall.

"My archives have long operated as a safehouse," the King said as they came to a pause before the portico. He turned, gauging her reaction. "It is unwise for you to reside anywhere that lacks magical protection."

"Right," Raegan said, her voice sticking to the sides of her throat as the realization settled over her shoulders.

She'd known this was coming. She'd passed the point of no return, and now she couldn't have her old life back. Tipping her chin up, Raegan gazed at the strip of sky visible between the surrounding buildings. To her embarrassment, her eyes blurred with tears again.

"Do you know what you need right now?" the King asked. "It is understandable if you do not. We can return to my archives, and you may rest until you are more clear-headed."

"I'll need my meds and clothes and probably a few other things from my apartment," Raegan managed to get out, not looking at him, hating how pathetic she sounded. "But for now, I would really like a shower and to lie down."

"Of course," the King said and then gestured to the portico. "Are you ready to depart?"

A strange part of Raegan whispered—or, pleaded, really—that no, she was not. She turned to look at the entrance of the alleyway and watched another school bus putter by. Could this be the last time she belonged to the same world as the children on that bus and its driver seated at the wheel, in full control of where they drove next?

It was not that normalcy suddenly held any appeal. It was that she'd always imagined taking charge of how the stranger worlds bled into her own. Foolishly, she'd never thought that the wilder things would wrap themselves around her like marionette strings. But here Raegan was, crisscrossed in vines and threads and shadows.

Not having the will to speak aloud, she simply nodded her head. Then she allowed the King to sweep her into the ink-spill mouth of the portico and whatever awaited them beyond.

Chapter Thirty-Two

"And you're just going to let me stay *here*?" Raegan asked, annoyed that a hint of awe made its way into her voice.

But it was hard not to appreciate the space around her, and besides, it certainly felt less dangerous than appreciating the King himself. Instead of admiring ocean eyes and powerful shoulders, Raegan looked around the room again, taking in the stone walls and large fireplace, then the soaring ceiling studded with exposed beams. Ancient tapestries adorned the far wall, depicting decadent feasts and sprawling forests. A corner bookshelf towered a few paces from the fireplace, heavy with leatherbound volumes.

"Yes," the King replied evenly from where he stood at the entryway, leaning against the doorframe. "These are the safe-house quarters I offered."

It seemed impossible that the archives had been hiding so much during her first visit, but upon their return from the Oracle's Temple, Raegan discovered that the long wall beside the reading area concealed a door. When the right words were spoken, the door opened and led to a corridor housing a number of guest chambers.

"What's the toll? Will I owe something in return?" Raegan asked, fatigue seeping into her voice. The soft-looking bed dressed in cozy flannels across the room seemed at odds with what the Fey usually offered mortals in all the stories she'd ever read.

"I said I would ensure your safety," the King replied, pushing off the doorframe to stand straight as an arrow. "You cannot return to your home. I offer this freely in its stead."

She told herself she'd imagined the tiny flicker of hurt that crossed his features for a moment, or that he had engineered it. She was dealing with the Sidhe, after all, which made her want to examine every loophole and contort her thinking to keep up with the wily, ancient beings. But right now, she just couldn't. The day had been too long, her body was too weary, and even her tongue felt heavy. Her jaw hurt, surely from grinding her teeth all day.

"I appreciate it," she said eventually, looking down at her shoes, looking anywhere but at him.

"I will remain in the archive portion," the King replied. "If you should require anything, or want to discuss something, you may seek me."

And then he was gone, slipping away into the shadows of the stone hallway. Raegan was left with a door slowly creaking closed and the silence of the space around her. She took a deep breath. The air carried the same scent as the King's office—warm smoke, shimmering chestnut and a deep, bitter vanilla.

Raegan chewed the inside of her cheek, considering her options. She could chase after him and demand answers. But she couldn't form the questions no matter how many times she practiced them in her head. An unearthly beautiful, unimaginably powerful, and terribly ancient Fey king showed up and was not only willing to help her, but also *knew* her, felt something for her, brought memories rushing to the surface . . .

If someone asked Raegan for her opinion on such a situation, she'd laugh in their face and say they were being tricked by the Fair Folk—a tale as old as time. It didn't matter how real any of it felt or how badly she wanted him. Believing any of it was a fool's game, and she'd never been a fucking fool.

So she took three deep breaths, pulled off her boots, and went to investigate the bathroom instead.

"Holy shit," Raegan murmured, looking around the space with wide eyes.

Like so much of the archives and the King's office, it felt like she could've designed it herself. Light from two sconces danced over the stone walls and floors. A large claw-foot tub lounged in the far corner, and a rainfall showerhead sprouted from the wall above it. Beside the tub, fluffy towels were piled high on an antique chair, a bar of soap in pretty paper wrapping balanced on top.

She didn't bother looking at the rest of the room. Raegan marched to the edge of the tub, cranked the spigot until the water was almost too hot, and then stripped, discarding her clothes on the floor without a second glance.

The bliss of the hot water sliding around her skin pulled a long sigh from her mouth. Her eyes closed in a matter of seconds. For the first time all day, her shoulders sagged and her jaw relaxed.

Raegan told herself she'd get out when the water cooled off. But the minutes slipped away from her on silken strands and by the time she was feeling a bit better—and had become rather pruney, too—the water temperature hadn't dropped. In fact, sweat began to cling to the back of her neck and her hairline.

"Magic," she muttered, frustrated at herself for thinking a bathtub in a Fey king's accommodations would do something so mundane as get cold.

She gathered her hair up with one hand and stood, a groan escaping her at the pull of muscles and catching of joints. After washing up, she rinsed off and pulled a towel from the chair. Then Raegan stepped out of the tub, confused to find her clothes were no longer in their unceremonious pile on the floor. Instead, a quick glance around the bathroom revealed her garments neatly folded on the vanity, nestled between two porcelain sinks. She distantly wondered if there was some kind of tidying enchantment at work, but when she approached the vanity to dress, something else entirely caught her attention.

A small piece of paper, folded over more than once, sat atop her sweater. Raegan frowned and darted for the note, as if it might change its mind and flutter away. She stood there, naked and damp, water droplets still adorning her collarbone and the soft slopes of her belly, and unfolded the paper.

Typed upon it was a list of locations, pros and cons noted beneath each place in an indented paragraph. Raegan furrowed her brow, trying to understand and failing—until she saw the scribbled, handwritten message at the bottom.

Don't contact Bronwyn. Will break Cormac's cloaking. She's safe.

And then it all came flooding back to her—the piece of paper Maelona had unfolded at the café, talking about places Raegan might live a life away from the Protectorate, the Fey, and everything else that she was now firmly steeped in. She traced damp, shaking fingers over the words Maelona had somehow managed to write in all of the mayhem. And then she sighed, letting the note flutter onto the vanity.

At least her mother was safe. Both Maelona and the King seemed to think so, which she supposed was the best evaluation she'd ever get. But she had not considered that even contacting her mom would break the spellwork her father had so painstakingly set to keep their family safe. She didn't know why her father would leave the book in the basement and the spell in the lockbox if the simple act of her doing magic could endanger everyone. With a heavy sigh, Raegan let her head fall back, tilting her chin toward the ceiling.

Oh. Of course. Whatever her dad had done was

segmented, designed to keep working on one side even if the other broke—as if he knew Raegan would never be able to resist the siren song, or at least he didn't wish to risk it. She thought back to the way her mom couldn't even see the book he'd left for her, and she wondered if he'd concealed it from Bronwyn, leaving it visible only to Raegan's eyes. Because her father had *known* her, had recognized that same glinting strangeness in his daughter.

Fresh grief rolled through Raegan's chest, but she told herself to focus on dressing instead of dissolving into tears. Gingerly moving the note to the side, she unfolded her sweater. When she pulled it over her head, it smelled like she had just gotten it out of the dryer. She lifted the hem and took a deep inhale of the fabric. Yes—definitely laundered, definitely accomplished by whatever enchantment was woven over the bathroom.

The simple gift of clean clothing on clean skin helped Raegan refocus, shoving the torment down for at least a little bit longer. Plucking Maelona's note from the vanity, she walked out of the bathroom and searched the room for writing paper and a pen. After a few minutes, several curses, and at least fifty percent more drama than necessary, Raegan emerged triumphant with a cracked leather notebook and a 1960s-era pack of sharpened pencils.

She darted for the worn-in leather couch in front of the fireplace. Curling her legs up underneath her, she began to write down everything she knew. It only filled up about half a page, which was depressing to look at. She drew a line beneath the information and, in the new section below, wrote out what she remembered of the Prophecy.

"When the world is split in two," she muttered under her breath, the words she scribbled keeping pace with her voice, "the Maeve of thirteen from over the hill—not beneath—will complete the work of the one who came before. She will walk beside the exiled King and turn back the Timekeeper. And so the Gates shall open."

Or something like that. It was close enough to try to dissect each line.

"World split in two"—current state of affairs, the Gates separating the world with magic and the world without.

"Maeve of thirteen"—me, it seems. My middle name is Maeve. Born January 13th.

"From over the hill"—a human; not someone from beneath the hill, i.e. the Fey. Also, my last name, obviously.

"Work of the one who came before"—

Raegan froze. Information crystallized quickly in her mind, connections jumping together now that she had finally been able to follow her process of putting words to paper.

"Fuck," she said to no one, drawing out the word. Adrenaline shot through her veins, hot and energizing. God, she hoped she was right about this.

Raegan stood, her breathing hard and quick as she tucked the notebook into her pocket. She willed her heart rate to slow down, but it only climbed higher, thumping louder and louder in her chest and then her throat. She made for the door, ignoring her discarded boots, and sprinted down the corridor that led back to the archives.

She was almost surprised when she found the King there, exactly where he'd said he would be, standing at the worktable and examining a large piece of parchment. He had removed his suit jacket and rolled his sleeves to the elbow, exposing the coiled muscles of his forearms. A few buttons were loosened at the top of his shirt as well, she noticed.

Raegan forced herself to focus as the King looked over at

her. He said nothing, eyes shadowed in the low, warm light of the archives.

With one last deep breath, she stepped forward from the threshold, arms at her sides, shoulders back and spine straight. "I am in possession of something the Prophecy needs to come true," she said. "And if you want to see it, we need to renegotiate our deal."

CHAPTER THIRTY-THREE

Adrenaline pounded loudly in her eardrums. Her heart climbed another inch in her throat every second the King said nothing at all. He only watched her, not even shifting from his stance: palms flat and shoulder-width apart, supporting his weight as he leaned over the table.

For what felt like the thousandth time in only a few hours, Raegan told herself not to look away from his infinite, ice-gray eyes.

"If any other mortal claimed to be in possession of something so earth-shattering," the King finally said, one brow arching, "I would likely disregard it entirely."

Raegan permitted herself a tiny smile and walked closer, clasping her hands behind her back. "But I'm not just any mortal, am I?" she asked, stopping a few paces from him. With a sigh, she hinged at the hips to lean over the worktable. Then she rested her elbow on the well-worn surface, propping her chin up on her hand. "So you can't just disregard it, I suppose."

The King's gaze dripped from her eyes to her mouth, from her mouth to her collarbones, and then lower still. He blinked slowly before meeting her gaze once more, head tilted and sculptural lips parted. Something dangerously close to a challenge flickered across his expression.

"Oh, I certainly can," he replied with a shrug of his powerful shoulders. Then the King returned to studying the manuscript unrolled in front of him.

Normally, being so easily dismissed would infuriate Raegan. But from the King, it wasn't just a simple dismissal. Instead, it felt like a gauntlet drop. But more than that—as loath as she was to trust this particular instinct of hers—it felt a hell of a lot like flirting.

And so, with a confidence instilled solely by the fact that the Unseelie King had not only refrained from killing her but also possibly flirted with her, Raegan slid closer. Then she reached over and tapped the middle of the manuscript he was inspecting with one hand. "Hey," she said, her voice lower now. "I was not done speaking with you."

Without raising his head, the King looked at her sidelong, his lips parting again. A thrumming uncurled in the center of Raegan's body, the beat of it so thick and sweet that it took all of her willpower to ignore the sensation. She wanted to blame it on the King's magic, on some kind of thrall or enchantment, but she knew without a single doubt that the desire she felt for the dark-eyed, lithe, and dangerous creature belonged to her alone.

"Nice try," she said, lifting her eyebrows appreciatively, her hand still splayed over the manuscript, "but it will take more than some pretty eyes to distract me."

To his credit, the King hit her with the most sensual half-smile she had probably ever seen, the curve of his mouth saying more than words ever could. Open desire claimed the cavity of her chest, sending daggers of heat into her flesh.

"You find my eyes pretty?" he murmured, mirroring her stance now, dropping his weight to his elbows and propping his chin up on one large hand.

Raegan watched him, eyes narrowed, trying to decide how she wanted to proceed. If she played too far into his response, she'd get caught up in it all and probably attempt to climb the High King of the Unseelie Court like a particularly broad tree.

So she moved to diffuse instead, even though the fire kindling in her belly begged for the opposite. "I'm trying to speak *seriously* at the moment," Raegan continued, removing her hand from the manuscript, looking at the ancient Fey as if he were a very naughty little boy. "I know what a certain section of the Prophecy is referring to. I would wager it's the part you haven't been able to puzzle out."

The King immediately stood up to his full height, crossing his arms. Raegan had to hand it to him—the cool, slick composure was back so quickly it was hard not to be impressed, though she preferred the molten core that lingered beneath.

"A bold wager," he told her, reaching for a steaming teacup set off at the end of the table and taking a drink. Raegan did her best not to notice how deft his hands were despite their size—how a bone china teacup, its construction so thin and delicate that light shone through it, was not reduced to ash between his fingers. She wondered how she would fare there.

"I've been called bold before," Raegan replied with a dazzling grin, standing up straight and sliding her hands into her pockets. In the background, a fireplace she hadn't noticed before popped and sputtered, scattering molasses-colored light into the imposing space. "My request is simple."

"And yet I still do not know what you can offer me," the King said, one dark brow arching, his voice dripping from his mouth like honey.

"The work of the one who came before," was all Raegan said.

It was all she needed to say. This was the moment she had been building toward, trying her best during all the foreplay to not directly mention it, studying the King's expression the entire time, wagering that she just might be able to catch enough of a glimpse to know if she was correct.

And catch it she did—there and gone in his eyes, quick as a comet, but Raegan saw what she was looking for. Just the tiniest flash of interest, barely more than a glint that could've been attributed to the light of the nearby fire. But she also noticed the way the King's eyes narrowed ever so slightly, as if he had found something worth studying further. Raegan had absolutely no idea why she felt she could read him this clearly, but she did.

"You can save your protests," she said with a wave of her hand. "I *know* you, and I know you haven't the foggiest what that part of the Prophecy means."

The words tumbled out before she could stop them, leaving Raegan and the King regarding each other in the golden, softly wavering light. A wave of emotion crested at the back of her throat, thick with a longing so bottomless that for a heartbeat Raegan was not sure if she had ever felt anything else.

Against all odds, the King saved her. "Let us say I *am* stumbling over that section of the Prophecy," he said, diplomatic and regal, steepling his fingers. "And let us say that you, a mortal who only discovered all of this existed a few hours ago, somehow holds the answer. What do you desire in return?"

Raegan's breath caught in her throat. Oh, what a loaded word—*desire*. There was much she desired, so many things she hungered for that had never been hers to taste.

"I desire," she managed, willing herself to finish the sentence in the way she knew she must, "for you to be on my side. Through all of this. I don't want simply your agreement to act in specific ways I must painstakingly hash out. I want you. On my side."

Those had not been the words she'd meant to use. She had

no desire to reveal the depths of the ferocious hunger uncoiling low in her belly.

The King took too long to answer. She watched his chest rise and fall, his breath harder and faster than the situation called for.

"I am the High King of the Unseelie Court," he said, the words correct but the tone all wrong, a pale imitation of the cool, unaffected Fey being she'd first met. "I cannot act against the interests of my court. Not even if I desired your offering. Which I . . . which I do not."

Raegan did everything in her power to bite back a grin as she watched the fairy king stumble over his words. She had him. Triumph and lust mingled in her veins, thick as ambrosia.

"I thought you might say that," she replied with a shrug, fighting to display indifference. "I don't blame you. I would simply show you if I could, but the necessary object is at my apartment, where I believe you were quite insistent I do *not* go."

And then the King moved—faster, so much hopelessly faster than she could track—to stand right before her, mere inches separating them. Autumn rain and woodsmoke rolled over her senses. "Overhill," the King said, looking down at her, his head cocked in a way that brought to mind large predatory birds. "Are you attempting to lure me to a location the Protectorate is also familiar with?"

Fuck. She hadn't considered that part, which she supposed was exactly what she deserved for thinking this idea through for all of thirty seconds. Raegan's mind raced, trying to find the right words to smooth this misunderstanding over. Apparently, she did not speak fast enough, because suddenly the King caught her jaw between his long fingers and leaned down so their eyes were level.

"Do not," he said, his voice a low murmur, "become more trouble than you are worth."

Her flight or fight should have been screaming. It wasn't.

The King's touch was, against all sense, gentle. Considering the situation, she'd expect his fingers to dig into her flesh, for the King to force her to look directly at him. None of those things were happening. She had the sudden, distinct impression that if she only took a single step back, he would release her entirely.

And yet she stayed exactly where she was. "Precisely how much trouble *am* I worth?" Raegan asked, raising her eyes to meet his oceanic gaze.

The King's breath caught in his throat, and she fought the urge to slam her mouth against his. The keening in her core erupted into a howl. He held her gaze, the muscles in his jaw catching. She pressed the advantage, grabbing the wrist of the hand he had on her chin. Beneath her fingers, she felt his cool skin, and beneath that, his racing pulse.

"Answer me," Raegan demanded.

The King studied her but did not release his grasp—nor Raegan hers—and she watched as something like a forest fire rolled over his features. All at once, she became aware that her skin was touching the King's in two separate places, mostly on account of the way her mind bucked and boiled like a sudden squall.

Just before her vision clouded over completely, the King let go of her, straightening. "Get your shoes," he told her.

"What?" Raegan asked despite herself, the word coming out in a high-pitched, bewildered tone.

The King rolled up the manuscript on the table and slid it into a leather case before reaching for his teacup and draining the remaining liquid. "We are going to see if you are telling the truth," he replied, making eye contact with her as he began to roll his shirt sleeves back down, "or if you are going to die tonight."

Chapter Thirty-Four

Out on the sidewalk, beneath the dark sweeps of the autumnal evening, the King offered Raegan his arm. She took it despite the very credible death threat he'd made no more than five minutes prior. Mostly because—if she was being honest—he looked very good in his charcoal wool overcoat and black three-piece suit.

"You people take your manners so seriously one moment," Raegan grumbled, falling in step beside him, "and then threaten to kill people the next. It's absurd."

She told herself she'd imagined the way one corner of his mouth curved up, a trick of the neighborhood's nighttime dress of murky streetlight, cigarette smoke and antique shadows.

"I have always found it polite," the King replied, looking over at her, "to be clear about one's intentions."

"Oh, yes, you're extremely clear-cut and straightforward," Raegan snorted in reply, rolling her eyes.

He said nothing, and for a moment she thought she'd offended him—goddamn fairy kings—but then she actually thought about it.

"Fine," she added, quickening her step to match his much longer ones as they crossed the street. "I'm not *aware* of any misdirection. But I guess you all can't lie, or whatever. Right?"

The King made a low sound of consideration from somewhere deep in his chest that did not help dissuade Raegan from wanting him to slam her into a wall and fuck her as hard as he could. She swallowed and looked down, trying to focus on avoiding cracks in the sidewalk.

"Your people think we cannot," the King eventually offered, sounding amused with himself.

Raegan swatted at his shoulder in response, releasing a dramatic, exasperated sigh. Again, she told herself that it was only the skittering light of the streetlamps that made her think he had smiled. She shook her head and slid her free hand into her pocket, fingers meeting the cool surface of her phone. All the levity of the moment swept out like a tidal wave. Her real life still existed somewhere. Steeling herself, she checked her home screen.

Predictably, more texts from Henry. Another voice memo from Saanvi, then an hour later, a simple text that read, *you okay?* A missed call from her mother. No text follow-up, though, so there wasn't an emergency.

Anxiety knotted in her stomach as she stared at her screen, trying to decide what to do and what was real. Her steps became more like stomps, and she saw the King tilt his gaze in her direction, though he said nothing. Raegan gritted her teeth. She was finally, *finally*, on a quest. Why couldn't everyone leave her the hell alone?

"Is everything alright?" the King asked, his voice coming from close to her ear, like he had leaned toward her to speak.

In response, Raegan let out a derisive laugh. "Obviously not," she replied, biting down on the inside of her cheek. "But it's all dumb mortal stuff. I doubt you'd care."

In the passing glow of the streetlight, she watched the

King's expression stiffen. "Per our bargain, I am required to care about your well-being," he replied, some of the previous languor seeping out of his tone. "That being the case, if something is troubling you, I will do my best to assist."

Raegan told herself to breathe for a few seconds, but sorrow had been brewing inside her all day, and now it had fermented into anger. "Fuck off," she spat at the King, tilting her chin up at him. "You could probably fix every problem in the world with a wave of your fancy fucking faerie hand, and yet you haven't, have you? You're here because you want the Gates open. Let's not pretend otherwise, yeah?"

Her words were as much a reminder for herself as they were barbs for the King. It didn't matter that just now, as they walked arm-in-arm, their bodies slotted together perfectly, like they'd been made from the same stardust. It didn't matter that, against all reason, the King seemed capable of seeing the truth of her beyond all the layers of bluster and misdirection. And it certainly didn't matter that Raegan was probably more attracted to him than she had ever been to anyone else in her entire life.

The King slammed to a standstill in the middle of the sidewalk, so abrupt that Raegan tripped a little. She looked up at him, ready to spit venom, but the expression on his face cut off the words in her throat. His eyes were an ocean in a storm, the muscles of his jaw standing out harshly beneath his pale skin, dark brows drawn together.

"Do not mistake me, Overhill," the King replied, his voice like black ice. "I have done everything in my power—and more —to remedy the plight my people face. It consumes me. If our liberation were so simple an exercise, understand I would have done it, no matter the cost, a millennium ago."

Raegan realized with a shaking breath that she'd actually made him angry, possibly for the first time. For once, nothing about the King was slick or calculated or cunning. Of all places, it was here in the glow of a French café to her left, among its outdoor bistro tables, that he had drawn himself up like a snake about to strike. And of all things, it was over the idea that he had not done everything he could.

Interesting.

"Look, I didn't mean to offend you," Raegan attempted, but one look from the King cut her off.

"And for *you*?" he continued, glowering down at her, the intensity of his gaze palpable on her skin. "For you, I have—"

He halted, swallowing the words, looking away from her, sharp profile glowing against the dusk sky. Before Raegan could say anything, he began to walk again, pulling her along with him. She followed a few steps in silence, glancing over to see the storm still brewing across the King's features. How she wanted to poke and prod, to see what would make the thunder rumble and the lightning strike.

But she had the strangest feeling she would be pouring salt in her own wounds somehow, like maybe she and the King shared the same tender, aching places. She spent the next block clenching her jaw, telling herself that the idea was not only infinitely stupid but also impossible.

And yet it did not leave her.

"We will be taking the underground," the King said, his tone again clipped and professional. "I would like to engage in as little magic as possible."

Raegan nodded but did not reply, reaching her free hand out to trail her fingers along the iron fence of a church courtyard to her right. Up ahead, a sycamore tree draped over the gate, dappling the sidewalk with scraps of red and yellow silk, an autumnal fairy carpet. She took a deep breath and then another, the familiar scent of cigarettes and car exhaust and cool air soothing her a bit.

They slipped past a rowdy group of bar goers wearing matching t-shirts, and then the King led Raegan to the mouth of the subway entrance. She slipped her arm tighter into his, a response to the evening bustle of the station and the threat of the Protectorate, and absolutely nothing else.

Jogging down the stairs to keep time with the King's long strides, Raegan asked, "Does doing less magic make it harder to find us?"

"Precisely," the King replied, casting a wary eye out around the belly of the subway station. The daily commuter traffic was over, but the night had descended cool and crisp, so the city would surely be bulging at the seams.

Raegan tracked his gaze, understanding that the time of day actually made it harder to see who didn't belong. Restaurant workers mixed with corporate professionals headed home from happy hour, night shift nurses stepping off subway cars behind fresh-to-the-city college students. At least during rush hour, miserable as it may have been, the Protectorate would've been easier to spot.

"This way," she said, gesturing toward the correct platform to return to her apartment. They walked through the turnstiles, Raegan amused to find that instead of tapping a pass, the King simply waved his hand over the scanner. Forced to shuffle through side-by-side to maintain physical contact, she wondered if they looked like two people so in love that they couldn't bear to forgo touch for even a moment. She wondered what that might feel like.

When they reached the platform, which was blessedly quiet and relatively empty, the memory of seeing the King for the first time from the subway car lodged itself between Raegan's ribs. A wave of emotion caught at the back of her throat, and despite the layers of fabric between them, she suddenly felt overwhelmed by the King's proximity.

An express train flew through the station, all screeching metal and howling wind. When it passed, Raegan busied herself with reading the flier that had settled like a strewn leaf at her feet. For a few seconds, she was convinced the text was in a language she could not read. But bewilderingly, she realized the flier was very much printed in English, advertising a flea market.

"Did you see me, too?" Raegan asked, having no idea where the courage to say the words came from. "A few days ago, on the train? At the City Hall station?"

She was not in the habit of asking questions she did not already know—or at least suspect—the answers to, but this hushed inquiry made in the dim, gray-walled cavern of the subway platform shattered that rule. She had no idea how the Unseelie King might answer her, and even more so, Raegan had no idea what the implications of that answer would be.

He turned to her, his brow creased, looking impossibly lonely and tired. His gaze met hers and then drifted away, only to return again. "Yes," he replied, the word coming out hoarse and empty, a dried-out husk.

Raegan's heart was beating faster, and time seemed to have slowed down, as if it were moving around her in a circle instead of dragging her forward on its usual current. At least twenty words tried to climb her dry, aching throat before she thought of the right ones.

"What is going on here?" she asked, her voice low and reverent even though they were now alone on the platform. "Beyond the rest. What is going on underneath?"

His perfect alabaster skin nearly sallow in the green-hued lighting, a phantom wind kicking up the ends of his overcoat, the King almost looked familiar. Something surfaced from the depths of his gray eyes that Raegan thought she might have seen a thousand times before. And then it blinked out of existence.

"Let us stay focused on what is to come, not what has already passed," he replied, cool but not unkind, straightening the line of his shoulders.

Raegan's every instinct was, of course, to push and pry. But instead, she was overcome with a bone-deep exhaustion. Time felt strange again. Hadn't they been on this platform for

at least a hundred years? Everything she did felt like a repeat—
the way civilizations are built on top of the bones of the ones
that came before, just for those cities to fall, too, and provide
stable footing for the next swell of humanity.

So instead, she simply fixed her eyes on the track and
waited for the train to come.

Chapter Thirty-Five

Raegan and the King boarded the subway without speaking to each other. The car was barely half-full, and she pulled him toward the open seats at the back, away from the other riders. They settled onto the worn vinyl, Raegan's left arm and shoulder pressed up against him. She told herself some degree of physical contact eased his burden of hiding them away from prying eyes, but there was absolutely no reason to lean into his warm, sturdy mass.

The subway lurched into motion, sending an empty coffee cup skittering across the floor. Something hung between the two of them—something they had been talking about on the platform, Raegan thought. Though she couldn't get her head around exactly *what*. She dragged her right hand through her hair. It had been a long day. Of course she felt a bit scrambled.

In a completely different world, the sway of the subway car might lull her into drowsiness, and she might rest her head against the King's substantial shoulder.

Instead, she straightened and cleared her throat. "What should I expect?" Raegan asked, as if that would quell the anxiety twisting her insides.

"It is likely your living quarters have already been

disturbed," the King replied, looking over at her. "If that is so, you will feel violated and angry—a normal response. Beyond that, I doubt we will get through this evening without a Protectorate interaction."

A chill seared its way down her spine. Why had she been thinking they'd just take a friendly jaunt to her apartment and back? Of course this was going to be unpleasant, and she chided herself for imagining otherwise.

"Stay close, follow my instructions," the King added, his voice low and intense, "and no harm will come to you."

She sucked on her teeth and slunk farther down in the slippery seat. How badly she wanted to trust him. It would be so much easier to stop fighting the tide that pulled her toward him, telling her they had always kept each other safe. But he was an immortal Fey king and she was a mere mortal woman, and she'd read that story often enough to know where it usually ended.

So Raegan just nodded, letting the back of her head rest on the top of the seat. She stretched her legs out in front of her, crossed at the ankles, and watched another passenger farther up in the car who was busy knitting. The needles moved back and forth, weaving smaller, separate strands into one singular, grander thing.

"This is it," Raegan said to the King when the subway slowed a few minutes later, pulling into her station. She sat up and slid her arm through his without a word. Together, they walked onto the platform and then up the stairs, avoiding the debris that always seemed to line every crevice and corner in her city.

Anxiety coiled thick and sour in her stomach with every step. She couldn't shake the feeling that she was abandoning the safety of her nest for the terrors of the wide world outside. But letting the King go alone wasn't an option— her father's spell was her only foothold, and it was a weak one at that. How hard would it be for an ancient Fey being to simply take the sheets of parchment from her, if he wanted?

As they reached the top of the subway stairs, Raegan turned to examine the King in the glow of the evening. Above him, the moon—a slim, elegant crescent—had emerged into the sky. Two otherworldly things side-by-side that she could see but not fully comprehend.

"This way," she said, trying to pull him across the street. But the King didn't budge against her weight. She looked over her shoulder at him, eyes narrowed.

"We cannot march in down the sidewalk," he told her, one eyebrow arched. Then he gestured to the side, where the worn awning of a closed deli created a velvety swathe of darkness on the walkway.

Raegan followed him with skeptical, tender steps, a hidden part of her wishing they were ducking into the shadows for another reason entirely.

Once the dimness had swallowed them, the King spoke again. "If you permit it, I would like for you to show me the way to your home," he said. "To remain less noticeable, I will be employing a cruder method that requires me to touch you. Do I have your consent?"

Raegan had to bite her tongue to stop the word "yes" from leaving her mouth immediately. Because of *course* he had her consent—the dark-haired, lithe-limbed creature knew her body better than anyone, had touched every inch of her a thousand times before.

She let out a long exhale, looking down at her shoes, barely distinguishable from the sidewalk in the awning's shadow. Regardless of how she felt, Raegan would be damned before she gave any Fey blanket consent like that.

"You have my consent to touch me for this specific situation and only to aid your knowledge of reaching my apartment in the safest way possible considering the threat of the Protectorate," Raegan finally replied, raising her gaze to his.

Even in the dark, she found his storm-gray eyes with ease. "But I retain the right to revoke that consent at any time."

A flash of white—a smile, she realized—and then she felt the King step in closer to her. "Well done," he murmured, a rumble in his chest. Then his large, powerful hands were upon her.

Raegan suppressed the roll of pleasure that moved through her body as the King's fingers brushed the place where her jaw met her neck. Both of his hands moved upward in a gentle swoop, coming to cradle the back of her head. She swallowed hard and tried to think of anything but the way their bodies pressed together, all her soft curves against his hard angles.

"Please picture the route to your home," the King commanded, though there was a slight hitch in his voice. Raegan furiously told herself it was only because he was concentrating and not because of her.

Biting down on the inside of her cheek, she walked the first few blocks in her mind's eye with minimal issue, carefully mapping every turn and footstep. As she drew closer to her front door, she no longer walked the path alone; instead, the presence of the King became undeniable. Heavy, dark, certain, and relentless, half a step behind her, so like her dream in the autumn meadow with the river in the distance—

The King pulled back suddenly, one hand falling to her shoulder, the other pinching the bridge of his nose. Though the dimness made it difficult to be certain, she thought his eyes might be squeezed shut, hard.

"Sorry," Raegan murmured, heat rising to her cheeks.

"It is alright," the King replied, not looking at her. "What are the remaining directions?"

She told him the final two turns and then gave a description of her building. He nodded, looking out from beneath the awning and into the night.

"Are you ready?" the King asked, his tone solemn now.

"I mean, I guess," Raegan replied with a shrug. "I have no real idea what I'm getting myself into. So fuck it."

He turned back, gaze meeting hers again. A cold steel lingered in his expression. "I will not allow any harm to come to you," the King said, the line of his shoulders and the clench of his jaw so fierce that she had no choice but to believe him.

Before Raegan could say anything, he slipped his arm back through hers and swept them out into the night. The first few blocks passed slow and tense. The King moved methodically, sticking to the shadows, doubling back, stopping and waiting at odd intervals.

"There is only one entrance, yes?" he asked a block from her apartment.

"Yeah," Raegan replied with a nod, distracted. It was hard not to see every pedestrian they passed as possible Protectorate. Even the pack of overgrown frat boys on the last street felt suspect to her—it'd be a damn good disguise, wouldn't it?

Beside her, the King grumbled something about fire hazards. Any other time she'd demand how in god's name an Unseelie regent had an opinion on human safety codes, but at the moment, her heart was in her throat, and it took every ounce of her willpower to keep walking. She felt violated. The idea that the familiar comforts of her neighborhood—the soaring alleyways and imposing industrial buildings and over-grown weeds woven into chain-link fences like a patchwork quilt—could all suddenly become a threat was terrifying. And infuriating. How much more did the Protectorate plan to take from her?

"Steady," the King murmured beside her, as if he had continued access to her thoughts.

She hated how much the scant syllables spoken in his low, melodic voice actually did soothe her. *Steady.* All she had to do was stay the course. Raegan skirted a piece of free furniture left out on the sidewalk, feeling some of her anger solidifying into determination. Though mortal, she was still a force to be reckoned with, and she had a literal Fey king at her side.

Approximately three seconds later, the King dragged her into an alleyway, shattering the veneer she'd been constructing. Raegan didn't even have a moment to catch her breath before he pulled her into his chest, his back against the stucco wall.

"Be silent," the King said between his teeth, the words just barely audible. She nodded, wondering how loudly her heart was beating. Whether it was in response to the potential threat or to the way the front of her body was flush against the King, one of his strong arms tightly wound around her waist, was anyone's guess. Black pepper and autumn leaves filled her senses, banishing the alley's scent of damp rot.

Too soon, the King released her and pushed off the wall. Backlit by the streetlamp, his strong features stood out against the night, his eyes nearly black, chin tilted up as if he could catch the Protectorate's scent in the air.

"We must be quick," he said after a few moments, looking over at her. "Your neighborhood is infested."

"Protectorate?" Raegan asked, just to be sure, in a near-whisper.

The King nodded, impossibly regal even in an alleyway filled with trash and knee-high weeds. "I will offer them a distraction," he told her. "And then we will move."

He reached deep into his pocket and retrieved a long, elegant vial—not dissimilar to an antique perfume bottle. From the vial, he pulled something so gossamer-thin that Raegan could barely make it out in the dim light. Then he cupped it in his hand and blew on it gently, sending the object spinning into the air like a wish made on a dandelion.

Raegan opened her mouth to ask if an ancient organization dedicated to fighting the Fair Folk would really fall for something so simple as a distraction. But then the ground shivered beneath her, like someone had run their fingers along the back of an attention-hungry feline. She felt *something* stretch, claws experimentally flexed.

In the distance, beyond the ever-present murmur of sirens and car radios and the hum of the subway below, a roar shattered the night. The sound of it cut right into Raegan's body, like a cold wind through a flimsy shirt.

"What the fuck," she muttered despite herself.

"*Cath Palug*," the King replied, his voice cool and even, like she'd asked about the weather. "She gifted me three of her whiskers some time ago. A debt paid."

Raegan's head snapped toward the King so fast she thought she might've given herself whiplash. "The giant cat?" she demanded. "Didn't Sir Kay kill it, like, hundreds of years ago?"

The King tipped his head back and laughed as if the idea of a human knight killing a monstrous faerie cat was the most amusing thing he'd ever heard. And then, without answering, he grabbed Raegan by the wrist and pulled her headlong into the night.

Chapter Thirty-Six

As Raegan yanked the door to her apartment building closed behind her, another roar cleaved the night in two. She wavered for a moment at the bottom of the stairs, breathing hard, holding one hand up to the King in a request to wait. Of course, he appeared entirely unfazed by their sprint across multiple blocks.

"Okay," she wheezed, gesturing toward the long, steep flight of stairs before her.

His hand still locked around her wrist, the King plunged toward the stairs. She imagined he would've made it to her door in half the time without his mortal baggage in tow. On the landing, she tried to slow her breathing as she dug into her pocket for her keys.

But then the King pressed a few fingertips to her door, and it creaked open.

"Did you . . . .?" Raegan breathed, fear shooting through her chest.

"No," he replied with a grim shake of his head. "The Protectorate has already been here."

Raegan set her jaw, following the King into her apartment. He closed the door behind her, running his hands along the frame and speaking in low, monotonous tones—magic, surely, she thought. She told herself she was safe enough to process what she saw before her for at least a few seconds.

Her coffee table was overturned, the underside cut into as if she could've hidden secrets within the particle board. Her couch was gutted, all the stuffing yanked out and sorted through before being left in a heap. The bookshelves had fared no better, nor had the books upon them. Raegan looked away before the sight of her books treated so roughly brought tears to her eyes.

All the cabinets in her kitchen were wide open, some of her vintage plates scattered on the countertops. Strange symbols shimmered on the little window above the sink. She forced herself to take one long breath in through her nose and out through her mouth. It got caught somewhere halfway up her lungs and came out instead as a sputtering huff of anger.

And then she remembered—of course, her father's spell-work. Raegan spun on her heel, her skin pricked by a thousand white-hot needles, and dove for her work bag. Its contents had been rifled through, her belongings strewn across the floor. She turned in a few fruitless circles before spotting the manila folder poking out from a pile of books. With the King still at work by her door, she half-ran, half-fell toward the folder.

"Thank fucking god," Raegan muttered upon examining the spellcraft papers. Everything seemed to be intact, so she clutched it to her chest, her body filled with utter relief that she hadn't failed her father.

Swiping at the tears that spilled hotly onto her cheekbones, Raegan examined the pile of books the manila folder had been sorted into—modern fiction and memoir, investigative crime, drier journalistic texts. She let out a sharp exhale, hoping that meant somehow, against all reason, the Protectorate had ruled her father's spellpapers as being insignificant.

"I see you have found that which you seek," the King said from behind her.

Raegan rocked back on her heels, wrapping her arms around her chest, the papers pinned against her. "Why didn't the Protectorate take them?" she asked, the question posed mostly at herself.

Behind her, the King remained silent, though she could've sworn she felt his gaze on her for a few intense seconds. She squeezed her eyes shut, her mind racing. What a crossroads she faced—if she was wrong to show the King her father's spellwork, everything would be over. She'd be left behind as the stronger, older, better beings went on their quest. Perhaps he'd be kind enough to wipe her memory. Or perhaps the cruel faerie king would leave her with the knowledge that she had been so, *so* close but the door had closed in her face and she would never again feel the winds of myth in her sails.

Raegan counted to three, letting her gut decide for her. Every muscle in her body tense and coiled, she stood and turned to face the King, offering him the folder. Time stood still as he reached forward—delicate, gentle, as if the spellpapers might turn to dust—and flipped the folder open without removing it from Raegan's grasp.

He examined the first page, brow furrowing. Then his gaze slowly met hers. For a long, harrowing moment, Raegan didn't understand the expression on his face—until her stomach dropped, and she realized it was rage.

"Overhill," he said, "I do not understand. You are showing me a blank piece of parchment, are you not?"

For some reason doubting herself, Raegan glanced down at the paper, half-surprised to find the ornately detailed illustration of the Gates still there, the scrawled notes still littering the margins.

"No?" she asked, her hands beginning to shake. "It's not blank to me. It wasn't blank to Rainer."

Her next thought—standing there in a ransacked apartment, a manila folder clutched in her hands like a lifeline—was that she'd gone absolutely fucking insane. So insane that her own delusions were incapable of perceiving what she plainly saw before her.

Terrified, Raegan raised her gaze back to the King and instead found amusement, of all things, simmering across his features.

"Your father is in a class of his own," he said with a slight shake of his head, the corners of his mouth curving upward. "You will need to permit me to see what is contained within this parchment. Kelpies are oathed to different rules and less constrained than those who sit upon a court throne or those who are sworn to the Timekeeper."

Her head spun. If her dad had laid a spell on the papers to conceal their contents, *should* she give a goddamn Fey lord the ability to view them? Her mouth went dry, her throat aching. The world condensed to the folder she held in her hands and the King standing before her.

A clamor split the air, closer this time, the windows in the apartment shaking. Her teeth rattled, and then the moment shattered like broken glass, scattering in glimmering pieces on the floor.

Reflexively, Raegan closed the folder and pulled the papers tight against her chest, taking one large step back from the King. "Tell me what the fuck is going on here," she said, her voice choked with a thousand emotions she could not begin to identify. "Not the Protectorate, not my father. Tell me what is going on between *us*. The truth."

She expected the King to draw himself up, to examine her with cold eyes, for his mouth to curl into a snarl.

Instead, his shoulders sagged and he dragged a hand through his dark hair. "Overhill, we do not have the time," the King replied, exasperated, gesturing toward the door and all the horrors that clearly lay beyond it. "And besides, that was not the deal."

"Well, I'm changing the fucking deal," Raegan near-shouted, holding the folder aloft and shaking it for good measure. "You want what's in this folder? You want me to let you see it? Amend the fucking deal! I want you on my side, protecting me, protecting this quest, without having to watch my language every goddamn second to satisfy your Fey bullshit. And I want you to tell me why I've had these weird dreams all my life and these inexplicable feelings and why when *you* showed up, everything went fucking insane."

She paused for a deep breath, and the King only watched her, his expression careful and guarded. So she kept going.

"And all you have to do is touch me and I lose my mind, like there's too many thoughts and emotions inside of me and I'm going to burst!" she shouted, a bit louder than intended. "Not to mention all the crazy shit Cordelia and the Keeper were saying, like you and I have some sort of past, but of course that *should* be completely impossible. It doesn't feel that way, though—and sometimes I even think I remember. It's right there, so clear, if only I could say it out loud. And then two seconds later, it's gone, just sand falling between my fingers. Am I losing my mind, or is something happening?"

Raegan pressed her lips together, breathing hard, staring up at the King. She could keep going—part of her wanted to —but she'd asked the question that had been stuck in her throat for too long now. She'd gotten it out of herself, like a particularly stubborn weed with deep, deep roots.

"Your sanity is sound," the King told her, his voice gone into that soft, silvered tone he had used back at the Temple of the Oracle. "There are other powers at work. Though I would prefer to leave the past buried, I am willing to discuss all of it with you further, but *not* here—we are not safe."

He shifted his weight, glancing over his shoulder for another moment, as if something outside had uncoiled or intensified. She hesitated, pulling the folder tighter against her chest.

"Show me one page," the King suggested, beginning to look exasperated, the cruel gleam returning to his eyes. "Only one. I understand that you believe if you show me everything, I will no longer need you."

Raegan opened her mouth and closed it again. The windows of her apartment shook hard again, the dirty silverware in her sink rattling. Every second she squandered standing here was one less they could use to escape the Protectorate, and this did not seem like a good time to test the King's limitations. Besides, Maelona—or perhaps the shell of what had once been Maelona—seemed testament enough to the Protectorate's power, and frankly, that horrified Raegan.

"Fine," she snapped, opening the folder again and taking a step forward. She paused, looking for the right words, only half-surprised when they came to her easily, like she already knew them. "High King of the Unseelie Court, I invite you to view one—and *only* one—of these cloaked pages to judge whether you wish to alter our agreement. Any additional pages will remain obscured from your eyes until I permit otherwise, and only after said agreement alterations are sealed."

For a split second, the King looked at her as if she might be the sun. Then he stepped forward, hands clasped behind his back, towering and imposing in the low-ceilinged space of her apartment. Raegan's entire world held still as she watched his eyes rove over the page. Like the kelpie, his cold composure held steady for a few moments, her heart thumping noisily in her chest all the while. Then his dark brows drew together and something like confused awe flooded his expression.

The Unseelie King looked up and considered her, the darkness clinging to his shoulders like a cloak, looking for all the world like he had just stepped out of a nightmare.

"I accept your offering," he said, inhuman and ageless as the shadows whispered around him. "While I remain ever faithful to my court and the Unseelie Throne, I align myself with you, Raegan Maeve Overhill, in pursuit of your interests."

Blood pounded in Raegan's ears. For a halting moment, she wondered—far too late—about the consequences of putting her father's spellcraft in the hands of such an ancient and terrifying power.

But then instinct flared in Raegan, bright as the first fireflies after a long winter. She was Gods-touched, Fate-kissed, a Prophecy running wild within her. A sense of rightness fell onto her shoulders like armor. For the first time in her life, she felt she was exactly where she was supposed to be.

CHAPTER THIRTY-SEVEN

Raegan might have lived in that moment—spun from pure gold, honeyed and mythic—for an entire age, were it not for the series of explosions that echoed from outside.

"We need to depart," the King said as their eyes met. "*Now.*"

She nodded hurriedly, grabbing her laptop and notebooks from the coffee table and stuffing them into her bag, followed by her father's mythology book, his spellwork tucked between its pages. Then she darted into the kitchen, opening the cabinet by the sink and grabbing her medications.

"You know, no one's going to believe that's just fireworks," Raegan said as she ran into her bedroom. "Someone's gonna call the cops."

The King followed her, wavering at the doorway. In the corner of her eye, she thought she might have caught discomfort in his expression. "Mortals are not privy to what is occurring," he replied, his voice tight.

"That's convenient," Raegan replied, reaching under her bed for her duffle bag, which seemed to have either caught on something or was heavier than she remembered. "Could you be useful instead of just standing there?" She chucked her duffle onto her bed, standing to find the King's imperious look had returned, arched eyebrow and all.

"Could you pack slightly faster than your current glacial pace?" the King returned.

Raegan rolled her eyes at him and pulled her nightstand open with too much force, shaking the lamp and photo frames that sat atop its surface. She grabbed socks and underwear by the fistful and shoved them into her duffle. "Has anyone told you that you're incredibly annoying?" she demanded, moving onto the next drawer. She paused, wondering what bras were best for an entire quest. Her tits hurt just going down the fucking stairs. "I would *love* to punch you in the face right now." She didn't dare sneak a glance at him, though she didn't think he had moved.

"You would be unable to reach," the King replied, ice-cold.

"Fuck you," Raegan said out of reflex, this sharp-tongued banter with him dangerously natural. She awaited his response but heard nothing, so with a huff, she grabbed a few different bras—underwired, heavy-duty athletic, comfort—and turned to face him.

The King no longer stood at the doorway; instead, he had stepped into her room without making a sound. His gaze connected with a framed art print on her wall, one she'd thrifted a number of years ago. A maiden with Pre-Raphaelite waves of red hair leaned over a small balcony, offering her token to a dark-haired knight astride a powerful black destrier.

As she watched him consider the art, something unfolded inside Raegan like an old letter opened for the first time in decades. A heartbeat later, the King seemed to startle, as if he hadn't realized she was looking at him. His regal exterior and metal exoskeleton materialized a few seconds too late, and for the briefest of moments, Raegan saw past it all.

And beneath, there was only pain. Pain so bottomless and suffering so endless that the color of his eyes no longer seemed like an ocean or a storm but instead, the grayed-out hue of misery itself.

"Oberon," she murmured, her hands falling useless at her sides.

He examined her, sculptural mouth parting. For a moment, she was so sure whatever he said next would change everything, bring all the pieces together, and send her to her knees, weeping with relief.

But instead, the entire building shook and the King's expression closed. "Hurry," he said, raw and urgent. "Let me keep you safe. Please."

Something about his tone made Raegan shut her mouth and nod. She shoved jeans, sweaters, joggers, and tees into the duffle, then grabbed toiletries from the bathroom. When she returned, the King had left her bedroom, lingering in the small living room. She stepped toward him gingerly, having the strangest feeling that even such a powerful creature could—at some point—break.

He turned, holding out his hand—elegant, long-fingered, lightly calloused. A wave of foreign emotion slammed against Raegan and she almost reached out to place her hand in his. But then she understood, hefting her duffle from the ground and handing it over to the King. His fingers closed around the handle as if the bag carried no weight at all.

"Do you have everything you need?" the King asked, like he was trying to be careful, perhaps even gentle.

Her brows drew together, and then she grasped his meaning, sweeping a glance around the apartment: the suncatchers and keys in the window, the tucked-away kitchen, the dead houseplants, her quiet sanctum. "I won't be able to come back, will I?" Raegan asked.

"No," the King replied with a slow shake of his head. "No, I think it is best you do not."

"Right," she said, a hoarse echo. She grabbed two undisturbed photo frames from the bookshelf—her favorite portrait of her father and one at her college graduation with her mother—and slid them into her work bag before handing that to the King as well. "Yeah. I have everything."

At her confirmation, the King did something with his lithe hands. Her eyes tried and failed to track the movement as both her bags shrank down into something smaller. Not in a funny kids' movie kind of way—it was like the fabric came alive and knitted itself into something else, a mass of snakes writhing about. But the event was over before Raegan could analyze it further, and he handed her a leather luggage tag with her initials on it.

She took the tag and tucked it into her pocket, trying to take a deep breath. The attempt was interrupted by the King reaching over and engulfing her hand in his much larger one. The feeling of his skin on hers threatened to capsize Raegan's sanity, but there was also a deep-seated, worn-in comfort beneath the chaos.

"Stay close," he murmured, "and please do as I say. You will be safe. I promise."

Outside, the air soured around her, that teeth-rattling feeling coming from nearly every direction. The block was empty save for the moths crowding around the streetlights. She thought the King would direct them from shadowy corner to dark nook, but instead, he strode directly down the sidewalk. His movements were haughty, no hiding or sneaking, muscular shoulders back, strides long and languid. She tried to match his confidence, but her heart hammered in her chest, so she wrapped one hand around her knife, pulling it from her waistband and sliding it into her pocket.

"You are familiar with the viaduct, yes?" the King asked, his voice low and serious.

"Yes," she replied, the raw wind nearly taking her words.

"When I tell you to run," the King said, his eyes narrowing in concentration as he scanned their surroundings, "go there."

Raegan nodded, gritting her teeth, surprised to find no

distrust clawing up from the pit of her stomach. A voice in her head insisted with absolute certainty that the raven-haired Fey would never harm her. With a sharp inhale, she pushed that thought aside and focused on what she knew for sure—their covenant was real, concrete, and it should hold.

Any additional time to consider her next move was cut short when a man in a rumpled suit appeared on the sidewalk ahead of them, his form backlit by the streetlamp. Her entire body tensed.

"Not yet," the King murmured into her hair, just loud enough that she could hear it. Raegan could only hope she had bet on the right eldritch terror.

Something invisible rocketed past them, tearing the air apart as it went, releasing a horrible screeching sound like nature itself could not bear the wrongness of its existence. She had to tell herself not to flee with each step.

"Steady," the King said. "Not yet. Let me give you more cover."

Her blood pounded. The air smelled of burnt hair and rusted metal, her world condensing to this one city block lined with a developer's chain-link fence and crumbling old row houses, broken glass winking in the streetlights.

The man in the suit bellowed something, and Raegan was surprised to find it was her own name. "We only want to help," he continued, his London accent crisp. "We do not want you to bring more shame on your family."

The King did not stop, nor did he speak, until they were only a few paces from the man in the suit. Up close, he had lank blond hair, long limbs, and a pointed, hawk-like face. He also looked, at least to Raegan, like he was trying very hard to disguise his deep-seated terror. His brow pinched together and then released, fear flooding his eyes like a tide, in and out, in and out.

"While it is always a delight to spill *Gwarcheidwad* blood,"

the King said, slick as an eel, "we have pre-existing commitments for the evening."

The man said nothing, his lips pressed together. On some
instinct, Raegan swept her gaze out and around the area,
seeing what the King must've been waiting for: more Protectorate emerging from the mist. Though many of their suits
looked for all the world like off-the-rack Brooks Brothers, their
accouterments were anything but. Chainmail and chest plates
sat atop navy wool blazers, gloved but ordinary human hands
wrapped around brutal axes, maces, spears, and swords—all
iron, she had little doubt.

And then she felt the King slide his hand from hers.
Raegan's entire body seized, knowing what word was going to
leave his mouth next, and hoping to god she would actually be
able to do it. Time stretched long, far too elastic, entire lifetimes fitting into each of her breaths.

The King splayed his hand on her back and spoke a series
of words that she knew to be an incantation; she could feel the
hum of the magic in her bones.

"Where did she go?" the man in the suit demanded, nearly
jumping out of his skin, eyes darting to and fro. "What did
you do to her?"

And then the King's voice in her ear: "*Run.*"

To her absolute shock, Raegan did. Her body took off,
bolting for the viaduct, which was not far. Farther than she'd
like to run, sure, but the adrenaline made her feel as though
she could cover any distance.

Behind her, Raegan heard what sounded like a small
explosion, a bone-rending scream, and then laughter.

The King's laughter.

She kept going, rounding the corner and diving into an
alley she knew cut through to the cross street she was headed
for. The nighttime autumn air was blessedly cool on her face,
and she felt like the city was opening up for her, guiding her
through its streets to safety. Raegan blew past someone in a

yellow puffer coat walking a bunch of small dogs and then cut off a bus pulling away from a stop, doing whatever she could to cross the busy street faster.

Her short, heavy breaths fell in time with the sound of her boots hitting the pavement until she turned down the street that held her destination and finally slowed, winded. She hazarded a look over her shoulder but saw nothing. Ahead, the abandoned High Line railway soared above her, a weed-devoured ramp rising up to connect it to the street level. A chain-link fence surrounded the entrance, but she was sure another denizen of her city had freshly taken bolt cutters to it, like always.

She jogged along the fence line, trying to find an opening with only the weak moonlight as a guide. Growing frustrated, she ran her hand along the chain-link instead and finally found a cut. She crouched down, preparing to wiggle through. The tall grasses and weeds on the viaduct would provide better cover, she thought, and the height of the ramp would give her a good view of what might be coming.

Raegan was halfway through when two hands roughly grabbed her—not the King's, she knew instantly. Digging her heels into the loose, rocky soil, she tried to get leverage, but with nothing to hold onto, she was yanked back through the fence and deposited onto the uneven pavement below.

She rolled, banged her knee hard, and then staggered to her feet. In the weak, murky light, she could make out a mountain of a man before her—brown hair cropped close, pockmarked skin, a heavy brow and deep-set eyes. He'd been at the café, too. Unlike the others, he wore no chainmail, though Raegan felt fiercely sure he always did. He was familiar in a way that made her stomach lurch.

Bedwyr. Something buried deep inside of her seethed with rage, like she'd waited lifetimes for revenge.

The man took one look at her and spat on the ground. Then he lunged. Raegan tried to use his size against him, but he was far, far faster than he should've been. He got an arm around her neck in less than a second. She raised her heel and stomped hard on one of his feet, but he merely grunted and yanked her back against his chest. Raegan hissed threats of violence, trying to kick his groin, but he simply lifted her off the ground so her legs flailed uselessly. But even with her arms pinned to her sides, she thought she might still be able to reach her knife in her pocket. Raegan centered herself.

"Let me go, you fucking asshole," she screamed, slamming the back of her head into his nose. He spat a curse this time, revealing a thick British accent. She shouted an insult in response, struggling hard against him, doing anything she could to conceal the movement of her hand into her pocket.

Then, slinking out of the darkness, came a voice as low and dark as the night itself. "If you dare to harm her, I will slit your belly open and invite the *Cŵn Annwn* to feast upon your entrails."

Chapter Thirty-Eight

The man did not release Raegan, but his grip slackened, some kind of involuntary response to a threat from the Unseelie throne itself. She sucked air into her lungs, feeling a surge of adrenaline return as she looked up and saw the King.

Really, entirely, truly saw *him*, not the guise he had been wearing. The being just a few steps from her and her captor was exactly as her father's book had described: the last of his kind, a destroyer of worlds. Pitch-black shadows knitted themselves into armor over the King's body, obscuring his clothing entirely. Despite the impossibility of it, Raegan could make out arm bracers that came to viciously sharp points, a longsword with a heavy hilt, and a dark sweep of chainmail across his shoulders. All made of slinking, slippery shadows, plumes of black ink humming with deadly energy.

She felt her captor's breath hitch.

"Haven't seen this version in a while," the man said, jiggling Raegan like he was showing off the keys to a brand-new car. "Always been my favorite. Maybe it's just nostalgia."

She watched the King readjust his grip on the shadow-blade and realized very quickly that he was not the type to trade insults back and forth with the enemy. Well, she certainly wasn't going to wait around either, then. With her captor's attention understandably focused on the ancient being of nightmares standing before him, Raegan finally got a good grasp on her folding knife. She slid it from her pocket, flipped it open, gathered all the backward momentum she could and then slammed the blade into the man's stomach.

He let loose a horrible scream and dropped her, much like a child does when the animal they picked up unexpectedly sinks fangs into flesh. Despite her best efforts, Raegan was not prepared for such a definitive response, and she stumbled forward, her face about to meet the chewed-up pavement.

The King caught her by the upper arm with his free hand. All the forward-moving energy sent her straight into his chest, where she discovered that his armor felt just like cold metal, despite its unearthly origins.

He steadied her, his arm sliding around her waist. "Did you *stab* him?" the King wanted to know. Having caught her breath, Raegan turned to look at her would-be captor, who was still standing but barely, blood flowing freely from a wound in his gut.

"Yes," Raegan replied, holding up her soiled knife with all the glee of a kindergartener at show-and-tell. Somewhere through the man's anguished moans and her own breathing, so loud that it seemed fundamentally impossible, she noticed the King's powerful arm was still around her waist.

Raegan looked up at him in the gloom of the alley, his features illuminated by the wan, steel-gray moonlight. His mouth curved into the no-man's-land between a smirk and a smile. She ached for nothing but to drag his lips down to hers.

"Beautiful," the King said, only just louder than a murmur, and Raegan had no idea if he was speaking about her assault on the Protectorate man or . . . *her*. Heart racing with fear and adrenaline and desire all at once, she said nothing, for once in her life not wanting to disturb the moment.

But that familiar teeth-rattling wail made its way up the alley, followed closely by shouts. Whatever had slipped onto the King's features drained away, his mask of cool composure sliding back into place.

"We must move," he told her. "Are you unhurt? I am sorry my concealment on you did not hold for longer."

"Yeah, I'm fine," Raegan said, still breathless.

In response, the King nodded, grabbed her hand, and began to stride toward the viaduct's ramp. As they passed the Protectorate man bleeding out on the pavement, the King reached down in one fluid motion, brushing his fingers against the man's forehead. Raegan felt something push or maybe pulse, and then the King kept walking, having barely broken his stride.

When they reached the chain-link fence, he spoke a word and the barrier tore down the center like old wallpaper splitting at the seam. He stepped through the gap and turned to assist Raegan through the shorn metal edges. Then they began to walk up the incline, the King's firm grip still on her hand. She almost wanted to say she disliked it. But she could not.

As they walked, the grass and weeds grew taller, approaching Raegan's chest and then growing even higher. For a moment, she was worried about navigating the terrain, but then she saw how the plants bowed to the King as he went by—and by extension, cleared a path for her as well.

Ten thousand things fought to leap from her tongue, mind running too quickly for her mouth to keep up. Her hands were maybe shaking, she realized, and her knees felt a bit like goo. Even after a few more steps, her body didn't seem to have realized they were out of imminent danger—her heart still thundered madly in her chest.

"D-did you heal that man?" Raegan asked, reverting to her place of calm: acquiring knowledge.

"Certainly not," the King replied, looking at her sideways. "I made him forget that he had witnessed either of us, only our friend *Cath Palug*. If I was successful with the others, no Protectorate operative will remember sighting us tonight, though I cannot be sure."

Raegan did not know how to respond to that, not exactly. In a way, she was glad the King had not healed the man. But she supposed she had only been so willing to stab him because she had assumed magic would make even a dangerous wound heal easily.

A closer shout went up from behind them, and Raegan glanced over her shoulder, thoughts broken as fear skittered through her body.

"We are fine," the King replied, slowing his pace for a moment to look at her. "We should not be fools, of course, and we must continue to make haste. But this is a wild place. And wild places are still mine."

Nodding, Raegan bit down on her lip. There was no denying the feral nature of the viaduct, even in the middle of a densely populated neighborhood so close to Center City. Nature had taken over every inch of the man-made structure. Vines coiled like elegant tattoos around patinated steel, and up ahead even an oak tree had taken root. As clouds shifted away from the moon above them, Raegan noticed the fluttering wings of moths and other creatures. The tiny insects created a halo around the King's head, paying homage with each beat of their crystalline wings.

When the ramp leveled out and they reached the main High Line, the flying things dispersed, disappearing back into the gray velvet of the night.

"Just through here," the King said.

His grip on her hand softening, he led Raegan diagonally across the High Line to the ruins of an old storage building. Graffiti adorned the walls in jewel tones. She admired a huge loop of blood-red cursive as they slipped around the corner of the structure. Shock vibrated through her as she caught sight of a black crown with seven points on a wall they passed. The rendering was far from ornate, but the synchronicity of it made her reach out her hand and trail her fingers along it. If the King noticed, he said nothing.

When Raegan set her sights ahead of her again, she found a familiar shape. A series of huge, old-growth wisteria vines knotted themselves into a pointed arch, using two interior columns of the abandoned building for support. Distantly, she heard a soft drip of condensation. Despite the cool air outside, the atmosphere inside was warmer, damper, bringing to mind reptilian enclosures.

"I may not be able to shield you from as much portal sickness as before," the King said, leading the way around a giant crumble of cement and rebar. He came to a halt before the wisteria portico.

"I'll live," Raegan grumbled, though she glanced over at him, eyes narrowed, looking for signs that the King was taxed. In truth, she expected to find none, but his posture had slackened and he appeared to be keeping as much weight off one leg as possible.

"Were you injured?" she asked, having not even thought it possible. She ran her eyes up and down the King's form. The shadow-armor had dispersed, and she imaged that a wound should be obvious through his assortment of fine wools.

The King looked at her, something that was both a grimace and a playful smile moving across his mouth. "Just now?" he asked, arching a brow. "No. I was not injured. But in earlier battles? Yes, many times."

"I suppose," Raegan mused, watching him closely, "that it's easy to forget you have worn the same body all these years. I didn't think of a cumulative toll."

Something flashed in his eyes that she did not understand, though it hardly seemed to matter as the King looked away and moved toward the portico. Raegan stayed beside him, her hand still in his as a tremor ran down her spine. She twisted, gazing over her shoulder. She did not like the feel of the vast expanse at her back, the weed-choked railroad and open black sky. At the precise moment that the itch of being watched turned into sheer foreboding, Raegan saw the King freeze, his free hand mere inches from the middle of the portico.

"Something is wrong," he told her in a low tone, tilting his head back, as if to catch a scent of the enemy in the air.

"Look!" Raegan exclaimed, pointing to her discovery at the base of the wisteria vines. Hidden by the weeds and crumbled concrete, the bottom of the vines was blackened, sickly with disease. Now that she looked closer, she could see the upper reaches were parched and dry.

The King said something under his breath in a language she suspected was ancient and long-dead, though she knew without a doubt his words were a curse.

"Come," he said, turning on his heel and taking a large stride back toward the way they'd come. Raegan leapt over a pile of rebar to keep up, her heart beginning to thump around in her chest again, a wet towel in a washing machine.

He paused at the threshold of the structure, scanning the horizon. Beyond the tallest weeds on the viaduct, Raegan could see the familiar skyline lit up against inky darkness. Looking at the view had always comforted her, but tonight it felt distant, like a homeland she had once known but could no longer return to.

"Did they do something to it? To the portal?" Raegan asked, keeping her voice low.

The King did not look at her, but he nodded. "I did not think they could enter such a place," he murmured, his body like an arrow nocked and ready to fly.

"It used to be a railroad," she said, looking up at him, brow creased. "Doesn't it matter what things used to be just as much as what they are now?"

At that, he swung his gaze to meet hers, eyes black in the gloom. "Yes," the King answered. "I suppose it does."

With that, he slid into the waiting shadows, pulling

Raegan along with him. The King set a fair pace, she thought, almost as if he was finally accommodating for her much shorter legs. They moved through the crumbling structures and high grass of the viaduct, doubling back around to the large area by the ramp.

The King moved slower then, shooting Raegan a terrible look when she accidentally sent a few rocks skipping across the ground. He pulled her a few more paces forward and then, out of nowhere, spun her into his arms as if they were dancers and not fugitives. Raegan found herself crushed between the corroded metal wall of a storage shed and the imposing, muscled frame of the King, her nose bumping into his chest.

"Make no sound," he advised, barely more than a whisper, easily mistaken for a rustle of the tall grass in the night breeze. Raegan nodded, trying to stop her hands from shaking. In an effort to stay calm, she took in a long, slow breath, heavy with the smell of rotted leaves and condensation and rusted things.

Her heart ran away in her chest at the sound of two voices just outside the shed. Looking up, she saw the King's attention snap to the location of the voices, so much like a predator sighting its prey. Raegan swallowed hard and told herself to breathe. She was in the company of the Unseelie King. He could handle whatever the Protectorate wished to throw at them.

But she couldn't forget the way he kept weight off his left knee or how tired he looked. It made sense. The King was doing magic in a world that had none. Raegan wondered, not easing the growing panic in her chest at all, how much he had left in him.

A twig snapped close—much too close—and the King stepped in even closer. Raegan's panic momentarily abated at the sensation of his long, powerful leg sliding between her own. She found herself caught at the crossroads of desire and terror.

The King raised his free hand—the one not holding hers

—and made a small movement. Farther down the viaduct, a loud, metallic clang sounded. Though she could not see anything, her sight line blocked by the King's body, Raegan heard two sets of footsteps barrel out of the shed, chasing the phantom noise.

Without a moment of hesitation, the King pulled away from the wall, nearly dragging her behind him as he slipped around the opposite corner, keeping to the outer ring of five-foot tall weeds. With a jolt, Raegan saw that there were other Protectorate people up on the viaduct. She had only emotionally prepared herself for the two, but she could see at least four more gathered around like a hunting party, iron spears gripped hard in gloved hands. She tried to remind herself they were likely looking for the faerie cat, not the Unseelie King and his mortal companion.

But then one turned in their direction and Raegan froze, as if she had suddenly grown roots instead of legs. The King had size and weight to his advantage, and so he merely yanked her off balance until she followed him. Fear gripped her—she was so sure they had been sighted. But as the King led her through the grass, she realized the Protectorate woman had in fact not seen them at all; it was simply a terrifying coincidence.

Instead of taking the ramp to the sidewalk, the King led Raegan to an access ladder that ended significantly far from the ground. Its surface was chewed over with rust, and Raegan was fairly certain she saw it sway in the breeze.

"Are you fucking insane?" she hissed at him.

The King looked at her and nodded, almost gleefully. Then he pulled her into his arms and leapt.

CHAPTER THIRTY-NINE

"Jesus fucking *Christ*," Raegan hissed the moment her feet were solidly on the ground. "Was that necessary?"

The King looked down at her. "There were at least six Protectorate operatives," he replied. "Yes, it was necessary."

Raegan glanced up, expecting menacing faces peering over the edge of the viaduct's hulking iron mass. But only the underbelly of the trestle greeted her: ever-damp, decorated with graffiti. She let out a long breath.

"We will have to walk back," the King told her, gesturing to the broken sidewalk and litter-lined gutter across the street. "I do not wish to risk attracting any additional attention."

Raegan nodded, moving automatically to entwine her arm with his—certainly a more natural pose than trotting around a busy neighborhood with his hand clamped around hers. They moved off into the night, walking in silence. Best to focus on their surroundings, Raegan thought, and keep a sharp eye out for anything suspicious, any change in the atmosphere that spoke of that terrible, air-shattering magic. To call it magic felt wrong entirely. Whatever powers the

Protectorate wielded seemed more like an abomination to her.

An abomination that she hoped she was free from for the evening as they crossed back into the King's neighborhood some time later, having taken any would-be followers on a merry and exhausting jaunt through the commercial district. Now they strolled down a popular series of blocks lined with restaurants and bars, the kind of place that had twinkling lights strung up in the trees and live music slinking out into the night.

And yet it was exactly there that Raegan felt the hairs on the back of her neck rise up. She saw no one out of the ordinary and certainly did not feel that teeth-hammering magic. But a spike of white-hot fear pierced her chest all the same, her hands suddenly clammy.

"We need to get off the street now," the King said, his voice low and intense, dark eyes examining the block.

"There's a bookstore up ahead," Raegan said, trying to stay focused. "It's big on the inside. Lots of places to hide."

"Of course," he replied, nodding. "The one with the cats."

That described at least half the bookstores in the city, but Raegan could not bring the correction to her lips. She felt like a tiny mouse rushing through a field, hoping to reach safety before an owl's talons sunk into her flesh. The remaining distance to the bookshop stretched comically in her mind, a horrible funhouse mirror that turned half a block into ten miles.

But they reached the front doors, which the King pulled open, ushering Raegan inside. Relief sang hymns in her chest. The friendly mess of the shop welcomed her back with open arms. Bookcases reached high toward the ceiling, packed full of titles in haphazard organization. The fat orange cat snoozed upon his usual chair tucked away in the corner, a piece of sheet music beneath his paws as if he had been examining the composition before drifting into sleep.

"There's a second floor," Raegan said, taking the lead and pulling the King along behind her.

For a moment, she worried about how the King would fare with his size trying to navigate the narrow, winding rows of shelves. Then she remembered he was a big boy, more than a thousand years old in fact, and plunged into the maze of towering bookcases. By the time they reached the stairs to the second floor, she had tripped over two piles of books and almost run into another browser, while the King had disturbed a grand total of nothing.

At the top of the stairs, the second floor greeted the pair gently, enveloping them in a quiet, dusty, book-scented hug. The lower level had been dotted with other customers, but up here, silence hung in the antique eaves of the old building. The hair on the back of her neck was still raised, foreboding thick in her ribcage.

"Over here," she said, sticking to the outer ring of the shelves as she navigated to the small room of vinyls at the very back of the shop.

When they crossed the threshold, she loosened her grip on the King's arm, trying to slip into the feeling of safety she had so often felt within the confines of a bookshop. But she could not muster it now, her mouth dry, her heart pounding. Not with the Protectorate prowling the street outside, not with all that lay before her—and not with the King.

He certainly did not make her feel safe. He made her blood race and her pulse throb and her heart ask questions her mind did not know how to even begin answering. In the dim, dusty light of the shop, she turned to look at him, only to find the King's gaze was trained out through the doorway, reminding her of hunting dogs catching scent of their prey.

"They are nearly here," was all he said.

Time skittered strangely, the dark walls lined with CDs replaced by cold gray stone. Words hung off the tip of

Raegan's tongue like the last drop of tea, *I am yours until they come*. She shook her head to chase the thought away.

"I need you close," the King said, his powerful arms wrapping around her waist as he stepped back behind a towering display rack. "I need to conceal us, but I am in pain and tiring."

Raegan nodded, mute, her heart careening for another reason entirely, as the King pulled her against his chest for the third time that evening. She fit into his arms like a lost key, and the temptation to place her cheek against his chest and hear his familiar heartbeat was unbearable.

"Why do I know you?" she asked the King, the words leaving her mouth in a hoarse whisper. It was the question she had wanted to ask since the moment she saw him, the words that had pounded against the back of her throat in that subway car.

The King inhaled, a muscle in his jaw jumping as he watched her. She hated the way he said nothing. She wanted to scream at him or maybe shake him until she understood, until this slinking, dark howl within her stopped its raw keening.

"I imagine you already know," the King said, his words surfacing slowly. "Or that at the very least, you have begun to suspect."

Raegan didn't feel like she knew anything. Or rather, she felt like she knew things—knew everything, knew too much—and yet *understood* nothing. Actually recalling what she might know would require digging through endless, unlabeled filing cabinets in her mind. Feeling raw and tired beyond belief, she let her forehead drop against the King's chest. She felt him freeze, all hard, unyielding muscle. But then one of his hands alighted on her hair, gentle as a butterfly.

The framed illustration in her room he'd been looking at sprung back into her mind. She remembered when she'd found it at the thrift store, some alien feeling rising in her as she had traced over the woman and the horse with her fingertips. The knight's face was not visible in the piece, his back to the viewer, and he wore no colors or a shield that would perhaps give more hint to his identity. It mattered not—the artwork was compelling either way. Raegan had nearly been able to taste the dust rising from the street, and smell the horses and the flowers trampled underfoot when she'd first seen it.

She looked up at the King, no words leaving her mouth, but a question forming all the same—not one that she was sure she could even put into words. Whatever she wished to ask was formless, fathomless, as unknowable as the anonymous knight upon his black horse.

The King's hand slid from her hair, brushing her jawline. Her heart skidded to a halt, breathing terse and quick, as an unfathomably old longing uncoiled in her belly. With a weathered sigh, the King cupped the side of her face in his powerful palm, fingertips skimming her temple. But still, he said nothing.

"Tell me," she begged, her voice quivering. She was both mortified and astonished to find she could taste the wet, bitter salt of tears upon her lips when she spoke.

To her surprise, the King closed his eyes and complied, exhaustion as heavy as a mantle on his shoulders. When he spoke, his voice reminded Raegan of torn velvet. "You keep coming back," he said, as if that explained anything. "Always mortal. Always doomed. And yet you will not cease."

The words hit her with a palpable weight and her body wavered into the nearest display case. A million voices screamed inside her head, each vying to be louder than the rest. Raegan heard nothing but noise: the clash of ancient battles and the thundering of hooves and the swell of a symphony and the lap of river waters upon sandy shores.

She looked back up at the King, wanting more—*needing* more, knowing despite all reason that the being before her held the keys to everything she yearned for. There had always been a door in Raegan's heart, and she had spent her life trying to fill it with things that were not door-shaped.

Just as she opened her mouth to speak, two other browsers entered the room, chatting amicably. The King yanked his hand away from her, placing it against the wall to brace himself instead, shifting weight off his left leg. One of the browsers—tall, lean, wearing a patched denim jacket—looked over at Raegan and the King, somehow aware in the way only strangers are that a moment had been broken, dropped like an egg onto tile floors.

"Come," the King said, his tone low. "The Protectorate has moved on, and this is no conversation for public spaces."

Aware that tears were still streaming down her face, Raegan nodded, mute, and slipped her arm into the King's. She didn't know if it was because of the unholy, impossible thing hidden deep inside her, or simply because of the length and difficulty of the day she had just survived, but she had to fight the urge to turn toward the King, bury her face in his chest, and weep. But the fear of such vulnerability churned sour in her stomach, so she kept moving, letting her body remember to walk and breathe on its own.

Somehow, they returned to the King's archives and safehouse without incident, though he was insistent about sticking to alleys and shadowy side streets just in case. They walked in silence through the front door, the vestibule, the office, and then through that strange corridor that spat them out into the huge room full of books and shelves and hidden things.

"Please, sit," the King said, gesturing to a pair of worn-in leather chairs perched at the edge of the fireplace.

Raegan stared at the cozy scene for a moment, dumbfounded—apparently, the archives kept much of itself concealed unless the King permitted otherwise. She lowered herself into a chair and stared at the fire, aware that he was moving around the space behind her. It took all of her willpower not to turn and watch him. Instead, she gritted her teeth and examined what else the archives had decided to reveal: a kitchenette in the far corner, equipped with a tea kettle, espresso machine, mismatched mugs and saucers, as well as a mini fridge beneath the counter.

She realized that the King seemed to intentionally glamour away any parts of his space a visitor might find too cozy. Like he didn't want anyone getting too close. Like it was easier to keep everyone at arm's length. Raegan sighed. She could understand that.

Movement stirred in her peripheral vision as the King settled into the chair beside her. In the firelight, the hollows of his face were sharp and deep, as if he hadn't slept in many, many years. He'd removed his suit jacket and waistcoat, leaving only his dark shirt, sleeves rolled to the elbows. Her blood pounding, she watched the tendons in his forearm tighten and release as he stared into the fireplace. Then, gazing straight ahead, almost as if he could not bear to look at her, the King began to speak.

"You and I, Overhill, have known each other for a millennium."

CHAPTER FORTY

The King's voice was flat and even, as if he were reciting words from a teleprompter or reading aloud from a memorized script. Raegan dared not speak— she found herself trying to limit even her breathing.

"Sometimes we pass by each other with hardly a ripple," he continued. "Other times, like the situation we have found ourselves in now, we are hopelessly entwined at the root."

Raegan felt as though someone had simultaneously poured cold water all over her and pricked her with a million hot needles. Her mouth was painfully dry. Something about her heart seemed brittle all of a sudden. For once in her life, she had nothing to say.

The King crossed his ankle over his knee, still not looking at her, the firelight dancing up and down the feral places of his face. Raegan preferred it this way, too. The words leaving his mouth were difficult enough; she was not sure she could also look into his eyes while he said them.

"The closest concept your people have is reincarnation," the King said, a hint of condescension creeping into his voice. "It is exceedingly rare, despite the casual way mortals speak of it. For most, including the Fey, death is the final door. But not for you. Death cannot seem to hold you down. It can barely get its hands around you for more than a moment or two."

This was the most Raegan had heard the King speak without further prompting, and she became surer and surer with each passing moment that this speech had etched itself onto his bones.

"We have broken vows for one another," he continued, listless. "We have fought beside one another. We have crossed oceans for one another."

Raegan's heart hammered so furiously in her chest that it frightened her. The King's words explained *everything*. Not just the strange, intense way he made her feel but also what she had experienced since childhood—the recurring dreams, the strange memories, the way sometimes she'd know things she should not, or reach to grab at skirts that were not there as she began to ascend a set of stairs. His words explained what she had always known to be true, the fantasy she'd harbored deep in her marrow even when she became too old to believe such things.

She swallowed hard as she felt the King's eyes fall upon her. Dampness gathered on her palms. Steeling herself, she turned to meet his gaze and found a sea of simmering cruelty, hewn over a thousand years of torment.

"In dozens of lifetimes, I allowed you to consume too much of me. I suppose it is only human to attempt to taste the divine," the King said, his voice a dagger, the line of his shoulders turning predatory.

Raegan held his gaze, alien things clamoring in her chest, no words materializing. So she said nothing, and instead let him fill the firelight-soaked space that hung between them.

The King took a sharp inhale before he turned away from her. "The Protectorate captured me because of you. You wished to play the hero, and foolishly, I went after you. I thought I could not live without you," he said, his tone hollow. "I know better now."

The chill of his words settled over Raegan like a frost. She needed warmth; she craved something that was not caustic and over-brewed by time.

Beside her, the King raked a hand through his dark hair, jaw tense. "We lost the war. You were executed. The Protectorate kept me. I am unsure how long. They tried every way they could come up with to kill me. When they saw they would be unsuccessful and it would only give my court time to retaliate, they exiled me, closed the Gates forever, and invited the Timekeeper to devour this half of the world."

The King stretched, panther-like, his hands coming to rest on the arms on his chair. He dug into the leather, long fingers flexing.

"In the two hundred years since, you have occasionally returned to destroy any chance I have at reclaiming my throne," he said. The fire sputtered low, one log reduced to embers, and he stood, moving to collect more kindling from beside the hearth. "I have to hope you will not poison everything this time, too."

Raegan's stomach dropped, sourness gathering at the back of her throat. The King crouched to feed the fire, his large frame nearly blocking out all the light. Then he straightened and turned to face her, silhouetted by the flames.

"And more so," he continued, crossing his arms, "I have to hope I will not *allow* you to. I am a better king when I do not know your touch, when my flesh does not crave yours."

Raegan knew all of it to be true the same way she knew her middle name was Maeve and the sky was blue and her mother was from Caernarfon. But the way he said it, so accusingly, looming over her, backlit by flame, was infuriating.

She crossed her arms, mirroring him. "Your flesh is safe, Oberon," she sneered, pouring all the venom she could into the few short words. "All I want is to find my father. I'll use you to that end and nothing else."

It was a lie and she knew it, but she said it anyway, because if finding her dad was no longer her north star, then what was? *Who* was? This ancient thing before her, all sharp angles and jagged edges? He'd cut her just now, so deep that far too much of her anger had been replaced with hurt. In fact, she felt like she could choke on it.

"You know," Raegan said, leaning back in her chair, examining her nails as if she had not just been scraped raw, "I'm going to need you to prove what you're saying. Because I think I'd feel something more for you if all this were true. Sure, I might fuck you, but you're talking about a lot more than that—you're talking star-crossed *love*."

She let out a haughty laugh instead of a tearstained scream, eyes sliding toward the King as he settled back into his chair. The impassivity on his features stoked her anger, and she relished it.

"Fairy magic is quite a drug, I hear," she continued, watching him closely for any sign her knives had hit their mark. "Making a human believe they've been entangled with you for a thousand years is a touch romantic for your kind, but it's awfully clever, and it'd be careless of me to let such a wild statement go unverified. I mean, you *are* a monster, after all."

The King tried to hide it, but he flinched. She slunk back in her chair again, mouth twisting into some dark shadow of a victorious smile. Tilting her head, she looked over at him, eyebrows raised expectantly, wondering if she'd have to deliver another barb to prod him into speaking.

But the King cleared his throat. "What process do you require?" he asked, cold and professional, steepling his fingers.

The Fey could not read minds. Raegan was sure of it because she remembered asking her father one afternoon, wondering what god-like power the Fair Folk did not have. It was obvious, too, in a way—all that guile would hardly be worth the effort if one could simply peer into another's mind.

Okay, she was *pretty* sure.

Raegan glanced at the King and saw he was waiting for her to speak. She told herself it was a deeply inconvenient time to like that about him.

"I have a recurring dream," she began, the tip of her tongue darting out to moisten her dry lips. Her idea was sound, but there was something in speaking about her dream that suddenly felt like uncovering a fresh wound. "It's autumn. I'm walking across a field. I smell woodsmoke. Someone's walking beside me, just out of sight. If anything of this is true, then I imagine it's *you*. Tell me, Unseelie King, which side of me are you walking on, and what are we walking toward?"

The King leaned across his seat toward her, propping one elbow on the arm of his chair. She tried not to let the few additional inches of closeness have its intended impact, but now she could smell him, the damp stone and black pepper and swirling woodsmoke.

"I am on your left," he replied, his gaze unwavering, "and we are walking toward a winding river. Its shores are narrow and sandy. The mountains rise up just beyond it in the distance. The forest begins on the far bank."

Raegan thought she had braced herself for it, but hearing the King describe the landscape of her recurring dream—so private she had never told anyone but her parents about it— made everything else he had said become blisteringly and irrevocably real.

"What are we doing there?" she asked, softening her tone, hoping that he wouldn't shut down completely now that she wanted something. "It feels so . . . important. Dreadful. Grim. But important." It had felt like the purpose she'd been searching for her entire life, but Raegan wouldn't give him that.

The King considered her and then shook his head, turning back to the hearth. "There is only so much that it is safe to tell you," he said, the words flat and trodden-upon, like he'd already said them a million times. "After you were executed and I exiled, you had a Seal placed on your magic and your memory during your next return. I know not if it was out of selflessness—to keep my people's secrets safe—or simply your own weakness. Too much knowledge of your memories risks the integrity of the Seal. For it to break on its own, instead of being removed, would almost certainly induce madness, rendering you useless to me."

Raegan spoke before even thinking, lurching forward in her chair, her heart pounding. "So remove it. *Now*."

Again, the King shook his head, leaning on his knees, staring into the fire. "Only the one who placed it can remove it," he replied. "And no one has heard from her in at least a hundred years. Seals are one of the few magics that remain even after the creator's death, so it is possible it cannot be removed at all. Even the way magic is leaving this side of the world will not degrade its integrity."

Raegan nearly threw herself out of her chair in frustration. A thousand years of knowledge, of memory, of magic, and most importantly of *herself*—of all the pieces she had always known she was missing, locked away by her own doing and now right here at the tips of her fingers, yet still unreachable.

"Who was it?" Raegan hissed. "At least tell me her name."

The King glanced at her sideways, evaluating her, a look in his eyes like he did not think she could handle whatever came next.

Then he sighed and said, "Baba Yaga."

CHAPTER FORTY-ONE

He had to be lying, Raegan thought. Some kind of cruel trick on the stupid little mortal foolish enough to get in his way.

"Baba Yaga," she echoed, the last syllable choked by an incredulous laugh. "Right. Of course."

She waited for a sly knife between the ribs. But the King said nothing. He looked more statue than living thing, gaze directed at the fire, all the unnaturally sharp points of his frame—the shoulders, the jaw, the cheekbones—etched in the shadows of the wide, dark space. He was not something anyone could hold or caress or, god forbid, attempt to love.

He was no longer the man from her dreamscape's café or the knight walking beside her toward the river or the lithe, dark-haired lover tangled in her bedsheets. He was not her once-in-a-hundred-lifetimes, and she was not his.

Not anymore.

A bottomless sorrow enveloped her, the edges folding in on themselves, and Raegan felt something deep inside her fracture. She had managed to lose a grand and beautiful impossibility—a love that haunted her from one life to the next, echoing across space and time. Her throat closed off, and she dropped her head into her hands, fingers digging into her scalp. Emptiness lurched from the corners of the room. Her vision blurred.

It was just like Layla had said when they'd broken up. Raegan was too hard to love. Even for the person who had done so for centuries, until he just couldn't take it any longer. She bit down hard on the inside of her cheek, willing herself not to cry. Not here. Not in front of him.

Somewhere beyond the furious beating of her own wounded heart and the low blaze of the fire, bells sounded—soft, ethereal, like dappled light on the forest floor. Beside her, the King rose. She did not look up, twisting away from him as if she couldn't stand the mere sight of him. She heard him exhale.

"Excuse me," the King said, clipped. "I am receiving an urgent call."

Raegan said nothing, gratitude and grief mingling in her ribcage as the King strode across the room, disappearing into the shadowy hallway. When she was sure he was gone, she raised her head, dragging the backs of her hands across her eyes. She fought to prepare something to say when he'd return —anything at all that wasn't about what had transpired between them across the millennium. Self-disgust roiled in her stomach at the thought, but Raegan knew she was not strong enough to continue this line of discussion without breaking down.

"It's a fucking trick," she whispered to herself, surprised at the raw, desperate tone of her own voice. "A faerie trick. Nothing more."

She said it again and again, hoping the shape of those words might become more familiar in her mouth than anything else involving the Unseelie King. By the time she heard his footfall, she almost believed her own lies.

"If you would like to remain under the protection of the

Unseelie Court," he said, breaking the silence, his mask firmly back in place, "I need to examine your father's spellcraft."

Raegan turned to him, movements sharp, her mind racing. "What is that supposed to mean?" she demanded, springing to her feet, grateful for a different reason to be angry. "What about our agreement?"

The King folded his arms in a way that made his powerful shoulders seem all the more apparent. He looked down at her as if she were the most tiresome toddler on the entire planet. "Keep up, Overhill," he said, one hand making sharp, elegant articulations in the air beside him. "You have my aid, my protection, my word. Not my Court's."

"I didn't realize that Fey courts were fucking democracies," Raegan scoffed, rolling her eyes at the very idea that the King did not rule with an iron fist.

To her surprise and discomfort, the King smiled, the expression made all the more unsettling by the way the firelight sent shadows slinking across his face. "There is undoubtedly much you do not understand about the Unseelie Court," he murmured, his voice low and soft, somehow more dangerous for it. "Do you wish to experience the darkness of our depths, or would you prefer to deliver on your promise?"

Despite herself, a delicate chill traced cold fingers up Raegan's back. She swallowed hard, a primal instinct woven deep into her marrow urging her to run and never look back. But she stood her ground, hands balling into fists at her side, her skin gone clammy. "Fine," she replied. "Let me put my things away, and then I'll show you. It'll only take a minute."

The King examined Raegan, hawkish, his weight shifting toward her, as if he had sensed her body's desire to run. For a long, simmering moment, they held each other's gazes. Fear and heat uncoiled in Raegan's belly, the combination both unreasonable and delicious.

"A moment to settle in," the King agreed, dragging his gaze

from her eyes all the way down to the bottom of her feet. Then he turned on his heel and stalked to his worktable.

Not willing to push her luck, Raegan turned and disappeared into the guest quarters. Once she was safely behind the door to her chambers, she pulled the luggage tag from her pocket. She turned it over in her hands, suspicious, before deciding to just lay it on the couch and see what happened. Before her eyes, the small leather item twisted and morphed back into her duffle and work bag.

Raegan let out a tired sigh, incapable of thinking about the mechanics further. She pulled her father's spellwork from her work bag and held it against her chest for a long moment. Then she reached into her bag to begin unpacking her things. But a thought hit her violently—what was the point? When would she next have to flee?

So instead, Raegan zipped her bag back up and hesitantly returned to the archives. When she arrived, the King was placing two coffee cups and saucers onto the long, gleaming worktable. He had switched on a row of old-fashioned reading lamps, the green glass and brass frames glinting in the firelight.

Raegan paused for a moment at the edge of the table, her father's spellcraft clutched in her arms. She inhaled, taking in the arched bookcases behind the King, crafted from a gorgeous dark brown wood that almost appeared black in the low light. The Art Nouveau-patterned rug beneath the worktable unfurled in leafy scrolls of deep emerald green. The rich smell of espresso perfected the scene. In so many ways, these surroundings seemed handpicked to soothe her. But of course, Raegan felt no peace. She was not sure she had felt peace in many, many years.

The King cleared his throat, and she shook off the thoughts that had settled onto her shoulders, pulling the nearest ceramic mug closer. It looked like a latte, but she didn't care. As long as there was plenty of caffeine, she'd be happy.

"Here," Raegan said, placing the spellcraft sheets onto the table without ceremony. Her eyes trained on the King, she brought the mug to her mouth, savoring the flavor.

He pushed his own coffee aside, leaning over the table toward the spellcraft. "May I?" he asked, looking up at her, his hand hovering over the closed folder. She furrowed her brow, not understanding—the spellcraft had been part of their deal, and yet he still requested permission to touch it.

"Yes," Raegan confirmed, ignoring the deft movements of his powerful hands, taking another long pull from her coffee. "And you are permitted to view all of it this time."

By the time she settled the cup back onto its saucer, the King had laid out all seven pages on the table. Raegan watched silently as he shuffled them a few times, changing the order, peering closer at certain elements. After a few moments, he reached for a nearby storage shelf, plucking a leather-bound notebook and fountain pen from it. Then he studied each page in turn, making notes as he went. Raegan was struck by how similar his process of understanding and unraveling seemed to her own. She shoved that thought aside. He was a tool to find her father; nothing more.

But she drew closer all the same, peeking around the King. He seemed absorbed in deciphering a symbol etched in the margins of one page. She took another step, leaning over his arm, so close—too close—that their hips almost brushed. The King's concentration seemed to snap, and without moving the rest of his body, he turned his head to face her. The intensity of his gaze made Raegan's heart pulsate, warmth rebelliously pooling in her belly.

"What can I do? To help, I mean?" she asked, shifting back and taking another sip of her coffee, struggling to remain focused and unaffected by the Fey being beside her. A task was a necessary distraction, and besides, anything could be another step closer to finding her father.

"Remind me of your occupation?" the King requested, his

full attention settled on her, as electrifying as it was disconcerting.

"I'm a journalist," she replied, trying to keep her tone steady.

He made a low noise of approval that sent the heat in Raegan's core roaring through her body. Then he reached across the table, pulled a book from a pile he must have gathered earlier, and offered it to her. Eyes narrowed, she took it, careful not to allow their fingertips to brush.

"Could you research this symbol?" he asked, gesturing to a glyph in the margins. "It may be incidental. I do not want to waste too much time on it, but ignoring it entirely would be foolish."

Raegan looked down at the clothbound book he had handed her, turning it over in her hands. It was a collection of symbols, glyphs and runes commonly and not-so-commonly used in spellcraft.

"Sure," she replied with a shrug, tucking the book under her arm. "Do you have more paper and pens?"

Already back to the spell papers, his attention gone from her as quickly as it had arrived, the King gestured to a nearby shelf. Raegan let out a breath and dug around for a pen she liked, snatching a spiral-bound notebook from a small cache of writing pads. Then she leaned in toward the King again, hoping to copy the symbol for ease of researching.

"You are quite close despite ample workspace," he snapped at her, none of that heady softness in his voice, only sharp irritation.

"Oh, fuck off," she grumbled, casting him a sideways look. "You're hogging all the spell papers. I'm trying to copy the symbol down so I can, you know, actually research it."

The King straightened, one hand flat on the table to support his weight, the other reaching up to pinch the bridge of his nose. Raegan found the mannerism sharply familiar, the ache of it seeping deep into her heart.

"I am sorry," he said, eyes meeting hers. "I am in a good deal of pain. I prefer my physical space when it reaches this intensity, which only occurred recently. You had no way of knowing."

Raegan was taken aback by both the admission and the honesty. She looked at him for a moment, wondering if this was some kind of play or ploy. But the crease in his brow was as real as anything, and she'd already caught the way he moved with occasional discomfort more than once.

"It's okay," she said, holding his gaze. "Thanks for telling me. Does this happen a lot? Being in this much pain?"

The moment the words left her mouth, she realized she already knew the answer. The King looked away, a rueful, bitter half-smile sliding across his angular features. He drummed his fingers on the table as if he were making a decision. Raegan waited, letting the silence settle in around them, only the fireplace crackling and popping in the distance, the smell of old books and gleaming woods and tanned leathers dancing on the edges of her senses.

"Yes, it does," he replied finally, looking at her again. "I am always in some degree of pain, often severe. I would appreciate you not mentioning this to anyone. Many would see it as weakness."

"Sure," she murmured. "Of course."

She felt so keenly then the gap between them. The King had survived all these years, no rest, no fresh starts, no new bodies; she had slept and awoken anew again and again. Before she could voice this feeling, or even say anything else at all, the openness on his face dissipated like morning fog, gone in an instant. It stung. But it was a useful reminder to sharpen herself against their shared past, to bring her walls up higher.

"See what you can find on the symbol," the King said, looking back down at the spellcraft again.

Raegan didn't need to be told. She'd already opened the book, skimming the table of contents, grateful for anything to look at that wasn't him. She didn't mind the work, even at the late hour. It was a foothold, a familiarity, a place where her body might not sing his name.

She wasn't sure how long it had been—only that she was eight notations and a page of theory notes deep—when she saw the King wave his hand in her peripheral vision. A chair appeared at her side, as well as his, both the perfect height to sit at the worktable. She settled into hers gratefully.

Another half-page of notes later, the words of the book began to blur. She sat back and stretched her arms above her head, not able to hide her yawn.

The King caught her gaze, sidelong. "It is nearly three in the morning," he said, examining her. "Perhaps you should retire to your room to rest."

Frustration skittered through her body; neither of them appeared to have found anything earth-shattering so far. Raegan clenched her jaw, about to spit back that she wasn't done just yet, but then the opportunity to be away from him washed over her with a bitter kind of relief.

Infuriatingly, the King read her as easily as the three books he'd been paging through. "Rest," he urged, sitting back in his chair. "Join me here tomorrow morning when you awaken?"

"Sure," she said with a shrug, getting to her feet, body stiff. She snatched the notebook she'd been using from the table, wondering if she should also take her father's spellwork, when a thought hit her. "Wait. Where do *you* live?"

"Not here," the King replied blandly. "You will require a morning meal, yes?"

Raegan rolled her eyes, pushing her chair in and taking a few steps toward the guest chambers before answering. "Humans need three meals a day," she replied, looking at him over her shoulder. "Not sure how you can't keep that straight. Oh, and tea. I'll need a lot of tea."

Without another glance, Raegan slipped through the door to the living quarters and padded down the hall to her room.

She undressed as she walked to the bed—socks, sweater, pants, bra—and rooted through her bag for the first comfy things she could find.

She knew she should use the time away from the King to plot and plan and be ready for all that was to come, but the moment she was curled beneath the soft flannel sheets, sleep overcame her. Lost somewhere in the drowsy twilight, she thanked whatever god oversaw this small mercy. To stay awake, she knew, was to weep for all that she had lost, and she did not know if she would ever be able to stop once she began.

So she tumbled headfirst into oblivion, hoping to find a gentle, quiet darkness. But she found nothing gentle, nothing quiet. Only darkness.

CHAPTER FORTY-TWO

It was a familiar landscape that awaited her: the wide, deep river, craggy mountains, and gray skies of her recurring dream. A deep sense of dread laced with iron-willed purpose coiled in her stomach like a snake. She knew this dream, knew it as well as she knew anything at all. But something was different this time, like a rock had been overturned to show what slept beneath.

An autumn breeze blew, heavy with the scent of woodsmoke. Leaves crunched underfoot, and she had the sense of a cloak over her shoulders. Someone walked next to her, trailing a bit behind, but she knew them. She never doubted for a moment that they would remain at her side no matter the cost.

When she reached the riverbank, a lucid part of her reeled, recognizing that the dream had never allowed her to plumb its depths before. But the tide of the dream was stronger than that tiny lucid spark, and all she heard was her companion pleading for her to leave it be, that what she was doing would never be worth the price.

She ignored them, dropping to her knees at the riverbank, carving strange spirals deep into the mud, whispering something under her breath. Time stretched and dilated—an eternity could've passed—but then she was covered in mud and a scintillating spiral overtook the bank before her, its curves sinuous and strange.

"This will take far too much from you," the voice behind her said, and that lucid part of her froze because she knew that voice —would know it anywhere.

Of course, of course, it was the King's.

She wanted to turn around, to ensure her hearing had not deceived her, but the dream had its own life and sway, and before she knew it, her dream-body was shedding her cloak, and then her skirts and kirtle before unbuckling a belt and pulling off her boots. Only when she wore nothing at all, free of the weight of the mud-soaked cloth, did she wade into the river. It should have been cold. But she felt nothing.

When she reached the middle of the river, she threw her head back and screamed, all unbridled rage and half-mad desperation. The sound was a summoning, something that reached beyond words, something old and deep and lonely. It strained at her vocal cords, like it might tear her throat in two. But she was strong—more than strong enough to command this darkling cry.

Her hands were open, she realized, held perpendicular to her torso, the river's current lapping over her palms. Suddenly, there was a foreign weight in her grasp. She looked down.

It was a shield made of the most peculiar material, so brown it was almost black, slick like river silt, sharp like old magick, and heavy as folklore. It had no seams or thin spots, as if it had been carved from one solid piece. The shield was formidable, heavy, uncleavable. She kissed its surface and bowed to the river. Then her dream-body turned toward the shore.

And there he was, without a doubt. The King stood there on the banks.

Younger, the lucid-her realized, with no lines around the eyes, no hint of silver in his inky black hair. He should, she thought, look terrified of the woman whose body she was in, *naked and covered in river silt, emerging from the water with a conjured shield the color of dried blood.*

The King did not. He was looking at her like he had never seen anything so magnificent in his entire life, like perhaps he never would again.

She reached the bank, strides carrying her to the King. He did not throw a cloak over her shoulders, did not pull her shivering body close, because she was not cold and she did not need him to keep her warm. She spoke his name—but that name wasn't Oberon, she noticed, too late to catch what she had said—and handed him the shield, her muscles beginning to falter under its weight.

He took it, their eyes locked, and the second his fingers touched the shield, she felt it—the Fatesong in her chest, the knowledge that she would see this to the end. Together, they could try to change the ending.

The King-with-a-different-name slid the shield over his arm, holding it across his chest like a knight already in his mausoleum. She reached for him, her mouth meeting his, the cool surface of the shield between them coming to rest on her breastbone. He tasted, she thought, of mead and judgment and Fate. For the briefest of moments, the shield shone like wet blood before he let it rest against his side.

She fit her body against his, her bare skin pressed to the rough cloth of his garments, his hard muscle just beneath. Only then did he pull her close, arm sliding around her waist, palm open on her soft belly, bowing his head to bring his brow to her shoulder.

She parted her lips to remind him, mouth moving against his ear,

"You will be the one to end this."

And then a strange series of gentle booms resounded in the dreamscape, melting away the river and the King and the shield.

Raegan awoke, sitting straight up, her heart racing quick

as a current. She found herself back in the guest chambers of the archives, flannel sheets tangled around her legs. The sound was much more mundane than it had seemed in her dream—just someone knocking on the door to her room. It had to be the King. She could probably pretend she was still asleep.

But the Seal and the Protectorate and the dream and her father's spellcraft . . . all the strange and terrible things that pulled at her with pleading hands, a labyrinth waiting to be walked.

Groggy, Raegan forced herself to her feet, shuffling toward the door and pulling it open. She found the King on the other side of the threshold, much as she had expected.

"Is everything okay?" she asked, pushing auburn curls away from her face. Her heart hammered mercilessly in her chest at the sight of him.

The King took her in with his usual cool, calm demeanor. He was dressed in an impeccable three-piece suit, its shade a deep, dark green. It did wonders for his pale complexion. He looked infuriatingly well-rested and unspeakably attractive.

Raegan, by contrast, surely had an entire rat's nest on her head, as she hadn't even remembered to braid her hair before sleeping. Her joggers were covered with a downy layer of lint from the flannel sheets and her thin camisole was intended for sleep only. She wished she had grabbed a sweatshirt or told him she'd be there in a moment. She wished she had done anything but obey the part of her that wished to see him as quickly as possible.

"I am sorry to disturb you," the King said. "You have slept for the entire day. It is nearly nine in the evening. I only wanted to ensure you were alright."

Dumbfounded, Raegan said nothing for a long moment. She could not remember the last time she'd slept for so long, not even when her depression was at its worst and leaving her bed felt like an impossible task.

"Shit," she eventually said. "I guess I was tired."

"As long as you are alive and well," the King replied, like it would only be mildly inconvenient if he had found her corpse instead. "When you have rested adequately, we have a number of items to discuss." His words should have been generous, but his voice had a sour undertone, lips curling mockingly.

"I did flood an entire café and discover the world is nothing like it seems," Raegan said in defense of herself, leaning against the doorframe. Her mind moved more slowly than she liked, the dream haunting the corners of her vision like a double exposure.

"Yes," the King replied, amusement sliding across his features. "The result of pent-up abilities. It would take you another thirty years to do something similar again."

He said it back-handedly, as if it were of no great interest. But Raegan noticed that the mention of what she had done made the King look at her differently, like he was remembering who she had once been. She caught his gaze tracking down her frame for a heartbeat. The way her body reacted—heart surging, desire kindling low in her belly—was as strong as if he had physically touched her.

"I will be in the reading room," the King said, his tone clipped now, weight shifted away from her. "Please continue to rest if that is what you require."

Then he turned and continued down the hallway, gait as effortless and graceful as Raegan had ever seen it. She closed the door, pressing her back against it for a long moment, eyes squeezed shut, lips pressed together. Her body yearned for the King in a way she had never experienced before—like there was a tightly-locked chest inside her and he was the only one with the key. And god, she wanted him to open her wide, to feel those powerful hands run down her body and then slide inside . . .

Raegan opened her eyes and forced a long inhale. A quest yawned wide and hungry. She couldn't allow something as simple as lust to distract her. Not even for the person she defied death for again and again.

She dragged herself across the room to root through her bag for something to wear, doing her best not to think about whatever it was that she and the King had once had together. Love had always been a tricky thing for her. She had found out very early that people could disappear at any time, gone forever without a trace. Love was like opening a door, and Raegan was worried that if she stepped through, she'd only find another empty grave.

She abandoned that sharp-edged thought, dressing in soft, oversized clothing before heading into the bathroom to take her meds and brush her teeth. Even though the King claimed she'd slept for nearly an entire day, the face in the mirror did not look any less exhausted. Dark circles curved like bruises beneath her eyes.

She leaned forward, meeting her reflection's eyes in the mirror. As of this moment, she was unchanged. Raegan supposed that, at some point, this journey might mark her. No one escaped a fairytale unaltered. Perhaps, she considered, she would know she was approaching the end when her reflection held something beyond herself.

"More things you don't have the bandwidth to consider right now," she chided herself, trudging over to the coffee table to retrieve her notebook and pen.

When she arrived at the archives, the King was awaiting her, seated at the long, gleaming worktable. "There is hot water in the kettle," he told her, not looking up from the book he was reading.

Raegan, as always, went where the caffeine was. Along the kitchenette's counter, she found not only a freshly boiled kettle but also a platter with pastries and fruit. She prepared a cup of tea and a plate for herself, then went to sit with the King. For the briefest of moments, the scent of woodsmoke and black pepper and rain nearly pulled her back into the dream entirely, and she found herself standing on the river-bank with the shield and the long, hard length of his body pressed against hers.

"Had some pretty intense dreams last night," she said, trying to keep her tone level. "I think that's why I slept so long."

The King didn't bother to look up. "It is good you were able to rest."

Annoyed for a reason she couldn't quite place, Raegan reached for her tea. The bergamot and Ceylon covered up any lingering scent she associated with the King, which she was grateful for. But the dream still clung to her, digging fingers into her flesh, and she could not release it from the waking world.

"It . . . finished, I guess, for the first time I can remember," she said, staring straight ahead, tracing her fingers along the teacup's mouth. "There was the river, and I conjured a shield and . . . you. You were there. Younger. Different name."

At that, the King finally looked up, but there was no surprise or confusion in his features. Raegan was no fool and had picked up that he was not particularly emotive, but she would have expected at least a trace of *something*.

Then the King released a breath, the line of his shoulders sagging. "I know," he said, holding her gaze in a way that once again made her realize how ancient he was, his gray eyes fath-omless. "I know, Overhill. I too had the dream last night."

CHAPTER FORTY-THREE

A hush settled over the vast, dim space, broken only by the hitch in Raegan's breathing. She didn't think she had even gotten her mind around the experience yet, and now she had to wonder if the King had been there, too. The same lucid splinter caught in the skin of his dreaming body.

"It is unusual that you can recall such an early memory," the King said, closing his book, the weight of his full attention now on Raegan's shoulders, not unlike a heavy fur cloak.

"It's a memory, then?" she managed to ask, her late breakfast and hot cup of tea forgotten.

He nodded, watching her so closely that it almost made Raegan shrink away—his searching eyes an abyss gazing back at her, hungry and endless. A thought came to her, quick as a bead of blood after a thorn's prick.

"Are you looking for *her*?" she asked in a raw whisper.

For a moment, the enormity of the King's sorrow was so plain that she wondered how he could possibly carry its weight. His grief called to her own, and the immense loss she had felt last night swept onto her shores again. She wanted to throw herself on the ground and weep, to beg and bargain, to forgo everything and forsake everyone if only she could have him back.

Instead, Raegan looked away from the King, wishing she had never said anything about the dream at all, wishing she had forgotten it the moment she opened her eyes, wishing Death would just fucking keep her next time.

"My father's spell," she mumbled, gesturing toward it. "What does it do? And will it help me find him?"

The King took a long pull of tea, looking almost grateful for her redirection. His mask of cool composure had returned. "It is an attempt to reach the Gates," he replied, as if the past few moments hadn't happened at all, "unlike any others I have seen before, which is no short list. If this is the 'work of the one who came before,' and if that refers to your father, then finding him and fulfilling the Prophecy could be one and the same."

Raegan chewed on the inside of her cheek, happy to be lost in thought. She opened her notebook and asked him to continue. He complied, explaining that the spellcraft was dangerous, as the Gates existed on the far side of the In-Between, ruled by the Timekeeper. There was no guarantee of destroying the Gates themselves, or even staying alive long enough to do anything at all.

"Hold on," she said, a massive headache blooming behind her eyes. She drained what was left in her teacup. "I've heard the Timekeeper mentioned a few times. Who is that, exactly?"

For a moment, surprise flickered on the King's face, but then he seemed to recall the nature of Raegan's memory. "An old god," he told her, choosing his words slowly. "He demanded worship and sacrifice from the early mortals in Cymru, so my people imprisoned him beneath the Isles. Years later, the men that would become the Protectorate freed him in exchange for defeating the Tylwyth Teg and creating the Gates."

Raegan nodded, scribbling a few lines in her notebook,

desperately trying to ignore the way the King had shifted in his seat to face her, his eyes tracking her movements. She set her jaw and forced herself to be a reporter right now—nothing more. "Why would the Protectorate free him?" she asked, tapping her pen against the worktable. "If the Fey felt imprisoning him was necessary, it seems like he would be bad news for us humans."

A rueful expression moved across the King's face as he pushed his teacup away. "Time," he said, as if that explained everything. "He is the god of time. My people are exceedingly long-lived, if not immortal. What need do we have to bargain for more years? Mortals, though—oh, the deals and sacrifices they will make for just a little more time. Particularly during the days when the Fair Folk walked ageless among them."

Raegan's headache all but exploded, and she squeezed her eyes shut, her pen falling limp against her notepad. *Everything* was about time, was it not? Her own life revolved around how fast she could file a story, how quickly the mayor's office would call her back, who got the scoop on the latest scandal first. Wasn't everyone just selling their precious, sacred time for wages because it was the only way to survive?

"Wait," she said, her mind turning over in her aching skull. "Are you saying that men were mad the Fey were more powerful than them, so they released Kronos, and now we have fucking *capitalism*?"

Amusement sparked in the King's gaze, making Raegan's stomach flip. He leaned forward onto the table on his forearms, startlingly close to her hands. "More or less," he replied, eyes dropping to her notebook for a moment.

"Okay," Raegan said, scribbling down more and then flipping to a new page. "Thanks. So back to my father's spell. Why is it so interesting to you? Because of the Prophecy? You didn't seem particularly happy about that."

The King sighed, unfolding to stand. Then he turned his back to the worktable, staring out into the cavernous space. In the silence, Raegan noticed slinking notes of classical music floating above the ever-present murmur of the fireplace.

"I have been named in Prophecies before," he finally said, crossing his arms. "I find I do not like the loss of agency. No, the Prophecy is not why. Though I admit it lends weight."

Raegan opened her mouth to ask more, but he kept speaking, his gaze falling to the large, yellowed pieces of parchment spread out like a door on the table.

"This," he continued, gesturing to her father's spellcraft, "is different because it calls for an anchor already placed within the Timekeeper's realm. Completing this spellcraft requires two people who share blood or an oath of some kind. The first is a sacrifice; they make a bargain with the Timekeeper. When he comes to collect his due, he takes them to the In-Between to slowly feast upon whatever years they have left. That establishes a tether—or perhaps a lighthouse, if you will."

The King paused, and Raegan wondered if it was because of how furiously she was writing. She wished she had thought to bring a recorder; her hand was cramping.

"Sort of like selling your soul to the devil?" she asked, putting her pen down for a minute to massage the base of her thumb. "You make a bargain to be, let's say, a great musician for ten years, but then your soul goes to hell."

"Yes," the King said, rearranging a stack of beautiful leather-bound books on the end of the table. "The Devil is a fascinating figure in human folklore. There is little doubt a large part of his behavior and character are directly lifted from the Timekeeper."

"Okay," Raegan said, tucking one leg underneath her as she turned to a fresh page. "And then the second person uses the tether to locate and enter the Timekeeper's realm, I'm guessing?"

· · ·

The King said nothing, looking over at her with a guarded expression. She gazed back blankly, confusion swarming about in her mind. And then it came to her, heavy as laced boots on a drowning man.

"Oh," she murmured, her heart plummeting to the bottom of her stomach. "My dad is the tether."

The way he disappeared without a trace. The way even Nyx's scrying glass could not afford them more than the barest of glances: her father's face behind a window. The way the King and Cordelia both thought he was within a primordial being's realm. The way the spellcraft had been waiting for her all these years—for its second dance partner.

Raegan dropped her head into her hands, only the soft mustiness of the books and the crackle of the fireplace still perceivable. And then she lost herself in the memory of her father's encounter with the tweed-suited man on the train platform. She recalled his obsession with it in aching detail— the way the tale had haunted her, always just on the edge of her vision. Squeezing her eyes shut, she staved off tears as she remembered how insistently her father always told that story.

Like she would need to know every detail because the entirety of magic hung in the balance. "Fuck," Raegan huffed into her clammy palms.

"I am suspicious of why a mortal would go to these extremes," the King said from somewhere in her periphery. "And I am always suspicious of a Prophecy. But this spellcraft is a true chance, and I have given far more for far lesser hopes. Of course, you will be unable to complete the spell without your Seal removed, and even then, it remains to be seen how quickly your capabilities will return. Make no mistake: this venture is dangerous."

She raised her head, propping her chin with her hands and staring out into the vastness of the archives. The center pathway twisted and then disappeared into shadows, the sconces along the walls shimmering like orange jewels. And yet among all these nameless and unknown treasures, the seven pieces of parchment on the table might be the most precious of them all.

If she was strong enough to follow the trail her father had left behind. A few days ago, Raegan would've never doubted that. But now she'd existed in this darker, stranger world for barely any time at all and had needed to sleep for an absurd amount of time to recover—almost an entire goddamn day.

And then, just like that, a thought of the more mundane variety paralyzed her. "Wait," she said, her voice hoarse as she turned to look at the King. "You said I slept for almost a day. What day of the week is today? It's not Sunday, right?"

"Yes," he answered, sharp and sure. "It is Sunday."

Raegan leaned back in her chair, both hands coming up to cover her face again. Nausea swirled in her abdomen, and damp, prickly anxiety swept through her. "I should've gone to work," she moaned from behind her hands. "Fuck me."

"Did you not handle your affairs?" the King asked, the condescending calm of his voice among the calamity of her realization making her furious.

"No, Oberon!" Raegan shouted, slamming her hands on the table. "No, weirdly enough, I wasn't exactly thinking about the future, considering the kelpie and my dad and the Protectorate and the Prophecy and you! I was sort of playing it by ear for a bit there! How could I *possibly* forget about my fucking *job* when I've spent the last twenty-four hours thinking I was going to die or be abducted or tricked into some terrible agreement with a faerie king?"

She stared at him, breathing hard, feeling the anger seep red across her face and chest.

"I suppose that is reasonable," the King conceded after a moment's pause, seemingly not at all fazed by her outburst.

Raegan dug into her pocket for her phone, letting out a furious, half-strangled shriek when she realized it was back in the living quarters. She stood, her chair scraping discordantly against the stone floor.

"Can I be of assistance?" the King asked in such a polite voice that she wanted to throw something at him.

"I need my phone so I can . . ." she spat in reply, trailing off, trying to think, "say I've been tremendously sick, I guess?"

He straightened and took a step forward in one long, fluid movement, more shadow than flesh. "Please follow me to my office. It is impossible to receive service here due to the wards."

Raegan trailed behind the King as he headed for the hallway leading away from the reading room, muttering about wards under her breath. Of course, her phone didn't work here. How else could she have slept so long without Henry, and probably Saanvi, calling her about eighty times?

When they arrived at his office, the King gestured toward an old-fashioned landline telephone set atop a filing cabinet. She stared at it, the realization that there was no point calling in sick for the day crashing down around her.

Raegan knew that she'd be gone much longer than that. She knew she might not even come back at all. What to say, she wondered, to the people she planned to leave behind in a world broken in half?

And all those years ago, had her father wondered the exact same thing?

CHAPTER FORTY-FOUR

Raegan set the telephone handset back in its cradle, her hands trembling. She'd been so distraught when speaking with Henry that he'd had virtually no choice but to believe her—to believe that the old darkness had returned again, and now one of his best reporters faced inpatient hospitalization at a mental health facility. Just for a few weeks, she'd sworn a number of times, as if speaking the timeline into existence would make it come true. As if locating an ancient folkloric witch, regaining her lost memory, and then marching into an unknown realm to fight a god would take but a few weeks.

The reading room stood empty when Raegan returned, and she sank into one of the chairs that faced the fireplace, pulling her knees to her chest. Its warmth did not seem to reach her. The realization that following this thread of Fate required leaving people behind sent a palpable chill over her skin. Henry had promised he'd contact Bronwyn after Raegan made up some lie about only being granted so much time on the phone. But still, she'd be the second person her mother loved to leave in this way.

A soft stirring to her right—like that feeling in the air just before a thunderstorm rolls in—pulled her from her thoughts. Raising her head, she found the King standing a few feet away.

He met her gaze and then lowered himself into the chair beside her. "I have arranged a meeting with an informant offering details on Baba Yaga's whereabouts," he said, the firelight flickering across his high cheekbones and aquiline nose.

"Okay," she breathed, twisting in her seat to face him. "And? Feels like there's a catch here."

His eyes slid to hers, broad chest rising with a deep inhale. A log crashed against the grate in the fireplace, making her jump. "The informant is a member of the Seelie Court," the King said, a wry amusement pulling at the sides of his mouth. "They will only meet on neutral ground, and they specifically want to see *you*."

Something unfolded inside her, light as a moth's wing, beaded in dew. Then it dissipated as quickly as it had arrived, a dove-colored wisp of smoke. She tongued the inside of her cheek, focusing on the King's words. "Fine," she said, meeting his gaze. "So we go. I assume it's within your abilities to keep me safe from any nonsense the Seelie Court might have in mind?"

As she spoke, Raegan remembered one of the footnotes in her father's mythology book—that the Seelie Court had not fought at Camlann, and if they had, the battle may have turned out entirely differently. She had a feeling that the past thousand years had done little to erase any contention.

The King scoffed in response, getting to his feet. Her mouth went hopelessly dry as she watched him re-button his jacket as he stood, the deft movement of his powerful hands kindling desire in her core.

"It matters not," he said, striding toward the worktable, where he picked up a stack of books. "You are not going. There are too many variables at a place like Gossamer—too much delicate politics."

He placed the stack of books on the table beside her,

bringing his body close to hers—almost as if he hoped to distract her from the dismissal. It nearly worked, the fire in Raegan's belly building to an inferno, black pepper and damp stone slinking into her senses. But her anger was just as quick to spark.

"What?" she demanded, looking up at him, settling clenched fists on each side of the chair's arms. "Of course I'm coming. The Seelie Court wants to see *me*. Handle the fucking politics, Oberon. Aren't you a goddamn king?"

There was something about speaking those words aloud that tugged at her—a silken rope wrapped around her wrist, as if to pull her back when she wandered too far away. Briefly, a vision of an impossibly long table in a forest laden high with fruits and golden goblets and a million lit candles sprang to her mind. Before she could examine it, the moment danced away.

Beside her, the King let out a low sigh, plucking the top book—a pretty volume with gold gilt lettering and dark floral cloth—from the pile. He ran his hand over it, his gaze meeting hers again. "You will be safe here," he said, his authoritative tone displaying how accustomed he was to being obeyed. "For all my power and influence, Gossamer is neutral ground and the Protectorate has your scent. I would be a fool to promise I can absolutely guarantee your safety."

He cut himself off, something shifting in his expression. Then the King stepped in toward Raegan, gently pulling on her wrist until her clenched palm faced upward toward the ceiling. He slipped his long fingers beneath her tightly-curled ones, prying with a light touch until she unfurled them. Despite everything, the brush of his skin against hers was a cool breeze after a thousand scorching summers.

The King pressed the gold gilt-lettered book into her open palm. His much larger hand engulfed hers as he closed her fingers around the volume before reaching for her other wrist. All the while, Raegan's heart throbbed dangerously beneath the delicate skin of her throat. Her eyes were level with the King's broad shoulders, and there was nothing she could do to stop her mind from imagining the corded muscles beneath the deep green cloth.

She could have tried to look away, but Raegan was afraid that if she did, her gaze would drift upwards, past the King's strong jaw and to his full, beautiful mouth. Then she would have no choice but to imagine the feel of his lips against hers, and she was not sure she could survive that.

The King's powerful hand slid around her wrist, his touch gentle but indecently firm, fingertips brushing the sensitive softness on the underside of her forearm. He brought her other hand to the book—though she desired so desperately instead for him to pin her hands above her head and lower the hard expanse of his body against hers, to draw all the forgotten things out of her by sheer, unrelenting force alone.

"Stay here," the King commanded, and for once in her life, Raegan wanted nothing more than to yield and to be rewarded for her obedience. "Read. Sleep. I will return with information about Baba Yaga."

Intoxicated by his touch, her skin yearning for his, the low thrum of his voice spreading fire through her core, she almost listened. Almost.

"No," she said, raising her eyes to his, their noses mere inches apart. "This is about me, too."

His expression darkened, the beautiful eyes narrowing, a muscle in his jaw clenching. "You will stay here," he repeated, his hands now applying pressure on hers, as if he could physically press her into doing what he wished. "You are *safe* here."

"I said I'm coming," she snapped, leaning forward and sliding her legs off the seat, knees brushing his legs.

"I am the High King of the Unseelie Court," he countered, his voice as low and dark as she'd ever heard it. He seemed to welcome her physical aggression, removing his hands from hers to grip the chair's arms, pinning her in on every side. "And I said you will stay here."

As the King spoke, he drew closer, lowering the weight and power of his immortal body toward her much softer, weaker, mortal one. Raegan could feel the heat of his skin through the layers of clothing that separated them. She wondered if he could sense how mercilessly her blood pounded for him, a siren song that begged with each breath to simply give in.

But then the tidal wave of anger broke upon Raegan's shores, all white-hot and indignant, fueled by a feeling of complete and utter helplessness. Any words she could conjure died on her tongue—and so without another single intelligent thought, she tightened her grip on the book the King had pressed into her hands and chucked it over his shoulder at the opposite wall. It made a soft thud on impact, the pages crinkling against the stone, spine crumpling as it landed in a heap on the ground below.

"Get a grip, High King!" Raegan shouted, surprised at how loudly her voice rang out in the space. "Do you honestly think I'm going to stay behind to read and knit or what-fucking-ever because you can't handle your own shit? Because that's what this is. I'm finally back, and you can't handle the idea that something might happen to me. Guess what? Something *always* happens to me. You're always going to lose me. Get used to the goddamn pain."

Her voice broke on the last sentence, the air in her lungs depleted. But the King didn't even flinch. No matter what she flung at him, he never retreated like everyone else always did. Instead, he held himself in exactly the same place, his body hovering above hers, arms caging her in.

"*Fine,*" the King spat at her, his lip curling with fury.

Raegan hadn't even processed that she had bent the Unseelie King to her will before he caught her jaw between the fingers of one hand, holding her gaze with those deep gray eyes.

"Get dressed," he snarled, the planes of his face growing increasingly feral in a way that should have sent fear skittering through Raegan's body, though she only felt heat and need, coiled so tightly she thought she might explode. "I hope you have something in that bag appropriate for the finest Fey club on this continent."

She held his gaze. "And if I don't?"

He offered her a dagger of a smile. "I could make you a beautiful gown from a handful of oak leaves, but personal enchantments aren't permitted at Gossamer, so the moment you step through the doors, you'd be quite . . . exposed."

The challenge sang across Raegan's skin, and she shoved off the chair. Only at the last moment did the King release his grasp, stepping just to the side, allowing her to slip by.

She took a few strides toward the living quarters and then turned to examine him over her shoulder. "I can see what you've been thinking about in your spare time," she said with a dangerous grin before heading to the passage into the guest chambers.

Reaching her room, Raegan slammed her shoulder into the door, barging inside. For obvious reasons, she hadn't thought to pack any formal clothing that would come even close to matching the King's perfect suiting. Anger and damp hot lust swirled through her body as she began to dig into her overnight bag. Frustratingly, her best options appeared to be leggings with tumbled leather panels and a long, sheer sweater.

But then her hand hit an unfamiliar textile at the bottom of the bag. Curious, Raegan pulled it from the depths, gasping out loud when she saw her favorite dress: a tight, black, midi-length piece with a low neckline, corset-style bodice and a long-sleeved, closely-fitted sheer shrug that cut away from the bust. It was wrinkled, and she had absolutely no idea how it had gotten in there—not until she dug deeper and found a pair of pointed-toe heels with long leather ties that wound up the leg. And then it hit her: she'd visited a college friend last month to see his new apartment in New York, and he had insisted they go out to a club his colleague had been promoting. She'd probably just shoved the bag under her bed after the trip without unpacking.

Feeling powerful, Raegan ducked into the bathroom and began to sort through her haphazardly packed bag of toiletries. At the bottom, she found an ancient kohl pencil she'd thought she'd thrown out a long time ago. It would do. She was elated to find that a tube of mascara and a bottle of ibuprofen had made its way into the random assortment as well.

She downed three pills for her headache and then turned to examine the bathroom floor, remembering how the room had appeared to clean and fold her clothing the night before. Skeptical, she gently put her dress on the ground and then turned back to the mirror.

There, she scrutinized her complexion, taking in the redness around her eyes and the unusually pale shade her golden-hued, freckled skin had taken on. Leaning toward the mirror, Raegan traced the kohl in a sideways V-shape from the outward corner of her eye, smudging it with her fingers until it created a dark, grunge-y cat-eye effect. She applied mascara and then used a tube of lip gloss, both for its intended purpose and also to add a little highlight and dimension to her cheekbones.

"Not bad," Raegan said appraisingly, dampening her hands under the faucet to lightly reshape her long curls. When she looked back up, her dress was hanging by a hook on the back of the door, perfectly pressed.

She found a black lace thong that sort of matched the nicest bra she'd brought with her, and then she was pulling on the dress and stepping into her heels. She stopped to appraise herself in the mirror: hot and deadly, all curves and contrast. A few years ago, she would have lamented the way her stomach was far from flat beneath the tight dress and second-guessed the amount of cleavage on display. But now that she had a Fey king's life to ruin, it all felt perfectly right.

Her blood hummed as she exited the room and strode down the hallway. When Raegan emerged into the reading room, she found the King sitting in front of the fire, the book she had thrown against the wall between his hands. He did not acknowledge her, his gaze directed at the dancing shapes of the hearth. But as she drew closer, Raegan saw the King's gray eyes slide to her, and then down her frame—pausing for a heartbeat in all the right places. His right hand clenched for the barest of moments.

Nothing sensible or wise won out. None of Raegan's street smarts or even a basic regard for her physical safety was able to overcome the thick, beating desire that consumed every inch of her body. So she prowled to the King, planting one hand on either side of the chair, just as he'd done to her. For good measure, she slid her knee onto the chair's seat, right between his thighs.

"Is this good enough?" Raegan asked him, one eyebrow arched, staring down at him.

The King took his time, as he always seemed to, and she tried not to be consumed by thoughts of what else he might do slowly, achingly. His face was impassive as he dragged his eyes from her generous thighs to her soft waist before lingering tauntingly at her bust, and then finally meeting her gaze. "It will do," he replied, bored, unaffected, but his grip on the book she'd thrown tightened. "Do leave my books out of your tantrums in the future."

Without a second thought, Raegan pounced. "Oh, I'm so sorry about your book," she replied, tilting her head to one side, heavy auburn curls falling over her shoulder. "I suppose they are your only company, aren't they?"

Apparently she would have to cut deeper, because the King only sighed, trailing a few fingers down the book's spine. She said nothing, watching him, lips slightly parted. Raegan was rewarded for her efforts when she saw the King's control slip, just a hair, his eyes greedily dipping to her body for a moment or two.

"This title is quite rare," he replied, gaze holding hers again, molten amusement in his expression. "It should be treated with more care. There are some things, Overhill, that demand a finer, more experienced touch."

Heat swept through Raegan. She needed to hike up her dress and wrap her legs around him. She needed to feel the flex of his hard muscle against her body, to remember where the scars etched his skin and to place her mouth on every single one.

She leaned closer, pressing her leg against the King's inner thigh. "I'm not used to being gentle," she breathed. "You'll have to show me what you mean."

His beautiful mouth curved up ever so slightly, and Raegan could've sworn she saw his breath hitch, the rhythm of his broad chest interrupted for a split second. The King removed one hand from his book, reaching over to slide his fingers up the inside of her arm. The rest of the room faded, all of her attention on two things: the memories sparking in her mind, and the frenzied hunger with which she desired the being before her.

But then the King unfolded, rising to his feet like a shadow peeling off a wall, leaving Raegan unbalanced, her leg still between his, dizzy and half-mad with want. One arm sliding around her waist, his palm open against the small of her back, the King steadied Raegan as if it were simply the gentlemanly thing to do. "Come," he said, looking down at her, knowing exactly what he was doing, as always. "We are due at Gossamer."

Chapter Forty-Five

Just outside the King's archives, the moon hung heavy and silver in the sky. A breeze swept down the cobblestones, bringing a tiny tornado of leaves along for the ride. The coffee shop across the street was closed up tightly, and a BYO café farther down the block glowed with warm fairy lights, tiny tables spilled out onto the street, the sounds of wine-drunk patrons just barely reaching Raegan's ears.

"My court's security councilor, the Lady Andronica, will not forgive me if we step outside of the highest wards," the King said, his voice rich as honey in the autumn night, "so she has approved a compromise."

Raegan followed his gaze to what appeared to be a normal taxi idling at the curb. No one occupied the driver's seat, at least not any kind of being that was visible to her eyes. She took a deep breath, filling her lungs with the woodsmoke-rain scent of the King and the crispness of autumn air. At least five questions about the compromise and Lady Andronica sprang to her mind, but she found she hardly cared about the answers, her attention firmly placed elsewhere.

The King opened the passenger door for her, and she

ducked inside, preparing to slide across the leather seats like she would have done with any of her friends. But the High King of the Unseelie Court was not her friend or anything even remotely close to it, and he closed the door behind her before coming around to the other side and joining her in the backseat.

Shortly thereafter, the taxi ambled away from the curb, still no driver in sight. Getting into the car had hiked the slit on Raegan's dress higher, and she was pleased to see the King immediately take notice. It was as if he had been trying to avoid seeing her as a flesh-and-blood being this entire time, and now she had given him no choice in the matter. Raegan leaned toward him, enjoying the power such a thought gave her.

"Tell me about what to expect," she requested, smoothing her dress across her thighs.

The shadowy weight of the King's attention draped across her shoulders. "The Seelie Court is useful when it wants to be," he replied, studying her. "A warning, their informants tend to be twice as flirtatious as they are helpful."

"That seems to be your type," she said, narrowing her eyes, twisting her torso toward him. In this confined space, Raegan's desire threatened to consume her entirely. "What exactly *is* your type?"

The King's sculpted lips parted then, an exhale escaping before he looked away. She waited for him to say something, but no response came, so Raegan pressed her thigh against his. At that, he turned back to her, a playfulness moving across his mouth that would've made her light-headed if not for the sadness shadowing it.

"I imagine," he began, the words a low rumble in his chest as his long-limbed body began to bow around hers, "you already know the answer. Do you intend to make me say it aloud?"

How many times had someone panted in her ear that they

wanted to fuck her or would make her scream or whatever bullshit so many men seemed to think was even remotely stimulating? But here *he* was, using language that was hardly profane in any way, and yet the heat and tension between her legs was building to a sheer torment.

"After all these years?" she asked, fighting for control. "I've ruined your life how many times and you *still* want me that badly? A little pathetic, honestly."

For a moment, Raegan felt his muscles stiffen against her, like he had been struck by a blow. She bit down on the inside of her cheek, watching him, wondering if she had gone too far. It wouldn't be the first time she had dug a bit too deep, claws too sharp for play.

But then the King slackened, the pressure and weight of his heavy muscle back against her build again, and she saw the corner of his mouth curve upward. Relief flooded her. No, not too far. And, some distant memory reminded Raegan that he had always been able to withstand her edges, jagged as broken glass.

The cab slowed to a stop, and she studied the view out the window to see if anything looked familiar. She had been sure it would—after all, she knew the city so well—but the landscape that greeted her looked nothing like anything she'd ever seen. Raegan found echoes of her city in the sparkling schist-stone walls and the elegant turrets, but there was something other-worldly about whatever waited for her beyond the taxi doors, something dark and slinking that reminded her of the King.

She felt the heat of him leave her side before she noticed that he had exited the cab, looping around to, once again, open the door. The King helped her out, every touch lingering for half a heartbeat longer than necessary. When she stood on the sidewalk, Raegan could see a long stone pathway leading to a large black door, the top of its expanse swooping into a sharp curve.

Above it, she was surprised to see neon lettering that

spelled out "Gossamer" in a looping, archaic-looking script. Either side of the pathway was closed in by the neighboring buildings' towering walls.

All her thoughts swept away when the King slipped his arm around her waist, fingers splayed across the curves of her belly. With their bodies fitted together like lost puzzle pieces, they walked to Gossamer's entrance. Raegan fought to stay alert, to keep her wits about her and her distrust sharpened, but every passing moment bracketed by the King's hard wall of muscle made it harder and harder.

The large, arched doors opened easily at the King's touch, which she could understand. Raegan found herself surprised that the entrance to a heavily warded Fey club was so simple, but things made more sense when she found herself in a vestibule. Another set of doors waited at the far end, a hulking Fey, larger than even the King, stood guard. Their features had that sharp, feral look Raegan had come to recognize. Dark locs gathered at the base of their skull. In the dim halfway space, lit only by rows of candles that lined the alcoves high above, the guard's obsidian skin gleamed like a midnight eclipse.

"My liege," the Fey said, bowing their head at the King.

"Kamau," the King replied, something like humor seeping into his tone. "Andronica pulled many strings for tonight, it seems."

At that, Kamau burst into a deep, golden, belly laugh, crossing their massive arms. Raegan noticed their skin was adorned with tattoos, details hard to make out in the low light.

"You know Andronica," Kamau replied. "She's mad you left the safehouse at all. But Baba Yaga must be found. So I am here if you need anything."

Raegan looked up at the King and was surprised to see him actually smile—bright, disarming, and utterly dangerous.

"There is no one else I would rather have at my side," he replied, before turning toward Raegan and introducing her to

Kamau, who turned out to be one of the Unseelie Court's most formidable knights.

Raegan's interest was piqued; the good-natured gleam in Kamau's deep brown eyes did not exactly square with war and murder. But that quick assessment was about as far as she got before the King pulled her even closer and stepped through the second set of doors into Gossamer.

Considering that the entirety of their short ride had been spent trying not to do something ridiculous like climb on top of him, Raegan had not taken sufficient time to prepare herself for what a hidden, magically warded Fey club might look like.

"If you do not close your mouth," the King murmured in her ear, "you will look quite unsophisticated, which is decidedly *not* my type."

Raegan wished his sentence had ended in something a bit different, but she still tried to look less awed by the grand space. It was no easy task. The ceiling sprang away from her, reaching up into an inky black abyss. Vines and branches climbed the walls in effortlessly beautiful patterns, the leafier limbs creating a forest canopy above. Soft pinpricks of light, alarmingly similar to a spray of stars on a clear night, reached through the leaves. Intricate chandeliers of wild brambles were suspended throughout the club, the molasses glow of candlelight flickering from within.

"Fuck," Raegan said under her breath, allowing the King to pull her into the deeper recesses of the beautifully impossible place. "How is this even possible with the Gates?"

"Pocket realms," the King replied, his tone breezy as they made their way through the crowd. "A number of them existed here before the Gates—including my archives. They were created with the old magic, and so they remain. For now. If the residual magic leaves this world entirely, it is likely they will collapse into nothing."

Despite her general obsession with fact-finding, Raegan was only half listening. Yes, this place was a stunning mystery, but . . . the patrons themselves had grabbed her attention. Some were like Oberon and Cordelia and Kamau—sharp-featured, their beauty hard and feral, with graceful limbs and dark eyes. Others sported skin the color of tide pools or iridescent, beetle-like wings. Unlike human clubs, the din was not unbearable. Raegan imagined there had to be magic at work. She could hear the King murmur in her ear, but the space still held the echo and vibration of a packed bar—all the excitement and atmosphere with none of the frustrating inability to flirt or tell someone to fuck off.

The King had no trouble weaving through the throng of Fey to his intended destination. The moment anyone sighted him, heads bowed and conversation slowed. Raegan even caught a few curtseys. She did not escape attention, either—eyes slid over her, a probing kind of interest, not malicious but not kind, either. She was hardly bothered amongst all the wonder. Every fabric she brushed by felt divine. Everyone smelled positively delicious in different ways: a silver-haired slip of a being in a gown made of petals wore lily of the valley, whereas a dark-skinned Fey with a dazzling smile in a shimmering, golden suit smelled of amber, spiced wine and honey.

In a few moments, Raegan caught sight of what she presumed to be their destination: a long, curving bar that seemed to be made of living trees, their trunks meticulously wound together. The bar top itself shimmered like labradorite or an abalone shell. Beyond the busy hustling of the bartenders, a wall of quicksilver—endlessly more magnificent than a mundane mirror—stretched up to the ceiling. Decadent, beautiful bottles lined the elegant metal shelves, filled with liquids that Raegan couldn't even begin to identify.

The King chose two open seats toward the end of the bar, where curving branches tucked into a velvety wall before beginning the climb upwards to meet their brethren. She was sure nearly anyone here would have volunteered their seat for the Unseelie King, but it did not seem to be his style to accept.

She slid onto a stool made of the same twisting limbs as the bar, its flat seat topped with a velvet pillow in one of the jewel tones the Fey seemed to favor. The King sat beside her, raising a hand to a bartender who had already noticed them despite the packed space. Someone on the King's other side greeted him exuberantly, and he turned to respond. In the meantime, Raegan swept her gaze around the room, noticing the alcoves along the walls where more candles burned with a flickering, golden light. A few hallways led off from the main room, but darkness cloaked their depths like a velvet curtain, leaving only the initial bramble arch visible.

She was just turning back to the bar when she abruptly came face-to-face with a tanned Fey to her left, standing much too close. His corn silk hair was swept up and away from his forehead, and his eyes were a disconcerting absinthe green. Just like all the other Fey she'd encountered, his features were nearly human, but not—that strange, skittering otherness so clearly marking them as something else.

The shit-stirring grin on the Fey's face, though, was completely mundane. She'd seen it a hundred other times in a hundred other places, and it was not something that usually went away by being ignored. So Raegan rested one arm on the bar, her back to the King, who was still engaged with someone, and cocked an eyebrow at the blond.

In response, the Fey also placed his hand on the bar top, angling his body around her, a poor attempt at boxing her in. "You here with anyone, Red?" the blond asked, as if he was the first person to ever nickname a redhead in such a way. Raegan wondered if he was relatively young or if he had somehow squandered immortality by remaining so stupid.

At the precise moment that she opened her mouth to reply, the blond's entire face crashed—the grin wiped off as if it had never been there. She watched the Fey swallow hard as his green-eyed gaze shifted to look over Raegan's shoulder. As if fear had prevented him from remembering the existence of his limbs, the blond snatched his hand off the bar top a few beats too late.

"Fuck," the Fey stranger stammered. "I—I didn't know she was here with y-you, High King. I do m-most humbly b-beg you and your lady's pardon."

Raegan had little doubt about what was going on behind her. Her mental image was more or less confirmed when the King's voice, low and dark as dusk, came from just over her shoulder.

"So then *beg*."

Despite the deadly chill in his voice, or perhaps because of it, desire dug its claws deeper into her flesh. She leveled her gaze at the stranger, pleased to see naked terror in his expression as he began to fumble through a series of strained apologies and pleas. His voice shook harder with each sentence.

Then the King's hands slid around Raegan's waist, and every nerve ending she possessed liquified. Hunger drummed in her core. His mouth brushed her ear, and there was nothing she could do to contain the shiver that ran down her body.

"Is he forgiven?" the King asked, the words thick as honey.

Raegan thought about saying no, about seeing how much violence the Unseelie King would enact on her behalf and if the blood would make her desire grow tighter and sweeter. With effort, she pushed the temptation down. "Yes," she said, narrowing her eyes at the blond. "For now. You should go before I change my mind."

The offending Fey melted into the throng of bodies, gone in seconds, leaving Raegan at the King's mercy. His large hands still engulfed her waist, and she could feel his chest at her back. She clamped her jaw so tight she thought a tooth might crack.

The King pulled one hand away, which was enough for Raegan's mind to clear a little. But such clarity lasted only a moment, as he used his free hand to reach for the lip of her stool and pull it closer to his. Trying and failing to push the thrumming of her unmet hunger to the side, Raegan turned to face the bar—and the King.

"I apologize," he said with a small shake of his head. "Seelie scum."

The entire lengths of their thighs were pressed together, the curves of Raegan's hip meeting the sharp, muscled points of the King. She could hardly breathe. "I sort of wanted to ask you to kill him," she found herself saying. "But I thought that might complicate the situation, considering what we're here for. Also would've seemed generally uncool of me, I guess."

His eyes slid to her, the ghost of a smile moving across his mouth. But before he could say anything, two drinks were placed on the bar before them.

"Did you order for me?" she asked, indignant, turning to look at him full-on.

"I would never dream of it," he replied, pushing one glass closer to her. "It is a Fey bar, Overhill. The bartenders know what you want."

She offered only an arch laugh in response, picking up the old-fashioned glass offered to her and examining the molasses-brown liquid within. It looked like a negroni—and a well-made one at that—which was exactly what she had planned to order.

But she could not stop her eyes from slipping to the dark-eyed, raven-haired being beside her. Because at this moment, all Raegan really wanted was the King.

CHAPTER FORTY-SIX

She forced herself to take a sip of her drink anyway, though alcohol was sure to only make matters worse. The flavors fell on her tongue in a way she had never experienced before. Brows furrowed, Raegan held the glass up in front of her as if she could stare at the drink until it told her its secrets. When it did not, she shrugged and took another sip. And then another much longer one for good measure.

"Now what?" she asked, looking at the King in her peripheral vision.

"We wait," he replied in a hushed tone, twisting on the stool to face her. "And we pretend that we are having a wonderful time, certainly not here for any ulterior motives, like clandestine meetings."

"Ahh," she said with a smile. "I suppose no one has a bad time out with you, do they?"

The King smirked, making no attempt to hide it, and the way his mouth moved into the expression made Raegan even more desperate to feel his lips against her skin. Maybe she could get someone to punch her in the face or throw a drink at her. Maybe that would reduce the absolute frenzy her body had worked itself into during the past hour.

"I think not," he said, taking a sip of his own drink, a stormy-colored liquid in a lowball glass. "But I would encourage you to share your thoughts."

"I should've grabbed my notepad," Raegan teased, looking at him sideways, all the questions she'd jotted down rushing into her mind. "Oh, that reminds me, does iron not impact you the way basically every folktale implies it will?"

Maybe treating the King like an interview subject would make this easier. If she could only focus on the facts, on rooting out information and finding the patterns that were sure to exist, perhaps she would be able to avoid the unyielding temptation to fuck him.

"That sort of information," the King replied, tracing a line in his glass's condensation with a fingertip, "is quite privileged."

"We came here in a car, and we've been on the subway together," Raegan deadpanned in response, her body turning to face him before she even realized what was happening.

The King sighed as if she had caught him in some elaborate lie he'd spent months planning, raising his gaze to meet hers. "Yes, technically it does," he replied, his expression open. "But nearly all Fey born on this side of the Gates are immune. We are a resilient people."

Raegan propped her elbow on the bar, resting her chin on her hand. This information was interesting, and more importantly, it was an excellent distraction from how close the King's body was to hers. "But you?" she asked. "And other older Fey who weren't born here?"

The King raised his glass in a mock toast, one eyebrow arched. "We have grown accustomed to the pain," he told her, downing a large portion of his drink. The King handling something with dark humor seemed a bit jovial by his usual standards, which made Raegan even more curious.

"In addition to your existing pain?" she asked, not able to stop the pity that seeped into her tone.

He stiffened at the slight change in her voice, forcing Raegan to wonder exactly how attuned he was to her. She put *that* question away for later, a few loud shrieks momentarily distracting her. Over the King's shoulder, she saw a group of pretty, green-skinned girls who did not even look to be of drinking age dancing beside the bar. She reasoned that they were all probably older than the city she had been raised in.

"Pain has been my constant companion since I was very young," the King said sharply, though the admission surprised Raegan. "It is of little concern."

She shrugged, taking another sip of her drink. "Sure."

And just like that, a chasm opened between them. The levity evaporated and the King did not lean into her any longer, though he hadn't exactly pulled away, either. Raegan wondered how difficult it was to explain the same things to the same person over and over. To feel for a moment that something lost had finally been regained, only for one question to destroy the illusion.

"Hey," Raegan tried, leaning her shoulder into his for a moment. "I was wondering. It's fine if you don't want to talk about it. But uh, I was curious what I looked like, the first time we met? And what was I like in general?"

He turned to look at her, his features more guarded, the line of his shoulders returning to that familiar predatory stance. But then his gaze softened, eyes drifting across her frame—not leering or hungry, simply taking stock. Perhaps counting the freckles on her cheeks or examining the precise shape of her collarbones. "Like this," he said, a muscle in his jaw leaping as the words left his mouth. One powerful hand gestured noncommittally toward her.

She tilted her head, lifting an eyebrow, not wanting to push him too far but still hungry for more. His dark eyes drifted back to her, heat slinking into his expression. Her body responded immediately: heart increasing its pace, stomach flipping, desire uncoiling.

"You were this," Oberon repeated, the words soft. "You were . . . *just* like this."

A gentle ache spread across her chest as the implications of his response unfolded. Something other than lust awoke within her, alighting on soft wings. It was old and so very tender, laced through with grief. She reached her hand toward his, yearning for the familiar map of veins and tendons. But she could not bear to meet his eyes—the feeling that bloomed within her was crystalline, and one mistake would shatter it into a million pieces. She did not think she could endure its shards lodged forevermore in her chest.

A heartbeat before her skin brushed his, a bartender appeared, reaching across the shimmering surface for their empty glasses. The moment burst. Raegan dropped her hand into her lap, her heart thudding thickly. She pressed her lips together, looking down, trying to get her shit together. In her peripheral vision she saw the bartender buff a damp spot, and the King shift his weight forward as if to obscure something. An old instinct raised its head, and the moment the interaction ended, she lifted her gaze to the King's, inquiring wordlessly.

Leaning toward her, his broad shoulders blocking her line of sight, the King held his closed fist between them. As his long fingers unfurled, Raegan knew what would be waiting in his palm even before her eyes registered the object in the dim, scintillating candlelight.

In the King's open hand was a velvety, downy wisp of an owl feather. She inhaled, some alien meaning settling over her shoulders, like her body could feel the importance even as her mind scrambled for concrete answers.

Then the King closed his fingers, sliding his hand—elegant, natural—into his pocket instead, leaning toward her. "It would be best," he said, speaking in a low tone, "if this looked as natural as possible. Please forgive any liberties I take."

Raegan tried to nod as imperceptibly as possible, thoughts racing. Beside her, the King unfolded to his full height, a shadow elongated by dusk. She turned to face him, tilting her head back to meet his eyes.

The King gazed down at her with heavy-lidded desire, the feral planes of his features shifting the expression into something ravenous and dangerous. Raegan's heart rate spiked, her arousal hot and swift. Then his fingertips were at her chin. This time, she didn't even bother trying to resist the urge to lean into his touch—after all, she was only doing her part to convince any onlookers of their ploy. His long fingers slipped into her hair, warm palm against her cheek.

And then his dark eyes met hers, a question lingering there. She shifted her weight toward him, placing one hand on his chest. *Yes*, she wanted to scream—of course he could kiss her. For show or sincerity, she didn't care. Her entire body burned for him, the heat between her legs damp and torturous. A hundred heartbeats in the space of one, and then the King swept low to bring his mouth to hers, hand cradling the back of her skull as if their bodies had met in this way a thousand times before.

His kiss was cavalier and urgent at once, conveying both cold indifference and heated desire. He tasted like mead and folklore and darkness. Snippets of memories exploded behind Raegan's eyes. She returned his kiss like it might save her from drowning, or awaken her from an enchanted slumber. Her blood turned to fire in her veins when she felt his other hand slide around her waist, fingers clutching at the fabric of her dress.

And then because it meant nothing at all, the King pulled away, though he slid his hand into hers and tugged gently. Raegan gave in as she suspected she always had, following the path he carved through the silken rush of Fey bodies. For a moment or two, she wondered if perhaps they were too obvi-ous, too conspicuous, but then she realized just how much she had been utterly absorbed in him. Banquette seating lined the back walls, occupied by what appeared to be mostly tangles of mismatched limbs. More than one couple or group out on the floor had moved far beyond talking or dancing. A Fey club, Raegan realized, was sure to be about sex or violence—perhaps both—and in this case, she was grateful it was only the former. At least at the moment.

The dark hallway was a cool relief from the throb of bodies on the floor. They walked side-by-side, hands still entwined, through the labyrinth of hallways. Beeswax pillars provided flickering light from tiny, rounded alcoves. The low sounds spilling from behind closed doors on either side of the hall revealed the nature of the tucked-away spaces.

Up ahead, the King slowed at a door, leaning over to snuff the candle beside it, sending smoke coiling into the air. Then he led Raegan over the threshold. She found the interior was not unlike the rest of Gossamer—candles burned in alcoves, heavy with dripping wax. The branches that climbed the walls were laden with pale pink flowers. One corner offered a rather excessive pile of fresh silken sheets and pillows, while the other was taken up entirely by an open water closet crafted from shimmery tiles. It featured multiple showerheads and an enor-mous claw-foot tub. Just to Raegan's right was a long velvet chaise and a darkly lacquered side table.

It was all very beautiful and impressive, lightly scented with jasmine and oud, though she thought a dispossessed people might be better off putting such effort into things like revenge. But then she realized creating such a stunning space just for the sake of joy and pleasure was, in a lot of ways, an enormous and glorious "fuck you."

When she returned her attention to the King, he had stepped away from her, his hand slipping out of her grasp. She watched without a word as he strode over to the side table.

From an elegant pitcher, he poured two glasses of what Raegan desperately hoped was water. When the King handed a glass to her, he did not meet her gaze and seemed to do everything in his power to stop their fingers from brushing.

And just like that, all of the heat and desire evaporated from the room as Raegan wondered if every flirtatious touch and lingering look this entire evening—even *before* arriving at Gossamer—had only been to manufacture the charade that would conceal their movements and intentions. Her stomach plummeted, the cool condensation of the glass jarring against her warm fingers. Was the thick and honeyed lust she felt for the King entirely one-sided? Why hadn't she bothered to ask herself before if this ancient Fey being was playing her like a fiddle again and again and again, across time and space and eternity?

And worst of all, Raegan wondered if the strange feeling that had unfolded in her chest for a moment back at the bar could be crushed now that she recalled the sweetness of its bloom.

CHAPTER FORTY-SEVEN

A gentle knock sounded on the door before Raegan could tumble any deeper into that bittersweet tenderness. With a sideways glance, the King strode to the door, opening it only a small margin. A few low words were exchanged—not in a language she could understand—and then he stepped back, ushering someone inside.

A tall female-presenting person with closely cropped silvery-blonde hair stood silent before her, golden eyes meeting Raegan's. Their frame was somehow sinewy and soft at once, the duality beautifully showcased by a short silk dress in a rich cream color. The keyhole neckline offered a flash of bronze skin, and the attached cape cascading down their back was trimmed in sashaying rows of fringe, something about the movement reminiscent of an owl's wings.

With a start, Raegan realized she was looking at the woman from the alley, the one she'd seen just after Maelona had shoved her out the back door. The woman with the owl-like gaze and familiar voice. The woman who had turned a key in Raegan's chest and unlocked something old and slumbering.

"Overhill," the King said, his voice deep and rich, though his expression was guarded. "You may recall—"

"Blodeuwedd," Raegan breathed, the syllables catching in the middle. Tears stung at her eyes, longing climbing up her throat with sharp talons.

The woman's impassive, elegant features burst open, a flower in bloom, and she plunged toward Raegan. Though no tangible memories revealed themselves, Raegan found herself falling into the embrace all the same. Within Blodeuwedd's arms, she found the feeling of wholeness—crisp as an autumn afternoon and twice as golden. Sobs untangled from her ribcage, saturating the gorgeous fabric of the woman's dress.

"*Renhines pennaf*," Blodeuwedd said in a tear-choked whisper, tucking the crown of Raegan's head beneath her chin. "My queen is returned. After all these years."

All at once, Raegan remembered an injured owl in the sacred oak glade, and the surprise when the snowy-feathered bird with a bandaged wing became an unconscious woman in her arms. Not during that first life with the river and the shield and the younger King, but a different one, many years later. Something more pushed at the membrane of her Seal, so tangible that she could feel the sensation on her skin. But the locks held, leaving her with a vast ocean of nameless emotion.

Blodeuwedd pulled back, her strong hands coming to cup either side of Raegan's face. "I like this hair," she murmured, sniffling. "Though I am less confident in my ability to help you care for it. I'll learn."

Behind Blodeuwedd, the King said something in that lilting language—almost Welsh, but not quite—and took a step forward. "Please be mindful of the Seal," he added in English, gaze falling onto Raegan.

Blodeuwedd looked back at him over her shoulder, nodding through the tears that cascaded down her face. And then she drew away, pulling the warmth of her hands from Raegan's face, leaving behind a sensation of clouds passing over the spring sun, obscuring the first real radiance after a long winter. "I understand," she said, dragging the heels of her palms across her face to wipe stray tears, "that you seek Baba Yaga."

The King moved then, peeling away from the shadows that clung to him, coming to stand beside Raegan. He leaned his weight against the tall, lacquered side table. She wondered if it was an attempt to appear casual about the information, or if the pain stitched into his skin had heightened its cacophony. "Does she live?" the King asked, direct.

Raegan glanced over to find that the predatory line in his shoulders wasn't present, and she hoped that it meant he trusted Blodeuwedd. Raegan certainly did, absolutely and irrevocably, the intensity of their connection so deep that she could not conjure a shred of doubt.

Blodeuwedd looked between them, her gaze turning hard for a moment. "Is this truly what the two of you wish?" she murmured, her voice like a May breeze through a thicket of yellow broom flowers. "You don't have to take up this mantle over and over again."

The King met her offering with a harsh laugh, though he made no attempt to hide the exhaustion it exposed. "When have the three of us ever been afforded wishes?" he asked, sounding wistful, wrung out. The words settled like stones at the bottom of Raegan's stomach.

Blodeuwedd winced, looking down at her feet for a moment. She let out a long breath and then tilted her chin up, lovely round face like a moon in the dim candlelight. "I can direct you to Baba Yaga," she continued, looking between Raegan and the King. "This is an eventuality she and I once prepared for, but the years have passed and she has grown more reclusive. I think she buried her hope long ago. But you may yet be able to reach her."

With those last words, Blodeuwedd's gaze landed on Raegan. She understood the meaning innately; it was Raegan who would have to remind the folkloric witch of the hope she had once harbored. Perhaps it was still there, an ember in a forgotten hearth.

In the silence, Blodeuwedd examined her, the golden eyes gone owlish, hunting for something hidden behind Raegan's expression.

"This is what I want," Raegan assured her. "This is what I've always wanted. Let me mend what has been broken."

"Then you must go very soon," Blodeuwedd replied. "The Protectorate is inflamed, hungry. Even with your great power, Oberon, you'll need assistance to leave the city safely. My court cannot know I've consulted with you, nor can anyone become aware of the other like-minded Seelie souls who have aided this effort."

Beside her, the King bowed his head in agreement, as noble and regal as anything Raegan had ever seen. Anticipation and terror, and the slick, bravehearted thrill of a quest galloped through her veins.

"You have my gratitude, Blodeuwedd," the King said, holding the woman's gaze. "Anything you require, know that you need only ask."

Pride and pleasure at the King's words flushed Blodeuwedd's skin. She said something in that lilting, musical language, reaching out for Raegan. Emotion curled thickly in her chest as she accepted Blodeuwedd's hand, the woman's skin pleasantly cool in her feverish grasp.

"You and I were both flowers plucked by greedy hands," Blodeuwedd said, her words fervent, eyes holding Raegan's. "They thought they might contain us in pretty vases or breed us for more blooms. But the plucking turned us into something else, didn't it? Something with wings and talons. Do not forget that."

Blodeuwedd pressed an object into Raegan's palm—a dry, bundled softness of some sort—and then stepped forward. With a long, swooping sigh reminiscent of feathered wings in the air, she bowed her head to rest her forehead against Raegan's. Something in the very fiber of her being released a breath for the first time in hundreds of years.

"Do not forget," the woman murmured again.

"I won't," Raegan promised, the words wobbling on her tongue. "Thank you. For everything."

At that, Blodeuwedd pulled away, looking at Raegan for another moment, eyes brimming over with tears. "I will arrange with Andronica," she said, her gaze lifting to the King. "Rest. Prepare. The less you tax yourselves before this, the better."

With that, Blodeuwedd turned on her heel, the silken cream cape swooping out behind her as two long strides carried her to the threshold. She opened the door and slipped out into the hallway. The King closed the door behind her, waving his hand over the latch. Something in the air shimmered like an oil spill before disappearing completely.

Raegan looked down, examining what Blodeuwedd had given her: seven short sprigs of a green-stemmed plant with halos of small, white flowers. Meadowsweet, she realized. Something pushed against her Seal, and she raised the blooms to her nose. Images danced in her mind: a sun-drenched courtyard and the sound of a woman's laugh; a dagger encrusted with sapphires, a garnet bead of blood on its tip; rolling hills veiled in meadowsweet lace; the weight of a great bird on her shoulder, talons gripping the velvet of her gown. Again, that feeling of softly spun wholeness washed over her, golden and sacred.

Memories tugged at her with pleading hands, and her body pitched with vertigo. Raegan tucked the meadowsweet bundle into her sleeve and looked up, trying to anchor herself back into the stone-clad room with wisteria vines climbing the walls.

Instead, she found only the dark, heavy, ravenous gaze of the King. He had turned back toward her and was now leaning against the door. The realization that she was alone with him—truly alone, and freshly cursed with the knowledge of what his kiss felt like—blazed across her skin like wildfire.

"What now?" she asked, hoping for any direction that would distract her from the incessant thrum in her belly.

"We wait here briefly until our safe passage is prepared," the King replied, his eyes narrowed, scrutinizing her from across the room. "And then we return to the archives to ready ourselves for the road that awaits."

Frustration at his vague response flared in her, a welcome bitterness to cut the saccharine bloom. Raegan turned away from him, trying to take inventory like her therapist always suggested. She noted the tiredness in her limbs, and the confusion, and the complex web of emotions. She leaned onto the table, her feet and ankles beginning to protest the pain inflicted by her high-heeled shoes. With a short, harsh exhale, she glanced over her shoulder at the velvet chaise lounge. It was the only place to recline in the room that did not feel so blatant about its purpose.

Raegan straightened and took a step toward it, only for her heel to catch on the uneven stone floor. She tripped. Maybe in different shoes she would've caught herself on the edge of the side table, but in the lace-up pumps, she rolled one ankle. Pain shot through her leg, and she cursed, the sound coming out louder than she'd meant it to. Teeth gritted, she attempted to adapt, shifting her weight to her good side and reaching down to unwrap the many loops of the leather ties that crisscrossed her ankle and her calf. If she could just yank the damn things off, she'd limp away to the chaise.

Raegan caught the King in her peripheral vision—the glorious sweep of him, his skin like moonlight against the dark green suit, his movements all strange grace—and cursed for another reason entirely. She tried not to look like she was struggling. She did not succeed.

"May I be of assistance?" the King asked, his shadow falling over her.

Raegan braced herself and looked up, wild tangles of hair falling into her face. And then those oceanic eyes met hers and a thousand winged-things began to buzz in her chest.

"I'm fine," she said, the words coming out strangled. "I just tripped."

"Your shoes seem oddly designed to impede movement," the King told her, his voice dry. She could just make out one arched eyebrow from her uncomfortable, doubled-over stance.

"Yeah, but they look hot," Raegan replied without thinking. "And, uh, you are stupidly tall. If I hadn't worn heels tonight, you would've had to squat every time you wanted to say something to me."

As she loosened the top knot of the leather ties, she heard the King laugh—a low rumble from his chest, husky around the edges. She tried not to pay attention to the way her body responded: all uncoiling heat. The King said nothing else, though Raegan didn't think he had walked away. Besides, woodsmoke slunk into her senses now, heady with rain-damp stone.

Pain provided a useful distraction, the ankle she hadn't rolled now screaming out in protest from bearing all of her weight. Raegan prayed for her blood to rush in any other direction as she yanked at the leather knot, which was not coming undone.

"Overhill," came the King's voice again, even drier this time. "You appear to be struggling."

"Yeah," Raegan snapped, though not unkindly. "I think I rolled my ankle, and I want to get this goddamn shoe off, but I need to sit like *right now* because it fucking hurts."

And then he was close, so close—she could've just leaned to the side and found herself pressed against him.

"May I?"

She straightened, attempting to push hair out of her face,

but a number of curls stubbornly curtailed her vision. "Sure," Raegan replied, thinking that some help would get her safely to the other side of the room quicker.

Both of the King's large, powerful hands slid around her waist. The gentle pressure of his fingertips against her curves unspooled the thick lengths of desire that she had tried her best to shove in a box and drown in a lake. The King lifted her as if she weighed nothing—Raegan did *not* weigh nothing—and placed her on the side table. Between the immediate alleviation in pain and the sensation of his touch, she let out a low sigh before she could restrain the sound.

At least the King possessed the decency to take a step to the side, remaining nearby in case she continued to require assistance, but not so close that Raegan lost her mind entirely.

"Thanks," she mumbled, not daring to look at him. Instead, she scooted farther back on the table with her palms and then drew the pained ankle up and onto her knee. The hem of her tight dress traveled with the movement, sliding up from her mid-calf to her thigh. She continued to work on the knot of leather she had tied herself only a few hours ago to no avail, feeling like a giant idiot. And also, like she came closer and closer to doing something stupid with each passing breath. "Sorry," she said, letting her eyes slide to the King.

He stood a few feet away, his arms crossed in a way that made her wonder, yet again, about the muscular build of his shoulders hidden beneath the suit. And he *watched* her, every bit the faerie lord condescendingly examining a mortal and their silly little habits.

"The knot," she explained, pulling the leather ties away from the swell of her calf. "It's stuck. I promise I know how to take a shoe off."

The King's full mouth moved at that sentence, lips parting slightly, as if he were picking his best barb. Under the glow of the candles lining alcoves in the walls, his eyes were endless pools in which Raegan would happily drown. Her hands went still on the ties, and she remembered all over again that she was alone with him, his very real body only inches away, and hers already conveniently placed on a piece of furniture at the correct height for a multitude of activities.

A shimmer in the shadows and the King moved toward Raegan, as if he had been thinking the very same thing.

"It is excruciating," he said in a low voice, "to watch you."

And the King reached for her.

CHAPTER FORTY-EIGHT

Raegan's breath caught in her throat, all the slinking, swollen pressure in her unwinding. But then the King's hand met only the leather tie at her calf, his fingers—god, she needed to stop watching them so closely—deftly separating the strands. He held his arms straight out, keeping his body as far away from her as possible. His skin never brushed hers as he untied the knot. Raegan wondered if he was trying just as hard to keep his desire under control as she was. The thought manifested like a flare of heat, but the King moved away immediately, retreating a few steps back, shoving his hands in his pockets as if he could not trust them uncaged.

She swallowed, her mouth dry. "Thanks," she said, high, wispy. And then, before she could stop herself—the ache in her bones far too much to withstand—she added, "Probably won't be able to get the other one undone, either."

Raegan watched the King cycle through his next choice, every thought so clear on his face. For a moment, she felt acutely that she knew him, that she had always known him. That a room full of people would see nothing in his expression while she could read a hundred stories laid bare on those high, sharp cheekbones and oceanic eyes and feral brow.

Without a word, the King approached her, and Raegan's core curled in on itself. Something dark and lovely simmered across his features. His movements were sharp and predatory, and god, how she wished to be devoured. He said nothing, though she may not have heard it over the sound of her heart careening in her chest, and began to untie her other shoe. Perhaps she was imagining it, fulfilling her own wishes even as reality unfolded differently, but the King took less care this time. The back of his hand brushed the bare skin of her calf, sending goosebumps racing up her leg. He stood closer, facing her now, bowed over her frame instead of approaching from the side.

Raegan fought it, she truly did, but the instinct to part her legs for him was too strong, an ancient and unyielding urge that had followed her senselessly across time and space. The King released the knot, this time unwinding the thin leather ties from her leg as opposed to just letting the shoe clatter to the floor. The lightest brush—so easily accidental—of his touch sent Raegan's heart leaping into her throat, the ache buried deep within her singing louder and louder.

Beneath the high, shadowed ceiling, spirited away from the world she knew, little felt real to her except for the King. Suddenly, she was enveloped in him, a door opening within her that allowed the past to slip out, gowned in black velvet:

A wild look in his eyes and blood on his jaw, striding toward her across the ruins of some empty stone hall. Then the glint of firelight against the dark swoop of a forest, her bare back arched into a woolen blanket, powerful hands wrapped around her thighs, her own fingers grasping at silken threads of familiar raven hair. A sunset turning his pale skin golden, tall stalks of heather crushed beneath her boots as she caught up to him atop a light-soaked hill, grabbing a fistful of his loose, linen shirt and pulling his larger body toward hers.

And now here: the pain in her feet dulled, the surface of the table warming beneath her skin, the heat of him just an arm's reach away, an infinite need spreading everywhere he had not yet touched her in this life.

A name bloomed on Raegan's tongue, old and dead everywhere except for within this room, and she watched him look at her as if he were seeing her for the first time. His body gave into hers, eyes searching her face for something she thought she may finally be able to give him. Blistering desire erupted within her, and she reached out, filling her fist with the fabric of his suit jacket, a poor replacement for his flesh. There, in a place that was not a place, in a time outside of time, the King gazed down at Raegan.

He gazed down at her as if he would sacrifice everything for her and hate himself all the while. All these years spent trapped in the same spiral, tirelessly mapping the labyrinth but never finding its exit, having no one but himself to blame, and yet and yet *and yet . . .*

So Raegan did the only thing she could, which was to clutch both sides of his jacket and pull herself to him. Her mouth crashed against the King's in desperate, keening want. He met her with bottomless need, wrapping his hands around her waist as she threaded her fingers into his hair. Every place her body met his form came alive with yearning awareness, as if she had never quite understood what it meant to be flesh and blood until this moment.

All Raegan's unmet desires turned molten within her as she wrapped her legs around the King's hips, pulling him closer. Even in the maddening way they both hungered for each other—as if they had only ever known starvation—his movements were impossibly elegant. The sensation of his hands sliding up her legs and bringing the fabric of her dress along with him was nothing short of divine.

The King's mouth trailed to her jaw and then her throat, hands wrapped around the tops of her thighs. She tipped her head back, a soft moan escaping her parted lips. The sound deepened as he slid a hand beneath her knee, pulling her closer to the edge of the table. Her legs opened wider for him, the fabric of his suit scraping deliciously along the delicate skin of her inner thighs.

Their hips slotted together, her aching softness pressed against his hard desire, as Raegan fumbled with the buttons on his dress shirt. She released another breathless moan as the King's hand moved to cup her heavy breast, his lips trailing down from her collarbone. Arching her back with anticipation, her need for him crescendoed beyond reason, all of her weak and throbbing.

And then it was gone. The heat of him retreated, his larger frame no longer pressing into hers. More dazed than she wanted to admit, Raegan watched him slide out from between her legs, gently pulling her dress back into place as he went.

Her heart hammered as she watched the King step away, his eyes shut. The hand that had just touched her with so much hunger moved, instead, to pinch the bridge of his nose.

"I am sorry," the King said in a strained, hoarse tone. "You have done nothing wrong. It is me. I—I cannot."

Raegan curled her hands together, fingernails biting into her flesh as she watched him.

Eventually, the King's dark eyes met hers. "Not again," he said softly, shaking his head. "Never again."

She opened her mouth and closed it when no words came out. She could not decide what she wanted: to hurl venom, to beg, to ask for more ways to understand. So she said nothing, her heart in her throat.

"I want you," he murmured. "I always do. But you make me weak. There is no other way to say it." At least he had the decency to look at her when he said it. But it did little to assuage the way Raegan's anger turned over in her stomach, sour and sharp.

"I make you weak?" she scoffed. "It seems like I'm the only way to make you *whole* again."

More than anything, she wanted him to correct himself, to elaborate with rose-colored sentences. If only the King explained his words correctly, she thought, then she could keep her rising wave of rage under control. She waited, picking at her cuticles until she produced a single drop of crimson.

"Perhaps," the King replied, leveling a cool gaze at her. "Perhaps in this life, things could be different. But I have little reason to believe so. You have always made me feel too deeply —in ways that my people are not meant to feel. I was created for a purpose. You get in the way of that purpose."

Raegan tasted blood and bile, and she stared across the few feet that separated them, her heartbeat thundering in her ears. "And yet you keep coming back to me," she snarled, lacing her words with as much poison as possible. "Like a beaten little dog, you come back to be made weaker again and again."

The King sighed, dragging a hand down his face. He looked nowhere near as upset as Raegan would've liked. She wanted him to feel as she did, like she'd been gutted.

"This time is the first in many years," he told her, beginning to pace, though his tone was measured, as if he were presenting at some corporate function. "I have made it a habit to stay far away from you."

The implications of his words sunk into Raegan like a knife. The only person that could make any sense of the alien feelings and the ancient yearning and the incoherent longing had stayed away—and on purpose? The King had made it a habit to abandon her to polluted half-lives where all she did was ache, always looking for an answer to the older things that lived inside her?

"*What*?" Raegan spat, anger covering up the hurt, hoping to god she could muster enough rage to hide how much she needed him. She sat up straighter, her hands curling inward, nails cutting into her flesh. "For how long, Oberon? How long have you been discarding me?"

"Since the Gates closed fully," the King replied, holding her gaze. "Since I was exiled."

She thought it might've been easier if he'd sounded guilty when he said it, or if he'd spoken the words with some kind of haughty pleasure at injuring her. But the King had not. He'd told her the simple truth when she'd asked for it, and somehow it hurt all the more for that.

"That's . . ." Raegan began, mortified to feel a sob clawing its way up her throat. "That's like hundreds of years. Hundreds of years you just . . . abandoned me. To this. Do you have any idea what it is to ache and ache and ache for something and not even know *what* it is?"

Her fingers raked at her own throat, as if she could tear out all that she had endured and throw it into his arms for him to contend with instead.

"I wake up from dreams I can't remember with strange names in my mouth," Raegan continued, her voice weary. "I know deep in my marrow that I have walked other worlds but no longer possess the keys to their doors. It's like I have loneliness stitched into my skin and you're the only person who knows how to remove it."

The King still watched her, not looking away for a moment, his chest rising faster with each word she said. He slid his hands from his pockets but only held them at his side, making none of the placating gestures she thought he might. "Please understand," the King began, moving like he might take a step toward her but thought better of it, "I know you. I have known you for more than a thousand years. I know your ache, for it is lodged just as deeply within me. And every time I lose you, the darkness inside me grows vaster. I cannot be with you again only to light your funeral pyre. I am sorry I am not strong enough."

Raegan bit down on her cheek, hoping for anything that

would stop her from digging claws into the softness the King had offered her. But no iron tainted her tongue, and wouldn't all of this be easier if she were not consumed by that strange, gentle feeling that only he had ever conjured within her?

"I didn't realize how seriously you were taking this," she laughed, the sound of it harsh even to her ears. "I'm stressed out and I wanted someone to fuck me. You were here. Don't flatter yourself. You are a means to an end, Oberon. I'll be delighted to discard you as soon as I possibly can."

Raegan wanted to take the words back as soon as they left her mouth, but pride soured in her stomach. The King only nodded, his features closing off as if he had shut a physical door. He looked away from her, his gaze falling somewhere near the far corner of the room.

"If I come back again, after this," Raegan continued before she realized she had even opened her mouth, "I hope I'll find someone else on the Unseelie throne, for the sake of your people. Someone who isn't made weak by a few kisses from a mortal woman."

In all truth, she had thought the Unseelie King would ignore her words. She'd thought he had surely heard worse, and would again, that such a low jab from her would hardly mean anything at all. But he turned back to her, his face contorted in rage. In hardly two steps, the King closed the distance between them, slamming his hands down on either side of her legs so hard that cracks appeared in the table's wooden surface.

The King's eyes were dark and wild, his features feral, everything about him the stuff of myth and nightmare. "*You* are the weakness," he snarled, so close to her that she could still feel the heat of him. "An infestation, a sickness, and how quickly you spread. Look at you—three decades you have squandered accepting that the world was what you were told it was, despite the ache in your chest that so clearly said otherwise."

He relented, only slightly, granting her no more than breathing room, his muscled frame still an impassable wall between her and a quiet place where she could tell herself that nothing he said was true.

"You admit that I am hardly more than a fleeting memory, a means to an end," he spat, cruel and appraising. "And yet you will happily forget about your supposedly beloved father long enough to share my bed. How very *weak*."

With that, he finally pushed off the table and away from her, taking several long strides until he stood by the door. Raegan watched the shadows stretch toward him, rolling like the front of a thunderstorm to their King's feet.

She waited a heartbeat for him to turn or to say anything at all, but then her throat closed off and she knew tears would be close to follow. And Raegan refused to cry in front of him. He had been willing to show her his soft undersides, but that was his error, not hers.

Gathering herself up, Raegan shifted her weight, trying to slowly lower herself to the floor, stretching her good ankle down first. Her bare foot met cold stone. She leaned into the movement experimentally, pleased to only find the usual kind of soreness from a night out in uncomfortable heels.

Then Raegan braced herself and placed the ankle she thought she'd rolled onto the ground. Surprise drew her eyebrows together when she felt no pain.

With his back to her, the King spoke again, his voice hard and even. "I addressed your injury," he said, not turning around. "Andronica will arrive shortly. Perhaps you would like to pull yourself together."

Anger swept through Raegan again, blind and white hot. She stomped forward and reached out to grab his arm. He moved at a terrifying speed, pulling his arm out of her reach as he swung to tower over her. The shadows tore themselves from the walls at his command, constricting and stretching into horrible shapes, demonic and ungodly things creeping in the gloom.

"Do not," the Unseelie King commanded, his voice ringing out from every inch of the room, "*ever* touch me again."

CHAPTER FORTY-NINE

Raegan wasn't afraid of him, though maybe she should have been. But it was not fear that moved through her chest. Instead, embittered sorrow pierced her breastbone. She spat something in return, not even sure of the words she spoke, and turned her back to him, desperately scanning the room for an escape.

By some small grace—either of Gossamer's or perhaps the King's—the water closet had grown walls, crafted from matching fish-scale tiles. A tall, elegant door with a wavy glass insert marked the entrance. She threw herself through it, slamming the door behind her. On the other side, a small seating area and vanity rendered in rich, shimmering ocean hues awaited her. With a ragged, tear-soaked sigh, Raegan lowered herself onto one of the seafoam velvet chairs.

"What a stupid choice for a fucking bathroom," she choked out, clawing at the fabric with her nails.

She pulled her legs to her chest, resting her forehead on her knees. Was this how it always was between them? Her hardheadedness running quick and hot, his cold-blooded nature just as inescapable as his sense of duty?

Wrapping her arms around herself, Raegan's levy broke

and she began to cry. She tried with all her might to be as quiet as possible, the idea of the King overhearing her too mortifying to even consider. When a headache began to thunder in her skull, she made herself stop. She got to her feet, feeling like a wrung-out dishrag.

Upon examination in the mirror, she found she didn't look much better. Her face was red and puffy, her eyelids ballooned to about twice their usual size, the kohl eyeliner she'd applied streaked. Raegan sighed, running the faucet—shaped like a golden swan, of course—until the water was pleasantly cool. She splashed her face and scrubbed at the kohl, trying not to drench her hair in the process.

A knock sounded at the door, sending her heart racing. She blotted her skin dry with an impossibly soft towel, trying to decide if she wanted to answer. Anger was still wrapped around her midsection, sorrow like a weight in the pit of her stomach. Would he expect an apology? Would he offer one? Could she make her mouth say, "I'm sorry," even if she wanted to? Or would it catch in her throat the same way "I love you" always did?

And yet the pull was still stronger than the push, so Raegan took a deep breath and opened the door.

It took her a few moments to realize that the person standing there was in fact not the King. Instead, a Fey woman stood there with the duffle bag Raegan had left at the archives, her arms crossed. A thick braid of gleaming black hair was draped over the shoulder of her fitted, nondescript black jacket. She was quite slender but powerfully built, an unpleasant expression on her sharp-featured face.

"Goddess's sake," she said in a velvety, deep-pitched voice. "Is it really you?"

Familiarity crept down Raegan's spine. She glanced at her bag, feeling a strong urge to simply grab her belongings and slam the door. "Sorry," she said instead. "I'm sure we know each other, but you may have heard my memory's sort of shit."

The Fey woman's expression pinched further, and she looked at Raegan with dead-eyed displeasure. "The situation has degraded, as it tends to when you are involved," the woman replied, almost certainly instead of a quip about how more than Raegan's memory was lacking. "It would be helpful if you could get changed into something more practical."

At that, Raegan snatched her bag from the faerie's feet, straightening to meet her gaze with an expressive display of distaste. "My apologies. *Some* of us don't attend formal affairs in our gym clothes," Raegan said, letting her eyes linger purposefully on the Fey woman's outfit.

In response, the woman openly sneered at her, so full of hostility that Raegan felt begrudging respect. "Seeing as your memory is as lacking as your insults," the woman replied, flipping her shining braid over her shoulder, "I'll remind you that I'm Andronica, security councilor and high knight of the Unseelie Court. We've met before, namely when you went against years of careful planning to play hero and got captured in the process, which led to the taking of our King, the closure of the Gates, and my exile into this hellscape."

Discomfort stirred in Raegan's stomach, and she swallowed. "Oh," was her only reply.

"Oh *indeed*," Andronica said, narrowing her dark eyes. "We'll talk in a few moments."

Then the Fey warrior turned on her heel, graceful as a ballerina and ten times as deadly, and stalked away. Raegan scanned the room quickly but didn't see the King. Gritting her teeth, she closed the door. She tossed her bag onto the stupid seafoam chair and unzipped it. Everything seemed to be in place—clothes, medications, notebook, and laptop, her work bag and its contents packed neatly inside the duffle. Heart pounding, she checked the side pocket. Relief rocketed through her when she found her father's spellpapers tucked safely inside.

For a moment, Raegan squeezed her eyes shut, pressing

her lips together. She could do this. Her feelings were just as irrelevant as whatever scraps of romance she had with the King. All that mattered was her father and her fate.

A few moments later, she was dressed in high-waisted, tapered black jeans, a long-sleeved tee with thumbholes, and her knee-high, lace-up boots. At the vanity, Raegan braided her hair, starting at the crown of her head.

"Right," she said to her own reflection. "Good enough."

Her duffle slung over her shoulder, Raegan exited the water closet, closing the door softly behind her. The room was empty of other living beings, though it had reconfigured itself. The velvet chaise and corner piled with silk sheets were gone; instead, a long table stretched down the middle of the space. A platter of bread, cheese, and fruit—all infinitely better-looking than any food she'd ever seen in her life—sat on its surface.

She ate ravenously, suddenly realizing exactly how hungry she was. When she'd finished, she stood and pulled out a chair. Placing her duffle into it, she leaned her forearms onto the chair's back. The universe afforded Raegan a few more moments of silence before the door opened.

Andronica arrived first, not even sparing Raegan a glance. Close behind her was Kamau, whose greeting was almost too cheery considering all that had transpired. Tension swelled in the room like an incoming wave, and then Blodeuwedd slipped inside, in the middle of a conversation with the King, who entered the space at her heels.

Raegan set her jaw and told herself to look literally anywhere else, but in the end, she could not. The King pulled the door closed, replying to Blodeuwedd—something about wards—but his ocean eyes slid to Raegan all the same. He held her gaze, his sentence trailing off, full mouth moving into a firm line.

She swallowed but did not avert her eyes. Her palms felt hot and damp, her heart thudding ferociously.

"Are you alright?" the King asked, looking at her in that

way of his—like no one else in the room existed at all. Her mouth went dry, and Raegan told herself that it was as much of an olive branch as anyone could possibly hope for from an ancient sovereign with god-like powers.

And yet her pride puffed its chest out like a preening lion, and she sneered. "Why wouldn't I be?" Raegan scoffed, arching an eyebrow.

He held her gaze for a moment longer, dark lashes dipping like a raven's wing. But she gave him nothing, crossing her arms. At that, the King relented, and with a shrug of his shoulders, he looked toward the table and moved for it. Andronica, Blodeuwedd, and Kamau had already taken a seat, so Raegan did, too.

The King did not sit. Instead, he came to the head of the table and rested his folded hands on the back of the chair. "Everything has gone to hell," he announced, some sly trace of dark humor ghosting his lips. "The Protectorate attacked an Unseelie sentry post for the first time since we came to this city last year, Blodeuwedd's faction has a turncoat, and apparently Baba Yaga's pocket realm will move halfway across the globe in six hours."

Raegan looked around the table, trying to gauge the temperature. Andronica looked pissed, but that didn't seem unusual. Kamau appeared troubled, their large hands tapping out a nervous staccato on the table's surface. Blodeuwedd hadn't stopped chewing on her lower lip since she'd walked through the door.

"If you are willing," he continued, his eyes falling on Raegan, "the recommendation from my most trusted advisors is to leave immediately."

Panic crowded out the air in her lungs. "Now?" she asked weakly, hating the sound of her own voice. "We're going to find Baba Yaga and try to remove my Seal right *now*?"

Across the table, Andronica snickered, not bothering to conceal the sound, though everyone ignored her.

"You can either leave now," Blodeuwedd added, her voice kind, "or go deep into hiding until things calm down, which could take a very long time."

Raegan tried to force a deep breath, dragging a hand through her hair. She felt feverish, anxiety gripping her shoulders with heavy hands. But she wanted this, didn't she?

"Why has the pace . . . accelerated?" she asked, doing her best to focus on information-gathering and not the intense pressure across her chest. "What happened?"

Andronica's eyes shot to Raegan, her expression full of long-held distrust. "*You* happened," she said, blunt and harsh, leaning across the table on her forearms. "The Protectorate is swarming this city, and our people might be exposed because of you."

"Now," Blodeuwedd began, "that's not entirely—"

The room rocked, as if some great beast had slammed into it. Candle soot dislodged from the alcoves and floated down to the floor like black snow. Kamau got to their feet in the same way a volcano erupts, launching themselves toward the doorway.

"Fuck," Andronica spat, rising to stand like a panther bored of sunbathing and ready to seek blood instead.

Blodeuwedd's eyes had gone wide, her fingers curling into her palms. Raegan looked to her for a cue, her muscles locked, but the golden-eyed woman's attention was settled on the King. He had leaned his head back, exposing the long expanse of his ivory neck, a deep breath pulling at his chest in an even stride. Then his chin was parallel to the ground again, and there was nothing in his expression but cold, brutal composure. "Overhill," he said, meeting her gaze, "we depart now for Baba Yaga."

It was a command, and Raegan balked instinctually, but the King had already turned to Kamau to address the Fey knight in that musical, lilting language. Andronica barked something in response, standing in front of the King as if she planned to physically stop him from leaving.

"Andronica," the King replied, switching back to English. "Caledfwlch did not end me. Neither did all the Protectorate's attempts. I have not diminished on this side of the Gates. I will be fine."

Andronica did not relinquish a single inch of space as Raegan watched the interaction closely, sliding the strap of her duffle over her shoulder and rising to stand. "How are you going to hold the wards *and* protect her?" Andronica demanded, her attention swinging away from the King to land squarely on Raegan. "You are unrestored, correct?"

Raegan seriously considered a smartass response, but she was intelligent enough to realize the Fey knight could realistically behead her before the King could do anything about it.

"Yes," Raegan replied, bracing herself.

Andronica's dark eyes flashed in the low light, her shoulders climbing closer to her ears with frustration. "Fate wastes all Her precious energy," she snarled, "to bring back something so *useless*—"

"Andronica," Kamau interrupted from their post by the door. "Maybe this is not helping?"

By the time Andronica had turned back to the King, he had laid a powerful hand on her shoulder, his expression gone serious, tenderness flitting about the edges. "You will hold the wards in my stead," he said, his voice heavy. "I know it is a burden."

Raegan watched Andronica's rich complexion pale as she looked up at the King with something that was not far off from fear.

"Before you protest," he continued, one dark brow arching, "do you believe I would ask for such a thing from you if you were not capable?"

Andronica ground her jaw as the Unseelie warrior recognized her king had just trapped her effortlessly. "Am I, though?" she asked, her words coming out in a long sigh. "You have trained me well. I have successfully held them when we've practiced. But *only* in practice, my liege, and with nothing else required of me. What if I'm not ready? If I fail, Gossamer will fall, the archives will become discoverable, and all our people's home warding will cease to exist."

"I am not tasking you with continuing your responsibilities *and* holding our people's wards," the King replied. "Kamau can oversee your work. Unless you do not believe they can?"

Raegan recognized that the King's words formed a genuine question. He had backed off from the pressure he'd put on Andronica, giving her a spot of leeway to exert her own influence, while also providing an escape route if she truly had doubts about her own abilities. Impressive.

"Yes, they can," she said so fiercely that a knot of admiration twinged in Raegan's chest. "Just as I can hold the wards. Go. Do what you must for all of us."

The King bowed his head to Andronica, bringing his brow to hers—much in the way Blodeuwedd had done earlier—as his powerful hand held the base of her skull. The knight and her liege stayed like that for a long moment. When they pulled apart, Andronica's shoulders were as straight and deadly as an arrow.

"Overhill," the King said, looking her way again. "Though I have little right, I will once again request that you follow me into the darker places of this world to see if we can find salvation there."

Raegan could say no. She could see what was salvageable of her little mundane life. She could try to find someone else to help search for her father. She could visit those places Maelona had written down and see if the Protectorate would leave her alone.

She could beg Fate to release her, petition Death to return her to the void, be done with magic and the gods and the Fey and all the wild, feral-hearted feelings this Unseelie King summoned from deep within her.

And yet, and yet, and yet . . .

Raegan took a few tentative steps toward the King, her blood beating like a war drum in her veins.

"To salvation, then."

Chapter Fifty

Raegan had not imagined that their transportation to Baba Yaga would be an ordinary sedan in a middling blue color. The underground garage at Gossamer held carriages crafted from orchid petals, and purring automobiles sleek as cheetahs, but the King had, for some reason, chosen an utterly mundane car. She slowed her pace as he unlocked the doors and tossed his bag onto the backseat.

"I want to remind you," the King said, looking at her over the frame of the vehicle, the weight of his attention pulling her from her thoughts, "that I will not force you to do this."

The statement surprised Raegan. For a moment, she only studied him, carefully considering what to say next. "What would you do?" she asked, crossing her arms. "If you were me?"

The King let out a low, humorless laugh, the sound of it absorbed almost immediately by the high, earthen walls that surrounded them. "If I were you," he echoed, "I would run."

She stared at him, ignoring the fear that crept along her spine. And then she scoffed. It was the last thing any sane mortal would do in the face of an ancient faerie king—but she was at least half-mad, and not precisely mortal, either.

"I don't want to run, Oberon," Raegan said, putting as much force into the words as she could. "I want to restore my memory, and then I want to hunt the Protectorate down and take back *everything* they stole from me."

The King's oceanic gaze consumed her for a long, skittering moment. And then he smiled, wolf-like and ravenous, the sight of it sending a bolt of exhilaration and desire into her chest. Before she could change her mind, Raegan yanked open the back door and threw her bag inside. She didn't dare look at him as she settled herself into the passenger seat, picking at her cuticles. The balance of the car shifted as he slid into the driver's side. The green numbers on the dashboard indicated midnight was approaching.

"Doesn't being in a car hurt?" Raegan asked as he reversed out of the parking spot. "You know, essentially an iron box?"

"Cars are made of steel and fiberglass these days," the King said, his tone distant. "Steel is iron mixed with carbon, rendering it less potent."

She nodded mutely and then sat in silence as he pulled out of the underground parking garage and onto a side street. The familiar city's shadows seemed to leer at her through the window. Raegan imagined the gloom of each alleyway filled with swarms of Protectorate, their soot-colored suits blending into the surroundings.

"You need not respond," the King began, flicking the windshield wipers on as rain suddenly spattered the windshield, "but I am sorry for what I said earlier. It was cruel, which I admit is not out of character for me. I often find it simpler to make you hate me. Then you leave, and I need only summon the strength to resist following."

Raegan let out a long breath, turning to rest her forehead on the cool, rain-streaked window. She'd rather stay angry at him. She'd rather put her Olympic-level grudge-holding to good use. She'd rather do anything than what every fiber of her body ached for—to accept his apology, offer her own, and maybe feel the hard, muscled weight of him once again.

Her stubborn pride, that red rash of rotting anger, won out in the end. Raegan said nothing, instead gazing out the window. She watched familiarity melt away as they took the bridge across the river. On the other side of the Delaware, the land was flat. The evening seemed to devour the end of the road somewhere in the distance, like they were driving straight into the mouth of some ancient beast cloaked in midnight.

A beast that may very well devour her whole.

An hour or more passed in silence. She would've preferred it strung tight with tension, but the quiet quickly became companionable and she could not find the desire to fight it.

"We have nearly arrived," the King said, jarring her. "Once we do, we will need to move quickly. Baba Yaga's pocket realm is currently in the Pine Barrens, but in only a few short hours, it will relocate to a remote Russian forest that would be significantly more difficult to reach."

Raegan had seen enough road signs to be pretty sure of their location, but she still felt faint amusement at the confirmation. Baba Yaga spending time in the Pine Barrens made almost too much sense. She'd love to tell her dad. One day, hopefully, she might.

"Stay close, stay sharp, and use your knife if you must," the King continued, turning to look at her for a moment. "Together we will see it through."

He spoke as if they were war-toughened comrades who had fought at each other's sides a hundred times before—which, of course, Raegan realized, they were. Their shared history, even if impossible to recall presently, steadied her.

"What's going to happen to me when the Seal is

removed?" she asked, looking down to see her hands were shaking. She settled them onto her thighs.

The King said nothing, as if the darkness had gobbled up her words. They'd passed through a few small towns, and the last one had long since turned into another winding two-lane road cutting straight through the heart of a forest.

"I do not know," he replied eventually. "Baba Yaga will be in a better position to answer this inquiry."

"Will I still . . ." Raegan set her jaw. ". . . still be me, I guess?"

At that, she felt the King's eyes fall on her for a stretched moment before he had to return his gaze to the road. "From what I understand," he said, "there are risks. You could go completely mad. You could fracture, developing alters for each life you lived, losing the interconnected nature of what you are. One of your lives could take over, erasing the rest. Ideally, the Seal will be peeled back and you will slowly integrate your memories over a period of time."

"And in that ideal scenario," she asked, resting her temple against the cool window, "I would be me but . . . more?"

"Yes," the King answered, drumming his fingers on the steering wheel. "You would have some degree of access to all your memories and knowledge, but you would remain."

"Right," Raegan murmured, closing her eyes against the thoughts buzzing in her skull. She hadn't expected to have so little time to wrap her mind around accepting that—if they even made it to Baba Yaga's doorstep—the removal of the Seal might be the end of Raegan Maeve Overhill. What chance did she stand against something infinitely older and more powerful awakening within her?

Of course doubt would creep in here, beyond the streets of her beloved city, beneath a vast canopy of rain-black trees and cloudy skies. She had cast herself entirely to the winds of Fate. There were a thousand questions she should ask. If her Seal was safely removed and they made it to the Gates, how would the world change with magic's release? What would become of mortals? How exactly had the Timekeeper tricked her ancestors in the first place? And were the Fey tricking her right now to get what they desired?

But all Raegan wanted to think about was her magic and her father, so her mouth stayed shut. Better to not know. Better to think only of the things that she had too long been denied.

The King pulled off the main road onto a meandering sandy lane that led deeper into the forest. Loose soil crunched under the tires. Pine trees loomed from all sides. In a few minutes, they reached a small parking lot that Raegan thought could be for a hiking trailhead, but she couldn't make out any signage. She sat motionless, trying to remind herself that she wanted this. She *did*. And yet . . .

"I'm terrified," she admitted to the King without meaning to, the realization leaving her mouth at the same moment as it clarified in her mind.

He looked toward her as he switched off the car's headlights. The moon broke through the cloud cover, illuminating his angular features. "You would be a fool if you were not," he said.

With that, the King turned the engine off and slid from the driver's seat. The smell of damp, sandy soil, resinous pine, and cold rain slunk in through the open door. Raegan let out a heavy breath, zipped up her leather jacket, and got out of the car.

"Here," the King said, handing her a luggage tag.

"Like from before?" she asked, thinking of the way he'd reduced the size of her overnight bag when she'd packed up her apartment.

The King nodded a confirmation, looking absolutely otherworldly and deadly beneath the moon's silver glow. He tucked a second luggage tag into the pocket of his own jacket, which matched the rest of his clothing—black, sleek, tactical.

"I would like to enchant your vision so you do not have to rely on me for sight in the darkness," he told her. "May I hold my hand over your eyes?"

"Yes," she replied, the word coming out a croak.

"Please keep your eyes open," he instructed, cupping one large hand over her vision, plunging her into darkness.

Raegan heard his deep voice move in a low, guttural cadence, and then his hand fell away. The world suddenly looked as if she had put on night vision goggles, but with more shades of gray than green. She swept her gaze through the forest clearing, amazed at how she could see individual rocks in the sand and the pine needles dusting the ground.

Raegan looked up at the King to say thanks and saw him —horrifying, cruel, unfathomably powerful, beyond ancient —looking over her shoulder with something that she thought might be fear. She blinked, forcing a sharp inhale. Could the Protectorate have found them already? How much could the King weather if they were to be hunted the entire path to Baba Yaga's door?

She had just about worked up the courage to turn around and face whatever made even the King react in such a way when his expression shifted, deep-seated hatred surfacing. She felt him wrap his fingers around her upper arm, pulling her close. He moved in a long, elegant step, placing himself between her and whatever lay ahead.

At the other end of the clearing, haloed in moonlight, stood something celestial. The stars themselves—just barely visible through gaps in the cloud cover—seemed to toss their shine down like flowers at the being's feet. Long silver hair flowed in a waterfall down their back, more tresses plaited like a crown around their head. Above their slender shoulders rose twin arches of snowy, downy feathers. Wings, Raegan realized in awe, like a swan's but much, much larger.

"Aranrhod," the King said, a picture of threadbare civility.

"My children," the being replied. Her voice was starfall,

turning wheels of silver, and everything that has been and everything that is yet to come. The sound of it seemed to shake the air around Her.

"Fate," Raegan breathed.

The being took a step closer to them, though She did not so much walk as glide. "I pulled your Threads," Fate said, "and you answered my call."

Raegan said nothing, her breath caught in her chest, blood pounding. The King's grip on her upper arm tightened.

"I have come," Fate said, standing just before them now, though Raegan never saw Her close the distance, "to offer you my blessing, for it is my path upon which you walk."

Up close, Raegan was startled to find echoes of the King's features in Fate's face. Not in a way that denoted relation so much as lineage—a shared otherworldliness that set them both far apart from humans.

"We receive your blessing," the King said after a moment's pause, though his tone was blank and hardened.

Fate inclined Her head, trails of silver hair running across Her shoulders like liquid metal. The world, it seemed, held still, all eyes turned to this forgotten clearing at the end of a rain-slick road.

"Good luck," Fate murmured, Her thin lips barely moving. "May you see this through. Seek the door Cormac Overhill left ajar."

Something like fire roared through Raegan's body at the mention of her father as Fate looked between the two of them with nearly colorless eyes, Her mouth moving into an austere smile. The being turned, the swoop of Her feathered wings lifting away from Her shoulders as if She were about to disappear back into the misty evening, leaving all the suffering and the terrible, never-ending ache to the smaller creatures crawling across the planet's surface like ants.

"Wait!" Raegan called, pushing the word out.

Though he said nothing, the King's fingers suddenly dug

into her flesh. Fate did not turn, but She gazed over one shoulder, the planes of Her face taking on that cold, feral look Raegan knew so well.

"What do you know about my father?" Raegan shouted, ripping her arm out of the King's grasp. "Tell me. Please."

"That is not for a little thing like you to know," Fate replied, Her tone cool. "He made his bargain, played his part."

A cold, horrible realization settled over her. "You put him on this path, didn't you?" Raegan demanded, her voice hoarse with fury and sorrow. "He just wanted magic back—*real* magic. And you used that against him to set all of this into motion."

Anger boiled in her stomach as she finally fit the pieces together. She knew she should stop. But a thousand years of anger was seeping into her bloodstream, and she thought it might poison her to death if she did not let it out.

"Do you enjoy watching us suffer?" Raegan screamed. Fate did not answer, the wind beginning to whip around the clearing. "Have you enjoyed spending the past thousand years grinding the two of us down into nothing but rage and indifference?"

"Little one," Fate said, though Her tone belied no kindness, "I do not expect a creature such as yourself to understand the grander workings, but you must have faith in the forces larger than you. This path is yours to walk. Any suffering is the result of your own failures."

"*Our* fucking failures?" Raegan yelled back, stepping toward the celestial being, the King forgotten behind her. "You are the architect. If we're failing, don't you think maybe it's because of you? Why don't you *do* something?"

At that, Fate's face darkened, silvered light shifting into the black of an eclipse. The feathers of Her wings shook and sharpened, downy white becoming jagged gray. "You've lived so long yet understand so little," Fate snarled, growing larger, the trees bending away from Her. "I am a function of the universe, essential to the fabric of the world. Imagine the enormous shock waves I would create if I were to interfere directly. No. Lower creatures such as yourself are the avatars by which I accomplish my great work."

To her surprise—and Fate's—Raegan threw her head back and laughed, the sound harsh and full of derision. "From the bottom of my heart, fuck you. I hate you."

It was true, and the realization of it almost broke Raegan. She had bent toward Fate all her life, begging for scraps, hoping to find that narrow Thread and walk upon it, a dutiful disciple. Something soured in her stomach, and standing here in the mist and the gloom, Raegan wondered if she had spent all these lives catering to the whims of a being that did not even have the decency to let her be unmade when the time came.

Fate said nothing, though She loomed over Raegan now, the smell of tarnished silver and sea winds thick on the breeze. Her pupils looked blown out, black seeping into Her colorless irises. The sight of it all should have stopped Raegan. But it did not.

"And what gave you the right to do what you've done to him?" Raegan demanded, gesturing back to the King, her voice loud and rough around the edges. "Look at *him*. He has kept to the path all these years, forced to watch his people fade if he does not play your game. Is that all you have to offer your chosen ones? An endless exhaustion we carry around our necks like a millstone? If that's the case, have the decency to end it. At least in death we will not have to feel your filthy fingers on our Threads."

Raegan's throat felt ragged, like she had swallowed broken glass, as she stared up into the face of Fate, the being's features as wide as the moon. Something caught the dim starlight, and she realized it was Her teeth—too many to count, gleaming like mother-of-pearl daggers.

"The Nameless One I cannot replace," Fate said, the force

of Her voice shattering the air, the earth quaking beneath Raegan's feet, the trees cowering in the distance. "But you, child? I could devour you whole and put another where you stand. You are far from special, hardly even Fate-touched. You were simply convenient and so eager, so very *desperate*, to serve me."

The being reached for Raegan with spidery hands wrapped in miles and miles of Threads, woven through Her crooked fingers like a web. That made Raegan the fly, it seemed, and she was tired of being the fly—her legs crumpled up and her wings crushed, all for the sake of fitting neatly into someone else's mouth. Raegan summoned every ounce of her bottomless rage. Then she threw her head back and screamed.

Fate could choke on her this time.

Everything happened at once.

Fate, Her Thread-bound hands at Raegan's neck. Water pulling in from the sky and the ground and the trees, forming a wave that looked more like a wall. The King at Raegan's side, his shadows interlacing with the streams of water. A voice, screaming—her voice, she realized, bloodcurdling and vast, the sound of something that has died a hundred times and can no longer summon fear for the inevitable.

And then nearly everything was gone, drained out of her like an emptied tidal pool, and Raegan thought that perhaps Fate had devoured her whole, unspun her Threads and put her back in the dark.

But she would not be so damp, Raegan thought, if that were true, and she did not think her throat would hurt in the void or that she would hear the beating of great snowy wings upon the air. Her vision returned in broken pieces: an empty clearing, a pool of thrashing water, a single white feather spiraling in the air.

Raegan stumbled back from the edge of the pool, the treads of her boots dragging in the wet sand. Her entire body tingled and buzzed, as if newly-discovered nerve endings were firing for the first time. Unsteady, she risked another step in retreat, only for her knees to buckle. But her back hit hard, solid warmth, and then arms closed around her.

"What have you done?" a voice demanded in her ear, thick and intense with barely contained anger. The warmth at her back disappeared as Raegan's world spun. She found herself face-to-face with a different eldritch terror: the exiled High King of the Unseelie Fey. His eyes were near-black in the gloom, face mere inches from hers. Rage sharpened his expression, the planes of his features gone feral and hungry.

The King pinned her against the cold steel of the car, his powerful hands gripping her by the shoulders. Raegan strained against his hold, her breathing ragged. But he did not relent. Instead, the King dug long, elegant fingers deeper into her skin. Her head swam. She should be terrified. But Raegan's heart skittered like a wild thing in her chest for an entirely different reason. Good sense always seemed to abandon her when it came to him.

"I did what I should've done a thousand fucking years ago," she responded, tilting her head back to meet his gaze. "Fuck her. Fuck destiny. Fuck all of it, Oberon. I'm so *angry*."

The King studied her with the ferocity of a predator searching for the tenderest morsel of flesh. She flinched when he moved suddenly—his hands left her shoulders, diving into her hair instead, the heat of his palms searing against her face. Raegan's breath caught, long-unmet hunger burning low in her belly even as part of her wondered if he planned to just snap her neck and be done with it all.

"With no training and your Seal still intact, you managed to reach past your Protectorate magic and use your true power to turn back a primordial being," the King said, his voice hoarse and uneven, his usual composure forsaken. His eyes were wild, broad chest rising with sharp, quick breaths. "You leave me no choice. You never do."

And then, against all reason, the King bent low and kissed her beneath the rain-shook sky. He met her mouth like a creature half-starved, his intensity pulling a soft gasp from Raegan. She returned the King's kiss without hesitation, reaching for him with the same hunger. But the King caught her wrist the moment she raised her arm, pinning it above her head, coaxing a moan from deep within her. Undeterred, she curled a few fingers into his waistband and yanked him closer with all her might. The ancient creature of shadow obliged, crushing his hips against hers before snatching her free hand in his and pinning that, too, against the cool metal of the car, their fingers intertwined.

His mouth trailed to her throat. Thick, heavy desire drummed loud between Raegan's legs, and she arched into him, desperate for more. The King released her hands, his own sliding to the slopes of her hips. His teeth grazed the sensitive skin of her neck, and she said his name in a low, breathy tone she hardly recognized as her own.

"I have spent so long trying to live without you," Oberon panted against her throat, the curve of her waist caught between his palms. "No more."

Before she could say anything, his mouth was on hers again, the intense heat of his kiss pulling all the breath from Raegan's body. His hands slipped beneath her shirt, fingertips brushing her bare skin. Goosebumps careened across her flesh. Of course a quest always sang to her so sweetly—she had spent a millennium traversing the alabaster valleys and sinewy mountains of this otherworldly being. Distantly, Raegan wondered what exaltation or purpose she might find in Baba Yaga's realm, or beyond, that could be greater than this dark, propulsive, eternal thing between her and the faerie king.

At that moment, he broke the kiss, his breathing ragged and unsteady. But the King did not move away from her; instead, he cradled her jaw in his lithe hands. When his eyes met hers, there was a storm there, as sharp-toothed as lightning.

"I am yours," the King murmured, each syllable dripping with gravity and something not unlike devotion, "and I will happily burn in the fires of your rage. You need only command me."

Raegan held his gaze for a long moment, the rest of the world forgotten. And then, finding no words to suffice, she grabbed the front of his jacket in her fists and dragged his mouth back to hers.

Some time later, the King spoke, his lips moving softly against her skin. "She will return. We have only delayed our punishment. We must go."

"Yeah," Raegan agreed, straightening, still a bit breathless. "Are you going to be alright? When the Protectorate comes, I mean?"

Something dangerous slipped across the King's features. He disentangled himself from her and began to walk toward the mouth of the woods, his footsteps hardly making a sound despite his size. Without a word, Raegan followed him, anxiety piercing her lungs.

"You may have noticed," he began, looking sideways at her, "that I have not needed to hold physical proximity in order to conceal our movements."

"Oh," she said. Because, with all the other shit that had been going on, no, she truly hadn't noticed. She was losing her touch.

The King paused for a moment at the place where the clearing turned into forest, placing one hand against the trunk of a large pine tree. Raegan heard a low hum that echoed out like a ripple, deeper and deeper into the woods beyond.

"I am, like all of my kind, limited by the lack of magic in this half of the world," he continued, beginning to navigate between the towering pines, following some direction or sense that she did not have. "But more than anything, I am limited by my commitments. At all times, I have held my people's protective wards. A great burden and a great honor."

Raegan kept pace with his longer strides, the forest closing in around them. The thick canopy above created a murky gloom that she imagined remained even on the brightest of days. Beneath her feet, the ground was spongy and blanketed with pine needles.

"But now," the King said, his voice huskier, as if the surroundings brought the wild out in him, "I am unburdened."

A delicate, delicious chill crept up Raegan's neck. In the perpetual dim of this barren forest, she was watching the Unseelie King unfold. It felt like witnessing a holy rite, or perhaps undertaking one. The darkness clung heavily to him, glorious and horrific, trees bowing as he walked by, raindrops not daring to land upon his shoulders. Maybe even Mother Nature herself preferred not to offend this particular faerie regent.

Raegan was not sure how long she followed the Unseelie King into the dark of the wood. She worried that she might be willing to follow him anywhere, his ferocity sweet as blackberry wine upon her tongue. Gone was the being who favored three-piece suits in fine wools and held his court within shadowed libraries smelling of citrus and vanilla dust. Instead, before Raegan was something positively feral, moving through the forest as though he were part of it—a predator finally released back into the wild.

Somewhere in the distance, a twig snapped. Raegan froze, her pulse thudding thickly in her veins.

The King slowed, pivoting in the direction of the sound, dark eyes roving. "Our quarry has joined us," he told her, voice drenched in bloodlust and years of unspent rage, "and Baba Yaga's door is nearby. She does not obscure the way."

Another muffled sound—a scuffle of a boot through the thicket of pine needles—drew the King's attention. He turned toward it hungrily. Raegan would have almost pitied the Protectorate had they not taken everything from her. She prayed his violence might alleviate her grief.

The King moved forward again, his pace faster now, long legs devouring the ground. Raegan realized he was leading the Protectorate deeper and deeper into the forest, making them think they were tracking a wounded animal—when in reality, they were walking right into the jaws of a beast. After a few more steps, he turned toward her, catching her gently by the arm. Raegan looked up at him, awaiting instructions. But for a moment he only studied her, almost as if he could not quite believe she was flesh and blood before him.

"Baba Yaga's door is ahead," the King told her, shaking off whatever had come over him. "The twisted black pine. You will know when you see it. Knock thrice and then enter. She is, in all likelihood, expecting you."

"Aren't we going together?" Raegan asked, pushing down the panic that arose at the idea of navigating Baba Yaga's realm alone.

"I will be right behind you," the King replied.

The great, impossible thing before her brought his forehead to hers, one hand sliding around her waist. She lived a thousand lives in that moment—nothing but the muted rainfall echoing around them. Then he pulled away, taking a few steps back from her. Shadows swept in from all directions, gathering at his feet like a pack of wolves.

"Go," the King said, solemn.

She nodded, her breath shaky. She swallowed hard and told herself not to say anything at all, unable to trust her tongue. With one last look at him, Raegan turned on her heel and made her way deeper into the forest. It did not take long to spot the twisted black pine: taller than the other trees, twice as thick, bent double with what could be rage or grief or hunger. Its trunk looped in a thick serpentine shape, branches reaching down instead of up. She stepped toward it, reverent.

And then that terrible sound of Protectorate magic shattered the air, a teeth-rattling wrongness. Despite herself, Raegan turned. Through the narrow hall of pines, she could see the King and at least twenty—if not more—soot-suited humans crawling out of the surrounding forest. She couldn't help it. She *had* to wait a few moments and make sure he would truly be alright.

One hand curled with knuckles already resting upon the tree's trunk, she bit down on her lower lip and waited. Blood bloomed on her tongue. The King held his ground as she'd thought he might, allowing the Protectorate to get so close that her heart lurched.

One of the Protectorate—a man at the front, built like a mountain—said something. The King threw his head back and laughed, the sound of it twisted and terrible. She realized the Protectorate man was the same one that had grabbed her by the viaduct. Something that Raegan didn't think was hers rose its head inside her sternum, hungry and eager. Time moved at half-pace. Her world condensed to the King in the distance and all the Protectorate—too many, surrounding him like flies.

And then: a crack, a split, and the sodden, pine-needle-strewn earth at the King's feet opened wide as a wound. Exposed roots roiled and rioted, reaching out like tentacles with their newfound freedom. The roots wrapped themselves around those frail human bodies, pulling a sizable amount of the Protectorate's force toward a gaping maw in the earth. They fought, Raegan could see—some throwing magic at the roots, others drawing more conventional weapons—but in the end it was all futile. With shouts and screams and a few pitiful, begging cries, they disappeared beneath the ground, the dark, shifting soil closing over their heads. The roots reached back out again, writhing with hunger.

"I do not wish to kill your people," the King said, and

when he did, all the roots stopped their slithering, holding still as if they had never been anything so horrific in the first place.

The Protectorate, too, held still. Even from her position by the twisted pine, Raegan could see the suits exchanging looks, faces pinched, fear clouding their expressions. They had never before seen the King unburdened, and now only a taste had left them willing to listen to the words of a faerie lord.

One of the Protectorate stepped forward, hands moving into what looked like an appeasing gesture. Their air-shattering magic stopped. Raegan held her breath.

"But I have done many things I did not wish to," the King said, and then the ground opened wider, the trees grew hungrier, and there was nothing in the air but the rending of flesh and cloth.

Chapter Fifty-Two

Little could have prepared Raegan for witnessing the full capacity of the Unseelie King. Violence came as easily to him as breathing. Roots snatched at ankles, slithering across damp soil with startling speed. When a smaller pine failed to snag the leg of one Protectorate, it simply bowed its head and impaled the man with its trunk.

She told herself to leave. She told herself to crush the triumphant bloodlust and throbbing arousal that bloomed within her as she watched the King tear the Protectorate operatives limb from limb. She gritted her teeth, running her gaze through the forest, trying to determine how many more from the Protectorate remained. Her fear for the King's well-being had diminished, trepidation of traversing Baba Yaga's realm alone rising to the forefront.

Perhaps if she held on for just a few more moments, she would not have to face whatever waited there by herself. The twisted black pine was so clearly a delineating marker. It was a place where anything left of who she had thought she was would fall away, and she'd be forced to see if her new skin could fit over her skeleton. So Raegan waited.

Until a flash of pinstripe caught her eye. With horror, she

found at least five Protectorate flanking her about a hundred feet off into the woods. She had hesitated, too fragile to enter Baba Yaga's realm alone, and now she had endangered both herself *and* the King. Reflex made her reach for the knife in her pocket. Old memories sparked, and she tried to dig for whatever she had summoned earlier against Fate, but nothing answered her call.

Heart pounding, a thousand ice-cold needles of dread pricking her skin, she shrank a step back against the twisted pine. Dread and indecision coiled in her stomach. She did not want to leave the King behind. But she was going to get herself killed if she stayed. Raegan told herself to stop being a coward and do the only thing she could. She knocked thrice on the twisted black pine, held utterly still for a moment, and then threw herself into the open space made by its contorted trunk. For a long, terrible moment, she only saw damp, pine-needle-strewn soil rushing at her, and all felt lost.

But then something stretched or snapped, and Raegan felt a harsh tug on her limbs. She slammed her eyes shut against the pain, and the world went black.

When she opened her eyes, the light was different: brighter, warmer. The tugging sensation had retreated, replaced by a sharp, sudden pain in her ribs. She coughed, raising her head to find the source of the discomfort.

As her eyes focused, Raegan saw a pair of worn leather boots and what she thought was the hem of a skirt the color of old blood. Bones were sewn into it. Then the pain again, sharper this time. She tried to climb to her feet but only managed to weakly roll over. The movement sloshed the bile in her stomach, and she vomited onto the ground, pine needles clinging painfully to her hands. When her sickness faded to a few dry heaves, she rocked onto her heels and wiped her mouth with the back of her hand.

"Why do you all always get sick?" someone asked. Their voice was heavily accented. Something Slavic, Raegan thought, but older and darker, thick as molasses. "Impressive, though. Fastest I've seen a mortal overcome realm illness. Though I suppose you're not *all* mortal, now, are you?"

Slowly pulling herself to her feet, Raegan turned to find the source of the voice: a ferocious-looking woman, her features gnarled and wrinkled, her nose beaked, the eyes black and sharp, bright as glass beads. Her sparse gray hair was in an intricate knot at the top of her head. A ragged black blouse was tucked into the bone-hemmed skirt beneath a wide leather belt. In her hands, the woman held a thick walking stick as gnarled as she was, which Raegan suspected had been the source of the stabbing pain in her ribs.

The woman was large, belly hanging over her belt and skin melting off her chin. Raegan found herself jealous of how this woman, if that's what she was, took up space. Jealous of the way she could enchant an entire realm into existence but did not bother or desire to turn herself into something slim and shiny.

Supporting herself with one hand on a nearby tree trunk, Raegan stood and made eye contact with the taller woman. "You're Baba Yaga, aren't you?" She supposed there was not really any point in asking. The being before her radiated power and smelled of acrid smoked bone, dried mugwort, and open flame.

"You know," the old witch said, her brow creasing in a way that almost read as concern, "I thought you'd come much sooner."

"Sooner?" Raegan echoed, her mouth dry. Something slinking and old—something that did not feel as though it properly belonged to her—appeared in the back of her mind, only to retreat into shadow before she could get a good hold on it. "Oh," she said. "Yeah. I was supposed to do that, wasn't I?"

Baba Yaga fixed her with a disappointed gaze that Raegan shrank under, just a little. Then the witch turned away, looking over her shoulder. "Come on," she said. "It's this way."

Wordlessly, Raegan followed the woman down a thin, packed dirt path that she hadn't noticed before. It snaked through the forest, vanishing almost entirely behind its own bends before reappearing again. The forest that surrounded the path was not the Jersey Pine Barrens. The trees towered much higher, many of their trunks too large for Raegan to wrap her arms around. Swamps ringed in thick, dark vegetation lingered to the right of the path, their waters black and murky. Heavy mist clung to the horizon. It felt primeval in the truest sense, untouched by perhaps anyone but Baba Yaga.

The air carried the scent of a distant bonfire, but beneath the smoke, the forest smelled richly of conifers, damp leaves, green ferns, and fungi. Raegan could've spent all day on this winding trail, marveling at the strange mushrooms and enormous oaks and knife-sharp swamp grasses. But instead, she kept her eyes on the back of the ancient witch leading the way. She marched, one foot in front of the other, until she lost track of how long she'd been walking the well-trodden dirt path.

Up head, something large materialized from the mist. She barely managed to hold back a gasp—it was Baba Yaga's hut. The structure was *exactly* like the illustrations Raegan had seen a million times—a simple, four-walled hut with a pitched roof perched on top of chicken legs. The legs were enormous, looking more like dinosaur claws than anything to do with a mundane farm animal.

A laugh bubbled out from the back of her throat, something between disbelief and triumph. Baba Yaga glanced at Raegan with a sharp eye but ultimately ignored her as they continued walking. The forest began to clear in a gradual, natural way, the larger trees tapering off into slender birches and then downy beds of ferns. The hut crouched in the center of the clearing, surrounded by a fence made of bone. At the top of each post, just as Raegan had imagined, sat a skull. She wondered if lights would flicker within the hollow bones once the man in the black clothing on the black horse rode past. Folklore settled onto her shoulders, heavy and imperfect and lovely.

"You are very late," Baba Yaga said, cutting Raegan's moment of awe short as she halted beside one of the hut's scaled legs. "Which complicates everything."

Raegan's gaze slid to the gray-haired witch, who'd crossed her arms over her patched black blouse, leaning onto the walking stick she had jammed into Raegan's ribs. "I know," Raegan murmured, things stirring in her belly, memories rising up unbidden. "I've tried before, you know. More than once."

Baba Yaga offered up only a scoffing noise, looking down her nose at Raegan. "So I heard," the witch replied. "I stay out of most things these days. I'm tired."

Raegan opened her mouth to say she was tired, too, but something sharp and gleaming in Baba Yaga's black eyes warned her away from making such a statement. So she closed her mouth and nodded, trying to look understanding.

Baba Yaga's mouth twisted, not unkindly, and she turned away from Raegan. Then the witch slammed the bottom of her walking stick into the soil three times. A moment later, the hut's legs folded, lowering the structure to the ground. Without looking back at Raegan, Baba Yaga ascended the rickety wooden steps to the door.

Raegan wavered, not daring to glance at the dark and wild wood behind her, but also understanding the implications of passing over a witch's threshold. There was only one reason to follow Baba Yaga through the burgundy-stained door, and that was to be unmade.

"Well," the witch called, looking at Raegan over her shoulder. "Are you coming or not?"

Raegan glanced up, setting her mouth into a firm line. For a moment, the world hung still. Then she nodded at Baba Yaga and followed the witch up the stairs, over the threshold, and into the darkness that hung from the eaves of the hut.

The inside was much larger than the outside. A fire roared in the massive stone-hewn hearth. A long table ran down the space to Raegan's right, a few mismatched chairs tucked beneath it. The air was thick with burnt herbs and strange rituals.

"Sit," Baba Yaga commanded, pointing one finger, curved with age, at the table.

Raegan, vaguely unsure if anything was even real anymore, slunk across the hut toward the table. The wide-plank floor creaked beneath her feet. She chose a chair with a wedge-shaped seat, three legs, and arms that were carved to look like two twin axes. The back of the chair rose up in a half-oval, decorated with ornate engravings. Raegan sank her body into it, realizing all at once how much her feet and knees hurt.

She turned and found Baba Yaga at the hearth, pulling a kettle away from the open fire. The witch placed an iron trivet on the table and set the kettle atop it before walking past Raegan into an open kitchen area. Mismatched shelves were affixed to the wall, and a narrow wooden counter held ceramic bowls and a large assortment of knives. She watched Baba Yaga retrieve two chipped teacups and saucers from a shelf.

Then the witch returned to the table, pouring dark, rich tea from the kettle. She slid one cup toward Raegan. She wrapped her hands around the mug, grateful for the comfort. The brew smelled of winter bonfires and crackling, smoky warmth, mellowed by a smooth, full-bodied richness.

"Remind me," Raegan began, her voice hoarse, "if it's alright. How did we meet?"

Baba Yaga came to a halt, the chair she had been sliding out for herself grating on the hardwood floor. Her black, stony eyes met Raegan's gaze. "Do you not remember?" the witch asked. Suspicion crept into her tone.

Raegan tilted her head, prodding at that dark softness inside her. Something surfaced. "It's hazy," she said, speaking slowly. "You were looking for a way out of something. An agreement? An arrangement? Not one you had made—one you had been bartered into."

Raegan had little idea if she were simply pulling from folklore or her actual memory, but for a split second, she saw Baba Yaga: a young woman striding up the path to a fence line, cloaked in a velvet cape marred with mud, her blonde hair in an intricate braid.

The witch said nothing for a long moment, sinking into the chair and stirring her tea. Raegan's heart began to pound at the thought of what something like Baba Yaga might do if she did not believe her.

But then the witch spoke. "It was a marriage," Baba Yaga said dryly. "*You* were the old Witch in the Wood then. I was a princess—hard to believe now—and I did not want the union. I had no use for a husband. You taught me the other ways, out there on your island I'd traveled so far to find, years ago. I did not marry, and I've never done another thing I did not wish since that day. I owed you a great debt."

Raegan noted the past tense, staring into her teacup for a moment before looking back across the table at Baba Yaga. "I imagine I already called that debt in with the Seal's placement," she said, running the tip of her tongue over her dry, chapped lips.

Baba Yaga's expression became grim, gaze drifting toward the window across from the table. "They hunted me, you know," the witch said, her tone far away. "The Round Table or the Protectorate or whatever they're called now. They've always hunted you through all your lives, and when they discovered your connection to the Białowieża Forest, they found me, too."

Guilt slipped pale, cold fingers between Raegan's ribs. It seemed that everyone foolish enough to entangle their lives with one of hers was never better off for it. "I'm sorry," Raegan said, but she was apologizing for someone she had once been, and that was a difficult thing to do, so her words came out hollow.

Baba Yaga shrugged, taking a long slurp of her tea. "A debt was owed," the witch said, her eyes meeting Raegan's again, "and I paid it. Now we are even, and I have lived long enough to discover my actions also concealed a budding Prophecy. Yes, girl, do not look at me like that. I heard it when the half-Oracle read it. Witches hear everything. And *real* magic—not this halfway, barely-there lie—is worth any risk. I remember this world before the Gates were closed all the way. It shimmered back then. Now it just fades away, farther and farther into the gray. You're supposed to fix it."

Raegan held the witch's gaze, her mouth going dry as her heart thudded, the sensation of her pulse thick in her throat. "So I'm told," she settled on saying, trying for a rueful smile.

But Baba Yaga only stared back, stone-faced, her small eyes like two pits.

Raegan sat up straight, sobering. "I only hope," she said, her voice hoarse now, "that I'm worth it."

"Hmmph," was all Baba Yaga said in reply, reaching for her teacup. She shifted her weight in the large chair she occupied, gaze returning to the window.

Raegan found herself looking, too, suddenly worried a threat may have appeared, but all she saw was the sprawling primeval forest. A hawk swooped by the window, a mouse writhing in its claws.

"You have returned to the King, yes?" Baba Yaga asked. "I

cannot imagine another reason he would be so close to my door."

Despite herself, Raegan's heart leapt in her throat, her fingers curling tighter around the chipped ceramic mug. "He's here?" she asked, the words coming out in a terse whisper.

The witch stared at her with those coal-black eyes, something not unlike disgust moving across her harsh features. "I have loved many strange and terrible things in my time," Baba Yaga said slowly, sounding out each word as though it were poison. "And even I have never understood how you managed to love him."

CHAPTER FIFTY-THREE

The words hung in the air, heavy as overripe fruit and rotting with accusation. Baba Yaga examined Raegan as she spoke. Maybe the witch expected her to look stung or even lash out in anger. But Raegan only sighed, pressing one hand to her forehead. Her skin felt clammy.

"Love is a bit strong," she replied, weary. "Only met him—or re-met, I guess—a few days ago, though it feels more like a year. Do you know if he's through your door yet, or just near it? The Protectorate came after us, of course, but . . . Fate also showed up."

At that, Baba Yaga reeled, her hands flying away from her mug, moving as if she might stand up and storm to the door. But then the witch appeared to collect herself, though her pockmarked hands curled into fists. "Aranrhod?" Baba Yaga demanded, keeping her voice low as if the downy-winged being could hear. "In the Pine Barrens? Near *my* door?"

Raegan nodded. The witch leaned back, tipping her head to look at the ceiling like it might hold some answers.

"How is She even here?" Raegan asked, watching Baba Yaga. "Aren't all the gods on the other side of the Gates?"

"That beast," Baba Yaga said eventually, her fingertips drumming on the table, "is one of the First. Not a goddess—much, much more. Nothing could contain Her, and I doubt even the Timekeeper would try. There are certain forces that keep this planet spinning on its axis, and Fate is one of them. She will slow the King down. I don't want to remove your Seal without him here, though it pains me to invite such an unnatural thing onto my lands."

Raegan added those bits of knowledge to her puzzle and took a sip of her tea. It was hot and bitter and exactly what she needed. Then she waited for Baba Yaga to speak. Her exhaustion sent her to the instincts built up over her years in journalism, and perhaps that wasn't a bad thing, even here, in the house of a famed and ancient witch.

"He is your tether," Baba Yaga said, her mouth forming around the words as if she'd eaten something vile. "The only similarity across all your lives. Already risky business removing a Seal that old. I'm not about to do it without a tether."

Raegan took another sip of her tea, setting the cup down on its saucer when Baba Yaga's eyes returned to examine her. "Then I suppose we wait," she said with a shrug. "What do you mean about him being unnatural?"

Baba Yaga's mouth turned downwards, sour. She sucked her teeth before replying. "He was made, not born," the witch answered, scrutinizing Raegan. "Two goddesses, an ancient Fey sword, the blood of the Unseelie Court's best warriors. That's why he has no true name."

Raegan desperately tried to file away these precious bits of information. She ached for her notepad and a pen, not trusting her exhausted mind.

"How did you find him, anyway?" Baba Yaga asked, as if her curiosity had gotten the better of her. "I heard he was doing his best to stay away from you."

Raegan met the witch's eyes and smirked, leaning back in

her chair for a luxurious stretch. "I'm relentless," she replied, crossing her arms.

At that Baba Yaga shifted again, almost like she saw something she recognized. Raegan took that as a sign to keep going. "It's a long story," she continued, stifling a yawn. "But I cornered him into a deal. And then we found out about the Prophecy, and I renegotiated. In my favor, of course."

Baba Yaga's eyes were appraising now instead of coldly examining, the set of her mouth not so hard. The witch's tongue darted out to moisten her lips. "I hope you hold the plait," she grumbled.

Raegan had no idea what she was talking about. Normally, that was something she'd withhold from showing on her face, but she'd been awake for too long with too little caffeine, and her poker face was not exactly at its best.

Baba Yaga, of course, pounced. "You do not hold it?" the witch wanted to know, leaning across the table toward her, the eyes dark and glimmering again. "*Never* let the faerie hold the bargain plait."

Raegan, beginning to see that something was very wrong here, brought her teacup to her mouth. She hoped the few seconds it took to have another sip would buy her some time. But it was hard to think clearly with the actual, real-life Baba Yaga staring her down from across the table. And Raegan very much wanted to know the information she was clearly missing. So she set her teacup back down and sighed.

"If you would be so kind," Raegan said, rubbing her temples, "what is a bargain plait? It seems I have fucked something up quite tremendously."

In response, Baba Yaga threw her head back and laughed —the sound like crows taking flight, old trees creaking in the wind, the first roar of a fresh bonfire. Any other time, Raegan's temper would have surely flared. But her exhaustion overpowered nearly everything, except for the gnawing worry she felt for the King.

"You fool," Baba Yaga said, wiping a tear from her eye as if Raegan's idiocy was the funniest thing she'd heard of in ages. "You have made no binding deal at all. Any bargain made with a faerie should end in a lock of their hair and a lock of yours being braided together. Otherwise, a bargain has no power. Faeries often try to maintain control over the bargain plait so they can destroy it, for the deal only holds as long as the plait does. But you did not even plait your hair together in the first place?"

Raegan considered this information, tracing the lip of her saucer with one finger. "They've done a really great job of keeping that bit out of human folklore accounts," she said eventually, eyes sliding to Baba Yaga.

The witch grinned at that, showing off blackened teeth. "Of course they have," Baba Yaga snorted. "Human folklore also says faeries can't lie. What a load of horseshit. Faeries lie as often as they damn well breathe. But now nearly everybody who even bothers to know a fuckin' thing about faeries believes it. Madness."

Raegan drained her tea, looking at the constellation of tiny tea leaf fragments scattered along the bottom of her cup. If Baba Yaga were telling the truth—and the witch did not strike Raegan as someone who needed to lie to trick or outsmart someone—that meant she'd never had a deal with the King at all. Not once was he sworn by any bargain to not harm her or act in her best interests.

And yet . . .

She chewed on the inside of her lip. She needed to sleep. She had no idea why the King would do such a thing. She had no idea how it was only twilight here in Baba Yaga's realm but had been well past midnight in New Jersey. She had no idea whether she was strong enough to withstand the removal of her Seal. She had no idea if her father awaited her at the end of this.

"Yeah," Raegan said eventually, dragging a hand through

her curls. "I'm kind of surprised he didn't just kill me. I mean, before we found out about the Prophecy, of course. Then, obviously, I became very useful to him."

Propping her chin on her hand, Raegan looked over at Baba Yaga, wondering what new level of scorn she'd receive from the witch based on that tidbit of information. But Baba Yaga hardly reacted, though one of her thin, nearly translucent eyebrows arched.

"You are the only living creature I could ever say this to with any degree of certainty," Baba Yaga said, leveling her gaze at Raegan, "but the Unseelie King would never harm you."

The words hit Raegan hard, an arrow to the weak spot in her armor. She had already known this to be true. She realized that maybe she had known it from the first time she'd met the King in this life. But hearing it said so matter-of-factly by a being who did not shy away from putting people's skulls on pikes was another thing entirely.

Raegan said nothing, holding Baba Yaga's black eyes, her breathing shallow.

"What an odd thing it must be," the witch continued, "to have something like him belong to you."

At that, Raegan bit down on her tongue so hard her eyes watered. She had no idea what game Baba Yaga was playing—if the witch was even playing a game at all—so she pushed her teacup to the side and folded her hands on the table. "I hardly think," she said slowly, "that either of us belongs to the other."

"No," Baba Yaga said, setting her mug down on its saucer with a clatter, a storm blowing over her face. "That is not what I said. In your marrow, before all the rest, you are like me. You are a witch. And we are the darkest parts of the forest and the woodsmoke on the wind when October comes roaring in. We belong to no one. We don't even belong to ourselves, not all of the time, and certainly not the way everyone thinks we do. We belong to the older curves, the deeper shadows, the quiet things that no man dares to know. But the King?"

The old witch cast her eyes to the window beside the door, her silhouette carved out by the hearth's light. "The King belongs to you. It is a strange thing, indeed."

Raegan, quite unsure of what else to do, looked out the window with the witch. She sat there in silence, only the sound of Baba Yaga's breathing and the fire crackling across the room filling the space. Sleep pulled at her with heavy hands and her eyelids drooped. Raegan was so tired that when she saw a black-cloaked rider on a black horse ride across the clearing below Baba Yaga's hut, she did not know whether it was real or not. At least, not until the witch spoke.

"Night has come," Baba Yaga said, getting to her feet, "and your King is not yet here. Let me show you to the bathhouse. You can sleep there. You stink too much of human cities for me to tolerate sharing my home with you for another second."

Raegan used all her effort to pull herself out of the chair, not even offended by Baba Yaga's comment. She wasn't sure how she was going to sleep in a bathroom, but frankly she would've accepted any place where she could lie down. A bathtub softened with some of the sweaters she'd packed would do.

Pulling herself to her feet, Raegan stood and followed the witch to the door. Upon reaching it, vertigo hit Raegan hard. She hadn't noticed, nor felt, the legs supporting the house stand up straight. The view out the window while sitting suddenly made sense, but her brain scrambled to process it all. When Baba Yaga plucked her walking stick from beside the door and tapped the hardwood floor three times, sending the massive legs back down to the ground, Raegan thought for a moment she might puke right on Baba Yaga's shoes.

She did not. The night outside was mercifully cool and fresh, the moon high above the trees, stars and galaxies twinkling. In any other place and any other time, Raegan might have lingered outside to enjoy a perfect autumnal evening. But her heart was too sick with worry and her head heavy and tired, so she trudged behind Baba Yaga down the hut's stairs and across the clearing.

Woodsmoke curled in the air—but not *his* woodsmoke—as Raegan walked. She took in the low, eerie light glimmering inside the skulls mounted on the fence—another thing she would have liked to stop and examine. But the darkness was thick and swift, and even Raegan was not sure she had the heart to navigate this place alone in the night.

Baba Yaga led her across the clearing and through a small grove of trees. At the end of the leafy hallway stood what looked to be a log cabin. Not exactly, Raegan could see in the dim light—or at least not what she'd usually call a log cabin in America. The roof rose in a sharp, pointed peak, much like Baba Yaga's hut, and the logs had been stripped of their bark and brined in age and fire soot. A chimney rose from one side, and a small door with an iron latch stood at the entrance.

"Here," Baba Yaga said, yanking the door open. "I'll send over supper. Don't expect anything fancy."

Raegan hadn't been expecting to be fed at all, and her stomach rumbled in pleasure. She peered into the bathhouse, not crossing the threshold. All she could see of the interior was firelight glinting off tile and age-worn logs. "Thank you," she said, turning to face the taller woman.

"I'll send the King when he arrives," Baba Yaga said, her tone appearing to curdle at the mere idea of having to speak with him. "And then we can go about removing your Seal. I said it's dangerous, and I meant it. You should know what you're risking: yourself. Madness is not only possible but likely. I can remove it, but I do not know who will wake up inside your body when I'm done."

The night stretched between them, a hundred emotions crawling up Raegan's throat. Her eyes blurred, and her stomach burned. She swallowed hard, looking up at the witch. "Baba," she whispered in the same way one might say "grandmother" or "please" or perhaps both.

Nothing in Baba Yaga's face changed, her shoulders still unrelenting, but she reached out and pressed Raegan's hands between her calloused palms. Emotion filled her dark, shining gaze. The witch's grip was tight—too tight—and Raegan was forced to wonder if this ancient, folkloric thing was afraid, too.

"Something feels different this time," Baba Yaga said eventually, sounding younger than what seemed possible. "So maybe it will be alright. Maybe."

Her hands squeezed Raegan's in a tight, warm embrace, and then she released the shorter woman from her grasp. Without another word, Baba Yaga turned on her heel and strode back through the grove of trees into the darkness that waited beyond. Raegan let out a long, shuddering breath, looking in through the open door of the bathhouse. There was no other option, she supposed.

Raegan entered carefully, waiting for her eyes to adjust to the dim light. The King's enchantment on her vision seemed to have worn off. Once inside, she raised her eyebrows in surprise. It seemed a great diminishment to call this space something as simple as the bathhouse. A long corridor ran parallel with the front of the building, white tile floors gleaming. Large bundles of dried plants hung at even intervals along the wall. Raegan took a deep breath. Something sharp, woodsy, and camphor-like met her nose—eucalyptus, she thought. She stepped through the hallway, pulling off her muddy boots and tucking them under a wooden bench built into the wall.

The main room offered a large stone fireplace that was already crackling with a beautiful flame—warm, bright, impossibly cozy. Two wooden lounge chairs were placed in front of the fire, each draped in blankets and furs. Candles lined the fireplace mantle. On the far end of the space was a pile of furs not dissimilar to the one in Baba Yaga's hut. The furs rested on a raised wooden platform, and Raegan imagined how quickly she could fall into slumber in a place like this, despite everything.

She moved to stand alongside the wall across from the fireplace and pulled her luggage tag from her pocket, placing it on another built-in wooden bench beside a stack of fluffy towels. While she waited for whatever magic was wound up in the object to release, she wandered toward the fireplace, noticing a large, open archway to its left. She stepped through, thinking she'd find a more traditional bathroom waiting for her.

Instead, an expansive room with gleaming tiles the color of smoke stretched out before her. The walls were crafted from the same stacked logs as the rest of the structure. Steam drifted lazily from the shimmering surface of a huge bath cut into the ground—accessed by a set of ornate, brightly colored tile stairs —ringed with lit pillar candles. Decorative tapestries hung from the walls, featuring scenes Raegan half-remembered from Slavic mythology and folklore. Plants exploded from every corner, turning what might have been a sterile, spa-like environment into something absolutely extraordinary. The room was somehow half-greenhouse, half-bathhouse, smelling of rich eucalyptus with glimmering water and mist-covered leaves. Raegan fell in love immediately.

She returned to the main room to find her suitcase on the bench and rifled through it to produce toiletries and some sleepwear. Then she stripped off her damp clothing, not having the energy to do more than leave it in a pile in front of the bench, grabbed a towel, and headed for the bath. She stepped in slowly, unsure of the temperature, but the water that met her skin was blissfully silky and perfectly hot. With a long sigh, Raegan walked down the remaining stairs and submerged herself up to her neck.

Finding a tiled bench built into the wall, she settled onto it, resting the back of her head against the lip of the bath. With only the sound of the fire crackling in the other room and the gentle ripple of the water, some of the more immediate stress seemed to slip away from her body. For now, she was at least physically safe.

A few minutes of peace, then guilt. Here she was, seeing the other side of the curtain, soaking in a divine bath, while her mother and her co-workers were no doubt worrying about her. The King was on a battlefield. Baba Yaga had a trial ahead of her that Raegan had brought directly to her door. Maelona could already be dead as a result of her attempts to help. Andronica could be crushed beneath the weight of holding the wards, pulling Kamau down with her. Blodeuwedd might endure punishment for treason if the Seelie Court became aware of her movements.

A ragged sigh escaped Raegan's mouth, ending in something more like a wounded cry. She squeezed her eyes shut and then forced herself to focus on scrubbing the evening from her body. Everyone had made their choices. Worlds were not repaired without carnage and consequences. Hadn't Raegan given up plenty, too? When the King reached Baba Yaga's realm—Raegan would not allow herself to start that thought with an "if"—she might lose herself entirely. Having a nice bath before possibly going completely mad didn't seem too selfish or luxurious.

Raegan held on to this halfway place of water, the main room just barely visible through the steam. So much life exploded in the bathhouse—from the tiles in bright hues of red and blue and yellow to the climbing vines and dark, waxy leaves of the plants. It felt like a place away from everything else. A place that Prophecies and owl-winged weavers of Fate and power-drunk mortal men could not touch. In her heart, Raegan knew that no such place existed, but blind hope had gotten her this far, so she held onto the idea and let it plant seeds within her.

CHAPTER FIFTY-FOUR

Raegan stayed in the bath until sweat began to bead on her forehead and the back of her neck. The thought of the King appearing when her clothes were already shed, her collarbones anointed in bathwater and firelight, was intoxicating, and she flirted with overheating before admitting defeat and sloshing up the stairs.

She grabbed a fluffy towel and wrapped herself in it, though she hardly needed the warmth. As she reached down to dry off her legs before walking into the main room, Raegan heard movement at the front of the bathhouse. Thinking it might be the meal Baba Yaga had promised, she padded toward the archway that divided the two main rooms.

The moment she approached the threshold, Raegan watched the door all but rip open. She froze, clutching her towel closer, wishing she had her knife on her and wondering if she could reach it in time. For a long, harrowing moment, there was only darkness on the other side of the door, complete and absolute. Her heart thudded hard in her chest. Then, materializing out of the night as if he were made of the same substance, came the King.

He stepped into the bathhouse like he had scented his

prey, eyes blackened with a feral gloom. Blood marred the left side of his jacket, and Raegan felt quite sure it was not his. Her breath caught in her throat. The King was horrifying and magnificent, not a stitch of humanity clinging to him.

His gaze roved to Raegan, and when he sighted her, he closed his eyes for a moment, inhaling like it was the first deep breath he'd taken in a long time. He stepped through the door, pulling it shut behind him. "I was not sure if you had made it through," the King said, his voice low and raw. Raegan watched his hand clench at his side. "Are you unharmed?"

"I'm fine," she said, blood drumming in her veins. "Didn't Baba Yaga tell you? I'm completely fine. It's you I've been worried about. Are you alright?"

The King took another step into the room and brought himself to a harsh halt, as if he were not fully in control of his body. Then he seemed to process her words and shook his head. "I did not speak with Baba Yaga."

Raegan's brows knit in confusion, and she tilted her head. "You didn't?" she inquired, wondering how he'd made it through the door without getting a solid stab in the ribs from Baba Yaga's stick.

"No," the King said, peeling off his jacket, which appeared to be damp with rain in addition to the blood. "I came straight to find you."

Raegan's breath hitched. She looked the King up and down, suddenly aware of what all his tightly coiled tension might've been about.

With a deep inhale, he came toward her, but only to hang his jacket by the roaring fire. Then he kneeled to unlace his boots, a muscle in his jaw leaping. "Did you learn anything when you spoke to Baba Yaga?" the King wanted to know, not looking at her. "You are, of course, not required to share it with me."

Raegan let out a long breath, leaning against the archway, trying not to think about the level of undress both of them were approaching. "She said the Seal wasn't meant to stay on this long," Raegan answered, watching his lithe movements, which made something as mundane as unlacing a shoe graceful. "So removing it is going to be dicey. But she'll do it. She wants to do it."

The King pulled off his boots and placed them by the fire before standing to look at her. His eyes were dark, bottomless pools in the dancing light of the hearth, his sharp features carved deeper by the shadows. Desire smoldered in Raegan's belly.

"What do *you* want?" he asked, gazing at her like nothing else existed in the world, sending her heart skittering faster.

Raegan should have wanted to demand answers about the false bargains he'd struck with her, or ask if Fate was coming for them, or do anything at all that was logical and smart and brave. All the things she'd thought she'd be if the world ever parted the veil for her. But she did not. She wanted the King to fuck her until the howling ache in her core finally subsided. And then, she wanted to tear apart every single person who had twisted magic and turned this once-beautiful world into a ruinous piece of cruel rock floating in dead space.

"With regard to the Seal?" Raegan asked, trying to keep her voice level. She forced herself to take a deep breath before answering, doing her best to shove aside the thick coil of lust wrapping itself around her midsection.

The King nodded and then pulled his damp sweater over his head, exposing a fitted gray t-shirt. Raegan lost track of her thoughts. Her eyes roamed across his sinful slopes of muscle, the sleeves of his shirt clinging tightly to the swell of his upper arms. She forced her gaze away, to the window on the other side of the room.

The King waited for her to answer. He did not prod her with more questions. He did not insert his thoughts. He did not rush her. And so, Raegan took a moment to think about the risks of removing the Seal, about the demands of Fate, about the tender bud that had pushed through her soil at Gossamer, and about the endless pit of rage burning in her chest.

It was, predictably, the rage that broke the surface, and the realization that came with it—one that had been unfolding in her for some time—stained everything in furious shades of red.

"I don't want to give a fuck about Fate anymore," Raegan said suddenly, fiercely, her fists curling as she met his gaze. "What do I actually want? I want to take everything back. I want my father. I want magic. I want *revenge*."

The King said nothing, again watching her like there was nothing else in the world. He prowled another step closer, his beautiful mouth parting slightly as he took her in. She became deeply aware that she wore nothing beneath the towel and that they were alone, tucked away from the world, and that tomorrow Raegan Maeve Overhill may cease to exist.

"And I want you, Oberon," she said, unable and unwilling to stop herself. "I want you as I always have: completely. Not in spite of what you are and not because of it, either. And I want you before the Seal is removed, before I might become someone else. Just once. Just once in this body, in this life, as *me*, I want you."

Immediately after speaking the words, she collapsed back against the archway. Her blood thrummed so loudly in her ears that the crackle and pop of the fireplace vanished. Time hung still as she waited for the King to say something—to say *anything*. Raegan felt as if she had sliced herself down the middle, displaying her still-glistening insides. She could only hope he would not choose to gut her again.

The King closed the distance between them in a heartbeat, reaching up above her head to rest one hand on the wall, looking down at Raegan in a way that made all the feelings she'd tried to smother throb and uncoil within her. With his other hand, the King reached out and took her jaw between his fingertips. His touch felt like a promise, and her body keened.

"You are my deepest wound," Oberon murmured, his eyes searching hers. "And yet I cannot live without the taste of blood in my mouth."

And then he kissed her, hard and unrelenting, his much larger body crushing hers against the wall. Raegan grabbed the front of his shirt, clawing her fingers into the fabric. Heat and need and a thousand years of longing exploded inside her, the gentle throbbing in her belly turning fast and wild.

Oberon's hand slid to her throat, fingers splayed, and she moaned, arching her body into his as she raked her nails down his chest. The rough groan he let out in response threatened to undo her entirely.

"Deny me," he rasped, his mouth moving against the delicate skin where her neck and jaw met. "It will hurt so much less in the end."

The husky timbre of the words sent a shiver across Raegan's skin. She had no intention of obeying. Instead, she let go of her towel, allowing it to pool around her feet, and then slid her hands to the hem of his shirt, yanking it upward with all her might.

"Make me remember you," she gasped as he pulled the garment over his head. "Whatever comes next, whoever I wake up as, make me *remember* you, Oberon."

A low, deep sound escaped from the back of his throat, and he gripped her waist so hard it hurt—beautiful, delicious pain. Raegan moaned as he lifted her from the ground, pinning her hips against the wall with his own. She dug into his shoulders with both hands, kissing him harder, as if her life depended on it.

Oberon slid his hand into her hair, his touch turning sensual and gentle.

She pulled back, breathing hard. "I don't want tenderness," she panted, wrapping her legs tighter around him. "I want *you*, Exiled King of the Unseelie Court. Give me your inhumanity and your cruelty. Leave your mark on me like a bloodstain."

His chest rose and fell against hers, his head tilted to the side as he examined her. Raegan watched something move across his face that both terrified and aroused her. Slick heat slid through her core. With a sound that could have just as easily come from a predator prowling the forest outside, the King tore her from the wall, his powerful arms wound around her so tightly she couldn't breathe.

He threw Raegan down on the bed of furs on the other side of the room, his body pinning hers against the soft bedding in an instant. She wanted him to leave handprints and bruises and any manner of ways to remember him. Oberon slid his arm beneath her leg, pulling hard to wrap it around his hips. Raegan obliged with her other limb, closing her thighs around him. The movement drew a low, strangled sound from his chest that immediately seared itself on her memory.

Oberon lifted himself up, arms bracketing either side of her head as he crushed his hips against hers, devouring the sound of her resulting moan with his kiss. Desperate and half-mad with need, she slipped one hand down his scarred torso, tracing the silken dusting of hair that led from his chest to his abdominals and then lower, lower.

The King's hand wrapped around her wrist with crushing, bruising power. She panted his name in a feverish murmur as he pinned her hand above her head, reaching to capture her other arm to do the same. "You said you wanted me," he said, mouth moving against her throat. "You already have me. You always did."

The King pulled away, pressing down harder on her wrists. Then he held her gaze, driving Raegan nearly out of her mind, the howl inside of her building like a blaze.

"But you do not belong to me," he continued, bringing his mouth back down to her throat, lips grazing her skin. "So you leave me no choice but to ruin you for any other lover you might take."

With tongue and teeth, the King mapped a trail down her body from her jaw to her breasts to her stomach—somehow both ferocious and languid at once—touching her in all the places she wanted to be touched. When he reached the apex of her legs, he released her wrists, drawing back to wrap his hands around the soft flesh of her generous thighs. The harsh pressure of his fingertips alone pulled another long, low moan from Raegan, her back arching with anticipation, blood drumming hard with desire.

As she looked down at him, the King's eyes found hers again. His lips moved along the inside of her thigh, gaze locked with hers. Then his mouth met the damp heat at her center, and she said his name like a prayer or a wish or a confession, her breath strangled in her throat.

"You will remember me whenever you are with anyone else," the King said, bringing his long, deft fingers to her core in the absence of his mouth. "When you pleasure yourself, you will remember me. No one will fill you or devour you or take you the way I do."

Raegan moaned again, louder this time, her heart pounding faster than she thought possible. When Oberon returned his mouth to her core, she grappled for him with blind hands, needing more. In response, he dug his fingers into her thighs, his capable tongue bringing her blisteringly close to orgasm in mere moments.

"Raegan," he said, his voice curling possessively around her name, "I want you to come for me."

"No," she panted, trying to sit up, reaching wildly for him. "Not without you inside me."

For a second, there was nothing but his hands around her thighs and the sound of her own breathing. Then Oberon straightened and dragged her toward him, his upper body coming to meet hers. One arm supporting his weight, he grabbed her by the jaw and kissed her as if it might save them both. Distantly, Raegan was surprised when he tasted only of himself—folklore, smoke, and mead. But she was more focused on winding her hands into his hair, begging and pleading for more against his mouth in a way she had never done before. She reached for his waistband, making quick work of stripping the cloth away from his body.

"Now," she implored, dragging her hands across his back. "Please. Oberon, *please*."

The King pressed her into the furs with the heavy weight of his muscled body, lining up their hips in exactly the way Raegan so desperately wanted. Then his hard length met her soft, wet heat, and her back arched against her will, pleasure and pain filling her entire body. Her mouth fell open at the same time she heard a strangled groan escape from Oberon. Then the feeling of his kiss returned, coupled with the full, thick intensity of him at her center, their bodies moving in the same rhythm.

Oberon allowed her to wrap her arms around his neck as he slid one hand into the juncture where their hips met. The careful movement of his fingers in exactly the right spot made Raegan's vision go white.

"More," she moaned, digging her nails into the top of his heavily muscled shoulder.

The King complied, pulling another ragged gasp from her mouth. "Raegan," he said, his voice low and raw and thick with need. "Come for me harder than you will for anyone else."

She did as he commanded, the pressure within her finally snapping, an orgasm shattering her—making her his, as much as he was hers. She said his name more times than she could count as he tangled his hands in her hair.

Once Raegan thought she might be able to feel her bones again, he rolled them over in one quick, sharp move of muscle, placing her on top. She missed the near-suffocating weight of his body immediately, but every inch of her was red-hot and she needed to breathe.

So she collapsed against his chest. Oberon slid both arms around her, one hand massaging the back of her neck. After a few long, gorgeous moments that Raegan tried to live in—their breathing in sync, her flushed cheek against his chest, her thighs still wrapped around him—she sat up halfway, meeting his gaze.

Again, as if he knew what she wanted just from the look in her eyes, Oberon gripped her hips hard, ravenously taking in her collarbone and soft stomach and generous curves. When he dragged his eyes back up to hers, Raegan's core pulsed wildly. He reached out and grabbed her wrists, placing her hands onto his chest, palms down. His touch trailed up her body until he reached her breast. There, Oberon teased her until she whimpered, rolling her hips against his.

She ran her eyes across his body—the elegant collarbones, deft sweep of powerful muscle, the dusting of raven hair across his chest, narrowing and darkening as it trailed down to the sharp cut of his hip bones, which formed a hard V. With all her might, she tried to memorize it.

Then she met his gaze again, finding his mouth slightly parted.

"Raegan," he said, both hands returning to her hips, a question tilting his low, deep voice upwards.

She would've done anything he asked. He possessed her completely and entirely.

"I want you," the King told her, "to give me your rage."

Fire roared through her body, and Raegan did as he bid.

CHAPTER FIFTY-FIVE

Much later, he carried her to the bath, not releasing her from his arms. As he settled onto the tiled bench, Oberon pulled her onto his lap, her back against his chest. Raegan sighed, low and long, resting her head against his shoulder. For once in her life, she was completely and utterly satisfied—no ache fluttered against her sternum, no yearning unfolding in her marrow. Raegan knew it wouldn't last, but she tried to savor it all the same.

She tucked her head under his chin, laying her cheek against his collarbone. The angle brought Oberon's shoulder into view—and more noticeably, the red marks her nails had left. She raised a hand, brushing the scratches with her fingertips. "I didn't hurt you, did I?" she murmured, though she knew it was probably a ridiculous question.

"No," he said into her hair, his hand tracing a set of bruises on her thigh she hadn't noticed yet. "Did I hurt *you*?"

"If you did, I liked it," Raegan replied, looking up at him to smirk. "Very much."

He lifted his hand to her jaw, brushing her lips with his thumb before leaning in to kiss her. It was soft, slow, sensual, his fingers sliding into her hair. The sensation of it awakened an entirely different feeling in Raegan, one she was not familiar with and did not wish to explore right at this very moment. But she kissed him back all the same, twisting to press herself against him.

And then Oberon just held her. He said nothing. He didn't have to. The feeling of him—real, corporeal, here—was all she needed. At some point, he unwrapped his arms from her waist to massage up her neck and into the base of her skull. Raegan melted into his touch, her eyelids growing heavy.

She'd never admit it, but she felt like a stray cat finally being offered a few scratches and a bowl of milk. Oberon had fucked her hard and relentlessly, exactly what she'd asked for and precisely what she'd needed. But as much as it confused her, Raegan also desperately wanted this aftercare. The feeling scared her. It had been something she was happy to administer, most of the time, but was ambivalent about receiving. The sex itself—the rush and the chase and the orgasms—was the part she liked.

And yet whatever was happening now, the way it seemed like Oberon encircled her completely with his larger frame—how could he be so fierce one moment, and so gentle the next—was just as good. Maybe even better.

Raegan shoved that thought aside. It was too confusing, and it might not even matter this time tomorrow.

"Would you like to get into bed?" Oberon asked in a low voice, providing a much-needed distraction.

"With you?" Raegan asked, stretching to sit up straight. "Absolutely."

He carried her out of the bath even though she reminded him twice that her legs did, in fact, still work and that it was very presumptuous of him to assume they didn't. But she still let him help her dry off, and she leaned on him for balance as she stepped into a pair of soft sleep joggers. He lay down with her, and she curled into his chest, his scent and his skin and his voice all so painfully familiar.

"Was it ever just like this?" Raegan asked, her voice thick with sleepiness. She felt his powerful hand alight softly on her hair. "You know. None of the rest. Just this?"

"I wish I could tell you the answer you want to hear," the King replied. A pang smarted inside her chest, but she hadn't been expecting anything else. "For now," he continued, wrapping an arm around her waist, "it can be, if you wish."

Emotion swelled in Raegan's throat, tears pricking her eyes. "For now," she echoed, "I would like that."

When she awoke the next morning, sunlight floated in gently from a nearby window. She was pleasantly sore in places that had not been sore in some time. The previous evening came back to her in a flood, and she shifted to roll over. As she did, a muscled arm snaked around her waist. Raegan smiled, trying to hide the expression in the pile of furs as Oberon pulled her against him, her back to his chest.

The smell of woodsmoke and damp stone enveloped her. For a lilting moment, she had little idea who she was or what century it might be. All she knew was the fragile feeling in her chest and the impossibly beautiful creature with his arm around her.

"If I had known telling Fate to fuck off got you so turned on, I would've done it a while ago," she murmured.

She waited for the sound of his laugh, but when she heard nothing, she twisted in his grasp, turning to face him. As she did, Raegan found only the kind of sorrow that would've drowned most people.

"You did, once before," Oberon told her as he brushed hair away from her face, his touch gentler than it had any right to be. "The first time we met, I was the doomed one. And you refused to accept the path Fate had placed me upon."

Raegan's breath hitched. She opened her mouth to ask a

question but realized she'd know soon enough and probably shouldn't risk further corrosion to the Seal. Long-dead things rattled their cages in her mind, but the locks held. For now.

"How did everything get so fucked up?" she wondered out loud, letting her head fall back onto the furs.

He did not answer—could not, she knew—but he held her tighter, as if to show Fate and Time and all the rest that he had little intention of letting her go. Raegan breathed in his scent, trying to memorize the scars across his chest. Each of them had a story and once upon a time, she had been able to read them like constellations.

Raegan traced one scar with a light touch, following its swoop to the top of Oberon's chest, just below his collarbone. There she saw the deep mauve slash she remembered noticing the night before. He flinched when she touched it, surprising her.

"Sorry," Raegan murmured into his skin. "What the hell did that to you?"

His hand landed on her hair again, somehow soft as a butterfly's wings. Another question he couldn't answer for the sake of her Seal. But something surfaced as she stared at the harsh puncture wound that had clearly just missed his heart.

Excalibur, whispered a voice from deep inside her. She examined the scar again, sleeping things stirring. For no reason at all, Raegan felt positive that this particular injury had been dealt by Excalibur. One of the world's most famous swords, made immortal by myth and legend. And still not capable of killing him.

"It is nearly time for us to meet Baba Yaga," Oberon murmured, his remorse-laced words breaking her thoughts.

"Right," she replied, not moving. She wanted whatever this was with him. She also wanted her power back, and more importantly, she wanted the ability to do something about her broken world. She reminded herself that removing the Seal could give her those things. If she didn't lose her mind, of course.

Raegan sat up when Oberon did, wrapping herself in a fur pelt. The fire still smoldered in the hearth, but she found the bathhouse colder this morning. When Oberon placed a plate of bread and fruit in front of her, she ate automatically. She tasted nothing. She stood and dressed, choosing comfortable clothes: tapered wool pants and a large, oversized sweater.

She found the King standing by the fire awaiting her, looking composed and deadly in well-tailored black clothing. But when her gaze met his, Oberon faltered, a muscle in his jaw leaping.

Raegan moved to stand beside him, her shoulder brushing his arm. "Why did you lie about the bargains?" she asked, staring into the fire, feeling so strangely sure that it didn't really matter all that much, even though she knew she should be furious.

The King sighed. "Because something felt different this time," he said, sliding his hands into his pockets, his words echoing Baba Yaga's, even if he didn't know it. "I wanted to keep you close, but I do not make decisions based on feelings. So when you offered me a reason, I took it. That said, I could not bind myself to you, considering our history and the Seal. I did give you my word, though, and I always honor my word."

Raegan's gaze slid to his again, her eyes narrowed.

"I *usually* honor my word," Oberon amended, a sly, cruel smile creeping onto his face. Then he shrugged. "I am what I am."

"Did you do something to me when I first came to see you?" she asked, trying to fill in all the remaining blanks, before she possibly became a blank herself.

"I took you home and eased your memory," he replied. "I apologize for the intrusion. You touched me without warning, and your mind reacted quite strongly. I was worried your Seal was at risk."

Raegan shifted her weight, pulling at a loose thread on her sweater. "You told me that we can't keep singing the same song or something," she mumbled, her eyes falling to the soot that ringed the hearth.

"And yet here I am, reminding you of its melody," Oberon said bitterly. "I am sorry I am not stronger. I did warn you. You make me weak."

Raegan stiffened at his words, remembering the way they'd cut into each other at Gossamer. But his tone was different, she realized, and a degree of awe laced it. Excalibur could not kill him. Nor could the Protectorate. Exile into a land without magic had hardly diminished him. But *she* did. In the worst way, the statement was a compliment—that she had the power to weaken a being molded by primordial forces, torn from the night sky itself.

In the distance, Raegan heard a bell tolling, low and lonely, more at home over a windswept moor than Baba Yaga's tangled green realm. But she knew the sound was for her all the same, a summoning of sorts, and she raised her gaze to the King.

"Please kiss me," she said. "Just once more. Before I go."

He did as she requested. It was the kind of kiss that spoke of extinguished flames and unyielding loss, a goodbye that stretched across eternities. Raegan kissed him back desperately, as if her rage and heat could keep both of them warm.

Oberon exhaled and rested his forehead against hers, hands still in her hair. She tried to memorize the feel of it all— hungry, as always, for everything she could not have. She closed her eyes against the weight of the sorrows she laid at his feet time and time again.

Then he murmured two words that sent light cascading into all her darkest places, locks falling away and doors flying open.

"Outlive me."

Suddenly, she was no longer in Baba Yaga's bathhouse but a wide, verdant field at the edge of the forest. She turned away from the woods, pointing at a tree and explaining something about its bark. A few feet behind her stood the King, resplendent with youth, his porcelain skin marked only by a few slight lines around his eyes, courtesy of riding in the sun all his life.

Then she stood at the mouth of a grand stone citadel, a large wooden door swinging open to allow her to walk through.

A clearing and a swan-winged woman and blackberry-stained lips.

A lightning-streaked sky, red as blood, a vast and terrible army at her side.

A man with pale eyes and pale hair, a sword on his belt that hummed with power.

A cottage with a thatched roof, her dried herbs lined up just the way she liked.

A feverish kiss from a towering, beautifully inhuman creature in black armor. His low, rich voice—like heather on the hills or dusk over the lake—murmuring against her skin, "Outlive me. I love you too much."

A feast, colorful banners hanging from the ceiling of a great stone hall, tables laden with food and wine. She stood in the corner beside a tall, gray-haired man, nervous but trying not to show it.

"Don't fret," the man was saying, looking at her with what she thought might be fondness. "It took many years for the nobles to acknowledge me at a feast, or even out in the market, despite me having spent the night ensuring their child did not succumb to fever."

The man took a long pull from his goblet, gaze darting over her shoulder. His thick brows rose in pleasant surprise, eyes mischievous when they returned to hers.

"At the very least," the man began, a smile tugging at his mouth, "you have someone's attention that no one else seems able to obtain, try as they might."

She looked at him, confused, and turned to glance behind

her. And there he *was, dressed in deep tones of steel blue that looked beautiful against his moonlight skin. His dark waves of raven hair were swept away from his face, tumbling down his neck. He wore a sword at his waist, and even from a few paces away, she knew he smelled of woodsmoke and black pepper and damp stone.*

He said her name, and she demurred politely, trying not to drown in his ocean eyes. Just behind him, the other people gathered in the hall looked on with a rapt sort of curiosity, as if this absurdly handsome knight did not always pay attention to the unmarried young ladies at feasts.

Then she returned the greeting, his name filling her mouth.

And suddenly, she remembered all of it—how it was the same name she'd said in the dream at the river, how there had been a changeling in King Arthur's court and almost none of it had happened like the stories said. She should know. She'd been there.

And so had he.

She raised her eyes to his, that same oceanic gray after all these years. And then, she said his name. Not a true name, no, but his first.

"*Mordred.*"

Chapter Fifty-Six

Everything that happened next was chaos. Her vision blinked in and out, and even though there was ground beneath her feet, it felt like she was constantly plummeting. Someone had been kind enough to lay her down on something soft, and then someone else was yelling, while the first person's voice kept getting lower and lower.

"How is it even possible?"

"It's *not*."

"Clearly, it is."

"I placed the goddamn Seal myself! Two little words shouldn't corrode it. Neither would fucking. Don't look at me like that. I'm no fool. You know as well as I do that she'd need extensive, specific knowledge of multiple lives. Despite my general distaste for you, I very much doubt you sat her down and walked her through everyone she's ever goddamn been. I certainly didn't say very much."

Then silence stretched long, except for the buzzing in her head, like a thousand bees ramming into her skull.

"If you do not salvage this, I will rip your little realm apart while you watch. Only once I have crushed the last of it between my teeth will I allow you to die."

More silence, then a wolfish whistle. "*Ебать*. I get threats all the time, but that's the first one I've taken seriously in a while. Well done. Now hush and let me save our girl."

Soft shuffling sounds, her chest caving in, her mind jumping and fracturing, mixing childhood memories with places she did not know, jumbling movies she'd seen with images of stone halls and brutal battles.

"Raegan, if you can hear me, we've hit a spot of trouble. I'm going to peel away your Seal, but it's corroded quite badly. To be frank with you, old friend, this is going to be brutal. Remember the old stories and look for the doors."

And then Raegan was Raegan again, at least a little, but she was also falling. Sort of. There was no up or down in this space, just blackness and a distinct sensation of rushing movement before her consciousness failed her, blinking out.

When Raegan woke, antiseptic lingered in the air, conjuring images of linoleum floors and watery light. She blinked her eyes open slowly. She was alone in a bare, quiet room. White sheets were pulled up to her waist, and a pale yellow blanket, wooly with pilling, stretched across her calves.

Shakily, she swung her legs off the edge of the bed and sat up. Her feet were encased in fuzzy socks with grippy pads on the bottom. Panic crowded her throat. Jaw clenched, she stared down at her lap, horrified to discover a plastic bracelet around her wrist, spelling out "RAEGAN OVERHILL, NO ALLERGIES."

No, no, no. Not again. Not like this.

The door across the room opened softly, and she snapped to attention.

"Oh, good, you're up," a kindly older man chimed from the doorway, backlit by overhead fluorescents. "I hope your head is feeling better. Your mother is here for a visit, but she said she could come back if your migraine is still an issue."

Raegan's tongue felt too thick in her mouth. "No," she said after a long pause. "No, I'm feeling better. I can see my mom."

"She's waiting for you out in the garden," said the man who she was trying to tell herself was not an orderly. She waited for him to walk away, but it became clear he would be escorting her. So she stood up, slid her feet into the slippers she knew would be next to the nightstand, and pulled the long cardigan off the edge of the bed frame.

And then Raegan followed the man out the door and down a hallway. She took in every sign, every person—anything and everything she could—to gain any kind of information. None of it made any sense at all. She had just been in Baba Yaga's bathhouse with an ancient Fey king.

As soon as that thought fully formed in her mind, Raegan burned with shame at how absurd it sounded. She tried to remember the feeling of the thick furs against her skin and the smell of the eucalyptus bundles and the taste of Oberon's kiss.

Before she could untangle anything further in her mind, the orderly led her into a small courtyard. Garden was a generous name for the space, which consisted of a few potted plants and an algae-choked fountain. Large gray cement walls surrounded it on all sides. She couldn't even smell plants or rocks out here—just antiseptic.

"I'll be back in a half an hour," said the orderly who she'd forgotten was there. And then he was gone, leaving Raegan to walk the remaining few yards to her mother, who was seated at a small café table that had seen better days.

"Hi, Mom," Raegan said, sliding onto the chair, finding her voice higher than she remembered, her heart hammering in her chest.

"Raegan," Bronwyn greeted. It was definitely her mother, Raegan was sure, the silver rings on her fingers and the worn mulberry sweater coat so familiar. She caught a whiff of her mom's perfume and calmed just a little.

"Nice to hear you call me mom," Bronwyn added, her tone harsh, confusing Raegan.

"Uh, right," Raegan said. "How are you?"

"Wow," Bronwyn replied, raising her eyebrows. "Maybe this is finally helping you. I'm doing okay. How are you?"

"I've been better," Raegan said, her throat closing off as tears threatened to descend upon her. "Mom, um, could I ask you some questions? There's some things I don't quite remember."

"Maybe you should talk to your doctor about that," Bronwyn said, looking concerned, which at least stung a little less.

"Oh, um, I'm on a new medication," Raegan ventured. "Some fogginess and memory loss might happen at first. And I just woke up. I had a bad migraine. So I was hoping it would be okay to bother you rather than take up time in my sessions?"

It sort of addled her that even now, riddled with confusion and fear, she could still lie that easily.

"Sure," Bronwyn said, her tone less guarded. "What do you not remember?"

"Uh, this sounds really bad, but how long have I been here?"

Her gut twisted as she watched the expression on her mother's face move into something that looked like sweet, sickly pity.

"Raegan, that's concerning," Bronwyn returned, looking toward the orderly by the courtyard entrance like she might run screaming to him because her daughter was unraveling again.

"I know," Raegan said, forcing a laugh. "I'm going to talk to my doctor as soon as you leave. I didn't want to miss your visit. I'm sure it's just the medicine." She forced a smile onto her face, feeling like her own puppeteer.

"You've been here almost a year, Raegan," her mother said,

eyes boring into hers. Bronwyn said each word slowly and deliberately, as if Raegan were either too stupid or too insane to understand. Her stomach flipped, and nausea threatened to overtake her. "It's almost November. You came here last October," Bronwyn continued, her eyes darting back to the orderly at the courtyard's entrance. "Do you remember? You, um, you were not feeling too well."

Raegan could not remember anything, a white wall of nothingness hitting her when she tried to recall anything from before waking up in that bed just a few moments ago.

"I think you should talk to your doctor," Bronwyn said finally when Raegan offered her nothing. "I don't want to upset you, and I'm not trained . . . I'm not trained to deal with this."

"Okay," Raegan breathed, her hands curling into fists so hard that her fingers hurt. "Uh, how's the house? Are you decorated for Halloween?" She would be clever and unafraid. She would poke and prod at this reality, testing its realness in exactly the same way it seemed to be testing her.

"Raegan, I don't decorate for Halloween, you know that," Bronwyn said, narrowing her eyes. "Are you okay?"

"I don't know, Mom," Raegan said hoarsely. "I really don't know. Um, have you talked to anyone at the paper?"

"The paper?" Bronwyn echoed, confusion crossing her features.

"You know, where I work," Raegan offered, her brows knitting together.

"Work?" her mother repeated. "Raegan, that's a bit strong for freelancing a few stories now and again. You haven't been well enough to work full-time since college."

Raegan's stomach dropped out from beneath her, and nausea swept over her in larger waves. With all her strength, she suppressed the rising panic. "Right," she said, drumming her fingers on the table, thinking. None of this was real. It couldn't be. "Uh, how are you doing?"

"You already asked me that," Bronwyn said, her tone flat.

"I mean, with the anniversary coming up."

Bronwyn waved Raegan's suggestion away with a swat of her hand through the still air. Her throat constricted as she resisted the urge to look up. Would she find some heinously painted ceiling depicting the open sky because she was not deemed sane enough to gaze upon the real one?

"That's a dramatic way of phrasing it," Bronwyn said after a pause. "I don't assign much meaning to the day your dad decided to leave us for someone else."

"Dad didn't leave . . . He's *missing*," Raegan said, her mouth dry. The iron grip she had on the panic faltered. It slid into her veins, hot and hungry.

"I think you need to talk to your doctor immediately. We've been through all of this before," Bronwyn said, closing the front of her sweater coat across her chest in that familiar way. "Cormac left us for another woman. You see him a couple of times a year. He hasn't visited you here because he can't handle it, but he's not missing. He's just an absolute asshole."

All of Raegan's control shattered, and her eyes welled with tears. A heavy weight settled on her chest, and breathing suddenly required all of her strength. Bronwyn watched her struggle, worry etching her features.

"I think I do need to talk to my doctor," Raegan sputtered. "I don't remember any of this, and I'm scared." Her voice hitched because now she *was* afraid—terrified, even.

Bronwyn softened for just a moment, reaching over to put a hand on her daughter's shoulder. "It's going to be okay," Bronwyn whispered, though Raegan wasn't sure which one of them she was saying it for. "Stay right here."

Raegan numbly watched her mom get up and walk toward the large glass doors, where a few orderlies were waiting. Two immediately walked over with her, and Raegan caught the edge of the conversation: "She doesn't remember anything. It's like all the work of the past year just went away."

Bronwyn's brown eyes were wide and shiny when Raegan stood. "They're going to take you to see your doctor," she confirmed.

"Okay, that's probably for the best," Raegan mumbled. "I guess I'll see you later?"

"I'll be back next month," Bronwyn confirmed, which sent a little dagger into Raegan's heart. A visit once a month? That's all her mom could spare?

The orderlies were gently guiding her away, so Raegan took a deep breath and asked, "Hey, um, where am I?"

"The Pines Center," the woman on her left said. "You're part of an inpatient program so you can feel better."

Raegan turned the name over in her head. "Where is it, like, physically?"

"You're in New Jersey," the male orderly said. He was the same one from before, she realized. "Just on the edge of the Pine Barrens."

Raegan bit down on the inside of her cheek, hoping for blood, hoping for pain, hoping for anything but what was in front of her. Fear crept up her spine, sly and slinking. Her mind had hidden the truth from her before. Otherwise, all of this would be so easy to dismiss. She'd been hospitalized in Boston during college. Not for a year, though. It was barely more than a week. In and out. She was fine, more or less.

Wasn't she?

Before Raegan could wrap her head around the situation, she arrived at the doors to her doctor's office. The male orderly ushered her inside. She dragged herself across the scuffed linoleum. Sitting there at the desk, shuffling some papers and calm as could be, was her editor, Henry Washington.

"Sit down, Raegan, sit down," he called in a gentle voice. "It sounds like you may not be feeling well today. I rearranged my schedule so we could talk."

It was too much for her to take, her body running cold like someone had dumped a bucket of ice water over her head. "Henry?" Raegan sputtered, sinking into the chair.

"Dr. Henry," he corrected, not unkindly. "Dr. Arman Henry. But I know in that story you're writing, I inspired . . . Henry Washington, isn't it?"

"I'm not that kind of writer," Raegan said, her mouth dry.

"What are you, then, Raegan?" Henry asked. "Do you remember why you're here?"

She spent a few precious moments trying to push past that blank white wall, or find a way to tear down this convincing reality built all around her. But then she looked at him again, and god, he looked so much like *her* Henry, and the pain of that realization snuffed out the last stitch of willpower.

"No," she finally said, quiet and small. "I have no idea at all."

CHAPTER FIFTY-SEVEN

Henry—Dr. Arman Henry, apparently—spent a few minutes explaining what Raegan had already assumed. She had been admitted to The Pines nearly a year ago following an episode that involved a complete split from reality, including lots of ranting and raving about the Fey and magic and the Gates. Henry didn't say it like that, but she got the point.

He was sorry to hear she was having trouble remembering and made a suggestion with an impressive amount of tact that the real Henry never would've had. Well, if her Henry was the real one. In all truth, Raegan did not know for sure.

"Maybe, because it's around the time of year your family changed in your youth *and* when you more recently joined us here, some of that old pain is being dredged up," he said, steepling his fingers. "And that's okay. Darkest before the dawn and all that. I think we should look at this as an opportunity to dig a little deeper."

Raegan kept alternating between obsessively listening to every word he was saying and trying to scan the room, looking for clues that this was made up. She didn't find any. It even smelled like an inpatient facility—the bleach and the fake floral air freshener and the aura of misery carefully scrubbed away. She looked down at her feet. If this was fake, they got the socks right too, down to the little grippy beads on the bottom.

So maybe this was real?

Suddenly, Raegan snapped back to attention because Henry had just said a name she had not expected to hear in this place. "I'm sorry—what did you say?"

"Oh, it's alright, Raegan," Henry said, unfolding his hands. "I brought up Oberon. The King."

Raegan's mouth went completely dry. "Oberon," she repeated, hollow.

"Yes, we've discussed before how he's essentially a stand-in for or a daydream of your perfect partner," Henry replied. "Unrealistic but aspirational in a lot of ways. Too good to even be human. He holds hallmarks of what we would identify as masculinity but isn't a man in the way we understand it, which sidesteps your issues with real, human men."

Her insides twisted. She thought she might be sick. "What?" Raegan settled on, the word coming out choked.

Henry sat back in his chair, examining her. Raegan tried to pull her thoughts together, tried to formulate something that felt close to logic. She reminded herself that the real Henry would've been familiar with her jokes about being attracted to all women and, like, four men, so the idea of someone male-presenting being her perfect partner would seem absurd to him.

Raegan rubbed her forehead. "Why are we talking about this?" she wanted to know.

"Does talking about it in this way make you feel defensive?" the doctor asked. "That he's imagined? Sometimes our imaginations can help us out, but it's important you realize no romantic partner has ever come to visit you. So we need to start deconstructing what's real to everyone else and what's only real to you. That doesn't make you bad or crazy. It only

467

means we need to be sure we can both agree on what parts are real, and what parts are just for you."

The man seemed less and less like Henry, his tone descending into something Raegan found hard not to equate with open condescension.

"How much does this place cost a week?" she demanded, pleasantly surprised by the amount of venom she'd summoned. "It better be cheap if this is the extent of your psychoanalytic skills."

"Okay, Raegan," Henry said, placing his hands on the desk. "I think we should take a break and maybe revisit this tomorrow. I know you were pretty confused earlier."

Henry got up from behind his desk to guide her by the elbow to the door. Raegan lifted her arm, not wanting whatever this thing actually was to touch her. She looked desperately around the office for anything at all that might indicate he was a fraud. Her eyes fell on a framed picture on the wall. It had a gold plate inscribed in looping calligraphy that read "our honeymoon." It still had a price sticker in the top right-hand corner and the photo inside was of a smiling couple. Maybe Henry just hadn't changed the stock photo yet, but it didn't look like one of those grayscale inserts. The couple was blonde, white, maybe in their thirties, standing in front of what looked like a vineyard. They weren't airbrushed or retouched.

And neither one of them was Henry. Because Henry was a single Black guy in his fifties.

He was rushing her through the door and into the hands of the orderlies, almost like he knew she was looking for something to break this construct. But Raegan's teeth had sunk in this now, and she twisted around. Her eyes locked onto the diploma hanging over his desk. It wasn't made out to anyone. All it said at the top was "The University."

Raegan threw her head back and laughed so hard that the orderlies exchanged glances. All of this was fucking fake. All of it. She didn't know why it was happening or what in the hell she could do about it. But she knew that everything around her was fake, and that meant the bathhouse and Baba Yaga and the quest and the King belonged to the real world. Her world.

The orderlies deposited Raegan in her room. In the lonely silence, she began to panic. What if she was just hallucinating to support her delusion? What if her mind was lying to her, showing her breadcrumbs where everyone else just saw regular photos and diplomas?

Raegan sat down on her bed, forcing herself to breathe, terrified by how fake everything looked, like cardboard cutouts. If this *was* the real world, she would never, ever be happy again. Panic and horror and that deep well of sorrow rose up her throat like a tidal wave.

"Okay, so then think, you dumb bitch," Raegan snarled at herself under her breath, running her hands through her hair so hard she yanked out a few strands.

Her mind remained horribly blank, as pale and stale as the space around her. She pulled her cardigan around her body, hoping that if she cocooned herself, she might emerge stronger and braver. As the fabric moved, something rustled in her left pocket.

All of Raegan's attention zeroed in, sharp as the point of a knife. Hand shaking, she delicately prodded her fingertips beneath the seam of the pocket. Something brushed her skin —soft, dry. Hope surged in her chest as Raegan pulled her hand away, cupping a bundle of meadowsweet in her palm.

Blodeuwedd.

Do not forget.

Raegan was on a quest. All quest-goers were tested, and this particular test was a classic. She'd seen it in a hundred stories, on the pages of her favorite books and on the screen of her parents' battered TV. She clutched the meadowsweet in her hand, the antiseptic smell banished by its springtime scent —green and fresh and full of life instead of this muted, quiet death.

She shot to her feet, beginning to pace. What had Baba Yaga said? To remember the old stories, to look for the doors. If she were trapped in some gray, shallow alternative world, what was the way out? What was the common thread through all of fantasy and folklore and old country stories? What was the escape hatch? The door?

And then, just like that, she knew. In a mad dash, her hands shaking, Raegan yanked off her sweater, pulling the arms inside out. She laid it on the bed and pulled off the white t-shirt next, turning it inside out as well. Then the flannel pants, then the socks, and for good measure, the sports bra and the underwear.

Feeling like a madwoman and standing naked in the small, dim room, Raegan began to re-dress with her clothing turned inside-out, starting at her feet and working her way up. When she reached the final piece of clothing, the long sweater, she gritted her teeth.

This had to work, or she would kill herself, she realized. If this world was real, she could not exist within its hollow margins, could not do its plain and simple bidding. Not after what she had touched, not after what she'd almost had. No matter whether it had been real or not. Raegan could not—would not—go back to a life without magic.

She stared at the sweater for a long time, longer than she'd care to admit, and then she bit her tongue so hard it almost bled and pulled the garment on, right arm first. As it settled over her shoulders, her heart pounded.

Steady, steady, steady, the meadowsweet clutched against her chest.

Nothing changed. Raegan fell into complete and utter despair. Nothing was real, nothing mattered, she was just sick and deluded and amounted to nothing. She was not some chosen hero. She had made it all up in her head to contend with her mediocrity, to apply a balm to the wound her father had left her with.

Her throat was closing off when she heard it.

A rumbling, or something akin to it, a low roll far off in the distance. It could've been thunder, except that it was October in the northeast. And besides, she could feel it in her bones, reverberating and humming.

And then suddenly, a crack began to form in the ground, right between her feet. It splintered and grew, climbing up the wall directly across from her and sliding onto the ceiling, tiny bits of plaster and drywall beginning to fall down like snow.

Fuck. She hoped she was not making this up, too.

There was no time to hesitate, Raegan knew, so she turned and fled for the door. It opened at her touch. Outside, the hallway was empty, the lights flickering strangely, the smell of acrid bone and herbs and damp stone thick in her nose. Without thinking twice, she sprinted down the hallway, down to the big double doors, and then, breathless and half-strangled by what might be, she threw them open and fell into the sunlight.

CHAPTER FIFTY-EIGHT

Everything she had ever been began to fall around her like stardust and ash and confetti. A sunset on a heathered hill. The view out of the top of a turret. A younger Oberon lifting his eyes to hers in a candlelit room. The hum and pulse of a battlefield. The familiar weight of a blade in her hands. The smell of smoking bone. A small room with a tarot reader. The green hills of an Earth that man had not dared to carve into just yet. The top of a battle-blackened hill, her scream raw in her throat. A river roaring and then parting around her, water rising high on either side. A gray courser beneath her, galloping hard through a forest.

Something, a film or a veil, peeled away from her. And then all the parts of her collided and her body felt like it was being split into a thousand pieces.

She saw the life where everything had begun, and the years when the snake had developed a taste for its own tail.

The ocean-eyed, raven-haired changeling created by two goddesses who feared that the old ways and magic were in danger. They implanted him in the court of a king who wished to unite the mortals of the Isles under one banner—the banner with a dragon rampart. The banner with a blade of iron forged specifically to shed Fey blood. The banner that posed a genuine threat to the Fair Folk and the gods and magic itself for the first time in history.

The hazel-eyed, fire-haired girl raised by the Druids deep in the woods after her parents cast her out for her magic, who'd shed her minor nobility in favor of the stranger, wilder things —only to be tasked with embedding herself in that same court to see if there would truly be war between the mortals and the Fey, and if so, how the Druids could survive it.

They were never on the same side, were never meant to be, and yet the changeling and the Druid girl subverted Fate, shifting the tides and nearly preventing the war that would tear the world in two.

They had failed, and now time slipped off the changeling entirely, while the soil called the Druid girl's name twice a century only to spit her back out.

She saw her first death and understood why the mountain of a man named Bedwyr made her stomach turn. That recurring dream, her body carried and dumped like refuse, was at his hands, ordered by his king. When men are afraid, they always kill the witches first. One day, when she was good and ready and more pressing matters had been attended to, she would ask the King to hold Bedwyr down while she carved out his insides.

The thought released something inside her, and then she saw everything else, too. The crows of war when they came cawing, leaving feathers outside her dwelling and pulling at her hair when she walked too deep into the forest.

The fierceness of the Fair Folk's resistance to the Protectorate rule of the Otherlands—humans infused with unnatural magic they should not have by a god who wanted dominion of a world that had never been his.

The weight of her own body as life left her, again and again and again.

The King, his shoulders draped in a black cloak, standing

before a dead door that once linked the realms together, snow falling all around him.

The rebellions and the dark places and the sunsets and the quiet moments in between. The way the King had been there for it all. The way his shadows had become a refuge for her.

Time, she could see, was not so much a straight line as it was snow falling everywhere all at once, gathering on treelines and weighing down the mountains. Here, she was as much Raegan as she was Nyneve as she was Titania as she was the Lady of the Rivers and the Deathless One and the Witch in the Wood. Everything seemed to bend and refract, reflecting right back at her and then out. A snake devouring its own tail.

She was infinite, maybe.

And then the light changed—directly overhead, casting no shadows. She was reaching her way across an endless dream, walking a tundra of a thousand lives, seeking the warmth of the one she now lived.

"It's this way," a voice called out.

Raegan turned on her heel, heart beating, and faced herself. Well, this woman didn't look anything like her—she had weathered skin and gray hair in a loose braid, leaning on a rough-hewn staff—but Raegan knew.

"Witch in the Wood," Raegan greeted.

"It is nice to see you again," the old woman answered. "I can lead you through this. Please don't be afraid. You're not stuck or trapped. You're just in between. You and I, we are very good at being in between."

"I fear I do need to get back," Raegan said, taking a step toward her.

"Oh, I know, I know," the old woman tutted. "I'll get you back. Come along."

So Raegan began to follow the Witch in the Wood through this frozen place, tracking her footsteps, the sun too bright for her eyes. She felt as though she should still be panicking, but she was calm, smooth as a still lake. She would see this through.

"You know, Raegan," the Witch of the Wood said, "time, it's not quite a straight line."

"I've noticed," Raegan said, her voice dry.

The Witch laughed. "I should've suspected you did," she replied. "Well, I'm only reminding you, I suppose. If I know, then you know. It's an important thing to remember. Time is happening all around us, all at once, never-ending. Where I once walked, so do you, and where you go, I will follow. Doors I have opened remain open, even if they do not appear so."

"I'll remember that," Raegan told her.

"Good," the old woman said. "It's very important you remember." The woman came to a stop for a moment. "How is he?"

Raegan did not need to ask. "He's tired."

"Ah. I suppose I can't blame him for that."

"No," Raegan agreed. "He knew who you were, by the way. When he found you in the woods, when the villagers wanted to burn you at the stake. I don't know if he ever told us directly, but he knew."

"I had a feeling," the Witch of the Wood said. "He remained with me for a touch too long to not have known." She began her procession again, somehow knowing where to go in this blank land. "I miss him."

"Where I go, you follow," Raegan reminded her.

The old woman turned and smiled at her. "Say hello to Baba Yaga for me," she said.

Suddenly, there was a door. It was ancient and wooden, curved at the top, with ornate iron details. Raegan could've sworn she had seen it before. Probably because she had. She had seen it a million times. In dreams, in museums, in photography books, in paintings. Always. Everywhere.

"What is this?" she wanted to know.

"A door," the old woman told her.

"I can see that. I mean . . . well, you know."

The Witch in the Wood shrugged. "Some things have no true name. Some things are too powerful."

Raegan did not have a chance to press her, a moment to ask more, because then the Witch in the Wood swung the door open and, before she could even think, she was walking through it. Walking back to her body and her revenge and her magic.

Raegan inhaled deeply, bringing the scent of a fire and fur pelts into her nose. She wiggled her fingers. They all worked. Her toes, too. There was still a pleasant, familiar soreness in her body. Her head hurt. Her lips were chapped, and her throat ached.

She took another deep breath and opened her eyes. A fire smoldered in a large stone hearth. She looked down at herself and saw she had been tucked into a pile of heavy pelts. Raegan reflexively identified the animals from which they'd come.

Realization dawned on her, heavy and bewildering. "Oh," she murmured, her eyes widening, wondering what else she might know, and also realizing that she was still very much herself.

With a soft groan, she rolled over. In less than a heartbeat, oceanic gray eyes met hers. The King leapt from his chair and knelt beside her, but he said nothing. Raegan heard Baba Yaga grunt as she rose from the other chair.

The witch loomed over Raegan, looking at her quizzically. "And who might you be?" Baba Yaga asked, her gaze slipping to the King for a heartbeat.

"Raegan Maeve Overhill," she replied, lifting her chin, surprised by the strength of her voice considering how sore her throat was. "And everyone else, I guess. But falling around me like snow or confetti or ash. It's all happening at once anyway, isn't it?"

Baba Yaga's black eyes glinted, her mouth moving into a very pleased smile.

"The Witch in the Wood sends her regards," Raegan told the old woman. "She is quite fond of you."

Baba Yaga beamed. "And I her," the witch replied, clapping a gnarled hand over her heart.

Then Raegan turned to the King, his expression so full of fragile, tentative hope that it almost broke her heart clean in half. Their eyes met, and Raegan tried to find words—she was good at words—but everything that came to mind failed to encompass what she was trying to say.

So instead, Raegan leaned forward, grabbed the front of his sweater, and pulled his mouth to hers. Baba Yaga whistled, ambling for the door as if they were going to tear each other's clothes off while she was still there.

But then Raegan broke the kiss, put her face to the King's chest and wept. She wept for all the sorrow she had known, for her lives that ended in pain and darkness, for her lives that never touched magic—so shallow and distant, she could hardly recall them, even now. She wept for all the misery she had witnessed and known. She wept for the reality she had almost believed was real—caught in her worst nightmare as the Seal's removal threatened to pull apart all her lives and trap them in separate tiny, gray boxes.

And most of all, she wept for the world—the one that had existed before the Gates and the Protectorate and the Time-keeper. And she wept at the rising, slinking terror that she might not be strong enough to bring that world back.

~

Baba Yaga insisted that Raegan and the King remain in her realm. The Protectorate had stopped sniffing and poking around her door, as she put it, so she could harbor them for a little longer. It would give Raegan time to rest and to begin unspooling her memory. Maintaining herself and her mind seemed to have come at the cost of her magic's immediate return. It was there, Baba Yaga kept saying. Without a doubt, Raegan could feel the difference. She finally possessed all of her pieces. But she had not yet figured out how to put them together. So not *quite* whole—but almost.

"Well," Baba Yaga said the second day after Raegan's Seal had been removed. "You could be raving mad. So what if you can't do magic just yet? It'll come. I can see it." She sat back in her chair, gesturing at the King, who stood before the hearth in her chicken-legged hut. "He can, too," she said, her voice louder, as if purposefully prodding Oberon to agree.

The King turned, taking in the two women. "I do," he said with a regal incline of his head. "As Baba Yaga said, it would be much worse if your abilities came back in full but your mind shattered."

"Then we'd probably have to kill you," Baba Yaga said cheerfully. "But we don't. Lucky, lucky!"

Raegan and the King shot Baba Yaga identical withering glances, but the old witch hardly cared. She just tut-tutted as if they were children—they both had hundreds of years on her —and then set off trying to explain all the ways eggshells were very useful to witches. Raegan took copious notes, to the point that her hand cramped. Of course she was beyond excited to be learning magic from the actual fucking Baba Yaga. And she could feel her power rising up in herself. Sometimes she could bring it to the surface of her skin. But never farther. In all truth, it was more infuriating than anything else, especially because if she focused, Raegan could recall the feeling of working magic. But only the memory.

Before Raegan even voiced anything, Oberon made sure to tell her that he was not disappointed in her and that he'd never expected everything to return immediately. The way he already knew what she might be feeling and took care to address it made butterflies stir in her stomach, aided by the waterfall of memories that often came to her when they were alone together. But it did not stop the sour feeling that arose from Raegan's own disappointment in herself.

Raegan realized she was not paying attention to Baba Yaga and jumped, forcing herself to sit up straight. The witch stopped speaking, eyeing Raegan with her small, dark eyes.

"You seem exhausted," the King said, suddenly beside her. She hadn't heard his footfall, though she did not know why that kept surprising her. "How do you feel?"

Raegan dragged a hand down her face, not understanding how someone that a solid part of the general population would not incorrectly identify as a monster had more emotional intelligence than most of the people she'd dated. "I'm exhausted," she admitted, embarrassed.

It had happened like this the night before, too—she'd hit a wall and she'd hit it hard. She didn't think it was all the information she was trying to absorb—she was good at that—but rather the weight of living with everything she'd seen. Everything she'd done. Everyone she'd been.

"Let's just finish up on the eggshells," Baba Yaga prodded, reaching out toward the mortar and pestle before the King's hand fell on the witch's shoulder.

"She is done, I think, for the day," Oberon said with that quiet authority of his. "You may recall that the years we wear can certainly be an advantage, but sometimes they become a hindrance. It is a lot of weight."

"Sorry," Raegan said to Baba Yaga, whose gaze softened when she heard Oberon's words.

"Yes, yes," the witch said, getting to her feet. "I know your warrior cannot hold the wards forever. I suppose I'm trying to stuff as much into as few days as possible."

"It is appreciated," the King replied, open and sincere.

As Raegan stood, her head went all woozy. Embarrassed,

she expressed that she needed to lie down. Baba Yaga promised the delivery of hot bowls of borscht to the bathhouse, and then Oberon led Raegan out the door. He offered her his arm the same way he had in the beginning of this journey, when he'd needed the physical proximity to glamour them better. But now it seemed to be a reflex, or a desire to feel her warmth. It made sense in a terrible, aching way. Raegan could remember enough to know for certain that the King had spent more time by her graves than walking at her side.

Which made her feel even guiltier about how the past two nights had gone. She would've loved to spend the evenings tangled up with his large, powerful body, forgetting anything else existed. But so far, Raegan had ended her days by weeping in the bath. Oberon had held her, sometimes for hours at a time. He hadn't tried to tell her it would get better, or that he was sorry, or that she needed to calm down. He'd just held her, running fingers through her hair or massaging her hands.

Raegan wasn't stupid. She knew it was partly because he simply did not feel things the way her human heart did. But the space he made for something he did not understand, and the way he always *saw* her, was breathtaking in the best way.

As they walked to the bathhouse, Raegan leaned her head against his arm and realized with a sudden shock—though it should not have been a shock, she supposed—that the King really did love her. Not blindly, not unconditionally. She remembered the lives where he either could not summon it, or could not bear it. But he always loved her when she was like this, when she was herself—a wild, keening howl of river water and magic and rage. His love was as strange and inhuman as he was—intense, deadly, unyielding. Raegan looked up at him, wanting to say something, to acknowledge that she cherished it. But as she did, the King's stride faltered and he stiffened.

A bee had settled onto the bathhouse door. It was larger than any bee Raegan had ever seen, its glassine wings the size of her hand. Instead of a buzzing or otherwise distinctively insectoid noise, the bee called with the low, haunting sound of a mourning dove.

As they approached, it swiveled its head. The bee looked at Raegan and then the King in turn with black eyes before releasing a few more sorrowful coos into the air.

"It appears," the King said, "that the Oracle has returned."

When the King finished speaking, the bee took off, the fading evening light shining through its stained-glass wings as it rose higher and higher into the sky. He said nothing, and he didn't have to, because now that the Seal was gone, Raegan understood the way of things.

"We must go," she murmured.

"You are exhausted," the King said, turning to look at her appraisingly—not a romantic partner trying to see what their lover needed, but a commander deciding if his warrior was up for battle. "The Protectorate's alarms will sound the moment we walk through Baba Yaga's door. No matter how well I glamour us, the twisted black pine has too much magic behind it."

She closed her eyes, tipping her head back, reminding herself to breathe. She knew she would be a hindrance if anything went wrong. "And that does not even account for Fate," Raegan mumbled. "If She is still angry."

The primordial winged being had not entered Baba Yaga's realm, though She certainly could have if She'd wished it. Oberon tensed at her question, the movement barely visible under the dark wing of dusk outside the bathhouse. A wolf howled in the distance, and Raegan saw the skulls on Baba Yaga's fence begin to glow.

"Fate's fury is often a brief flash," the King replied. "Do not misunderstand me, She will find a way to make us both pay for what you said. But not with physical violence. That is entirely too mundane for Her."

As he spoke, Raegan knew what he said was true in the same way she knew she had two feet and the sun rose in the east. Was her entire recurring, rebirthing existence not some exquisite torture for the way she had dared to defy Fate all those years ago by creating a shield for the changeling when there was only meant to be a sword for the king of men?

"Regardless," the King said, breaking Raegan's thoughts, "the Oracle is not asking for our presence. She is demanding it. A bee maiden's appearance is a summoning, and no doubt it is about the Prophecy."

Prophecies, Raegan understood now, were fickle things—not promises, not assurances, nothing at all but a place where the Threads shimmered, and Fate deemed something important enough to turn Her eye toward it.

"But Oracles are essentially Fate's high priestesses," Raegan said, turning to the King. "Will she want to help us? *Could* she even help? Or is this just another one of Fate's machinations?"

He smiled that low, dangerous smile, the expression of a dark and slippery thing that had survived for a millennium. "Octavia," the King began, reaching forward to open the bathhouse door for Raegan, "has her own plans. And more importantly, she owes me a debt."

She stepped into the bathhouse, not able to contain a smirk. *Of course* the Oracle, the Seer of All Threads, one of the most powerful beings on this side of the Gates—perhaps even both sides—owed the Unseelie King a debt.

Behind her, Oberon began to pack up the few articles of

his clothing that had migrated outside of his bag. Raegan supposed this meant they were leaving imminently and began to do the same. Less than ten minutes later, she stood with the King at the edges of Baba Yaga's thorny green realm, the bathhouse and the chicken-legged hut already moving into memory.

"Your work is deeply appreciated," Oberon was saying to Baba Yaga, his tone regal and kingly. "If the Gates fall, it will in many ways be thanks to you."

Baba Yaga stood with her hands on her hips and sniffed at his words.

"The Unseelie Court owes you a debt," the King added, only a little begrudgingly. At that, the witch grinned, pleased. The sight of her smile tugged at Raegan's heart, and she pulled the taller woman into her arms, breathing in her mugwort and smoked-bone scent.

"Try to stop dying all the time, my dear," Baba Yaga said, squeezing Raegan hard for a moment. "You know where to find me if you need me."

"When this is over," Raegan found herself saying, "I'll need you to help untangle the rest of me."

"I know," Baba Yaga said softly, stepping back from Raegan, one hand still on her shoulder. "The twisted black pine will always allow you through." Her eyes snapped to the King, the hard beadiness returning. "Not you, unnatural thing," she added, pointing a thick, curved finger at the Fey being. "Only *born* creatures in my realm from henceforth. No made monstrosities."

"It is your realm," the King said, sweeping into an impossibly elegant bow. "I will respect your wishes as its creatrix."

Baba Yaga stared at the King for a moment longer before her gaze slid to Raegan. "I will admit he is very charming," the witch said. "For an abomination."

Raegan laughed and pulled Baba Yaga into another fierce hug. When she turned away from the witch, who was striding back to the hut, she found Oberon kneeling on the damp earth, speaking an unknown language to a small pond surrounded by mossy rocks.

Raegan listened for a moment longer and found she *did* know the language—or at least, someone she had once been did—and understood he was calling forth a kelpie. Before she had a moment to brace herself for seeing one of those murderous fish-horses again, something came through the puddle, breaking the surface with such force that it shattered water droplets everywhere.

Dark as the ocean and dripping wet, a kelpie now stood beside the pond. It was enormous, easily six and a half feet at the shoulder, its strong neck cresting up and away. It was much, *much* larger than Raegan would have thought from her previous encounters. It was shaped like a horse, more or less, but gills gaped on its stomach and scales adorned its hindquarters. Its mane and tail were more like seaweed than hair, and its skin was shiny—slick and ridged.

When it turned, its dark eyes met hers briefly, and she realized who it was. "Rainer," Raegan said, her heart beginning to thud harder.

"Hello again," the kelpie replied.

"You know he was killing innocent people, right?" Raegan demanded of Oberon, who shot a glance at the kelpie.

"I already told you. It is in my nature," the kelpie said, swinging his massive head away. "Besides, you banished me from your city."

The King looked at Raegan, one dark eyebrow arched, then his gaze slid back to Rainer.

"A human with no training and a Seal on her memory banished the Scourge of the Isles?" the King wanted to know, appearing to be doing his best to suppress a smile.

"She knew the words well enough," Rainer grumbled. He shook his head and neck, much like a dog trying to remove water from its coat.

"I can understand your position," the King said after a beat of silence, looking toward Raegan. "But Rainer taking us through the Rivers is the only way we might escape detection and avoid starting yet another battle when we are trying to win the war."

An older understanding unfolded in the pit of Raegan's stomach as she stood in the kelpie's presence. She didn't like it. It was telling her that even the Rivers were constricted by humanity's encroachment, and there were so few places to be a kelpie these days. Rainer had to hunt. His instincts told him to survive, no matter the cost. A kelpie was ruled by water and shadow and not much else.

"It is in his nature," Raegan said with a sigh, pulling her leather jacket closed across her chest. "But don't kelpies usually murder you if you try to ride them?"

"Yes," Rainer answered. "But you are with the King. The King is my friend." Then the kelpie swung his head back around again and examined her. "You, too, are my friend, Lady Or'Afron. Do you not remember? I thought this time you would remember me, though of course, there are many times you do not."

Raegan looked at the kelpie, puzzled, searching through what felt like miles and miles of thread to find the right spool with the right life. And then she did, for a brief flash. Raegan was aboard the kelpie's broad back, one hand interlaced in his seaweed mane, the other brandishing a sword as they leapt from the sea directly into the thick of a battle on a driftwood-strewn shore.

"Oh," was all she said, looking at Rainer with fresh eyes.

The kelpie kneeled, all slow, elegant tides of movement, bringing his shoulders and back closer to the ground. She understood and strode toward Rainer but found that, though her mind recalled their shared past, her body did not have the muscle memory. What Raegan had intended to be a snappy, skilled mounting of the kelpie was more a desperate scramble, aided by Oberon, who steadied her and then pulled himself up behind her.

He wrapped one arm around Raegan's waist and placed his other hand on the kelpie's dark green shoulder. "Thank you, Rainer."

"Always, my King."

And then before she'd really had a moment to prepare, Rainer plunged forward, moving more like water across glass than a horse. Raegan thought it felt like freedom. She could not be sure how they were traveling—everything was a blur, and she couldn't tell if this was simply the forest or the Rivers. But the wind was in her hair, stinging her cheeks, and she told herself, just for a moment, to feel this temporary joy.

Before she knew it, Rainer had slowed, moving into a lofty trot. All around them, seaweed danced in long ribbons of dark green silk. Kelp forests billowed in the distance. The light came from above, filtered through the brackish waters into glimmering rays of blue-gold. Then the kelpie broke through the surface, and the otherworldly setting was gone.

Instead, Raegan sat astride Rainer beneath an overpass, graffiti climbing its walls. The ground beneath the kelpie's feet was strewn with Styrofoam bits and loose dirt. Somehow, though water dripped from Rainer's mane, she and Oberon were completely dry. Behind her, the King dismounted and then reached his hand up to assist her.

Wordlessly, Raegan climbed down and took in the large, muddy puddle a few feet behind Rainer's back hooves. It was barely an inch in depth, and yet it had opened a yawning mouth to the older, darker places.

"Thank you," the King said to the kelpie, inclining his head toward the ancient creature.

Rainer arched his thick neck, nostrils flaring. "You may repay me," the kelpie said, "by riding me into battle once more."

The King reached one hand out to Rainer's muscled neck,

palm flat. The kelpie swung its head around, meeting the King's gaze. Raegan held still as the Unseelie King and the kelpie shared something that was not for her—something of bloodlust and inhumanity and a terrible ache.

"It would be my honor," the King murmured. Then he seemed to remember the world around him all at once. Turning to Raegan, he took a large, almost-running step in her direction. "We must go," Oberon said, catching her by the wrist and striding out of the overpass's shadows and into the low, glinting afternoon sunlight beyond.

As they emerged, Raegan looked back, but Rainer was gone. She held her free hand over her eyes as a shade from the sun, realizing she recognized the neighborhood. The Oracle's temple was nearby. The King moved quickly, sticking to shadows whenever possible. In only a few blocks, Raegan found herself standing on the same sidewalk in front of the same tucked-away strip mall shop that held unimaginable things.

Everything was different from when she had first seen the dusty windows filled with houseplants and winking glass ornaments. When she had originally walked through those doors, she'd known so little—of herself, of the world.

"Are you ready?" the King asked from beside her.

Raegan let out a long breath, her throat tight and choked-off. No, she was not ready. When she'd managed to retain herself after the removal of the Seal, she'd also retained the parts of herself that still ached for Fate's approval. A common thread in nearly all her lives, which Raegan knew was likely no coincidence. But she felt it all the same. In truth, she did not know what she might do if she was no longer chosen and all of this had been for nothing.

"A Prophecy," the King reminded her, "is a fickle thing."

"I know," she murmured. "But there is a part of me that still needs it to be real. That needs all of this to have been for something. For Fate to have had some far-reaching plan, some Thread She had been following all of this time."

Beside her, Oberon said nothing, and Raegan felt that silence like a stone in her stomach. So she set her jaw and reached for the door.

Chapter Sixty

Inside, there was white marble and blue velvet and lush fruits in the abalone shell bowl and the smell of spring rain and far-off thunderstorms and fresh flowers. The long counter still stretched in a soft curve. It distressed Raegan how everything could change with no material reflection to mark the passage—not when she looked in the mirror and not when she moved about the world. It had been the same when her father disappeared. She remembered wondering how the sun could still rise in the same place when nothing was as it had ever been before.

"My liege and my lady," came the Keeper's smooth voice. He appeared at the counter, dressed in a crisp navy-blue suit, his glasses a brown horn-rimmed pair to complement the fabric. "I see you received the Thriae's call."

"We did," Oberon replied, leading the way across the expansive marble floor.

The Keeper inclined his head. "I will inform the Oracle of your arrival," he said, his gaze darting to Raegan for a moment.

They took each other in, Raegan assessing why he had

seemed so familiar in the first place, and the Keeper clearly looking for a sign that she was changed, altered, and remade by this Thread of Fate they all walked upon.

Apparently, he found it.

"Welcome back," the Keeper said to Raegan, the words weighted with meaning as they fell from his mouth. Then the tidy, besuited man disappeared behind a long length of velvet curtain into the hallways that Raegan knew snaked around the half-moon of a foyer. The ceiling still towered far above her, cloaked in the colors of a sunset, the constellations moving as she watched. But it all felt smaller, somehow. She had little time to think about it before the Keeper reappeared.

He stepped through the curtain, looking at Oberon and Raegan in turn. Then he cleared his throat. "I present to you the Oracle," the Keeper said, his voice grand, "the last of the original Pythia, anointed and ordained by Fate Herself."

A shape moved in the darkness of the hallway, and Raegan *felt* something, like a tidal wave or a great cloud passing over the sun. Then the Oracle appeared.

She was small, so much smaller than Raegan would have imagined. Her spine curved, one hand resting on a simple wooden cane. Her tiny frame was cloaked in billowing velvet, necklaces of gold and bone adorning her chest. The Oracle's skin was a deep umber, made all the richer by the color she wore: the blue that appeared to be common in this Temple, but deepened and darkened into a shade of blackberry. Her graying locs were gathered in a matching silk scarf.

The Oracle looked at Oberon, and then her eyes slid to Raegan. She moved out from behind the counter, coming to stand before the pair. Up close, the Oracle's features were softly wrinkled with age, making Raegan wonder exactly how impossibly ancient she must be. The immense power that the Oracle radiated almost made it difficult to breathe. She was eternal and absolute—qualities somehow made all the more terrifying by her small stature. Raegan was utterly transfixed. If she'd wanted to move, she was not sure she could've, not with the Oracle's gaze pinning her in place.

"I wish that my Apprentice had not offered you Fates-peak," the Oracle said, her voice melodic and velveted. "When we read Fate's prophecies, it calls Her attention, and then She strums Her fingers along our Threads to hear the sound of us."

Oberon said nothing, so Raegan did not, either. The Oracle reached into the depths of her velvet kaftan and retrieved something. Whatever it was, it was small and fragile, able to fit in her fist. The Oracle released a shuddering breath, her eyes squeezing shut for a moment. Then she opened her fingers.

Within her palm sat torn shreds of paper. For a moment, Raegan understood nothing at all, but then she peered closer and saw the crumpled thing was the Prophecy—the luna moth she had watched take to its paper wings and soar. And now here it was, broken, lifeless. Beside her, Oberon had gone entirely still.

"By going into the Vaults and retrieving the Prophecy, you accepted the path," the Oracle continued, her immense gaze falling upon the broken-winged moth. "You allowed Fate to put Her breath into your sails, to be a guiding wind beneath your wings. And then, from what I understand, you rebuked Her. So She took back what She had given you. Your Prophecy, your shimmering place among the Threads, the path you might've walked. Gone. Its wings are crushed."

The words slammed into Raegan's chest. Grief and fury and sorrow came crashing upon her shores. She felt as if wings had been ripped from her own back, crushed between great, powerful hands, and left hanging by tender shreds of flesh.

"I have exchanged my fair share of words with Aranrhod," the King said, breaking the thick silence that had settled across the foyer. "She has never crushed a Prophecy as punishment."

The Oracle's eyes slid to Oberon's, a knowing expression as sharp as a knife falling across her face. She tucked her hand and the forsaken Prophecy back into the billows of her velvet garment. In the distance, bells chimed, soft as silver water. The smell of lilacs and thunderstorms danced across Raegan's senses, but she felt as cold as the marble beneath her feet.

"You have never wanted what She offered you," the Oracle said, one thin eyebrow rising. "Like a misbehaving child, you were forced to continue accepting what you did not want. But this? You both wanted this. And so, She took it back."

Raegan was still herself, and because of that, anger had begun pounding louder than all her other emotions. She took a step toward the Oracle, her teeth grinding together. Though Raegan had at least a few inches on her, she felt much smaller than the velvet-cloaked being.

"Does She not want the Gates to fall?" Raegan demanded, hot fury curling around her words. "What is the *point* of any of this? Can't She—can't *you*—see the Threads extending for thousands of years, eternities maybe, and yet there are these constant games? *Why*?"

She found her fists were clenched at her side by the time she finished speaking, nails biting into the flesh of her palms. The Oracle's expression grew darker and darker with each passing word until Raegan felt as though she was attempting to stare down the entire universe. But the Oracle said nothing.

"Go on, then!" Raegan snarled. "Go ahead and tell me Fate has plans that I'm too stupid to understand. Tell me I should trust in Her. That I'm a silly child who is too easily frustrated. Tell me. I dare you."

"I am not your enemy," the Oracle said, at the same time as Raegan heard the King say her name in a softly threatening tone. "And as such, you will not speak to me in this way."

"Oh, I'm so sorry for my *tone*," Raegan snapped, advancing another step on the Oracle. "I'll make *sure* to—"

Her words fell away because two things happened at once.

The King's heavy grasp landed on her shoulder and pulled hard, and the Oracle began to levitate. Her velvet robes blew in an invisible wind, thrashing about as if a thunderstorm had appeared in the space of a heartbeat.

"Let us remind you that it is not *our* hands that string your Threads," the Oracle said, her words booming, coming in from all directions, hundreds of other voices joining in chorus. "Fate is a cruel and indifferent mistress. We Oracles—we Called Ones—are not Fate Herself. We see and we know and we advise. And if we are lucky, we get the chance to untangle and unloop. But we are not your enemy."

The Oracle, Raegan could see now, was vast and unbearable in her power. The small-statured woman before her was only one branch of a tree, one root of a plant—a piece of the Oracle visible to Raegan's eyes and understandable on this plane. Raegan cast her gaze at the floor, blood pounding thickly in her veins.

When the air seemed to loosen and the King's grip on her shoulder slackened, Raegan looked back up to find that the Oracle had returned to the ground, a small woman in a flowing velvet garment. But her dark, roving eyes still held the universe in them.

Raegan opened her mouth, but the King made a low sound of disapproval and the Oracle held up one weathered hand, silencing her.

"I do not deny the misery of your path," the Oracle said. "I know it well. You might remember that Oracles are called. We do not choose our fate, either. Instead, *She* chooses us as Her vessels, forces those of us with the gift of foresight to hold Her essence in our bones. I have no fondness for Her, but I certainly will not allow you to come into my Temple and treat me with disrespect, let alone as your enemy."

Silence hovered like a low-lying cloud as Raegan did her best to suffocate her still-smoldering anger.

"Please accept my apologies," the King said, his words uncharacteristically humble. "We had no right to treat you in this manner."

At that, the Oracle's eyes shot to the King, her face pinched. "I do not accept your apology because you have not transgressed," the Oracle said, looking the King up and down. "You have nothing to apologize for."

"I have brought a mortal with a recently Unsealed memory into your space," the King replied. Raegan turned to narrow her eyes at him. "Emotions are close to the surface and difficult to control in the days following a Seal's removal."

Anger coiled hot in Raegan's ribcage, fangs bared.

The Oracle's gaze fell on her, heavy and cool. "Do not infantilize your companion," the Oracle said to the King, her tone moving from righteous anger to flat annoyance. "After a thousand years walking this planet, fragmented as those years may have been, I would hope she has learned to master her emotions."

Raegan waited for the King to defend her. He did not. The fury inside of her threw its head back and hissed. She turned her attention back to the Oracle, feeling her face flush hotter and hotter. But then—something cold and swift, a slip of river water, rose up from a deeper, older place than the anger. It was icy and calculating, packed with all the force of rushing water. At its bottom, like a dragon curled asleep beneath an ancient waterway, was not anger or fury but *rage*. She relaxed her jaw and leaned into it, surprised by how easily the current took her.

"I apologize," Raegan said, meaning it. "I had no right to speak to you as I did. Truth be told, I am so, *so* angry that sometimes I forget who and what I'm actually angry at, and I take it out on whomever is in front of me at that moment."

She heard the King let out a small, low sigh at her shoulder.

The Oracle's face relaxed, the feeling of her gaze not as heavy as it had been before. "Anger is useful when we control it," she said. "But not when it controls us. Come. Sit."

The Oracle turned, moving toward the gorgeous sitting area that Raegan recalled from her previous visit. It simultaneously felt like no time and forever since she had last settled upon the emerald velvet couch and wondered how the world might part itself for her.

Oberon trailed after the Oracle, expecting Raegan to follow, so she did. The fury in her belly felt like someone had thrown a bucket of water over it—cold, indignant—wishing for more than anything to slink away and re-establish some dignity. Instead, she took a seat upon the couch, angling herself to face the Oracle, who had settled into a chair of magnificently twisted willow branches.

"Octavia," the King said, a question tilting his voice upwards as he lowered himself onto the couch beside Raegan. "I am always grateful for your counsel. But what is there to discuss if the Prophecy is broken?"

The Oracle perched on the edge of the willow chair, her hands folded on one knee. She considered both of them before speaking. "You were in possession of spellwork left to you by your father," she said, looking at Raegan. It was not a question. "Do you still maintain it?"

"Of course," Raegan breathed, her heart rate increasing.

"Fate has turned Her eye away from this Thread," the Oracle continued, voice lower now, a sacred sort of hush.

Beside her, Raegan heard Oberon take in a small, sharp breath. "What would you have us do, Oracle of Delphi?" the King breathed, his tone taking on the same reverent stillness.

The Oracle looked down at her hands, as if recalling the sight of the broken-winged Prophecy in her palms—hopeless and crushed, abandoned by the very force that breathed life into it.

"Do the spellcraft anyway," the Oracle said as she looked up, her features now a mask of long-simmering defiance. "Make your own fate."

497

Chapter Sixty-One

The Oracle's words beat like a war drum inside of Raegan, awakening things sleeping in river muck and lost to bonfires long ago extinguished. All of these lives, all of these years, and so many of them had not meant anything at all because she'd always bent to Fate. The only lives where she had made a dent—Nyneve in the place called Camelot, and Titania during the Uprising in the Otherlands—were when she had spat in Fate's face and pulled her own fortune from the silt.

"Yeah," Raegan breathed. "Okay. I'm in. But how long will it take me to be able to complete such delicate, complicated spellwork? There is an . . . urgency here, isn't there?"

Despite knowing that these events have been in motion for thousands of years, she had the strangest feeling that time was running out. Perhaps because her own clock was always resetting too soon.

"There is an urgency indeed," the Oracle agreed. "There always is with you, Lady of the Rivers. Your blood runs as quickly as a storm-swollen stream. The Prophecy is lost. Follow the spellwork instead."

The formal address made Raegan's mind swim, conjuring

"

images of low firelight and thatched roof cottages and an imposing gray stone citadel. Her vision blurred for a moment.

"Regardless of the Prophecy," the King said, his words pulling her back to the present, "Raegan is the only one who can follow the spellcraft. Her father is an anchor in the Timekeeper's realm, and only those sharing his blood or an oath can work the spell. And she is not ready." At those last words, spoken in a murmur, she felt the King's eyes land on her.

The Oracle sat back, her velvet caftan pooling around her. "Or are *you* not ready to risk losing her again?" she asked, her gaze heavy on the King. "Because you always will. That is the punishment. I had thought you were used to its sting."

Raegan turned to the King, who did not respond to the Oracle, though a muscle leapt in his jaw. "What punishment?" she asked, looking up at the Oracle.

"His creators made him on a day that was not a day, in a time that was outside of time, in a place that was not a place," the Oracle said, answering Raegan evenly and without hesitation. "He has no true name. Decisions such as these are transgressions against the forces that rule our universe. As such, his creators promised that he would assume the fate of the child he replaced to rebalance it all. And yet your bones do not rest on the plains of Camlann, do they, Unseelie King?"

Oberon held the Oracle's gaze and said nothing.

Then her dark, world-devouring eyes fell on Raegan. "Because *you* pulled a shield powerful enough to resist the Pendragon's blade for him from the old places in the river silt," the Oracle continued. "He lives forever and remembers. You die continuously and forget. A punishment that would have crushed the will and resiliency of anyone else, but you two are fools."

To Raegan's surprise, the Oracle's tone bordered on fondness when she called them fools. It did not stop the pain that embedded itself deep in her marrow at what the Oracle had just told them.

Her eyes slid to Oberon. Apparently, it was only a revelation for her, not the King.

He met her gaze. "Even when you remember other things," he began, quite composed for someone speaking of something so horrible, "you forget this part, the nature of what we are trapped in. That we exist within our very own ouroboros, doomed to keep repeating it."

Raegan's mouth was dry, and her throat smarted. Her chest felt hollow, as if something had reached its hands inside and scooped out anything red and alive. Swallowing hard, she fought to put this knowledge into a box that she could bury deep down somewhere. She had no more room for more sorrow, for more ache.

"If it is any consolation regarding the Prophecy," the Oracle said, her words sounding ten miles away, "the 'of thirteen' does not refer to your birthdate, but your age. The Threads *might* have still held the weight of this path, but you were supposed to start this Prophecy when you were thirteen, Raegan. Not now. These nuances are why only anointed Oracles offer Fatespeak."

Another blow to her chest, right where she was already tender, where there were gaps in her armor. "That makes me feel worse, actually," Raegan murmured without thinking.

No one comforted her. The conversation continued as if Raegan had not just discovered that she was not only useless but also an active obstruction. No wonder the King had treated her with such disdain and cruelty at first. Raegan's gaze drifted to him. Would he revert to it now that she could offer him nothing? Was this the most magical her life would ever be, held aloft by a now-abandoned Prophecy? Was everything downhill and mundane and ordinary from here on out?

"I need a minute," Raegan mumbled, getting to her feet and staggering for the door. Thankfully, the Keeper was not at the counter, and she ran across the glimmering marble floors, pushing out through the doors and into the cool autumn evening. Petrichor and fried rice met her nose. The flashing neon light of the pawn shop next door reflected off a puddle in the parking lot. She leaned against the building's wall and buried her head in her hands.

All of her grief and anger and ache was not some pull to a greater destiny or a Fate-touched path. It was meaningless. A punishment she would possibly repeat until the sun exploded and the entire universe was snuffed out. And despite all of it, Raegan knew that deep down, part of her still craved Fate. The remnants of that Fatesong—golden, looping, the most beautiful sound she had ever heard—still rang out in her chest alongside the pain, and she hungered for its splendor. When she had pulled the paper-winged Prophecy from the depths of the Temple's Vaults, it had all felt so clear and lucid. Everything was for a reason, and it had been such an overwhelming *relief*.

She would likely never hear a Fatesong again.

"Raegan." Her name came from beside her, though she had heard no approach. The King drifted across her vision, leaning against the Temple's wall beside her. "The ward only extends till the end of the walkway," he murmured, as if that were the reason he had followed her. She felt the warmth and weight of his arm meet her shoulder, and it broke the levy.

"I'm sorry, Mordred," Raegan sputtered at the King, barely holding back tears. "You bet on a losing dog. I can't offer you anything but more pain."

The King only watched her, eyes hooded by shadow. Raegan dragged the back of her hand across her face, roughly shoving away the tears. A sob caught in her throat, and her cheeks burned with shame.

"You made a mistake," she said, hot tears streaming freely down her face as she drew in ragged grasps. "I'm not what you thought I was."

The King turned to face her, closing her in against the

wall. She felt his long, cool fingers on her jaw, a gentle request to lift her chin and look at him.

"I was not sent to Camelot all those years ago to fall in love with a mortal," the King murmured, his dark eyes locked onto hers. "I jeopardized everything for you. I was prepared to betray everyone for you. You woke something within me I did not understand, nor could I bear to extinguish it."

Raegan's entire body braced for impact, though she knew it would come only in words—but those words would cut deeper than any dagger. Refusing to shut her eyes even though every fiber of her being begged for the release, she held the King's gaze.

"When you learned of the Fate I had stepped into, the Prophecy I inherited," he continued, "nothing could dampen your rage. You fought with everything you had to change the ending. And you *did*."

Her mind raced. She knew this already—she did not understand why the King was saying any of it again. Anxiety twisted in her chest.

"We have both, in some ways, accepted an ending," he said, leaning down closer to her. "Magic will die. My people will fade. You will amount to nothing with the Prophecy gone. Both of us will remain trapped in this cycle of grief."

His words lay like broken glass at her feet, and she did not think she could avoid cutting herself upon their edges.

"Instead of your sorrow," the King continued, his gaze boring into hers, "no matter how righteous it may be, I want something else from you. I want your rage."

Woodsmoke and damp stone and wild rain flooded her senses. His hand found hers, and she slid her fingers into his, gripping as hard as a drowning man would a buoy. Raegan took in a long, dangerous breath, pushing aside that artificial longing for Fate, reaching past her sadness and then her anger and then her grief.

Beneath the churning torment that thrashed within her

like an inferno, she found the still, placid waters of a river. The current there swept away everything in its path with calculating and nearly endless power. A river provided life, and a river offered death. One in each hand. Always just below a surface that belied the intensity beneath. Cold, surging, unimaginable power.

Raegan dipped her hand into the water. It sang to her, sweeter than she could possibly imagine, a deliciously dark symphony that filled her lungs and fortified her body. A song of the dark, rushing places, where all light is swept away. She tipped her head back and let the cold water and the river's song devour her whole—or perhaps, she devoured the river. Their edges ran together, lapping at the other's shores, because rivers gave life. And sometimes, they took it back.

Raegan opened her eyes to find the King still holding his vigil, their fingers intertwined, his forehead resting against hers. Her tears had dried. Her skin was finally cool, her face no longer flushed.

Something that was not her heart beat inside her chest, a flutter of paper wings that should have been dust in Fate's fist. And yet . . .

The King pulled back and gazed at her, eyes searching and then finding. "What are you going to do, Lady of the Rivers?"

Raegan drew herself up, pushing off the wall to stand straight, looking up at the King of the Unseelie Fey. "I'm going to change the ending."

Chapter Sixty-Two

Back inside the Temple, the Oracle and the Keeper gazed down at the spellcraft Raegan had laid out on the coffee table in the seating area. Oberon stood off to the side, his arms crossed. Raegan watched the Oracle and the Keeper circle the spellwork like sharks, taking in every detail. The Keeper's small mouth moved ever so slightly all the while, as if he were speaking to himself. He kept readjusting his circular, horn-rimmed glasses, and Raegan wondered what enchantments they offered.

Finally, the Oracle reached the large parchment with the illustration of the Gates, lines extending from multiple sections as if intersecting the structure. Then she let out a low whistle.

"I mean no offense," the Keeper said, standing up straight, folding his arms behind his back, "but your mortal, Protectorate-oathed father did not create this."

Raegan shrugged, taking a step toward the coffee table. "I'm not saying he did," she replied. "And for what it's worth, with my Seal removed, I find that nearly impossible to believe, as well."

"It is . . . old," the Oracle said, prowling around the coffee table again, her movement a three-beat gait with her cane. "But it is also new. Your father simply . . . possessed this?"

"I'm sure there's a story," Raegan said, the idea of her father's tales tugging at a tender spot inside of her. "But I don't know it. I think the Timekeeper, or someone working with the Timekeeper, came after him for having it. Just before he came to the States. I've been assuming he was fleeing the Protectorate, but I think it's more complicated than that."

The Oracle nodded, peering closer at one of the spell sheets.

"And you want to perform this craft, my liege?" the Keeper asked, his gaze wide with concern as he looked at Oberon. Raegan's attention snapped to the King, confusion creasing her brow.

"Who else would do it, Anakletos?" the Oracle asked, looking at the Keeper like he was a foolish little boy. "No one on this side of the Gates is powerful enough. No one on this side is . . . unnatural enough."

"Was I not created for situations such as these?" the King asked, only his eyes moving, rising to meet the Keeper. "Andronica will continue to hold the wards. Kamau will command the knights. Raegan and I will follow the spellcraft."

"Wait," Raegan said, holding up a hand and taking a step forward. The zipper pull on the sleeve of her leather jacket clinked, metal against metal. "You said back at the archives that this spell is so different because of an anchor, secured by blood or an oath. How do you share either with my father?"

Silence cloaked the space, the sound of running water slipping into the peripheries of Raegan's hearing. For a long moment, no one made eye contact with her.

"The King and your father do indeed share an oath," the Oracle said finally, leaning on her cane.

Raegan stared at her, dumbfounded. None of it made any sense. She turned to look at the King, expecting some convoluted lecture on the fluid complexities of real magic. Instead, he held her gaze with his ocean eyes. And in that split second she understood, and it threatened to crack her down the middle.

"Love," the King told her, his voice raw, like it was only the two of them in that vast marble room, "is as good an oath as any."

Emotions crashed heavily in Raegan's chest. He smiled at her—how could a smile be so sad, she wondered—and then turned back to the spellcraft laid out on the coffee table. She wanted to jump into his arms or maybe grab him by the hand and leave this place, make a life somewhere quiet and safe. Maybe all they needed—wanted—was each other.

But the Keeper began to speak of further preparations and Raegan remembered that her father and all of magic hung in the balance, and the Fair Folk were on the brink of extinction. She bit down on her tongue and looked at the Oracle, who was shaking her head at the Keeper's words. The paper-winged thing beat harder under Raegan's breastbone. If they were going to do this, it had to be now.

"Keeper," the Oracle finally said, her voice taking on that booming quality. "Any more talk, and you risk Her attention. Let it be done."

Pale beneath his bronze skin, the Keeper exhaled heavily and nodded. He took a few steps toward the back archway to lead Raegan and the King to the ceremony room that the Oracle thought would be the safest place to attempt the spell.

Which was how Raegan came to stand on the edge of a ritual circle's outer ring. The loops were marked with glyphs and symbols that made her brain buzz when she looked at them. Some she could recall, but others remained mysteries, even if she could draw up an impression of what they might do.

The room stood empty save for the circle, Raegan, a small chest of materials, and the King. No Fatesong trilled. None ever would. They made their own destiny now, and the only sound Raegan heard was the pounding of her blood and the whispers of doubt.

She watched the King pace the outer ring, stopping to make adjustments, sometimes in ink, sometimes in blood. Her father's spellwork was laid out on the floor a few feet from the circle, allowing Oberon to reference it as and when he needed.

Breathe. That's what Oberon told her to do while he prepared. Just breathe. A simple enough suggestion, but Raegan was having a very hard time. All of her choices, all the horrible things she knew, wrapped their hands around her throat and squeezed.

She looked around the blank room. High ceiling, marble floor, no windows. The door had essentially disappeared when she had closed it behind her. If she tried, she could perhaps pick out its seam along the wall, somewhere. It didn't matter, though. The room was warded to hell and back. They could only leave if they chose at the last minute to not attempt the spell at all, or if they managed to make it back from wherever it took them. The moment they opened the pathway to wherever the spellwork led, they would have no choice but to go forward.

In a few more days, the eighteenth anniversary of her father's disappearance would go by. And here Raegan was, disappearing herself. But what else could she do? Tell her mother that she was following in her father's footsteps? That she was doing what she needed to do, and to not be sad? To understand that some people are just not meant to be loved and held closely but to disappear into the sky?

There was nothing she could say to her mother or to Henry or to Saanvi or to anybody else that would make them understand. She shoved the heels of her palms into her eyes, trying to suffocate the feelings. When she pulled them away and her vision cleared, Raegan saw Oberon had finished working on the inner ring. She recognized the design immediately. It was depicted on the first sheet of her father's spellwork —she'd laid eyes on it in the bank only a few miles away. It could have been a different life, another timeline, for all she knew. It felt so very distant.

"Are you ready, Nyneve?" the King's voice landed on her like a heavy cloak, devouring her frame in black velvet as he spoke her name from that first life that had changed everything.

Raegan let out a shaky breath. "Honestly," she replied, looking up at him, "no."

Oberon moved toward her, skirting the ritual circle at the center of the room. "It feels almost . . . wrong, does it not?" he asked, tilting his head. "As if Fate is pushing us back onto our correct paths, restringing the Threads to conceal that the Prophecy ever existed."

She looked him up and down. There was no trace of the young knight she remembered loving. Only the Unseelie King stood before her—wolf-like, ravenous, deadly. She had little doubt of what he was focused on: sinking his teeth into Fate and reclaiming his Throne, regardless of the tender oath that made it possible for him to work this magic.

"Hey," Raegan said, reaching out to touch Oberon's arm, bringing his gaze to hers. "If I don't come back from this, it's fine. And maybe, unless you need me for some compelling reason, you should ignore me when I come back. Maybe you don't need all this sorrow. All this ache. Maybe you should find some other people and enjoy your immortality."

The King did not hesitate as he slid one hand along her jaw and up into her hair, his palm pressed flat against her cheek. "I have known many others in the years I have walked this earth," he told her, his gaze a dark inferno, "and yet I have tasted nothing as sweet as the sorrow you bring me, nothing as sacred as your faithless love."

Raegan flinched at his words, though she knew them to be true. He did not speak them with anger or judgment but as simple fact. She left him, always. But she always came back, too.

"You should know," Raegan began, the worlds trembling on her tongue, "that I really do lov—"

"Please," the King whispered, his fingertips passing over her lips. She had known him for so many years, long enough to know that the rough tone in his voice was the closest he ever came to begging. "Please do not say you love me."

Raegan met his eyes, hurt surely spilling over in her expression.

But then he brought his forehead to hers, his hand sliding around to cradle the back of her head. "If you do," the King said, his breath ghosting across her skin, "I think you will break me."

The penned sorrow climbed out of Raegan's chest, and she squeezed her eyes shut. She had cried enough. She had shed enough tears over the things she could not stop, and the people she could not save, and the Fateblessings she did not receive, and the Fatesong that she could no longer hear.

Enough.

"Fine," Raegan murmured against his lips. "To destiny, then."

"Let us make our own fate," the King replied, the steadiness of his tone strengthening Raegan. One last desperate hope. Fragile as a moth in a hurricane.

Then he kissed her in a way that took her breath away—pulling her whole body into his, as if he could slip her beneath his skin and keep her safe, like a secret. Raegan met him with the same red-hot hunger she always did, digging her fingers into his chest because if Fate was going to drag her down into the soil again, at least she would leave a mark. At least someone would know she had been here at all.

They broke apart. Raegan tried to smother the growing tenderness inside her with that cool, calm rage. But the King's mouth on hers after all these years of wanting him, of chasing shadows, of waking up with a name she did not know on her lips, turned her ache exquisite and all-encompassing.

"Maybe," the King breathed, forehead against hers, "in the next life . . ."

He did not need to say more. Raegan nodded, blinking back tears, and reached out her hand. The King placed his palm into hers, and with a soft flex of his other hand, he set the candles ablaze. They exploded into light and fire, starting with the largest candle directly in front of where they stood, moving clockwise until each flame crackled to life. The ancient smell of beeswax filled the room. Outside, the sun might have been rising.

All in all, the scene would almost have been beautiful were it not for the thousand years of pain and sorrow and strife that had led to this moment, this Thread, this slip in Time.

The King led her into the circle, both of them coming to stand in the middle. And then he did not hesitate. He began the rite. As he did, Raegan felt a hum that shook her entire being, threatening to dislodge the very marrow from her bones, sinking deep into her essence with barbed, hooked claws. It was *in* her, all around her, breathing in her ear and shouting in the distance, threatening to swallow her whole.

It was magic, she realized. *Real* magic. Not the small explosions she had mustered, or even the workings of Baba Yaga, and certainly not the battle magic of the Protectorate. This was something else. It was pure and dark and strange, pulled down from the sky as if this reality were just a fabric to be unwoven and restitched into something else.

The magic poured out of a single source: the King. For the first time since the removal of her Seal, Raegan was aware of how steeped he was in the oldest of magics—darkness. For a moment, he was nothing more than slinking shadows.

Then a door opened with the same pop she often felt in her ears when a plane descended. She had no choice but to walk through it, just as she did anytime a door showed itself to her. The door called to her, low and primal and vibrating, and she reached for it in the only way she knew how.

A flicker, and then the ceremony room at the Temple was gone. Instead, she and the King stood in an old train station. It was empty, almost like no one had ever touched it at all. Dark wood paneling along the walls devoured the light. Black iron benches marked the stone floor in severe lines. Raegan could detect no sound, no smell, nothing at all but the cold rage in the pit of her stomach and the hammering fear in her veins. Even the light was strange—colorless, slanted, dust particles swimming through it.

"Where are we?" Raegan asked Oberon. Though she supposed part of her already knew, might have known since she'd first touched the spellcraft in the bank's safe deposit room.

"I do not know," the King replied. "Despite its relatively modern appearance, this place—or plane, perhaps—is old. It has been painted over many, many times."

"Then we go forward into destiny," Raegan said, noticing their hands were still entwined. She stepped forward, and the King followed.

At the other end of the train station was an archway. It had been obscured when they first entered by a large clock tower that speared the middle of the space. The hands of the clock moved, but it made no sound. Raegan and the King stepped past it, eyeing it warily. But it was the archway that commanded attention.

Beyond the archway was nothing but bright unadulterated light. It too was incorrect—all white, coming from no one direction but everywhere all at once. Raegan walked toward it like all roads had always led her here and she was just remembering now that there had never been another escape.

When she approached the threshold, the King barked a warning, but it was too late—hadn't it always been too late for them both, anyhow—and the moment that strange, white light fell on Raegan, she suddenly found herself on the opposite side. A train platform greeted her. Just a square of raised brick, really, with one track and another clock tower. This clock had no hands at all and no numbers, either. Out here, the light twisted sepia, and everything gleamed raw and rust-red in the low light.

Raegan turned back and saw the King in the archway, unable to pass through it. Her heart raced wildly at the sight of a barrier bursting into existence and gleaming like an ax before throwing the King back into the depths of the station.

He said something, but she couldn't hear him, so she just watched, trying to decide what to do. She supposed she had been an idiot to think the universe would allow them to face this together, but she had hoped. Raegan saw his temper flare —rare, she knew—and he threw shadows at the barrier. For a moment, the entire archway was filled with nothing but his darkness, all light suffocated by the loops of black silk. But the barrier held.

Fear spiked deep into her body. What place could this be that a ward held back *him*? Fear escalated to terror, sorrow souring her stomach, and Raegan started to make her way back to the King.

Maybe they each saw different things. Maybe this space could be anything to anyone. But Raegan did not think it was a coincidence that this in-between looked exactly like the train platform in her father's story. The story that had been ringing in her bones since he'd first told it. The story that had kept her up at night and asked her what it meant to be human, and what it might mean if there was nothing else.

And then something shifted in the distance, like pressure popping or maybe an air bubble breaking, and Raegan could see that, down the rail line, far down around a bend, a train was approaching. Her cold, ancient rage slipped its fist around her terror and wrung its neck.

She looked at Mordred, and he looked at her, and maybe he already knew.

The train, despite having been in the distance just moments ago, was already pulling into the station. It slowed, the sound of the screeching brakes the only thing that reached Raegan's ears.

The train shuddered to a stop right in front of her, its sides heaving like an exhausted animal. Again, Raegan looked at the King and then back at the train.

She would never know which way was right.

The door slid open. Gloom loomed beyond it—a dead kind of dimness where even Time curled up and devoured its own tail. The sound of a train whistle split the air.

"All aboard," Raegan murmured under her breath, eyeing the steep set of stairs that led onto the train and then to the place that her father might be.

She looked back at her King. He stood on the other side of the barrier, his darkness sheathed. She almost smiled at that. He had always seen her, even when it hurt. The King held her gaze, his jaw set, spine straight. Raegan just looked at him for a moment, cherishing the slope of his shoulders and the oceanic depths of his eyes.

But a river only flowed in one direction.

The train whistle sounded again, louder this time, insistent, and Raegan turned back to see the gears around the wheels begin to skitter like beetles. A moment later, the train shifted, like it was about to begin moving again.

She took another step toward the train. She looked back at the King.

"Outlive me," she said to him, hoping perhaps the universe would take pity on her just this once and ferry the words to his ears. "Outlive me. I love you too much."

And then Raegan stepped up to the train door, just as her father had, just as her father always had, through every story and every re-telling, in every chance he had ever been given before they all turned to ash. And then, despite herself, she hesitated.

It was just a small pause—

one,

two,

three.

THE STORY ISN'T OVER YET

F ollow Raegan and the King's journey to the very end in the second half of the Fatebound Duology. Scan the code below to uncover what happens next, or visit https://tinyurl.com/mw54z3f5

Firstly, of course, I want to thank you, my dear reader. Thank you for following the Fatesong all the way through to this last page. I hope my book whispered to all your lonely, aching places. Picking up any book at all in a world with so many things to read is no small task, and to be willing to dive into a book this long—from a debut author, nonetheless—is a gift, and I thank you for it.

Like the book itself, this is going to be long. Sorry.

Thank you to Erin, Antara, Robert and Rachael—your talents for editing and art took my story and made it into a proper book.

Thank you to Jordon, the love of my life and my fierce supporter through thick and thin. It is no exaggeration to say I wouldn't have been able to write and publish this book without you—without your love, your emotional support, and your unfailing loyalty. I love you more, always.

To Allison, my dearest friend and biggest champion: there is little I can say here in a short paragraph that would accurately reflect what our friendship means to me. All the good parts of this book are thanks to you. You taught me how to write romance. You taught me that writing the stories we want to tell *and* considering what our readers desire are in fact not at odds with each other. I love you with all my heart and I can't wait to read every single glorious book you'll ever write. You're stuck with me until the very end.

To my mom, for always encouraging me to write since I was very small. Many people are parents, and from what I have seen, many people do a very poor job of it. Thank you for being so deeply kind in ways I still cannot fathom, and thank you for being one of my best friends.

To Lian, for being my rock, my voice of reason, my moral compass and my sweetest friend. Our daydreams of lovelier, wilder worlds have kept me going more days than I should admit. Thank you for always reminding me to stay soft in a world that turns us hard.

To Alyssa, for your wellspring of creativity and sunshine smile. There is no one I would rather walk through the Wissahickon with and discuss all matter of things. Thank you for reading my book and for seeing Raegan, and for always asking all the right questions.

To Ronan, for being a constant source of defiant joy and endless laughter—the kind that makes your belly hurt in the best way. Corpse crew forever.

To Paige, for persisting in being my friend since the TTN desks, even when I haven't made it easy. Thank you for seeing me, always, and for making me so many excellent pizzas.

To Charlie, for reading the debut novel of a random little worm you met on the internet. Thank you for championing this book even though you receive nothing in return. (Except for my endless gratitude and literally anything within my power to give you, of course.)

To Katrina, for being so obsessed with the King that I KNEW I had finally written him correctly.

To my little brother, for your humor and your enormous heart and for carrying the same heavy weight of compassion and justice that I do.

To my family, my friends, my ARC readers, my supporters who have stuck with me since the IRL days of Spiral—thank you. I'm so lucky to have too many of you to name, but know that I appreciate you endlessly.

And of course, thank you to the writers who inspire me most: Susanna Clarke, Tracey Deonn, Erin Morgenstern, Kelly Link, Neil Gaiman, Helen Oyeyemi, Allison Carr

Waechter, Holly Black, Elizabeth Hand, Lisette Marshall, Nicola Griffith, Lev Grossman, Arden Powell, Carmen Maria Machado and Tamora Pierce. None of you will ever read this, but it only feels fair to acknowledge your influence. Thank you for telling your stories.

About the Author

Victoria Mier is a queer, disabled author and suspected changeling. When she's not at her desk clacking away at the keyboard, you can most often find her deep in the Wissahickon, somewhere in a field with a horse named Castle, wandering the aisles of a thrift store, or on her couch with her two favorite people: her cat Calliope and her partner Jordon.

If you'd like to stay in touch, follow the links below:

WEBSITE: VICTORIAMIER.COM
INSTAGRAM: @BY_VICTORIAMIER
NEWSLETTER: THECHANGELING.SUBSTACK.COM

About the Artists

ROBERT KRAIZA is the cover artist, as well as the creator of the case laminate design. Robert is a tattoo artist and illustrator from Philadelphia, Pennsylvania. Drawing non-stop since he was a small child he dreamed of being a professional artist.

He worked as a fine artist and freelance illustrator for 10 years working primarily in watercolor, pen and ink, and sculpture. Shifting to tattooing in 2016, he currently works at True Hand Society, a tattoo and graphic design studio located in a renovated 150 year old church.

Drawing inspiration from the Art Nouveau movement, the Victorian era, and the history of his hometown of Philadelphia, Robert creates large scale whimsical tattoos and illustrations of the human figure, flora, and fauna with intricate framing. Robert was chosen as a designer for the US Mint Artist Infusion program in 2023 to create designs for coins and medals.

RACHAEL WARD created the title page and chapter header art. She is an illustrator and fantasy cartographer. Her work is inspired by early 20th century book illustrations, vintage botanical art, and the beauty and whimsy of classical fantasy worlds. She currently resides in Montreal, Canada, with her partner Ben and their little tabby cat Diadem. Discover more at www.cartographybird.com.

www.ingramcontent.com/pod-product-compliance
Lightning Source LLC
Chambersburg PA
CBHW060600300726
48975CB00005B/1393